Amy Trudeau

KIPPER'S GAME

BARBARA
EHRENREICH

KIPPER'S GAME

FARRAR STRAUS GIROUX · NEW YORK

LIBRARY OF CONGRESS CATALOGING-IN-PUBLICATION DATA
Ehrenreich, Barbara.
Kipper's game / Barbara Ehrenreich. — 1st ed.
p.   cm.
I. Title.
813'.54—dc20   PS3553.H65K55   1993
92-38614 CIP

KIPPER'S GAME

CHAPTER 1

The caterpillars first appeared in April, unannounced, a scientific wonder and subject of much high-level speculation. They were a grayish color, invisible against gravel or the usual curb-level debris of discarded newspapers, cans for recycling, broken toys. At first there were calls for action against the invaders, but by mid-May they excited little comment except when manifested in bulk and measured in pounds. In an expensive country suburb, a barn roof collapsed under their weight, revealing, to its outraged owner, the presence of several squatters—a woman and two men —whose crushed bodies were pulled out by the volunteer fire department and donated, unclaimed, to the university medical school.

It was the trees that the caterpillars were after, including the huge stoic elms Della looked out on from her kitchen window. The caterpillars attached themselves to the leaves, first turning them the deep gray of an unforgiving November, and then leaving them, at best, as lace. By June, most of the trees for miles around were bare, investing the sky with the brazenness of a sunny day in the dead of winter.

But there was not much sun, because the other constant that marked the change in Della's life was the haze. It seemed to her that it arrived to shut down the sky in the same week she found out her marriage was over, which she learned accidentally, by picking up the phone at 11:00 p.m., only to find that the line was occupied by two voices which seemed to know each other far better than she knew anyone, including her husband, who was one of the voices. The other voice, the female one, was teasing, cajoling, insistent. Leo's was fretful, agitated. She did not listen long enough to hear them in sequence. They seemed, rather, to be rushing toward each other, overlapping, cooperating in some sort of counterpoint, in the second before she said, "I'm sorry," although "sorry" was a pretty lame word for it.

After that night, the haze never fully lifted for weeks, and the sky became the color of milk, only less normal and reassuring. But she did not, in the first few seconds after she put down the phone, understand that this was the end of her marriage. It was something grotesque and unexpected, that was all. She leaned on the kitchen counter, waiting for Leo to come out of the den, where the other phone was, and watched an ant move across the counter toward the scent of water in the sink. More and more appliances these days have digital clocks, she had noticed—stoves, microwaves, automatic coffeemakers—giving them an appearance of intelligent expectation, as if they were also waiting, or moving purposefully on toward some destination of their own.

She watched the ant's progress against the forward motion of the clocks, caught in that place where things may still be reversible, where the door still seems to stand wide open to the safety of the minute before—before the police car arrives, before the roof collapses from the weight of gray, foreign life, the moment before time forks and one branch goes off gray and withered.

"Out of the blue" is how she would describe it to Miriam, but this was not true. It never is, unless you are willing to admit that the blue is not as empty as it seems when you are in it. Looking back, you can always see that it harbors some dark spot approaching from a distance and a direction where you would not normally think to look. Things had not been good between her and Leo for many months, a fact which Della blamed on herself and all the time she put into her mother's care, and then her mother's dying, and then all the work it takes for someone to be entirely dead in the sense of property and law. At the time Leo's distance seemed to represent deference for her involvement in these things, or, more likely, the natural shrinking of a man away from anything organic, like sickness, menstrual periods, or grief.

The night before the phone call she had been thinking of things to do that might reverse the situation. A confrontation, a hurt and studied coldness, perhaps a trip away for a few days, though where she might be welcome on such short notice, where a sudden visit might be thought natural, she could not imagine, for it was not like her to go anywhere overnight without great forethought and preparation. Or she might simply walk around the mall and have dinner by herself in a clean little place with croissant sandwiches, where a woman alone would not be a subject of prurient thoughts, would be only a shopper. Meanwhile, her not being home to make dinner would send a powerful signal of revulsion. Leo would have to confront her absence, which she had reason to believe was far more dignified and imposing than her presence.

But the mall was not the same as it was when she would take Steve there after school for a snack and a stop at the computer store, where, even when he was small, he was taken as seriously as if he were grown-up and had his own credit cards. There were other computer stores that Della sometimes drove him to, but she preferred the mall with its energy of acquisition and self-improvement. After Steve left home, though, the mall seemed to withdraw into introspection. Renovations were announced in upbeat PARDON OUR APPEARANCE! signs, but closings and dismantlings were also in progress, until the mall eventually reached a steady state of disrepair and abandoned promises. Huge drapes of plastic sheeting hung from the see-through plastic ceiling, which let in rain now, and starlings.

Paper cups and Styrofoam containers drifted along on the floor, piling up against the benches made deliberately uncomfortable to discourage teenagers and vagrants. From the aggressive interiors of the clothing shops, clerks looked out on the fake outdoors of the mall interior—a part of the world that had died, somehow, in captivity.

So she went to the mall only briefly, at around seven, for a sandwich and a turn through the department store, where it was perfectly natural to move indecisively from one section to another, fingering things or turning them over to look for the price. She would have walked longer in the mall, for the sake of walking, but there were so few people around at this hour that those who were present seemed to have been chosen on the basis of some subtle defect they shared. A boy of about ten caught her eye across a counter by breaking suddenly into an abrupt, sardonic laugh. She smiled slightly in complicity, but his face had shut down again, and when his mother pulled him away he did the laugh again, and then again from a greater distance, related to nothing.

■ ■ ■

The actual fight took no more than twenty minutes, and even that was probably more time than they needed. When Leo walked in she could see at once that he had already appropriated the anger that should, by right, have been hers. His face was shining with it. An illicit smile worked around the corners of his mouth, already smudged at this hour by liquor and something stronger. In the fifteen minutes on the phone after Della's intrusion, the teasing voice had worked changes in him. With this woman, you knew where you were. You were actually somewhere, moving along a line of development, involved. While Della was more of an environment, linked to the house and its comforts, but static. You could eat a whole meal with her and not remember anything that was said, the two of them opening their mouths only to eat or to speak about the food, words meeting bites until there was not even food to talk about.

"I would like a little privacy in my own home, if that's not asking too much," Leo started, leaning with one hand against the counter to establish his claim.

Della hung back in what she still believed was the moment before disaster. "My God, Leo, what's the big deal? I wasn't listening in. I was dialing the weather. How was I supposed to know you were on the phone at eleven o'clock at night?"

So far, she thought, I'm clean, I'm not involved. Nothing's going to happen. Leo went over to the cupboard in silence and poured himself a half glass of Scotch. Only two years ago he drank wine or rye, and now it was Scotch, a sign of change for anyone willing to see it. "Do you have to drink that? That's the fourth one tonight. No wonder you're so worked up."

"That's it, the fucking end." He finished the drink in one gulp and smashed the glass down on the ant, or by this time a related ant. "I can't live like this. Can't you see you ruin everything? You ruined Steve, yeah, the kid's a faggot, a drug addict, all we know. And you're ruining this"—the word came uneasily to him—"marriage. And you want to know why? Because you got nothing on your mind, nothing to do, day in, day out. You're not even interested in me. You're interested in the fucking dry cleaning, the fucking upholstery, your fucking faggot son . . ."

"All right," she said, heating up, "who was she?"

That was the signal, apparently, for doors that had been swinging loose on their hinges for decades along corridors connecting girls to old women, mothers to lost children, suddenly to slam shut in the new wind that was moving things. He swelled up with a righteousness he had been waiting all his adult life to fit into. Entitlement smoothed his face, red now with drink and a confused sense of destiny. "Didn't it ever occur to you, in your permanent trance state here, that someone could be interested in me as a human being?"

He looked at her defiantly, almost gloatingly, as if she were an authority figure in the process of public humiliation. "Well, you just mull that over, Della," he said, turning to leave the room. "You just think on that, huh? And in another twenty years or so maybe you'll figure out what's been going on here. Because you want to know the truth about you, Della? The truth is, you don't have a

life. You've got nothing going except whatever this is"—he waved
to include the kitchen and the hallway—"this monitoring operation. Monitoring and maintenance, that's what you've got going
here. Well, you want to know the good news? The good news is,
I'm still alive. What d'you think of that, huh? After twenty years
of this I'm still alive."

It was the idea that she wasn't interested in him that held Della
after he left the room and stamped, with a snorting sound, up the
steps, because here there might be legitimate blame and hence the
possibility of apology and renewal. Miriam had once asked her
what she knew about Leo's business, and Della had been surprised
by her own vagueness. He was, by his own description, an "entre-
preneur," though what he built up, traded, or invested in had become increasingly abstract over the years. There were involvements
with real estate, with "investment products," and now he worked
out of a rented office on what he called "business services," meaning
putting things together, people and products, setting things up.
Once, with manifest reluctance, he had asked Steve to help him
with a program for monitoring cash flow and debts. Steve helped
with equal reluctance on his part, and when Della asked him what
it looked like, from a programming angle, his dad's business, Steve
said, dumb, so dumb it strained his mind.

Of course she was more interested in Steve. But this hardly seemed
disloyal, since Steve was the one thing that redeemed their marriage.
When he was nine, Della was called in to the principal's office to
be told that her son had registered an IQ in the genius range. Steve
would need an enrichment program, which would be established
in the fall, budget permitting. The family would need counseling,
because this kind of gift was a fragile thing, easily shattered by the
unprepared parent, who would not know how to handle the odd
conjuncture of childish emotion and adult-level cognitive powers.
Della felt deeply affirmed, as she had when she was pregnant, radiant with invisible promise. But Leo had insisted that the test be
readministered, that they know for sure what they were dealing
with before they had a bunch of know-it-all shrinks breathing down
their necks, making the kid feel like a freak. Steve dutifully took

the test again, scoring a scant average, and when Della confronted him, he said, yes, he figured it was better not to let anyone know exactly what you had, because then they would want to take it away.

If Steve was an odd child, it was because of his extraordinary intelligence, Della reasoned, a feature which Leo never acknowledged and which even the school system seemed to lose sight of after years of listless performance on Steve's part. There was only one disconcerting event in his development. When Steve was fourteen he began to spend time with a classmate named Carl, meeting over their computers after school and communicating by modem until late into the night, while all four parents slept and assumed that their sons did also. Della tried to like Carl and include herself in some of their discussions, but they might as well have been passing notes behind her back, there was so little she could really follow. Then, when both boys were seventeen, Carl hanged himself from an exposed pipe in the basement of his home, leaving no note, not even a diskette.

Suicide casts an unflattering light on its survivors, for where death has found a niche, who knows what other extremities may have dwelt? There was some unpleasantness between the families, suspicions of a dare or of a game that went too far, though no one knew what the boys had been working on or playing with. Steve just seemed to withdraw more after Carl's death, spending more time alone with the computer or sometimes reading in his room till dawn. But Leo was transformed by the event, and came to regard his son as a criminal for whom only the crime had yet to be discovered.

After Steve left for college, and especially after he left their lives a second time for good, Della had addressed herself to finding what Leo called "a life." She hired a housekeeper and enrolled in courses at the university, which is where she met Miriam. Then, when her mother's mind began to fail, she was required, naturally, to fill in for it: making doctor's appointments, driving her mother to them, doing the shopping. It would have been easier if her mother could have moved in with them, but Leo rejected the idea outright. So she spent her time driving around the oblique triangle defined by her house, the campus, and her mother's house. One leg of the triangle was highway, bordered with just enough trees to contrive the impression of a rural immensity beyond, so that it might have been some other state far to the west. Another leg was a heavily trafficked four-lane street cluttered with shopping centers and free-standing stores with limited offerings, such as auto parts and lighting fixtures. The other leg, between the two houses, wound through neighborhoods whose blistery paint and unclipped shrubbery announced some shift in the economy, although Della could not remember what, exactly, the newspapers had taken to calling it.

■　■　■

When Leo came back downstairs, the hair around his face was wet from splashing himself with cold water. For a moment, coming down the steps, he had looked foolish, like a small boy in need of correction, but seeing Della still standing there, in what he liked to call the trance state, the place she had been slowly retreating to over the years, brought up his anger again. "I'm leaving, Della," he said, from the kitchen doorway, using her name to indicate that things had already moved onto the plane of legal interaction, beyond reach of tears or pleading. "I'm going to join the land of the living." He walked to the front door: "Not that you give a shit whether I live or die," and slammed out.

The rest of the night moved fast, as if propelled by diet pills. Della checked that all the doors were locked for the night and then checked again, including the windows. When there was nothing left to do for the house, a task defined itself. She brought the stack of family photo albums into the kitchen, turned on the overhead light, and began at the beginning, with the wedding pictures, moving through baby Steve, little boy Steve, toward the present, where the representations were fewer and more random: Steve posed in the front yard, ready to go off to college, the fat all gone from his face by then, which had grown thin and dark and ironic. Leo and Della dressed up for someone else's wedding, standing in front of one of Leo's new cars. Steve and Della together, him tall enough to put his arm around her shoulders, casually, both of them smiling at some joke he had told, some joke that Leo didn't get.

Photographs are the enemy of memory, usurping it with little slogans where whole essays should stand, and this was good, Della thought, because she was now an enemy too. At two in the morning she finished going through the albums and got up to get a pair of scissors. Then she went back through the albums with the scissors, cutting Leo out of every picture he appeared in and making a pile of his faces, some small and red, some large, clearly lined, demanding. For a long time she looked at the excised faces, moving them around on the table like pieces in a game, looking for the point of betrayal, seeing what might emerge from the different patterns she could make with them, but finding only their shiny surfaces, which repelled the light back up to her eyes.

After she had scraped the faces together in a pile and put the pile in an ashtray, she started back through the albums again. Here was a revised, improved, family of herself and Steve, moving jauntily through infancy, first day of school, sixth-grade graduation, unhindered by the headless body that now and then showed up in the margins. Leo drove him out, she allowed herself to think. This was the fact that Leo's departure uncovered. But cutting Leo out wouldn't bring Steve back. And for the first time she felt the white rage that precedes absolute loss: Steve is gone. The one special thing in her life, marking her off from every other sleepwalking woman in the mall, and now he was gone.

When the gray light from the window began to overpower the fluorescence, she fixed herself some coffee and a muffin and sat down to make a list. "1. Call Miriam," she wrote, and "2. Exterminator." But the list, so easily completed, frightened her. It was not at all clear how one began a day, just now, or determined when it was over. "One day at a time," they say, but this assumes that there are days, with visible edges, succeeding each other in proper sequence. Leo's leaving had already fused two of them together, and it was possible that the rest were already blending, ahead of her, into one smooth-walled tube through which she would be condemned to wander sleeplessly forever. For no matter what you thought of Leo, and Miriam had come close to saying straight out he was an asshole, he knew how to slice the substance of time into manageable segments: breakfast, dinner, evening, weekend. These, she saw with new respect, were the footholds by which people survive the ascent to wherever they are going, and without Leo, there was only a terrifying smoothness where no human foot could hope to rest. She took up the list again and wrote "3." Then left it blank.

■ ■ ■

After that, Miriam pretty much took over. She arrived a little after nine the morning after Leo left, bringing doughnuts and a vial of Valium. In the days while Della slept or sat in front of the television, Miriam dealt with lawyers, locksmiths, realtors. It was Della's decision to move out of the house, at least she had thought of it, but Miriam was in charge of the move, and brought in Maisy, the cleaning lady, for two days of packing and cleaning, at almost twice the normal pay. Miriam cooked too, or arranged the take-out food on the table for the three of them. There was something remotely mirthful about these meals, which Della strained to grasp. Miriam would light a cigarette after eating, in defiance of the de-parted Leo, who had outlawed smoking once he had given it up himself. Maisy would take a second helping, no need to rush, and from the look on her face Della could measure how far she had fallen: from the employer class, someone to be evaded and out-witted, to the level of common women.

After lunch on the second day of Maisy's presence, Della excused herself to go lie down, leaving Miriam and Maisy alone at the kitchen table. "You know what she needs," Miriam said, "she needs to get out of here, get a job, meet someone decent. This is not the end of the world. I mean, she's a good-looking woman. There are support groups for this."

Miriam had her own business, and her cards said "Programming Consultant," although what she mostly did was word processing for professors and graduate students at the university, dissertations, grant proposals. She was attracted to Della as a person of superior intelligence, but who had somehow failed to connect with the world. It was her theory that the very bright were inevitably slightly lazy, slightly off-key, it was so easy for them to coast, while the so-called stupid worked overtime to compensate and thus developed, by sheer will, a kind of second brain, layered over the imperfect one.

"I tell you what she needs," Maisy responded. "She doesn't need a man. She's been through men. She needs her boy. She needs to find that boy."

"But he's grown-up, don't you think." Miriam had not thought of Steve as a factor. He was in the past, something else for Della to move beyond. But Maisy had been around when Steve was still at home, while Miriam was still more or less a newcomer in Della's life. Maisy and Steve were friends, Della had said, if friendship is possible across such a distance of age and condition. Many times she had come home from some errand to find Maisy and Steve sitting in the kitchen, locked in what looked like an earnest discussion, the boy thin and tense and the large black woman.

"Not so grown-up he doesn't need a mother. A boy just drops out like that and no one goes out and looks for him. What kind of people. Blood doesn't end, you know, just because a door slams shut."

"Well, a whole year, he could be dead." Miriam shrugged. "The last thing Della needs."

Maisy waved her hand to push the thought away. "He's not your suicide type, her boy. For someone like Steve, the time to die, he would take that as his deadline, time to get it all done by. He'd be working toward that deadline, getting stuff done."

She paused to consider some unsolved problem in her mind. "And you look at those trees out there, maybe a deadline laid down for every simple fool on earth. Time running out. I could see that years ago, working in this neighborhood, when they built those houses on the corner. Tear down living trees to make a house out of dead ones they bring in. Kill some trees and bring dead ones in from somewhere to pile up over the grave. You put that together and you know it can't keep on going like that. You run out. And now with the caterpillars, we're all speeding to the end, got to get stuff done."

Miriam felt left out of some assumption here. "Well, what exactly did this kid ever do? Gets into one of the best colleges in the country, for computer science, God knows how, because his grades were nothing, and drops out, after less than two years, comes home, bums around, gets a job at the university—running errands for Dr. Leitbetter, I think, out at the Human Ecology Complex—then what? Vanishes into the mist."

"You be surprised what that boy is on to. Someday everybody's going to get a big surprise."

"Well, it doesn't help Della, does it?"

"Her son would, someone would find her son."

Miriam frowned. As far as she was concerned, Steve was no more related to Della's situation than the trees were, or the caterpillars. If you went around seeing everything connected, soon all the pieces would lock together into a whole, and where would you be? Standing outside, trying to follow the plot. It's the disconnections that provide the space for a person to move ahead in the world, make their own decisions. Leave yourself a clear path, this on this side, that on the other. But it couldn't hurt to check out some of the local computer bulletin boards for some trace of the lost boy, maybe post a message of her own.

"Only thing is," Maisy continued, rising with the dishes in one hand, "he wouldn't go by the name of Steve. He would go by the name of Kipper. I don't even know if she knows that. What he was doing, he said you need a code name, you don't want someone to jump in, try and take it over."

■   ■   ■

Upstairs, there were boxes in the hall, stacks of garment bags, a vacuum cleaner with its hose uncoiled. Della thought of sleeping, and then thought of sleeping as something she had done already, had tried and it hadn't worked. The boxes containing Leo's things had LEO written on them hugely in Magic Marker, like graffiti left by some spiteful child. She looked into her own bedroom—no, the master bedroom—and watched as it seemed to recede into the regrettable past. It was this strange receding of things that made her desperate to move. Even the kitchen with Maisy and Miriam in it could be seen only across a gap of years, perhaps decades, in which people unknown to her had grown up, moved on, or died, and others had forgotten their graves.

There were the twenty-eight Valium Miriam had given her and the seventeen sleeping pills she had found in the bottom of one of Leo's drawers. She had not made a decision about this, and was doing her best to prepare for the move like everyone else. In her version of the move, though, only the clothing and furniture and kitchenware continued on into the open spaces of the known future. She ended here, perhaps in what the others would still see as "this afternoon." But first there was something she had to do, the only goodbye that mattered, because Miriam would never understand anyway.

Steve's room, after the dimness of the hall, was unexpectedly, painfully, bright. Ordinarily, at this time of year, it would be shaded by the trees outside the window, but they were almost bare now and the white light from the sky was amplified by the white walls, once covered with odd scraps of paper—clippings, quotations, equations—now as mute and bare as the walls of a city after an unsuccessful uprising. Della stood there, waiting for some pattern to resolve itself out of the light and recall her son to her. What you see in a child is some aspect of yourself that genetic destiny has seen fit to memorialize. Many people are surprised to find that it is a current of defiance, long numbed by their own obedience to routine, bursting out in the young; or it could be a deep inertia of the will, which you had almost forgotten you were pushing against. The aspect of herself which Della had discovered in Steve was an undercurrent of impatience, an unexercised talent for obsession; although, of course, up to now, there had been no way for her to express any of this, outside of the eccentricities that seemed to have driven Leo away. The truth was, she had failed Steve. Capable of following him, she had held back. Unmoored to Leo's world, she had failed to enter the obvious alternative, failed even to imagine it. Carl's death had blighted that alternative, closed it to her, leaving her vague and unsteady.

Maisy must have cleaned the room regularly, because it was as dustless as the last time Della had come in, many months ago, searching for clues. She sat down at the built-in desk unit, facing the white wall where the computer screen should have been. Without looking, she knew the drawers to be empty of every scrap of paper, just a few felt-tipped pens rolling around among the rubber bands and paper clips. But in the middle drawer, which she had opened many times in the past to emptiness, she was surprised to find something black, looking at first like a poorly drawn capital letter against the whiteness. It was Steve's Walkman, and seeing it, she was seized with embarrassment, searching for its place in memory. Maisy, she thought, Maisy must have put it back here, she must be keeping it here for Steve. Once, not long after Steve had left, Della had returned from the dry cleaner and an aimless stop at the drugstore to find Maisy dusting the living room with Steve's Walkman on. So this is what Leo meant, Della had thought. Nothing was really safe with them, after all. You could not turn your back. But Maisy saved her from a confrontation by removing the earphones and saying pleasantly, "Hope you don't mind that I borrowed this. Your mind goes empty just staring at furniture."

"Of course not," Della said in a way she hoped was casual and friendly. You could not really tell what was friendly, though, and what might cause offense. Della had not known many black people, and it disturbed her that they could use their blackness as a veil pulled across their faces, discouraging any advance. "I like a little music myself, while I work."

"Not music," Maisy said, "talk."

Della had taken off her coat and set down the paper bag from the drugstore. There was nothing to do now but try to leave the room and find another room where Maisy had already finished up. "You could have it, you know. Steve's probably got himself another one by now." Maisy just shrugged and went on with the dusting.

The memory of this encounter still had the power to make Della uneasy. Experimentally, she slipped the earphones over her head. She had never worn a Walkman; women of her age—housewives—did not, although they probably had as much void to fill as anyone. Wearing earphones implied a certain disrespect for the immediate situation, an unseemly inattentiveness that hardly mattered now. She pressed the On button, expecting to have to fiddle inexpertly with the volume and tuning, but there was sound at once, a dark voice in her head, drawing her inward and away from the scalding whiteness.

". . . A man writes to me and says, Sister Bertha, I pray and pray and it don't seem to help. But I say, Why're you praying like that? What've you got hidden in your hands, you've got to keep them clasped so tight?

"Open your hands! You think they are empty, but they really are full!"

So this might be the source from which Maisy fashioned her composure. It was like listening in on something, hearing something so intimate and disconnected from any visual event. The voice was not smooth and educated, but neither was it—Della hesitated before thinking the word—black, and the fact that it was not from any extreme of social condition made her feel included. The extremism was all in what was being said, and it was like anything religious, appropriate to any situation, but especially to the one you happened to be in. Della had been married in the Church. She had gone to religious instruction every Wednesday as a child. But the instructions had always equivocated, presupposing faith. Sister Bertha's boldness took account of doubt, and cut right on by it.

"The law says, *Give it all away. Everything you've got, and follow me.* And when you've got nothing, then open up those hands and they'll be clean and empty: ready for the Lord!"

There was a moment of static, while Della held her breath. When the voice returned, it was calm, reflective.

"A woman writes to me; she says, 'Sister Bertha, I have fallen so low I can no longer see the light. First they threw me out of my apartment because the rent got too high and the welfare wouldn't pay. Then they say I can't get on welfare because I got no address.

Then they take my three little girls away for foster care, because they say I got no home and no money, I must be unfit. Sister Bertha, I'm asking you, give me some step to take before I lose my way.' "

The voice became gentle and urgent, hard to make out above the rising static:

"Sister, sister, if you're listening now, you have not fallen low, you have risen up. You are empty, is all, everything taken till you're hollowed out, so finally there is space in you for the Lord to dwell in, some room at last for Him. So open up your eyes, hold out those empty hands, stand up and . . ."

The door opened and Maisy looked in. Della stopped fiddling with the dial and slid the earphones to her shoulders. The static was complete now, the voice lived on only in her head. *Not fallen low, but risen up . . .*

". . . glass of iced tea," Maisy was saying as she entered the room, and then paused to consider the Walkman.

"It's funny, isn't it, how the sound seems to come from inside," Della said, still sitting, aware of her hands framing the tiny radio in her lap.

"You like music, it's the perfect thing," Maisy offered noncommittally, and they both went downstairs, where there were empty boxes waiting to be filled, sealed shut, and taken to an entirely new place.

CHAPTER 2

The walk from the parking lot to the Human Ecology Complex had been designed as an exercise in humility, Della believed, a warm-up for the day's work. She had been assigned to lot 16A, the farthest down the hill from the complex, which made it part-time home to the ten-year-old Plymouths and damaged vans of the maintenance crew, animal house workers, and kitchen staff. Ascending toward the complex, she passed first through lot 6, where technicians and secretaries parked, and finally to lot 3B, reserved for faculty and administration. The lot numbering system made no sense, she learned, because many more lots had been envisioned radiating out from a great domed stadium, to which the community would one day be invited to witness coded signals from space, should they be intercepted by the dish antennas reaching heavenward from the top of the complex. But funds had run out just after the foundation had been excavated, and in the spot where extraterrestrial greetings were to be announced, there was now only a mud-bottomed crater, filling with beer cans and index cards discarded at the end-of-the-semester interfraternity riot.

At the top of the hill, the Human Ecology Complex—called HEC and, in the lower circles of the academic hierarchy, Hell—rose in defiance of all architectural notions of harmonious coexistence, a challenge, in fact, to the very idea of "ecology." It was ten stories high, although the rest of the campus was low to the ground; and it was constructed of black glass, opaque from the outside, although most other university buildings were sober brick. The idea may have been that the outer surface of the complex, a collection of ten-story, green, mirror-like planes, would assemble its own environment out of the reflections of trees and neighboring buildings. But no trees had been planted, and no other buildings had arisen in years.

The first few mornings of her job in the complex, Della had gotten lost on her way to Dr. Hershey's lab. Miriam had given her a map when she had gone for her interview, but it turned out to be obsolete, so furiously was the building being redesigned internally or, in some sections, repaired. The ceiling of the animal house, for example, had fallen in only weeks ago, resulting in the death of one worker and the escape of many dozens of laboratory animals, including an iguana suffering from a rare, man-made cancer of the brain. Little was said about the worker, whose name was known only to Personnel anyway, but there were sightings of rabbits and mice in the poorly lit stairwells connecting one section of the complex to another, and rumors of a crazed iguana in the abandoned section known as the E Corridor—starving, as one joke went, because its tastes ran entirely to intelligent women.

Claire, Dr. Hershey's head technician, conducted the interview, shifting in her chair as she scanned the résumé Miriam had invented. "You've been out of work for a long time, you sure you're ready for this?"

Della was sure she was not ready but not sure she was entitled to an opinion. She had liked the concept of a job but had not expected it to rise up in front of her so suddenly. Miriam knew

Claire from her own years as a university employee, and was able to fix something up on a trial basis—nice boss, acceptable pay, three sick days a year. It would have been unthinkable to refuse. Della had been sleeping on Miriam's couch for more than a week now, eating Miriam's food, taking up time in the bathroom, trying to be unobtrusive because Miriam worked right in the apartment and sometimes emerged from the bedroom that was her office looking surprised to find Della still there, paging through magazines with the Walkman on her head. Sometimes Della caught a few minutes of Sister Bertha again, and felt lifted to some bright, high point above her grief. But it had probably been a mistake to mention Sister Bertha, because Miriam made a face and said it was time now for Della to get a grip on things, meaning a job to structure her life, an apartment of her own.

"You're sure you can handle data entry?"

Della was condensing, in her mind, an account of her computer experience with Steve, when Dr. Hershey strolled over, identifying himself by the name *Dr. Hershey* written on the radioactive film badge pinned to his lab coat. In fact, the lab used no radioisotopes, but the film badges conferred status—an acquaintance with danger—as did the lab coats, even on those, like Dr. Hershey, who seldom risked a stain except at lunchtime. "So you're interested in epidemiology?" he said, glancing at Della's résumé.

But he was already moving on, nodding remotely at the other technicians in his passage toward his office. Claire returned to her spiel. It was hard to find people with a talent for accuracy, she was saying. Popular music gives people the idea that a rough approximation will do, that a creative improvisation will always be applauded. This may be fine for some areas of life, but not for science, because the entire point of science is to make exact copies. She said this with a vehemence whose source Della could not imagine. The technician copies readings off the equipment into a notebook, Claire continued, not nearby numbers, or numbers she happens to be reminded of, but the same numbers that appear on the indicator, or wherever they appear. The exact ones.

Then she showed Della the computer and the cubicle that housed it. There were no windows and no posters on the walls, only a computer printout reading WAKE ME WHEN IT'S OVER taped to the wall, a message from Della's predecessor. Claire explained the work, or rather the microscopic fragment of the work that would be Della's, while Della nodded and thought of the more stimulating background information Miriam had given her.

Hershey was on the trail of a new disease, this much was known, although the early promise of something as big as AIDS had begun to fade. At least there had been no press conferences, and no call for the services of Dr. Leitbetter's staff of publicists, which had grown along with the height of the building, in preparation for a message from space or the announcement of a new epidemic. Leitbetter was the director of the Human Ecology Complex, though, five years ago, when Miriam had worked at the university, his title had only been Chairman of the Human Ecology Department. In the expansion from department to complex and from chairman to director, Leitbetter had swallowed up a number of hard-to-classify departments, projects, and faculty, Hershey among them. The enmity between the two men would have been more interesting if it had been more unusual, but almost all the senior faculty within the complex despised Leitbetter; some of them had even organized a faction within the faculty senate for the purpose of blocking his imperial designs. The trick, Miriam said, was to avoid Leitbetter, or anyone close to him, while at the same time not seeming to avoid him, or of course anyone close to him.

But once Della started working, the idea of offending anyone began to seem like a grandiose delusion carried over from her former life. She would arrive at the parking lot at eight, leaving a half hour for the walk to the complex and any indoor walking required by the elevators, at least one of which was out of service on any given weekday morning. If she got to the lab early enough, she would have coffee and listen to the technicians talk about dry-walling their basements and experiences they had had with the occult. Then she would enter the cubicle, where WAKE ME WHEN IT'S OVER remained on the wall, gaining the authority, through endurance, of an official statement from the administration.

It took her only two days to master the hierarchy of the lab and, by extension, the complex. At the top, of course, was Dr. Hershey, or his equivalent in a dozen other labs or departments, and just under him were two post-docs. Hershey had hoped for American post-docs, young men not unlike himself of fifteen years ago: tall, unpolished, sandy-haired young scientists from the Plains states, who would feel privileged to be invited to the Hersheys' on Sundays, where they would listen to Hershey's recordings of cicada songs with hand-rubbing enthusiasm and then help set up for the barbecue. But instead he had attracted an overweight Korean with no known interest outside of histology and a Pakistani woman of about thirty-five, a genius with the electron microscope, who had twice come over on Sundays and twice taken tearful offense at subjects related to her country, her religion, or the use of pork as a food. Just below the post-docs, though possibly, from some angles, at the same level, was Claire, followed by the two young female lab technicians, followed by the dishwasher, a morose middle-aged Hispanic woman who banged things and had been known to leave the water running.

The work itself required no exertion beyond the absentminded, nit-picking type of attention a mother applies to tightening shoelaces and checking zippers. If Claire was out of sight, Della would speed up for a few minutes, sending the digits onto the screen in a burst of keystrokes; then she would slow down for a moment of reverie. Leo had called three times since he left, and these conversations left Della with data of her own to process.

"Della, I think we need to talk," he would start in a patient tone. "I said some terrible things. I was strung out, what can I say, the stress. You wouldn't believe."

"If it's something the lawyer could deal with? I do have a lawyer."

"No, nothing with the lawyer. I'm talking about us, Della, what happened. There shouldn't be hard feelings. I was growing, you were growing. We were growing in different directions, is all. This is something two grownups can sit down over a drink . . ." Someone must have slipped a note in front of him, a paper to sign or okay.

"What direction was I growing in?"

"I don't know. Della, look, I discovered I wasn't growing at home. At home was a rerun, every night a rerun. That's why I had to make a transition. It wasn't you, Della, believe me, it wasn't you. I just wasn't growing anymore, and that happens, you die."

"Well, you must be enormous by now."

"Della, goddamn it, will you listen to what I'm trying to say. Do you have to go on the blink every time I try to communicate? And I have been trying to communicate, I don't know whether you ever noticed. Because, you know, the thing with you, you never got over Steve. You're in a world of your own, Della, you need professional help."

Later in the cubicle she would replay these conversations, looking for the undertone of compassion or regret that might give her the right to some sweetly tragic new conception of her loss. But grief had taken a vile turn after the first few days of blankness, hustling her from moment to moment, the instant corruption of one moment propelling her into the next. There had been times like this in the years of tension between Leo and Steve. She remembered a summer Sunday spent driving on the expressway, returning from a visit with one of Leo's brothers, when Leo had started in on Steve for one fault or another.

"I asked you a question," he said into the rearview mirror.

Steve continued to stare straight ahead, between their shoulders, out through the front windshield.

"I can't take this anymore, Della, what does it take to get a civil answer out of him? You got any idea?"

"You could cut out my tongue," Steve answered for himself, never taking his eyes off the point in the distance where parallel lines meet and all cars must eventually vanish. "You could cut it out and teach it to say anything you want. You could nail it to my forehead if you wanted, and watch it bleed to death."

They had pulled off at the first rest area, where father and son stalked off in opposite directions. Della remained by the car, watching a pregnant woman drag a bawling two-year-old across the parking lot, and in the stagnant afternoon heat the cries had seemed to be coming from the unborn child in the woman's belly. Looking back, it was hard to believe that she had continued to move through the day, to the house, which was overheated from having had all the windows shut, to a wan supper pulled together in the kitchen, and the mercy, finally, of night.

■ ■ ■

It was at the party that Della found her old professor Alex again, although she had not even counted him among the missing. Claire and the technicians took her along right after work to Dr. Leitbetter's main seminar room, a huge, high-ceilinged room on the tenth floor of the B tower. The oval seminar table which would ordinarily have dominated the room had been taken out for the occasion, and people were moving experimentally through the open space, confused by the absence of anything to keep them at fixed distances from each other. All of Leitbetter's immediate enemies had come, trailing their retinues of post-docs and technicians and emitting deep baritone barks of appreciation once they got to the punch.

Della was surprised to be invited, but Claire said the press might show up so Leitbetter needed a respectable-looking crowd, meaning everyone except the blue-collar employees, such as maintenance and cafeteria workers, who actually wore dark green. Della stood near the narrow, gray-tinted windows and studied the crackers on her paper plate. In dozens of uneasy social ventures with Leo, she had developed the rule of never appearing to look at the crowd, because if you look generically out at a group of people, someone is bound to show up at your side saying, "How's about a little smile, things couldn't be that bad now." The idea was to appear deeply engrossed, as she was now, forcing herself to visualize the tiny looms on which the salty strands were woven to make the crackers, when a pudgy man came over and cleared his throat.

"So what did you make of the lecture?"

"Was there a lecture? I had to work."

"Yeah, the lecture we're celebrating. Or actually the genius who gave it." He inclined his head toward a thin, curly-haired woman on the other side of the room. She was middle-aged, Della could see, but probably only in the eyes of others. In her own mind she was a twenty-four-year-old prodigy, full of naughtiness and sexy charm.

The paunchy man continued: "She said science is like literature, or maybe nature is like literature, I may have missed a transition here and there. Anyway, since it's like literature, it can be 'deconstructed,' that's her word, for hidden meanings. Very, very hot stuff, huh? Your so-called interface between biology and literary criticism. That's why Leitbetter brought her in, shows he's at the jagged edge."

"Nature has hidden meanings?"

"Yup, it's trying to tell us something. What's going on, you know, all this"—he waved his free hand to indicate the cosmos—"it's an effort at communication."

"And what is it trying to tell us?"

"Ah! You get right to the heart of the matter, don't you? The caterpillars, for example—she actually brought them in—are a parody of industrial pollution. Also a parody of social—what was it?—malaise. Which actually makes sense in a sick way. You see what they're doing now? They finish the leaves, then their little bodies get so fat they can't hold on anymore, and splat, they deconstruct themselves all over your freshly waxed car."

"So what do you think?"

"It's a bitch to clean up."

"No, about what it's trying to tell us."

"Look, attendance was practically mandatory for all of Hell. If Leitbetter keeps this shit up, he'll be found exsanguinated on his laboratory floor some morning, nothing but iguana tracks around. Pardon my French." He loaded a cracker with cheese and popped it in his mouth, scanning the room as he chewed. "Behold, there he is now, Richard Leitbetter, King of Hell."

Della recognized him from the television specials he had starred in, one called *Limits of the Knowable*, on whether the human brain was really adequate to comprehend the universe, or whether we might be like beetles trying to master cosmology. The other was on the historical evidence for extraterrestrial life, including an overview of what Leitbetter called the "legend of the Visitor," unusual,

God-related individuals who intrude from time to time, leaving their hosts numbed for centuries with surprise. It was possible to conclude that most humans were indeed like beetles, with a few exceptions like Einstein, Leif Eriksson, and possibly the narrator himself. In person, he had the same mannerisms as his larger, electronic self —a piercing stare meant to suggest ungovernable mental processes, mitigated by brief bursts of joviality. He was standing with one hand on the elbow of the lecturer, casting his eyes over the shoulder of the disordered-looking man who was trying to hold his attention.

"My God, isn't that Alex MacBride? I took a course from him," Della said, but the pudgy man had moved off toward the punch bowl.

Della shouldered her way through to the cluster around Dr. Leitbetter and stood there for a moment, hesitant to cut in, not sure whether Alex would recognize her.

". . . definitely not a Nazi, at least she wasn't what you would call a happy Nazi," Alex was saying. "So I don't think it's going to work . . ."

He turned around, prodded by Leitbetter's wandering gaze. "Della! This is Della Markson. The most brilliant student ever to join the narcoleptic hordes taking WOW, WOW 1 and 2, earning A + 's only because the registrar refused to record the double and triple pluses I actually awarded her. May I introduce Richard Leitbetter and our distinguished lecturer, Dr. uh . . ."

Leitbetter leaned forward toward Della in his jovial mode, prepared to accept her admiration. She couldn't be sure, but when he heard her full name his smile seemed to hit a snag for a second before continuing on to fill the lower half of his face. She had assumed that when Steve worked for him he had been insulated from the great man by a Claire, or a whole series of Claires, but maybe not.

"WOW? WOW 1 and 2? I love it," said the lecturer, waiting to be let in on the joke.

"Our core course for the non-science major. Very innovative. Actually Alex here had a hand in putting together the early WOW. World of Wonder. On the principle of meeting the student more than halfway, meeting the student right at his or her crib side, so to speak. Bigfoot, the Bermuda Triangle, life-after-death, sex-change operations—anything to tickle the curiosity of the post-technological suburban peasantry, seduce them into the possibility of orderly thought, right, Alex?"

"Della didn't take much seducing. A real round-heels, so to speak. So look, Dick, will you think about this Nazi problem? Before I waste any more time on this?"

But Leitbetter was already moving off, steering the lecturer by the elbow. "Forge ahead, Al. Progress report on Monday, okay? I'll see that Phyllis squeezes you in."

Alex reassembled his face into a smile and turned to look at his former student. "Well, what would you say to some pizza? I mean, if you don't have to run. There's nothing to hold us here, considering that the only thing to drink is cheap vodka in which innocent berries are being preserved against their will. A bite, okay? And you could tell me what you're doing in hell."

■   ■   ■

They drove to the restaurant in separate cars. Della arrived first and tried to think of whether there was some way to get through an hour or two without explaining the change in her living situation. That was not the kind of thing Alex would be interested in, nor, she guessed from the look of the place, did he care much about food. There was a bar against one wall and booths along the others, leaving a large space where there might once have been tables with waitresses sidling between them. Now the interior seemed unprotected against the yellowish light from the windows, which had come in searching for dust motes and premature wrinkles. She ordered tomato juice with a slice of lime, so it would seem like a real drink.

It was true that she had been the best student, though Miriam wasn't far behind, and the way WOW worked, there was no limit to what you could learn if you had the inclination. When she asked a hard question, Alex would answer, in a day or two, with a stack of books and reprints for her to read. Sometimes he would have coffee with the two women after class, enjoying the adulation he never got from the younger students, who were a hard bunch and closed off to information that was irrelevant to sex or the campus parking problem.

Eventually Leo had complained about the books and papers stacked on the dining-room table, and she had taken to studying more furtively. If he could have met Alex, he might have found some real grounds for jealousy, because Alex was a handsome man in a bruised, blond way, and he was also a beaten man, the two women were old enough to see, which gave him an aura of accessibility.

"You know, I think I still have a book of yours," she said after he had settled into the booth and repeated his delight at finding her after what? Two years? The interval had done him no more good than it had done her. From a distance, his tan suit looked dapper and summerish, but up close the stains came into focus. His hair was grayer than it had been, and his face was just beginning to bloat. A lush, had been Miriam's judgment; there are programs for people like that.

"Well, if I haven't missed it I must not need it. So tell me, did you get your degree?"

"No, I had to stop for a while. My mother got sick and then I, well, needed to get a job."

"Tsk tsk, Della, you should really finish: Do something, teach maybe."

"Oh, I'm doing something. I'm working for Dr. Hershey, data entry, things like that."

"Solid fellow, Hershey. Promising new disease, I understand."

"I'd rather be taking courses, but right now, you know, I had to get an apartment, so I have the rent and . . ." She trailed off, looking away.

"Hmm. Nasty business, finances. I know all about it."

They fell silent as the waitress leaned over them, wiped the table with a mildewed rag, and plunked down Alex's drink.

"Ah." Alex held up the glass admiringly. "So what have you been thinking? Really thinking about, as opposed to the little soul-crunching details of survival."

"Well. Okay. Can I ask you a question?"

"Ask anything," he said, with an expansive wave of the hand, "and if I don't know the answer, I can assure you the question will not be on the exam."

"Have you ever heard of someone called Sister Bertha?"

"Now, let me see, the nun who defied the Vatican by having an abortion?" He was leaning forward, obviously pleased that the conversation was taking an impersonal tack and that there would be no need to update the student-teacher relationship to anything more difficult and challenging. "Or the nun who immolated an entire classroom of orphans, as a protest against abortion?"

"I don't think a nun. Some kind of radio preacher, seems to be a pirate frequency . . ."

"You're not going religious on me, are you? The whole purpose of WOW, at least as Leitbetter conceived it, was to inoculate the innocent against the more savage forms of superstition."

"It's not a religion exactly. It's more like logic. I mean, if you take what religions say, and take that to its logical conclusion—"

"You want to order?" It was the waitress again. "Or another drink?"

"Another drink, by all means," Alex answered, then turning back to Della: "Leitbetter always has this effect on me—a desperate thirst."

"I don't think I liked him."

"You're not meant to. Your liking him wouldn't do him any good. I've known him since he was only a graduate student named Dick and he hates it that I didn't go along with the upgrade to Richard. He's not as bad as people think, though. He's probably much worse. Underneath the hustle is a grand plan, a vision that guides him; I hate to think of what." Alex lit a cigarette and used the cardboard backing of the matches to make scraping motions on the table, shoveling some invisible substance into a mound.

"Does it include Nazi hunting?" Della smiled. "Is that what you do now?"

"Yes, associate professors are now required, in addition to their normal course load and semiannual published paper, to bag a Nazi or two. No, it's some research. Charity, really, on his part; we all took a pay cut after the last wave of cutbacks and I took the unkindest cut of all. So Dick roped me into this project he has going, the *Biography of the Twentieth Century*." Alex pronounced the quotation marks fulsomely and leaned back to watch the questions gather on Della's face.

"I know, I know." He smiled. "It's a collection of biographies, articles really, on these obscure scientists Dick has come up with. The idea is that their lives illustrate the great contradictions of the twentieth century. The other idea is that I get paid $10,000 to put together an article on one Henry Relnik, an undistinguished physiologist from New Jersey who died in 1958. That brings me up to what I was earning five years ago; most people would call that good luck."

"Relnik was a Nazi?"

"That was the idea. He wrote some things on the need to improve science education, mobilize the underutilized potential of the human mind, etc., most of it quite atrocious. So there you have a great irony of the twentieth century in micro: a bridge between scientific humanism of the most noxious, sentimental variety—and *Mein Kampf*."

Alex swirled his drink before finishing it off, then held up the empty glass for the waitress to see. "Well, what am I going to do? I'm not exactly fighting off the job offers. The book contracts . . ."

The humility was new, Della noticed. It was not a quality which would have served him well in a classroom full of young people absorbed by the challenges of personal grooming—hair combing, fingernail examinations, the adjustment of belts and straps. Maybe he would ask her out again. "But you were talking about a woman," she said, "who wasn't a Nazi."

"His girlfriend, a German psychologist name of Dora Mueller.

Frau Professor Mueller until the Nazis ruled that women were not to use the titles *Doktor* or *Professor*. She's by far the more interesting of the two and probably the source of Relnik's ideas. So some faculty colleagues of Relnik's—he had tenure at this men's college in New Jersey, very small, Protestant denominational—started the rumor that Relnik was a Nazi sympathizer and possibly a German agent. Ruined him as far as research grants went. But from what I've managed to find out so far, he wasn't a Nazi, she wasn't a Nazi, and Leitbetter's lovely ironic link between Hitler and the New Age is based on nothing more than routine faculty backbiting. Of the kind which, if anyone was to take it seriously, would have Leitbetter himself demoted to cleaning mouse cages."

The subject returned to Leitbetter and Della looked for a way to mention Steve. The embarrassing thing was that she didn't know exactly what kind of work Steve had done for Leitbetter—computer programming, most likely, plus some unspecified research that had required driving around; to libraries, she assumed.

"It was a time when American science was just perfecting the brittle, know-nothing stance that we now know, of course, as science itself." Alex had skipped back to Relnik, and was addressing his drink as if it had raised certain questions. "But there were still men like Relnik, flakes we would call them now, who had the effrontery to cross disciplinary lines now and then, trailing vast questions of meaning and design. Today, a self-respecting physiologist would never go to a conference on the Future of Eropsychology (that was the Berlin meeting where Relnik met Dora); in fact, a self-respecting physiologist would be, at least, a neurophysiologist, slicing up cat brains to find where the visual signal ends up—a moot issue, one might think, in a dead cat, but modern science can only truly understand the dead, life being, for the most part, a complication, confusing the instruments, smudging the lenses."

Della let her attention wander to the bar, which was, oddly, the brightest area of the room, making the rest of the restaurant seem incidental, secondary to the larger purpose. A half dozen people sat around the bar, none of them talking, probably just glad to be out of the haze and into a light confident enough to cut shadows out of the air. One face held her. It was a man in his late twenties, just slightly overweight, with his hair pulled back in a high ponytail. That in itself was not unusual, but there was something in his face which seemed to refer to something not present, some problem or issue Della had briefly put out of her mind.

". . . unquestionably, the more brilliant of the two," Alex was saying, "and quite pretty, in the thoroughly composed way one is likely to find in photographs of the time. Blue eyes, wavy blond hair, and curvaceous eyebrows suggesting a sense of humor or at least a taste for the anomalous, which is almost as important. Even the name Dora Mueller has a certain Teutonic poetry to it, and there are hints that she had studied Freud, which was, of course, strictly verboten under the Brown Shirts. But apparently—and this all comes from one of Relnik's surviving colleagues, so who knows?—she thought Freud was barking up the wrong tree, zoning in on neurosis and psychosis. The thing to study, she thought, was joy: *Freude*, not Freud. Hitler, of course, had the last word on that."

The man with the ponytail got up from the bar, and Della could see the sloppy juncture between his T-shirt and his jeans, the heavy key chain hanging from his belt. It was clear now what he reminded her of; he was someone she had seen with Steve in the period after Steve had dropped out of college. He was a reminder of Steve. She excused herself and, for the second time that day, walked out across a room in the direction of someone Steve had known, Leitbetter and now this one. One thing was leading to another, propelled by an energy that had nothing to do with her, and when she stepped out from the booth, the room widened, asserting that the world is three-dimensional after all.

"So?" Alex said when she slid back into the booth. He had watched her move across the room with curiosity. You don't often find a woman who is good-looking without being aware of it, and hence seems to promise pleasure without the usual price of humiliation. He liked the short dark hair, curling in the heat, the sweet, tentative curve of smile. But the missing wedding ring was a warning sign. Alex imagined a one-bedroom apartment overlooking an intersection, freshly furnished and striving for pertness. There might be a half-full bottle of white wine in the refrigerator, some crème de menthe hidden deep in a cupboard. An offer of coffee. He would go home alone, as usual.

"I thought I recognized him. Someone my son knew. But he acted like . . . I don't know. Maybe he thought I was coming on to him."

■　　■　　■

Alex got home before ten and played back the calls on his answering machine. "Debbie" wanted a return call to the Atlanta area code on a "matter of urgent personal business." Obviously a collection agency. Finally the astringent tones of Leitbetter's Australian secretary. The meeting on the new WOW syllabus had been moved to the third-floor library because a leak had developed in the pipes next to seminar room 7A and repairs had been difficult to schedule. Same time, brown bag. She signed off with an insinuating "Toodle-oo!"

Now he could drink, freely and seriously. He wanted to put a deep channel of liquor between himself and the embarrassment of Leitbetter's brush-off. Of course, blabbing to an ex-student for two hours about the Relnik business was supposed to have the same effect, but it had only deepened the embarrassment. If he was really interested in Relnik he would have gone through the stack of documents that was still sitting on the floor next to the desk, testing his indifference. He was not a free agent anymore; he was Leitbetter's errand boy. Anyone in Human Ecology could see that he would have been out on the street long ago if Leitbetter hadn't found uses for him. Della probably took him for a maundering fool, and now drinking would no doubt lead to some fresh embarrassment, some undisguisable impairment, one disgrace generating another out of long habit and practice.

The room was dim, the sound of a TV in the next apartment serving as the only clock as it moved every day from the hysterical urgency of the game shows, to the ragged laughter of sit-coms, to, now, the responsible tones of what must be the eleven o'clock news.

Why do we always think of the passage of time in terms of ascending numbers? Alex strained to imagine the evening reversing from 11 to 7, not the sounds but only the numbers, going down instead of up. Impossible to think of moving ahead unless the numbers, some numbers anyway, go up. But why? When time moves ahead is something—other than entropy—actually increasing?

This was the good stage, before he got too murky to think, before the trips for the ice cubes became challenging enterprises, adventures in memory: where the chair was, where the light switch was, where the handle of the refrigerator was. And larger questions about the number of inches remaining in the current bottle and whether there was cash in the drawer for the next. For the only thing in his life that increased with the force and clarity of time's arrow was booze, the amount of it and the need for it, the glass filling and bottle emptying.

When Alex became aware of time again, after a few hours of sodden sleep, his head was aching and he was in a black swamp nailed down to earth by the stumps of ancient trees. The water level was subsiding in gasps, imparting to the scenery the rhythm of death and bringing him closer to the creatures beneath, huge swamp-bottom carps, rocking toward him with the motion of the water, hoping for a cadaver. Slowly he began to advance from tree stump to tree stump, heading toward the morning like the starved remnant of a guerrilla band emerging from the jungle toward the only clearing in sight, the enemy camp.

He had been worse than a fool, he had been rude. He would call Della and ask what it was about this Sister Something, the radio preacher. Or he would plunge right in and ask about the divorce that had given her this half-drowned look, so that it would not be surprising to see tendrils of seaweed snaking down from the dark curls that framed her face. Della: deliquescence: the tendency of certain salts to absorb water vapor straight from the air until they begin to sweat and finally vanish in a pool of their own making, so eager are they to dissolve.

He would make coffee and excavate the new pile of papers on

Relnik. This he knew was not redemption but the only substitute most of us have, the option of trying to actually be what we have been only pretending to be all along.

■ ■ ■

Della switched off the car radio, which was static on Sister Bertha's frequency anyway, and divided herself between reverie and speed. She would not be doing this, she was fairly sure, if Miriam had not as much as sent her. Miriam had been waiting up when Della got home the night before last, trying to look like a disapproving housemother. "He likes you, Della, anyone could see that. You were the teacher's pet."

"He needs a studio audience, that's all," Della said, and sipped her decaf for a moment. "Something funny happened."

"Oh ho! The first date and something funny happens."

"Not like that, give me a break. But I saw this guy at the bar, someone Steve once brought to the house. I'm positive. So I went up to him and I said, I think we've met, I was wondering if you might have heard from Kipper. I said that, I said 'Kipper.' And I was going to say 'I'm his mother,' but the guy looked scared or something. Maybe he thought I was, I don't know, going to be a pest. He just brushed me off and went out the door."

"He didn't say anything?"

"Yes, but I didn't get it. He looks at me and goes, 'Lady, I'm not into games anymore.' I just stood there like a jerk, I'm old enough to be his mother."

"He didn't recognize you?"

"I don't think so. Then he turned around on his way out, and this is the funny part. He said, 'If you're into games, try Homer.' Or Homer's."

Miriam shook her head. "You think because Leo rejected you everyone's rejecting you. That's a logical error: generalization. I learned that from Women in Transition. You'd get a lot out of it, Della, if you'd give it a chance."

"Yeah, well, it looked like rejection."

"But it could have been something else. Here, let me see that phone book."

And there it had been, between "Homer, Bertrand" and "Homer, J.": "Homer Electronics," with an address in a town five miles east of the university. Della looked down at the directions she had written out for herself on the car seat next to her, and in the half second her eyes were off the road, the truck that had been tailgating her lunged ahead, rocking her car with the violence of its passage.

The steering wheel was wet in her hands. She wiped her palms, one by one, on her slacks. There was a video game she had once watched Steve play. It was a matter of steering to keep the little image of an unmanned car on a road which whipped around out of its own free will while marauding vehicles flashed by with blazing guns. But the alarming part was the scenery: a desert of AstroTurf in which houses, villages, whole institutions peeped up on the horizon, grew until they reached the foreground, and then were swept under the lower edge of the screen. Only the sky was more or less constant, an unmodulated field of blue with no visible light source. Perfect little self-involved clouds moved across at regular intervals, bored by the carnage.

Steve loved video games, at least until he'd gotten his computer. She'd take him to the video arcade in the mall, with the little stool that he needed so he could see the screen and reach the controls. Della would watch over his shoulder, doling out the quarters, trying to follow the action on the screen. You don't have to play them more than two or three times, he would say, before you get the idea, the plan of the game, and he would try to explain, and Della would nod: That's good, Steve, that's really smart.

Her palms dried when she got to the exit and left the expressway. Now she was in a prosperous neighborhood, homes that might once have cost close to a half-million dollars. Once, maybe ten years ago, people had moved here with the simple plan of living the good life as defined by the more reasonable philosophers: love, work, play, responsibility, freedom, maintenance and repair. But from the look of things there had been disappointments. Spina bifida, Della imagined, daughters needing abortions before their sweet-sixteen parties, layoffs, demotions, useless sons getting home at dawn and vomiting in the flower beds. Still, the houses seemed committed to whatever it was their occupants had given up on, and Della drove slowly, with respect, toward the address from the phone book.

■ ■ ■

Homer, surprisingly, was Asian, or some kind of complicated mix. Della had been expecting someone large and sloppy-looking, like the man in the bar, but Homer was thin and well put together. He motioned her into a mostly empty space, like an urban loft, offering few visible concessions to the life of the body. Track lights ran around the ceiling, overpowering the thin light from the window. In better times it had been a two-car garage, but necessity had converted it into a freestanding apartment. Probably the rent paid property taxes on the adjacent house, which still had plastic sheeting over some of the upstairs windows, left over from winter.

"So you're Kipper's mom," he said with an edge of derision in his tone. Being someone's mom was always slightly silly, a reminder that even grown men, living in their own apartments, had once been drooling, stumbling fools. But Homer probably just meant to be polite. So the next question caught her off guard: "Can I see some ID?"

Della handed him her wallet and then winced at her naïveté. He didn't look like a thief; in fact, he looked a little monk-like, the way his shirt was done up all the way to the top, but then you never knew. He was flipping through cards housed in plastic, credit cards, video-club membership, check-cashing privileges in three supermarkets, and other souvenirs of married affluence. "There's a picture of him in there," she said, and he handed back the wallet, then studied the photo she dug out for him.

"Sorry," he said, looking up and stretching back in his chair. "But everyone seems to want Kipper these days. A guy came by yesterday, just since you called, it got me paranoid."

"What kind of guy?"

"I don't know, white guy."

"I'm just interested, if someone else is looking for Steve . . ." She returned the wallet to her purse and zipped it shut.

"Guy in a suit. He wanted to know everything about him: hobbies, sports, pets, favorite vacation spots. I said, That's easy, ha ha. The answer is none. None of the above. Kipper lived for one thing, we all know that. 'Purity of heart is to will one thing,' Kierkegaard said that. Well, man, Kipper was pure of heart."

"You say 'was.' Why do you say 'was'?"

"Was when he was here, that's all. I didn't mean anything by it. He's somewhere right now, right? But I don't know where."

"Then maybe you could tell me something about what he was working on. The 'one thing.' Because we had problems, in the last year, of communication. Steve and his father, for one thing, maybe Steve mentioned."

Della rubbed her upper arm nervously, as if the effort of talking had somehow injured it. There was no real reason for Homer to care. She didn't even know if this was his last name or his first, much less what he was thinking behind those tightly drawn features.

"He didn't talk about it, huh?"

"Maybe he thought I wouldn't understand. I mean, the technical part."

"Never had any patience with the uninitiated, did he?" Homer's smile was not fond.

"The reason I want to know is . . ." She looked around the room for a clue. Motherhood had once been a good enough reason for anything she wanted to do, a rationale for the space she took up, the food she ate. Leo was a thinner rationale, more on the level of an excuse. She was no longer sure what the system was, for justifying things, what claims she had. "My husband left me, Kipper's father."

Homer went over to the half-sized refrigerator in the far corner of the room and came back with two glasses of water. "It's filtered," he said, and they drank.

"Kipper and I were in the same . . . network, computer network, that's all. Anyway, at some point, he took off. Dropped out of sight."

"Just like that?"

Homer shrugged. "He was into this theory, you know, about what you could do with a computer to activate the brain, you know, push it to capacity. That was his thing."

From the look on Homer's face it was time to think of going, but there was something else, something connected with how she had gotten here. "Does this have something to do with games, I mean computer games?"

"Oh yeah, of course. It would have to be a game. Everyone is interested in games. The guy looking for Kipper, he was interested in games. Said he was from a computer game company. I have his card here somewhere. But the game was not the point of it. This is where people get Kipper wrong. The game was a means to an end."

"Which is?"

"Enlightenment: what else?" Homer laughed dryly. "The mystic goal of mankind. Except the mystics thought it came in a blinding flash. But the only way to get to it, this was Kipper's theory, is step by step. Everyone wants to skip the steps. But you can only get there, Kipper said, one move at a time. You see, the game provides the algorithm, the strategy for getting to the solution. If the game is good enough, of course, and he was getting to that. It takes you through the steps."

"So is this game, uh, available?"

Homer's face reverted to impatience. He looked at his fingernails and then turned his wrist and looked at his watch. "Look, I don't know any more. I don't know if he finished it. I wouldn't want to have anything to do with it if he did. You want to know what Kipper is up to, that's all right, you're his mom. But leave me out of it, okay?"

Della stood up and shouldered her purse strap. "Well, of course. You've been very helpful, but—"

"Okay, cool," Homer said, opening the door. "Let's just leave it at that."

CHAPTER 3

The apartment would be a new phase, Miriam had said, in which everything could be re-evaluated and assembled into a plan. Houses were no good for this because their very hollowness, after a point, sucked at a woman's soul and demanded certain efforts. But in a smaller scale of operations—one bedroom, a living-dining area—the importance of the tenant herself would come to the fore. Della had seen this effect in TV dramas, where women who might have seemed lost and irrelevant in a full-sized house gained wit and sex appeal as the walls drew more snugly in around them. From an apartment everything would look different. Cleaning would be an exercise in self-indulgence, and what others might see as loneliness would begin to resemble freedom.

They would have looked longer, but too many of the places involved personal stories of bankruptcy or cancer. Tightly wound real-estate women took them around, pointing out the design possibilities in a tile floor or arched doorway, exulting over southern exposures. Some places seemed to have been built to be empty, their walls straining outward to discourage the idea of furniture. In others the past tenants lived on in wallpaper stains and linoleum scratches: widows whose husbands' pensions allowed them to grow old in sleeveless housedresses, pairs of young secretaries poised for matrimony, groups of immigrant men sleeping four to a room, leaning out second-story windows when they wanted some privacy. There was a zone of impermanence, Della saw now, occupied by the unwed and underpaid, and with room in it for her.

The place they finally settled on was the second floor of a house that had been built for a standard-sized family whose other members had died or dispersed, leaving only the landlord downstairs. Just six months ago, he told her, on this very block, a woman had been raped in her bed, a nursing mother. She was okay except for some bruises, but the perpetrator had been charged with manslaughter, because the baby had been crushed between them, in the attack, and died of internal injuries.

These are just stories people tell in the suburbs, Miriam had said, myths, really, meant to maintain a high level of vigilance. Fear is something we do to ourselves with our heads. But the landlord had gone so far as to have an alarm system installed in his half of the house and a bedraggled dog on a chain in the yard. When he went out, to buy groceries or get prescriptions refilled, he left his radio on to simulate a human presence, and Della would be enlisted to share the heartbreak of some long-dead baritone, borne up to her on waves of big-band sound.

You could do something with this place, Miriam insisted. She had read about using plants to set up a biofield and coral tones to bring out the positive, plus things that could be done with mirrors. But from the day Della moved in, the furniture looked ill at ease, expectant, as though it had been called together for some project long since forgotten. There were no curtains up, and light was being gathered through the windows in unmanageable amounts, crowding out the air. The kitchen seemed only slightly safer. She thought of tidying up once the movers were gone, but each item left out on the counter challenged her to recall its place and function. Some things seem willing enough when they are being used, but put them aside for a while and an aloofness sets in. A list of instructions is implied—what this is, how it must be cleaned, the best method of storage—and these, as far as Della could see, had been omitted.

She was better off looking out the windows. From the living room she could see a featureless concrete warehouse at which over twenty men arrived every morning at seven, like conspirators summoned by a coded signal. She spent far more time, though, in the kitchen, where the window looked out on a water tower, a dull green bulb poised on stilts, higher than the house, but just far enough away to fit into the view framed by the window. All her life she had been seeing water towers, located irregularly along the side roads, without ever establishing their function. They stored water, she knew that, but now that she had one to study close at hand, she could identify no structure for adding water or, for that matter, draining it off. Leo would know, because he was good at things of a mechanical-industrial nature, but she would be the last to ask. And just possibly, even in a well-planned county, some things are built out of habit, and for no clear purpose, or because the budget allows it and some contractor, probably a man known to Leo, has demanded his due.

■   ■   ■

"Della, it's me." There was a throat-clearing sound. "Leo. How's it going?"

"Fine. Just fine." She could hear a staticky clicking sound, probably a remote control changing channels on a muted TV. He was at home then, his new home, watching a silent television set while he went through his calls.

"The shadow of an airplane passed over me. Yesterday. I was in the parking lot going for my car and then there was like this eclipse, just where I was standing. It spooked me, Della, it really did. I knew this guy, he was walking on the beach when an airplane went over him, the full shadow, and three weeks later he was dead. Hit-and-run."

"I'm sorry to hear."

"That was months ago, Della, the other guy. I'm talking about me, what happened yesterday."

"I know. The shadow." Maybe Leo had been threatened. He was in a line of work where a man might expect to be threatened some-day; that is, a line not easy to trace, an intention grown diffuse and possibly dangerous.

". . . a man gets to a point in his life," Leo was saying. The absence of clicks suggested some compelling scene, a car chase, a shooting, a disheveled couple sliding into bed. ". . . where you've been and where you're going. The basics, what it adds up to. I'm talking values, Della, what we give is what we get. There are mis-takes, I grant that, roads you take and roads, uh, not taken . . . Della?"

"Mmmh." The conversation was beginning to box her in. "Look, I'm going to have to get off, I'm expecting a call."

"Well, for Chrissake, don't let me take up your time. I just hope to God you're not seeing one of those pansy-ass professors." He filled in her silence with a series of clicks. "I just wondered"—he cleared his throat again—"if you happened to hear anything from Steve."

"No. Why?"

"Like I was saying, you get to a point, you know. You think maybe how much time do I have? Oh hell, Della, he's my son."

A nearly naked branch shook itself in the reflected light of the water tower. His son. This was a new concept. She felt her notion of Steve beginning to unravel. There was Leo's part, her part, some part lost with Carl, some part perhaps still belonging to Homer or others like him. Her part might be only the smallest fraction, a little boy long since superseded in the rush of things.

"Della?"

"I'll let you know."

"Great. Call me at the office. I'm there all the time." He must have switched off the mute, because a new voice, heavy with insinuation, cut in as they said goodbye: "So, Mario, this is a nice surprise, huh?" Followed by gunshots.

■　　■　　■

On Della's second Monday on the job Dr. Leitbetter issued a complex-wide call to a second lecture. Della went down with Claire and the two technicians, but got separated from them in the crowd filing into the auditorium just before noon, and ended up sitting in a row half filled with strangers. There was some horseplay and loud calls across the domed space until everyone found a seat. A few people had brought in illicit snacks, which they now unwrapped and placed on their laps, under the foldout desktops, because this was lunch hour and there was no reason to believe they would still have time to go to the cafeteria. One of the nice things about Dr. Hershey was that he told everyone to take a full lunch hour after the lecture, then he had gone into his office and shut the door behind him, refusing to take any part in it.

When the lights were in place and the cameramen stopped fidgeting with their equipment and appeared to relax, Dr. Leitbetter rose from a seat in the front row and walked across the stage to the podium, reflexively patting air with the hand nearest the audience in order to still any incipient applause. Della could see the gravity that settled over him in the presence of an audience, even an audience like this, half captive and half paid. Because most of the faculty refused to sit through the lecture again, all other personnel had been commandeered, except for a group of summer-school students who came voluntarily in exchange for free movie passes. Leitbetter stood beside the podium, resting one elbow on it, and seemed to scan the crowd for delinquent eaters and gigglers, but in fact the video lights were so bright that he saw only intersecting haloes against a background that might have been dark pebbles arranged in concentric arcs.

"As you know," he began, his hand stroking the light fixture on the podium, "the Human Ecology Complex is committed to the development of the fullest potential of all its . . . members." There was some audible conversation in Spanish as a group of men from the animal house settled into their seats, joking about the white lab coats they had been given to wear for the occasion. *"Maricón,"* could be heard, but for the most part not understood. Dr. Leitbetter tapped the light fixture to facilitate the settling down and continued.

"Today, a minor disappointment has turned into a happy opportunity, a learning opportunity, for all of us. Channel 3, which was unable to attend last week's lecture, due to the press of . . . events, asked if the lecture could be repeated for taping today. Fortunately, Dr. Caragiola was able to rearrange her busy schedule and oblige us. She is, as I am sure you know, a world-renowned scholar whose work has already wakened the literary world from its morbid self-absorption and brought a breath of air to those of us who toil in the more pragmatic realm of science. Note-taking is suggested. Bear in mind that at least one camera will be directed your way throughout."

Under the klieg lights Dr. Caragiola looked as young and whimsical as she had hoped to look at the party, and Della briefly joined half the audience in wondering if she was married and, if so, whether she had an interesting sex life. Anyone who had hoped for an opening joke or anecdote was quickly let down. Dr. Caragiola's idea of a witticism was to rotate the nouns around a preposition, so that "the relevance of structuralism" became the "structure of relevance" and the "dialectic of nature" became the "nature of dialectics," and so on.

"As a science," she was saying, with a complicitous smile, "literary criticism is in much the same condition as physics was before Newton, or biology before Mendel. We operate on hunches, vaguely remembered patterns of repetition; the fundamental laws remain unknown."

Next to Della, a thin woman pressed raisins between her fingers and brought them up to her lips with great circumspection. A man in front of her began to pitch forward into sleep. Since the problem that had developed with the complex's wiring, only last week, the ventilation was faint and wheezy. Everyone was sharing air now, and conscious of its density.

"But if the science of aesthetics lags," the amplified voice continued, "so too does the aesthetics of science. Scientists seek the 'elegant' solution. But"—Dr. Caragiola leaned forward and paused so that the audience could see this was a suspenseful moment—"who is setting the standards of beauty? Is it symmetry, simplicity? What is it that science seeks?"

There was a sighing in the auditorium. If this was the question, the answers would be a long time coming. Della began to doodle curving structures on the pad she had brought to simulate note-taking. Since the visit to Homer she had felt a slight shift toward greater focus. Only with Leo's call had it occurred to her what she was supposed to see in this new sharpness of things: what it was, was that she was not the only one who found in Steve's absence, well, an issue. There was the man who had been to see Homer, and now Leo with his newfound superstitions, Leo who had not asked about Steve in a full year. She began to work a larger pattern over the curving structures, pulling them in together toward the center of the paper, curve reinforcing curve.

"I have something for you," someone whispered to her in the heavily minted breath of a morning drinker. It was Alex, who had taken advantage of a temporary dimming of the lights, probably caused by another generator failure, to slip into the seat next to her. He was staring straight ahead with a look of mock amazement. "Isn't this something, huh? She's performing for us, we're perform-ing for her. Television has brought a much-needed symmetry to the lecture medium." Someone sitting in the row in front of them, a genuine professor in white lab coat, frowned over his shoulder.

"What do you have?" Della asked. She would have liked it to be something to eat.

"It's about Sister Bertha. I talked to this guy in Urban Anthro-pology. Can I see you after work?"

Della nodded carefully. The lecture was building toward some sort of climax. "Science is driven, then, by an unspoken meta-physical narrative of its own, a storyline that insists that the most economical answer is not only lovely but 'true.' But science awaits the harsh test of aesthetic judgment, a test which can no longer be postponed . . ."

There was a storm of heartfelt applause when she reached her final point and rounded it out with a modest "Thank you." A few people in the back bolted toward the doors, but Dr. Leitbetter had risen from his seat to say that Dr. Caragiola had kindly agreed to take a few questions. These were assigned in advance, Alex explained to Della. He had been offered one himself, something on the simultaneous interest in "codes" in both biology and literary theory, and whether this might point to a larger cultural metaphor, but he had begged out of it. A shaggy man near the front was fretting with his question, on possibly conflicting constructions of truth, which he read from a scrap of paper, and the audience settled back down in resignation.

"In science," Dr. Caragiola was answering him, "truth is what 'works.' But what about all the lovely, lazy theories that simply refuse to work? The inheritance of acquired characteristics, the ether, phlogiston? Are we to condemn them totally just because they refuse to lift a finger to propel our vehicles or improve our crops? How self-centered, really, and what a powerful argument for a thorough aesthetic re-evaluation."

Dr. Caragiola held her head at various angles, on the lookout for further questions, glad that her ready answers, some of them not entirely premeditated, were being recorded for the millions not now present. She raised her eyebrows toward a figure in the center of the auditorium and the cameras followed her gaze to a short-haired, overweight woman struggling to fold back the desktop and get to her feet. "I've been sitting here listening for one hour, and all I've been hearing is vanity and godlessness, godlessness and vanity." The voice shook at first with the challenge of addressing such a crowd, and then began to soar. "The Lamb has lain down with the lion, but I say to you: The Lamb shall rise up and slay the lion. And all those who have eaten of unclean meat, so shall they also burn. This is the story, the true story, and you know it!"

It was Claire, looking strangely pure and concentrated in the white light, in her white lab coat, fists at her sides. Next to her, the technicians sat rigid, staring blindly ahead. An ambiguous murmur started up, containing elements of approval as well as disgust, and one of the men from maintenance cupped his hands over his mouth and made a whooping sound. Dr. Caragiola leaned forward and squinted, trying to attach a face to the outburst. "Well, that's one narrative approach, anyway," she said, her face tightening sweetly around the words.

"Bullshit! It's the only story and anyone with eyes to see knows that!" Claire was in full voice now, careening ahead. "The Lamb has forgiven all, but his forgiveness is only the cleansing before the slaughter, when the Lamb shall rise up . . ."

Now Dr. Caragiola was holding on to the podium as if it had begun to rock. Other voices joined Claire's: ". . . unconscionable outburst!" and, from another part of the hall, "Amen, sister!" "Richard!" Dr. Caragiola hissed, audibly, but Dr. Leitbetter was already on his feet, striding up the stairs to the stage. "Thank you, thank you," he was saying, from his old position next to the podium, but he could not be heard above the hundred arguments that had broken out among the audience. A man in shirtsleeves yelled "Fundamentalist bitch" at Claire, who was pushing her way to the aisle. Someone else said "Sexist pigs," and candy wrappers flew from the back of the hall. The cameramen were intent now, signaling to each other, scanning for the action. Dr. Caragiola, still gripping the podium, turned to Dr. Leitbetter and said, at an angle to the microphone but clearly enough to be heard at the back of the auditorium, "You ruined this, you—"

■　　■　　■

"You have an appointment with Alex at three, Dr. Leitbetter, that's ten minutes from now." It was the voice of the speaker phone, a marvel of ventriloquism, and Leitbetter spoke back to the air, "Yes, yes, just let him on in when he comes." The appointment had been postponed because of the "outburst," as it was now officially known, which had taken up all his day after the lecture: talking to network executives, conferring with his loyalists among the faculty, attempting to soothe Dr. Caragiola, who had nonetheless sat in perfect silence all the way to the airport, refusing even to discuss his offer of a chair in the aesthetics of science.

But there was no point in wasting the minutes before Alex's arrival. Leitbetter switched on his desktop tape recorder, furrowed his brow, and coughed lightly. He did not like hand-held microphones for this purpose—the image of himself sitting alone with a squat black wand in his hand was disturbing somehow—but he had never become entirely comfortable talking straight into the emptiness either.

"We have not the time today to review the evidence, ignored or, tragically, suppressed by the stunted adolescent mind we know as 'science.' A mind that asks 'How? how?' but never 'Why?' "

He trailed off, frowned, replaying these sentences in his head. No good, stiff as cardboard.

He would be giving the William George Fleming lecture on the philosophy of science in three weeks, and the title he had made up, "The Research Institute as Cosmic Beacon," now seemed inspired: a means, he saw, of levitating himself above the multiplying torments of responsibility to his true position in the scheme of things.

He turned the recorder on again. "When I think of the cold disdain, the contempt, even, that has greeted the evidence, the rich and abundant evidence, for other inhabitants of the universe, beings greater than ourselves, for a Visitor who—"

Alex had stepped in and was looking around the room, lips pursed and eyebrows raised, finding no audience for Leitbetter's monologue.

"Come in, come in," Leitbetter said, still fussing with the tape recorder. Alex took a seat and waited in silence. The best policy, he had long since decided, was to ignore the wild-eyed, mawkish theories Leitbetter peddled on his public appearances. Visitors, indeed. A few weeks ago Leitbetter had given a press conference on the need to begin serious communication with extraterrestrial life —not just the usual baby-talk messages, the Pythagorean theorem and so forth, but the whole thing, all of human knowledge. Boil it down, express it in the binary system, start beaming it out right away. There is always the danger, Leitbetter had warned, that human life might self-destruct before the moment of contact, the arrival of the Visitor, so why not start now? A focused beam of X-rays, or maybe some other rays, pulsing out the value of pi, quantum states of the hydrogen atom, the genetic code, even the height of the Himalayas and the depth of the sea, in case you wanted the down-home touch.

"Just getting a few notes down, Al. You want cappuccino? Phyllis has a machine for cappuccino. Or bourbon-and-water, I could make that myself."

"Nah, I'm fine. Sorry to be late, but there was a spill on the eighth floor, hole in a radioactive waste storage drum; remarkably neat hole, I hear."

Leitbetter picked up a pen and balanced it between his fingertips, frowning while Alex described the route he'd had to take to avoid the cleanup effort, looping into Tower A by skywalk and then up the maintenance elevator, which had unfortunately stalled on the ninth floor for ten minutes before anyone could get to it.

"Yes, yes. And what do you hear out there?"

"Well, it certainly didn't look like normal chemical erosion."

"I mean about Monday, about the lecture. The little outburst. What are they saying?"

"I don't know, all kinds of things." Since Monday, in fact, the complex had seethed with argument, almost like a town meeting, although conducted piecemeal, in corridors, cafeteria lines, and over restroom sinks. New factions were imposed on old ones. Murmurs rose up, embodying theories and allegiances, then clashed against each other, like wavelets on some misdirected tide. Claire had her supporters, who were, sociologically speaking, drawn from the complex's middle stratum of employees—senior technicians, low-level engineers, administrative assistants. Dr. Caragiola, surprisingly, had supporters too, based largely among the tiny number of female faculty members and a handful of malcontents concerned about the social responsibility of science and its apparent abandonment by the Human Ecology Complex. There was also a small but potentially important third force, originating among the librarians and standing for the ideals of pluralism, tolerance, and patching things over.

"I mean the faculty," Leitbetter interrupted. "I suppose this is a big ha-ha."

"Well, it had its moments, particularly Channel 3's version, which I caught on the eleven o'clock news."

"It was Hershey, you know that." Leitbetter had the pen vibrating between two fingers, generating imperceptible winds.

"Come on, Dick, the woman is a nut, that's all. You should get out more often, the world is full of them. I was over at Urban Anthro last week: chiliasts, millenarianists, people who have had intimate contact with visitors from Alpha Centauri; followers of Isis, Loki, Quetzalcoatl; evangelical anorectics recruiting from health clubs; militant support groups for industrial diseases; Zoroastrians; you name it. The place is swarming with them. It's the times, that's all. UFO sightings, for example: up 30 percent in the last year alone. Number of people who've been taken aboard alien crafts and had their bodies delicately probed by tiny fingers: up 27 percent and rising."

"Hershey set her up. Anyone can see that."

"Dick, Dick, Hershey is a fucking civilian." This was their old word for non-scientists or, alternatively, 9-to-5 scientists who would stop an experiment because it was dinnertime or they had a school play to go to, people who associated obsession with a low-grade fever. "He's not that interested. He wants to be left alone with his disease."

"You're naïve, Alex." Leitbetter dry-laughed. "You have no responsibility to anyone but yourself, and obviously you don't take that very seriously. But I'm trying to build something here, doesn't anybody understand that?"

"I think that's generally recognized." Alex slid deeper into the armchair, aware that the seed of a headache, right under the skull behind his forehead, was beginning to prosper. "You still have that bourbon-and-water?"

"Of course." He waved across the huge gray plain of carpet to the wet bar that had been installed to meet the needs of Japanese businessmen and prime-time interviewers. "But not much time. Development Committee at four, and I have papers to go over first."

"It's about our old friend Henry Relnik, as I tried to tell you at the party last week."

"Yes, yes, what've you got for me?" Leitbetter sat back down and leaned forward, navigating the change of subject with the ease he was famous for. "Interesting," he had once told an interviewer, was not a word in his vocabulary, because it implied that some things were not interesting and that others were worthy of only mild puzzlement. While, in fact, to the scientific mind, all things sit pert and ready to inspire lifetimes of dedicated study.

"If Dora Mueller is supposed to be the Nazi connection, it isn't panning out. As far as I can tell, she loses her post at the university in '42 and gets a job at the Höhere Töchterschule, the girls' high school. Teaching hygiene. And while she's there she gets written up for attitudes unbecoming to *volkish* womanhood, or something like that. She wasn't a Nazi. For all we know, she was in the Resistance, for Chrissake, if there was a Resistance."

"Hmmm." Leitbetter appeared to be listening intently, but for some sound that had not yet been made.

"So there's no point to it, Dick. As much as I need it, I don't want to waste your money. This is not one of the great ironies of the twentieth century."

"Wait a minute, Al, you're not planning to let me down now, are you?" He had stilled his fingers by matching the tips, prayer-like, and bringing the ensemble up toward his face. "I have very major funding behind this, a source I really can't afford to disappoint. I would have done it myself, God knows, if it wasn't for . . . this." He inclined his head toward the desk, with its piles of correspondence, article reprints, lecture notes.

The pain was now stamping against Alex's skull, adding to the expectation of perpetual failure. "I'm only telling you"—he paused to sip—"what I found. What I found is that the original hypothesis doesn't hold up, and when the original hypothesis doesn't hold up, it's generally time to rethink. So I would say, scrap Relnik, Mueller, the whole business. Give me someone else, assuming you have a whole file of these types." He sipped again. "What do you think?"

"Oh, there's nothing to think." Leitbetter let a moment go by and then smiled abstractly. "If she wasn't a Nazi, she was a good German. Okay, maybe not even a good one. Still, the problem of evil, the responsibility of the average bricklayer . . . Perhaps the story gets a little richer, more nuanced, that's all." He stood up and looked at his watch. "But I need it soon, everything you can get: her theories, his theories, anything you can get on them. It's not just the funder. The publisher's breathing down my neck, Al. You're holding the whole thing up."

Alex left with a generous have-it-your-way gesture and then decided to use the incoming Development Committee as an excuse to loiter around Phyllis's desk until they had all gone in and shut the door to the inner office behind them. Phyllis was a large handsome blond woman hired for her accent, which was easily mistaken for British. For three years she had been one of Alex's major points of contact with the complex's gossip network, the same network that told him Phyllis flirted with everyone, evidently as a way of keeping in shape, and was no threat to a man's basic privacy.

"So you didn't try my cappuccino, Alex," she said, looking at him sidewise from her computer terminal. "When are you going to try my cappuccino? Hmmm?"

"Cappuccino is an alcohol antagonist, I have to use it very sparingly."

"Sure, and sex is a cure for hangovers."

"Well then, let me just get to the bottom of this drink and we'll see."

"Really. I read it somewhere. It's the vasodilating effect. Opens up the cerebral capillaries so the sun can shine in."

"Speaking of cerebration, I'm in a little trouble with the chief. A little late, actually, with my chapter for the *Biography of the Twentieth Century*, you remember that? And I was just wondering how many of the others had come in, to sort of see how I stand? I'm almost done, but if I thought I had another couple of weeks . . ."

She made a face by moving her pursed lips over toward one cheek. "I vaguely remember. File name BOTC. But nothing's come in on that."

"Nothing at all? No manuscripts? No thick manila envelopes?"

"Uh-uh, not on that."

"Well then, look, could you call up the list for me, of the other contributors? There's a guy—Robbins, Robertson? something like that, at Wisconsin?—who I might have a little overlap with, and I'd like to just check in with him, go over some points, if you could get me the list, names and addresses."

"Sure, sweetie, but not just this minute. I should have had this printed out for Development ten minutes ago. So scram, and I'll put it in your box for you, soon as I get a moment."

"You're a darling, Phyllis. I'd love to put something in your box too, you know."

"Out!"

But he was already in the windowless corridor, where a faltering fluorescent bulb, combined with the bourbon, was exciting the nucleus of a headache to exultant bursts of growth. The trick was to go over to the side of the pain, not to resist, for in some punitive system of physiology the pain was no doubt the booze-racked brain's attempt at healing. When he got to a working water fountain, he bent over and splashed his face, but the trip back to the upright position left him faint. There was no Robbins at Wisconsin, of course, but then, for reasons he couldn't even begin to fathom right now, Leitbetter had been the first to lie.

■   ■   ■

It was not Dr. Hershey's custom to think about religion during working hours, or any other time, for that matter, except for Sunday mornings between ten and noon, but the incident with Claire had forced the issue. He had known for some time now that she was low-church and opposed to abortion, evolution, female ordination, and all the other improvements on the primitive that gave the mainline denominations their strength and flexibility. He had even heard her refer to "the Lamb" once, in a hushed conversation with the dishwasher, who had merely wailed and crossed herself, failing to take up the challenge. But there was little in his own religious life to give him insight into a faith aligned with so much anger. For over a decade, his wife and he had patronized the same suburban church, where the sermons were as intricate as chamber music, and equally relaxing. Sitting with one arm pressed up against his wife's, he would open his mind to concepts like "transubstantiation" and "grace," where they would become the shifting terms in a somber new form of mathematics, private to him and deeply refreshing.

It was the disease, really, that forced the issue. He had never imagined that the subject of his research might someday reach out and find a point of contact within the human environment of the lab, but here it was. The disease had religious overtones, there was no denying it. In the final days before death, the skin grew shiny and thin in spots, breaking open at the slightest abrasion to emit a slow seepage of blood. The first reported death in San Carlos, Mexico, had in fact been covered in a supermarket tabloid, under the headline STIGMATA APPEAR ON SICK BOY: NERVOUS NEIGHBORS AWAIT SECOND COMING.

Hershey had shared the odd fact of the "stigmata" with the post-docs, chuckling a little at the folly of it, but since the tabloid had offered no dateline for the story, and since the accompanying photo might have been of a dying, malnourished child anywhere, the odor of sensationalism had not yet attached to his work. Nor would it ever, if he could help it. Yet the bleeding itself was a breach of boundaries, perfectly explainable, of course, but inevitably more disquieting than a surgical cut, this slow erosion of the skin. And now there was the unavoidable convergence of religious manias, the one surrounding the disease and the other centered on Claire, pointing to another breach, another potential point of leakage and fusion. Somewhere in all this was a menace alien to Hershey's orderly mind, a barely contained pollution, for where membranes break, or worlds that have been separate come too close, taboos may be the next to go, or courtesies and laws.

But what finally jolted Hershey to alertness was the appearance of the disease within his own country, in a town called Vista View: another boundary breached, and of this there was no longer any question. One child dead and a woman in the final stages, meaning at least a good supply of blood and tissue, reliably prepared by U.S. laboratory standards. At the Vista View end, there was an agreement to keep it quiet, call it flu or something, at least for a few weeks, until Hershey's people had a statement to make. He did not need trouble, bleeding Lambs or menopausal hysteria, with the pressure on full throttle.

So he began—subtly, he hoped—to rearrange the lines of communication within the lab. The technicians would continue with tissue slicing and microscopy, reporting directly to the Pakistani. Claire would be cut out of the information loop as much as possible, with the explanation that her skills were needed in a more hands-on sense, trying to infect the various animals he had chosen for this purpose. Della, who seemed intelligent enough, would carry more of the weight of information, scanning the literature for further outbreaks and entering new data as they came in. But first he conducted his own security check, startling Della with a summons to his office on an afternoon when Claire was off in the animal house, supposedly drawing blood, but actually, he was sure, carrying on with her constituents about the growing impatience of the Lamb.

He started by showing Della photos of the dead so far, the "holy relics" of the lab, as the Pakistani put it. This was to make it real enough, establish contact, as it were. No one could look at them and not be moved, he was counting on that.

"But they're so young," Della said. Actually, everyone made the same protest. "Young" was about the only distinguishing feature left on the blotched bodies, laid out coldly for autopsy.

"Right. Eleven to twenty, that's the age range we're dealing with."

"Is it always fatal?"

"As far as we know. But of course it's possible that there've been other cases that just haven't come to our attention yet."

"What do you think it is?"

"Well, who knows? We don't even know how it's transmitted yet: blood, feces, insect vectors, whatever." He sighed. "There are new diseases all the time coming out of the tropics. I go to the meetings: parasitology, tropical medicine. I've heard some dillies. But a disease that stays in the Third World isn't really going to amount to much. Even at epidemic strength, it won't support one small-size lab for more than a year. The grants just aren't there.

But our disease has just moved north, across the border, and that changes the picture."

He leaned back and regarded the map on the wall with satisfaction. "So you see how it is. We have a mystery on our hands, a hot potato. You're part of a very important effort here, I hope you know."

Della nodded and fiddled with the pencil in her hand. She had come in with a notepad, but nothing he had said so far seemed to translate into an actual instruction.

"We don't want anything to leak out prematurely, before we pin this thing down. We don't need the press breathing down our necks. Who knows? The Centers for Disease Control would snap it up just like that, and where would we be? But not everybody sees it this way. There are forces right here in the complex. Individuals." He paused, pulled a cigarette out of his breast pocket, and then returned it to the pack.

"You took a course from Alex MacBride, right?"

Della nodded again.

"I wouldn't share any of this with him."

"Of course not." Della took it as an accusation, the heat rising under her blouse. "I don't know him all that well, anyway."

Hershey rubbed his hands, signaling that the conversation was drawing to a satisfactory close. "Because it could go from him to other, uh, individuals." He rose to open the door for her. "People who don't know how to distinguish between science and spectacle. A line has to be drawn, because when you start bringing in other factors—the factor, for example, of personal ambition, of human . . ." He paused, not sure what word to put after "human." "You lose focus, that's all. The problem wins."

■　　■　　■

Alex went home with a plan for recovery: aspirin and sinus pills for the headache, orange juice and a sandwich for the shakes, coffee to cut through the mournful numbness that took over, most days, by early afternoon. Then he would see. But he was no sooner out of the deli than he remembered he had asked Della to meet him after work the other day, Monday. What had he done? Because he hadn't met Della or called her, or set a new time, or apologized. Monday evening joined various other patches of his life that had gone their own way, into obscurity. A sense of anxiety and loss set in, allying itself with the headache. He dug out the scrap of paper on which he had written her number, but there was no answer, just a series of rings set loose in an empty apartment.

Sobriety, at a certain point in the lifelong pursuit of its opposite, is like nothing so much as insomnia. You can cure it with the natural remedy or you can resign yourself for a while and try to find some way to pass the time. The coffee and the pills were adding a certain edge to things, which would be more congenial with a drink or two, but there was a reason to put up with it now.

Alex shut the venetian blinds, temporarily sealing his commitment to temperance. The view from his apartment was not conducive to effort, to the thought, even, of more modest forms of continuation. He could see boarded-up windows in the apartment house across the courtyard, the brown and balding lawn, a rusty tricycle at the curb, escaped garbage cans rolling in the street or, as it was optimistically titled, the "lane"; and the whole scene said: Oblivion is the superior state. What more proof do you require?

With the blinds shut it was possible to take up more manageable questions, like the matter of Leitbetter's little chore for him. Why was Leitbetter so interested in this Relnik business? To the point of implying that the other manuscripts were already in and that Alex was the last straggler? He sat in the dimmed room reviewing Leitbetter's character, an old exercise but not an easy one to finish. Success doesn't work for everyone is what it came down to, perhaps especially when the success is so far out of proportion to the effort extended. Even correcting for jealousy, it was fair to say that the work that launched Leitbetter, making him an academic celebrity by the age of thirty-five—friend of television producers, best-selling authors, and philanthropic business leaders—was derivative, mundane really. And that in itself could be the problem: never having taken the measure of his own mediocrity, Leitbetter was like an infant in a man-sized world, unacquainted with his limits.

Except that the answer to the Relnik puzzle might lie not with Leitbetter but with Relnik himself, a man who seemed to have accepted his mediocrity so agreeably and operated well within it. Alex uncovered the stack of Relnik-related papers Leitbetter had given him, weeks ago, when the project still seemed fresh and honest, and cleared off a place for them on his desk. He had skimmed through these papers before and found in them many incentives to drink. There were two categories, which Alex now sorted into file folders, to give himself a sense of progress. "Scientific," he labeled the first one, which contained a selection of Relnik's journal articles, mostly on the comparative morphology of the pituitary gland. Careful, patient work, but of the kind that produces, in the end, only one tiny grain of knowledge, which would have to be rolled together with thousands of other tiny grains before some larger structure emerged, for anyone with the wit to see it.

In the laboratory, Alex himself had been little more than a grain-maker, with his mind always straining ahead of the observable and experimentally possible. The truth was, although he liked to look back on his exertions at "the bench" as decent manual labor, he hated the lab, hated the obduracy of nature, always at such pains to conceal herself, to throw him off the track with contaminated samples, spoiled reagents, flickering, unstable instruments. He was just as glad that his grants had run out and that he had been lifted, by Leitbetter's ambitions, into some realm of thought unmenaced by observable fact, where infant speculations need not fear being crushed by the hard weight of counter-evidence.

Relnik had apparently experienced a similar liberation after the rumors about him put an end to his research grants, because the entries in the second file, arbitrarily labeled "Social," were smooth sheets of text, narratives without charts or diagrams: speeches, essays, articles in mongrel journals on "educational psychology" and "evolutionary neurobiology." Progressive education seemed to be the theme, with John Dewey cited here and there, offering reasonable grounds for hope. Learning is naturally pleasurable, or so Relnik had argued to various assemblages of educational administrators and school psychologists, no doubt still passing himself off as a working scientist. Educators must learn to enlist what Relnik called the "pleasure reaction." The traditional punitive methods inhibit the cognitive enterprise, and so on.

Good-natured pap, in Alex's view, though interestingly over-stated. Hunger had not driven the primitive human mind, Relnik asserted, any more than underpopulation stimulated animals to procreate. It was not only that the tool—that first great product of human intellect—brought food but that the conceptualization and creation of the tool brought pleasure. Joy was the great reinforcer, enticing the brain as well as the gonads.

Various forms of evidence were offered, few of which, Alex noted, would stand up in a modern journal. The headmaster of an un-named English boarding school reported that students who had been primed with a few jokes did far better with their irregular Greek verbs than did a class which had been threatened with an exam. There were similar reports on the learning ability of incar-cerated men versus a presumably well-matched group of vacation-ers. Conversely, people who had just successfully solved a puzzle or math problem were found, in standard tests, to take a more optimistic view of things than those who had given up in frustration. None of these studies, unfortunately, appeared to have ever been published.

Alex was reading doggedly, aware now of the chair against his back and the ache of disuse in his upper legs, underlining without any clear plan. "Curiosity is seldom recognized for what it is," Relnik had written, "a form of desire, linked to eros." And: "All great men of science share a single secret, the intense and secret pleasure of their work." Alex pictured a soul sweetened by disap-pointment, standing in front of a room full of wriggling under-graduates, willing them to learn.

Alex himself had at first been pleased to see his teaching load expand as his research grants ran out. Teaching meant more chance to read, always a disreputable activity among the hardcore lab men, who might scan the journals in the library for half an hour after lunch but were never seen carrying books. The students, however, were notoriously unreachable, even with the soft sensationalism of

WOW. It was almost worse when you did break through and some twenty-year-old would be moved to hold up her thin life for you: stories of indifferent parents, invariably divorced, of wan ambitions, pre-shrunk to fit the available careers, of extrasensory experiences involving dead celebrities and high-school friends.

Della had been a memorable exception. The first thing he had noticed was her eyes, brown and steady, tracking the line of thought so carefully she would forget to take notes, as if she had no interest in turning his words into her own possession. Things entered in through those eyes and came back in unexpected form: Why were all the heavenly bodies round, or spherical, that is? What could imaginary numbers be used to count? He would wrap this up and call her, apologize for the other day, try to engage her focus on this business, whatever it was, of the poor, wistful, dead Dr. Relnik.

Because there was no point in prolonging this. Leitbetter was wrong about Relnik, that was all, and too vain to admit it. There were Relniks all over the place, one-idea men, writing to people they didn't know, soliciting insignificant speaking engagements, boring and finally repelling their colleagues with their *idées fixes*. Alex dug out the cover note Leitbetter had attached to the Relnik files. He hadn't wanted to read it first because he didn't want Leitbetter's words in his mind, shadowing him as he read. But the note was brief: These were the papers a young assistant had managed to assemble a couple of summers ago. Leitbetter thought they were complete, as far as Relnik's published work went, but there was more—correspondence, for example, and lab notes—now in the possession of a distant relative of Relnik's, a grandniece, it seemed, living a few hours' drive away. An address followed, which Alex recognized as a town not too far down the freeway, once an attractive place but probably not doing so well this summer on account of the blight, the business with the trees.

It would be enough, Alex thought, to read the few samples of Relnik's unpublished work that came with the files, on the theory that an unpublished paper might function like a dream, offering an uncensored look into the poor man's mind. Alex fished out a fuzzy Xerox of a lengthy mimeograph entitled "The Pedagogical Implications of the Pleasure Principle." Perhaps Relnik had circulated it to a few of his colleagues, angling for encouragement. The language was too overblown and driven for normal academic use, pressing up against something, impatient with the obvious. "What is the trained mind," Relnik had written in the opening paragraph, "if not the mind trained to leap up and do tricks for its reward?"

"Pleasure" was no longer exactly the right word for this. Relnik seemed to be talking about discovery, not just learning, and the pleasure had taken on the grip of an addiction. Alex found himself circling whole sections, on what grounds he was not sure.

A conspiracy of silence surrounds this simple truth, so well known to the investigator, for the obvious reason that science must protect its austere image. Any hint of hedonism, it is surmised, would damage the scientist's reputation as an ascetic, pursuing truth for thoroughly dispassionate reasons. Yet who has not witnessed the stunned and radiant countenance of the investigator who, fresh from a successful experiment, bridging what had been separate islands of established knowledge, rushes forth from his microscope, from his laboratory bench . . .

The conspiracy begins in the nineteenth century, with the development of the modern university and the emergence of the scientist as bureaucrat, department chair, responsible citizen. Henceforth, science, dependent on huge gifts of public and philanthropic money, must present itself as a joyless enterprise . . .

Science education, it followed, must be designed to conceal the very possibility of joy, must be made as painful and tedious as possible, in order to throw the public off the scent. Only a tiny elite, among all those who undertake to learn, are ever admitted to the terms of the conspiracy: the unbridled hedonism that impels the search for truth.

But every mind is capable of the obsessive pleasure of the research man. Consider that quotidian phenomenon, so thoroughly neglected by research psychologists—"boredom." Boredom is experienced, if not by the dullest among us, by even those of low-to-middle intelligence. And what is boredom if not the systemic anhedonia of the understimulated mind, hungry not only for "novelty" but for new connections, linkages, the forging of which is the very meaning of "learning"?

Put quite plainly and crudely, the mind is a mechanism for masturbation. Deprived of better fodder, it will seek its satisfaction in any available puzzle, pulp mystery story, or game of wits. Science is only the best of its games, the most refined and compelling of its pleasures.

It was almost dark outside when Alex finished the mimeo, and the sound of canned laughter was pushing through the wall. Sitcoms already, meaning it was eight or later. Without even noticing it, he had gotten through his little period of temperance and on to a respectable drinking hour. And this was fortunate, because Relnik's unpublished thoughts sat awkwardly on the sober mind. Ravings, was Alex's general conclusion, half paranoid, half gleaming with the dank enthusiasms of a lonely, disappointed failure of a man. A non-scientist might get away with speculative excess on this scale, but for a scientist, it could only mean his mind had lost the capacity for the crisp either/or of logical proof, the delicate marshaling of confirmable evidence. The man was mad, and the question was, had Leitbetter known this all along?

It was possible to imagine Relnik's cracked thesis as a little joke, left there by Leitbetter for him to find, a postmodernist wink at the pomposities of science. The "great irony of the twentieth century" had nothing to do with Nazism. It was about science and madness: a mad, failed scientist whose madness consisted in the belief that the scientific establishment was a conspiracy of intellectual self-abusers. Dr. Caragiola, of course, would love it.

Alex poured himself a drink and let the whiskey's rough tongue explore the inside of his mouth. But was Leitbetter that subtle? Would he launch a whole project just to make some oddball point about reason and madness? Leitbetter was an appreciator of irony, of the nimble joke. But there was a difference between an appreciator and a perpetrator. The image arose of Leitbetter struggling for order at the ill-fated lecture, not getting the larger joke imposed by Claire on Caragiola's impenetrable witticisms, out of his depth. Leitbetter was a collector, not a creator.

Now there was a warmth in the room that had nothing to do with the heavy summer air outside. The only plausible inference was that Leitbetter had no idea, no idea at all, that Relnik was mad, that only Alex knew this now, and whatever near-dead colleagues of Relnik's survived today, if they were in a condition to remember anything. In which case Relnik's madness became one of those unaccountable factors, one of those tiny, persistent deviations no one wants to claim, like the deflection of starlight which had helped prove the theory of relativity and thus expanded the universe beyond anybody's prior dreams.

This led to the further thought, which seemed to dilate Alex's mind as it spread, that there were whole areas of experience, of knowledge, of human enterprise—whole terrains, really—over which Leitbetter and his sort had no control and could never hope to have. Relnik marked the boundary, beyond which lay open ground, the vast, dawn-lit mother country of surprise. The first surprise was that it was still there, fresh and waiting to be explored, after so many years of stupor and defeat. The second was that, mad as he was, and insignificant, Relnik might after all be right.

CHAPTER 4

With the security check at the main entrance, there was no way Della could miss anyone coming out of the complex. It had been Alex's idea to get together, but with a man there was always a margin of error. Last time he had forgotten, and this time too he might just go right on by to the parking lot, working on some problem in his head, unless she was standing there in his path. It would be different if she thought she could compete with other things he might be thinking of, but when she tried to see herself as a mental trace struggling to survive in someone else's mind, she came up only with a series of cancellations: attractive/not attractive, smart/dull, interesting/ordinary. There had been a more reliable collection of attributes once—young and pretty, she supposed, even promising—but they had gotten scattered along the way.

It was not that Della expected Alex to become a turning point, reversing the direction of her life. Expectations are one of the things we are called on to abandon, Sister Bertha said, like imaginings or anything else that seduces us from the actual situation. When she had last seen Alex, on an errand for Dr. Hershey that had taken her to the far end of the complex, he had told her that Sister Bertha was part of a trend, according to his friend in Urban Anthropology, a sign of the times. Not her precisely, because she had not yet surfaced into the realm of data, but others like her: low-income prophets preaching revolution, submission, and various intermediate solutions. There were dozens of them apparently, known to science, including a man on death row who advocated suicide as a shortcut to grace, and a former subway conductor with a congregation of flagellants. None of this, Alex had said, should detract from the wisdom of Sister Bertha's message, if that's what Della found in it, because even Jesus had been one of a whole flock of like-minded fellows—itinerant preachers, mystics, and ascetics— seeing the need or the opportunity for spiritual compliance. God when he takes physical form is prodigal in the forms that he takes. Alex had grinned: Look at Claire.

Only women were coming out through the security checkpoint now, technicians mostly, the young ones slim and petulant, the older ones plump and falsely eager. To look at them you would think it was youth that knew disappointment and middle age that was the season of deluded hope. And that might not be entirely off the mark, because the young at least could see what the middle-aged had become, while the middle-aged persisted in believing they were still young enough to expect good news. That might be the worst tragedy of youth, to look at one's elders and see how the story comes out.

Steve had once made her feel this, the humiliation of being an adult. She had gone into his room for a talk, after getting a call from one of the high-school teachers complaining about his attitude, which, it was said, lacked the most elementary orientation toward authority and the necessity for a downward flow of knowledge from old to young. Steve had been stretched out on his bed, reading a book, and he stared out the window while she repeated the message.

"So I have a bad attitude. I also have zits."

"Well, I'm just telling you," Della said, backing off. "Attitude isn't the big thing anyway, it's values. I wonder sometimes what you see yourself doing, you know, when you grow up."

"I see myself doing what I'm doing now, only I'll be better at it."

Della had found herself duty-bound to expand on the subject of values. We're put here to make a difference, to help in some way. Everyone finds their own way, according to their talents and ability, to make a contribution. A year or so ago, before Carl's death, this conversation would have been unnecessary, even ludicrous, but now Della felt obliged to make the effort.

"And how do you know you've 'helped'?" Steve wanted to know.

"Well, you try to make things better. You see if you can make things better for, uh, someone. For other people."

"And how do you know you've made it better for them?"

"Like if you volunteer or something, you can see, people are happier. It shows in their faces." Della offered this resolutely, although the only time she had volunteered, through the church, the elderly blind woman she had been sent to read to fell asleep five pages into the book, and Della had been left in a semidark room, reading to herself about how to make an inventory of your assets and learn to capitalize on your secret strengths.

"And how does it show? Do they smile?"

"Well, sometimes they do. Of course."

"So it's a matter of giving people pleasure, then, what you mean by values?"

"You could put it that way, yes, I suppose it comes down to that." She was hoping he would come up with an example of his own, some unsuspected tendency in need of reinforcement.

"So a prostitute, then, would be a good example of values?"

She made a second try, although the road along which she had hoped to lead him now seemed overgrown, hard to make out.

Pleasure is not the point, of course, there are sacrifices too. We give up some pleasure to give it to others. That's the essence of the whole thing, what we call morality, seeing beyond the pleasure of the moment, making a larger calculation.

"So why not just do what you want, then? The net result's the same, right? If what you're going by is the total amount of pleasure in the world?"

She should have raised him in the Church. Morality needs an institution of some kind to give it shelter. It was never meant to be alone outside with all the atheists and teenagers. She drew her breath and read off an answer from her mind: Pleasure is not the same as happiness. Happiness is not a five-minute thing. At some point you decide what is worthwhile and you try to bring your life into conformity with it. This is hard to see when you are young, but he would see, soon enough, the need for values, the need to live according to some plan, or for those who didn't have a plan, at least according to rules.

"You think so, Mom?" He seemed to appeal to her from some lost point of contiguity, when they had been pals against the world. "You really believe that?" Then he looked away out the window again. "You see that squirrel. What is it doing?"

"That's neither here nor there. We're talking about human beings with choices. It's just doing what it has to do."

"That's what I want to do, what I have to do. And you know, Mom?" He rolled back toward her and leaned on one elbow. "That's what you'd do too, if you knew what it was you had to do."

■   ■   ■

It was twenty after five, meaning that Alex wasn't coming and that, anyway, it would look foolish to still be waiting if he did show up. The date, if you could call it that, had stood at the end of the workday like a destination, and now there was no clear place to go.

Della headed out away from the building toward the walkway leading to the lower-level parking lots. Beyond the lots was open space, or what might have been open space if it had not been made busy by fragments of scaffolding and mounds of soil left by abandoned construction projects and ones which were not yet under way. There was a time when a woman in her situation would have taken vows and entered a convent. Always, as a girl, she had kept that possibility alive in her mind as a last resort, the only dignified response to annihilation. Was that what she was supposed to do, become a nun? She tried looking at things from a nun's remove: the stream of people going down the walkway like a dark cut in the gray landscape, everything bitterly bright as seen through a halo of renunciation.

Then, though she was walking, the air slowed down around her, growing thicker. Alex had forgotten her again, and even she sometimes had trouble remembering whose losses were being reckoned. She stopped and leaned against a car. When she stepped forward again, she was surprised to find that the hot late-afternoon air supported her without barring the way. But only until she got to the beginning of the walkway. Then the height, which she had never noticed before, perhaps because it purchased no view worth recalling, dismayed her, like a test of balance. She had to fight for control, but it was clear that fighting would only weaken her. If she went forward she would fall, if she fell she would be trampled. No one would notice except as something to scrape off their feet. The landscape would claim her. It was meant to win. Given enough time, everything was resorbed back into the earth.

After a minute, she moved forward again. Sister Bertha had warned of times like this, Sister Bertha who knew the exact geography of grief. A man had written to her, a man whose entire family had been destroyed in a tenement fire, saying he was afraid to go out because in the street the memory of his loss rose up like a hot wind, holding him motionless, and what was the matter with him, then, if he could not go out? Sister Bertha had said to stop blaming himself, the blast of pain came from outside himself and had nothing to do with his mind or the memories stored in it. This was the birth pain of the universe, screaming forever, from the first moment, out of the violent night from which all things proceed. Sometimes it found a human channel, a soul ready to contain it, and all that the chosen person could do was hold still, open his palms in prayer, and let God's pain pass through. Della would have liked to stand like this now, palms out and face to the empty sky, but something more than embarrassment held her back. All religions try the same thing, after all, to add a dimension of glamour to everyday grief.

■   ■   ■

"Better watch where you're going. The walkway's all slippery from the caterpillars." Della looked around as the paunchy man she had met at the party caught up to her, breathing fast from the exertion. "There should be warning signs. I told them: I slip and I sue."

"The caterpillars?" Della did not see any underfoot.

"Mmm-hmm. Isn't it interesting how nobody talks about them anymore? Yesterday's crisis is today's ho-hum."

"Oh, everyone's aware of them, don't you think?"

"If I organized a club, with membership based on awareness of the caterpillars—true awareness—it would be small enough to meet in my Toyota. Most people censor out the obvious because it doesn't make for good conversation, the result being that no one has the slightest idea what's going on in front of their nose."

"Well, just because people don't talk about them . . ." Della was not sure why she had taken the responsibility of reassuring him, but it was good to have an upright figure at her side. "What do you do?" she asked when he did not leave her at the faculty lot.

"Many things, don't we all? You mean, what do I do here? I'm in the business office, the soul of any great research facility; accounting, to be exact. The scientists study nature; I study the scientists: the inward flow of money, which must be matched, of course, with an outward flow of journal articles. Paper in, paper out. The green transformed to a delicate off-white . . . Watch out! You almost stepped in them!"

They stopped and regarded the small gray pile in their path. It was a clump that might have blown off a tree, if there were any trees around, or rolled out from the grass, turning to goo.

"You're right," Della conceded, "it could be dangerous."

"Not 'it,' they." He tapped her elbow for safety and they continued on down the walkway. "They're all in there, regrouping."

"What do you mean, regrouping?"

"How would I know what they do when they regroup? I'm an accountant, not an entomologist. But believe me, they're in there."

"Well, they're just going to be cleaned up by the groundsmen and, I don't know, thrown out."

"Thrown out where? Did you ever think about that? Into a dumpster somewhere that's already half full of caterpillar goo. You see, they're coming together, trying to reach a critical mass, and we're helping them. For all we know, this is just another stage in their life cycle: get born, climb up trees, eat leaves, fall down, turn to goo, get carted off, regroup, reaggregate, emerge as something new. Plenty of obvious parallels among the slime molds. But would anybody notice? No. Is anybody thinking about it? No. We're thinking about the vicious little Lamb of Jesus that got loose last week and kicked our dear Dr. Bedwetter in the butt."

Della made a sound of amusement. "Isn't that what Dr. Caragiola said, that the caterpillars have a meaning?"

"You don't think they have a meaning?"

Della had to admit she didn't know what it would be. There are plenty of things that come without comment. She was not, technically speaking, a religious person, in the sense of going to Mass, and it seemed to her that there must be things about which God has no opinion. But the paunchy man stopped in his tracks, forcing Della to stop also and face him.

"Think about it," he said, passing the fingers of one hand over his jowls. "They're not nice, right? They're not lethal, but they're not nice. So put it together."

"I don't see . . ."

"What it is," he was looking irritated, "is in the nature of a warning. Obviously."

Della took a half step back. There were blue stains on the fingers he had brought to his face, possibly the ink from a computer printer, and the pores on his cheeks were large and shiny in the afternoon heat. "Not nice is not necessarily a warning," she offered.

"Well, what do you think this is, then?" He used his foot to point toward another gray mass of caterpillar flesh, only a few feet ahead of them on the concrete. "A birthday card?"

■   ■   ■

Nothing that summer lived up to prior expectations of comfort or convenience. The brownouts came frequently and at unpredictable times, sometimes eliminating morning coffee and sometimes canceling the evening news. Even the traffic, Alex was discovering as he headed out to visit Relnik's grandniece, was coagulating, turning in on itself, like a migratory pattern destroyed by the absence of geographical cues and recognizable seasons.

He had left late because the outcome of the mission seemed preordained. There would be more of Relnik's dull science, his sloppy philosophical musings, and with luck some even more florid proofs of his madness. Alex indulged himself a little in the cheap satisfaction of imagining Leitbetter's chagrin. "I see," he would say with a twist to his mouth, tapping the desktop distractedly. "It's quite appalling. The rational mind derailed. I must apologize to you, Al, for this fool's errand." And Alex would be paid anyway, perhaps with a little extra thrown in, and the understanding that the episode was not to be bruited about the complex, where it would add to the already unkind perceptions.

Her name, interestingly, was Riane, and she seemed slightly surprised to see Alex at her door. She was younger than Alex had expected, not over thirty, and done out in a way that challenged you to keep on believing she was pretty: no makeup, hair cut alarmingly short, dressed in a T-shirt and baggy slacks. "Oh yeah, the professor" was her greeting. "Well, come on in." It was an ordinary tight little Cape Cod house, part of a treeless development that must once have lured thousands of impacted city dwellers with the promise of country living.

"You can sit over there," she said, but it was hard to see what she was offering. There were magazines on most available surfaces, glossy, expensive ones, as well as unemptied ashtrays and paper waste from take-out meals. Alex gingerly cleared away some unfolded laundry and sat on the couch.

"I'm an artist," Riane said, and Alex wondered if this was meant to be an explanation. She curled into a wingback canvas chair and studied him as he supposed an artist might, carefully but incuriously, concentrating on the angles and planes of light.

Alex went through the little speech he had devised. A belated realization of the significance of Dr. Relnik's contribution. The need for a thorough assessment, and also to bring the human side to light. A small grant and considerable enthusiasm from the publishing house which had recently done Jacques Monod and René Dubos; the biographies, that is. He was tempted to embellish, perhaps promote himself to a full professorship and add a couple of books to his credits, but he did not have full confidence in the cleanliness of his suit or the condition of his fingernails.

"I never knew Uncle Henry," she said, lounging back and stroking her calf.

Well, certainly, she would have been much too young. A shame too, considering the man's unquestioned brilliance, combined with his other contributions, in the area, for example, of educational theory. Alex wondered how long he would have to go on like this before asking to see the papers.

"Mother said he was a great man. I got the house from Mother. When I get a skylight put in, I'll really be able to get down to work. There's no point now, the light sucks."

"Your mother, uh, passed away recently?"

"Mmm." Riane sat up now, hugging one knee. "But I think she's still here in some way. Not all of her, but a kind of glaze, you can see it sometimes, forming on things. She didn't believe in death. She believed that an echo continues, of what you had been thinking in your life, some sort of electronic disturbance. You know anything about that?"

Tactfully, Alex conceded the possibility of reverberations. The body dies, but the pattern of thought no doubt continues. Something

Henry Relnik himself might have held to, it would be interesting to find out. There was so much still to know about the man, his many interests, his still fertile speculations. For example, one area he was hoping to explore and perhaps she would recall something her mother had said: did Dr. Relnik have any interest in politics?

Riane sagged back into the chair. "What do you mean, politics?"

A fair question these days. Alex approached the issue cautiously. Dr. Relnik spent a great deal of time in Germany with his woman friend, returning for summers well into the Third Reich. Did he have any feelings that he might perhaps have conveyed to Riane's mother, about what was happening there, the Nazis?

"He wasn't Jewish, if that's what you mean."

"Ah," said Alex, as if that cleared the matter up. "Well, do you remember anything else, any amusing stories, or little quirks, that might help illuminate the human side?"

"My mother was in communication with him right up to her death. She said he had moved onto the astral plane. That's the highest plane, you know."

Alex looked discreetly at his watch. Of course, the derangement, whatever it was, ran in the family. If she didn't mind, he would like to take a quick look-through and copy whatever was relevant.

Riane put one sneakered foot on the floor but did not get up. "You're younger than I thought you'd be."

"Healthy living, I guess." He smiled bravely.

"Mother always aimed for the astral plane."

He expressed his regret at having missed this estimable lady.

"I think sex is a shortcut," she said, reaching her hand under her T-shirt to massage her shoulder.

"Really? To the uh, astral plane?" He used his finger to paint a mustache in the sweat on his upper lip. There was no expression on her face. Nothing at all.

"Umm-hmm. I've always thought that, you know? Because it's so available."

Her hand had come back out and gone under one arm in such a way that her breast was pushed upward, making its own demands. If this was not some kind of a come-on, then he had lost the ability to read these things. Though it was also possible that the entire language had changed, behind his back, in the years he wasn't paying attention. A discussion of life after death might be the accepted preliminary. A thrusting nipple might be no more than punctuation. He needed to find his way back out, to the point where they were a few minutes ago.

"Ah, sex. You're so right. I teach a course called Comparative Sexuality: An International Perspective, in alternate years. Enrollment just keeps rising." Seeing her hand drop to her lap he gained confidence. "Yet it's odd if you think about it. The two key human sex hormones, testosterone and estrogen, are actually poisons. It's something any biologist thinks about sooner or later. Raise the dose just fractionally and you get cancer, in the case of estrogen; hirsutism and murderous violence in the case of testosterone. Sex and death—better yet, sex and disfigurement. Interesting that evolution would have arranged it that way, so that the sexual urge, in chemical form, would be poisonous . . ."

"Maybe there's a reason."

"Why the sex hormones are poisonous?"

"Yeah, to teach us not to be afraid of death." She stood up and shook out the leg she had been sitting on. "But let me get you the papers. What there is of them."

When she came back to the room she handed him a box tied in string. "Here you go, love letters." And she left the room again, to get the rest of the papers, Alex assumed.

They were indeed love letters, from Dora Mueller to Henry Relnik, dated 1938 to June 1943. Not a bad place to start, compared for example to Relnik's lab notes on the structure of the pituitary gland, which would probably be in the next box, and the letters had the undeniable appeal of being in English. He cleared a little space around himself and settled down to read.

Dora, at least, appeared to be sane. She had a fine, clear style delivered in a disciplined hand. Whole sections, devoted to heartfelt descriptions, could be skipped: low clouds settling around the mountains, the first light of dawn on the Schloss, the narrow streets decked out for Christmas, a hike she had taken to a highland meadow where herbs and wild mushrooms could be found. Alex slowed down just a little when she got to her work, which she always did, in every letter. Like Relnik, she seemed to be a brain-slicer, all the way from frogs to cats. There were problems of pro-curement. Sometimes she had to use animals that would not have been her first choice. Certain reagents were growing prohibitively expensive. A colleague had been less than cooperative with the electrostimulation equipment. Apparently she was trying to localize certain functions in the brain. Relnik must have been familiar with the general goals and hypotheses, since these were never mentioned.

If he was mad, she loved him no less for it. Always he was "*Liebchen*," "*mein Beliebter*," and so forth, in her only lapses into her native tongue. But other than missing her Henry and certain aniline dyes used in tissue staining, it was an enviable life: working and hiking, nature held captive in the laboratory and nature running free in the mountains. She saw the world through two sets of lenses, her microscope and the opera glasses she carried on her walks up into the countryside. A pure and sturdy existence, altogether a better deal than life inside the Human Ecology Complex. Then it occurred to Alex that the whole middle range of vision was missing, the part where other people live. Here, for example, was a letter dated September 3, 1939, roughly the time of the invasion of Poland, and Dora was reporting a touch of hay fever and a most interesting lecture on nervous conduction in the nematode.

Yet even if she did not read the newspapers, she must have seen Brown Shirts marching in the streets, roughing up the weak and impure of blood. And even if she managed never to walk in the streets, she must have been aware of the purge in the faculty of her own university, of Jews and the politically suspect. But Alex had to read a long way, and go back over some of the letters he had skimmed, to find some point of overlap with the world of known events. At one point she mentioned that the wife of a colleague had inexplicably committed suicide. Possibly the poor woman had some sound congenital reason for wanting to absent herself from the entire situation, though Dora did not speculate. The colleague had been back to the lab within two days of the tragedy, quiet but steady. We Germans, was Dora's comment, must be a stalwart people.

Alex felt his heart waver in defeat. She *was* a Nazi, or, what was equally chilling, she had simply never thought about the human world around her, and to her mind Nazism was a feature of the German landscape no more open to question than the run-down hills watching over the Rhine. And would it be any different if Leitbetter's operation were conducted under the auspices of a Fascist empire? A few concessions to the prevailing rhetoric, no doubt, but otherwise the same old quibbles over laboratory *Lebensraum*, the division of grant money, the order of names on articles.

Riane had come back in and was sitting in her old spot with a sketchpad and pencil. "Finding what you want?" she asked, looking up at him with her head lowered.

"It's hardly a matter of what I want." He gave a grim half smile implying resigned obedience to the demands of science. "One finds what one finds in this business."

"Do you ever want anything?" It would be easier if she smiled when she said this sort of thing, but it was the same unnervingly neutral gaze.

"Yes, as a matter of fact, a drink, very badly. If I could trouble you, that is."

They negotiated about his options, which were appallingly limited—rum and juice of some kind or Mexican beer—and she left him alone again with the letters. He had been moving forward in time, and at some point in 1942, apparently after Relnik's annual summer visit to Heidelberg, a new element entered in, a secret between the two lovers or at least something that Dora refrained from naming. She wrote of her excitement over "our project" and the need, nevertheless, to pursue it with great thoroughness and deliberation. She was quite sure of things on her side and had checked them over many times. The plan was sound, there was no reason for it not to work.

Riane returned with the drink and Alex regarded her, for the first time, appreciatively. "Very nice. I hope I'm not interrupting your work."

"I do collages."

"Mmm, I'd love to see them." He noticed for the first time that the walls were bare.

"It. There's only one at a time. I used to do more, cutting from magazines, but then I got more focused. Now I do one a year, and when it's done, I take it apart, piece by piece, and make a new one out of the pieces. It could be anything, so long as I can make it out of the pieces."

"Very ecologically minded," Alex said, half listening. His mind was on the lines he had just read: "Good news on our little project: the material will be ready soon . . ."

"That's not the reason," Riane was saying, glancing back and forth between Alex and her sketchpad. "I do it so there's nothing to buy. Nothing to sell. There's just one work and it only exists for a few hours a year. Otherwise it's in pieces, coming apart or coming together. See what I mean? You can see it but you can't own it."

Alex took another sly look at his watch. Well after five, which had been a deadline of some sort, but he could not remember what. This was no time to leave, with so much in the air. Leitbetter might like things "nuanced" but Alex preferred them sharply resolved. "Look," he tried, "I know I've taken up a lot of your time already, but I wonder if I could just take a quick look at the rest of the papers. I didn't really come here"—he threw in an agreeable laugh—"just for the love letters."

She was looking into his face but missing his eyes. "The rest of the papers?"

"Whatever you have. If you don't mind, that is."

"Mind what?"

"Getting them for me. I'll just whiz through, make a few notes, and . . ."

"There aren't any other papers."

Alex set down his glass. Then he picked it up again. The rum and the orange juice were in a power struggle which only he could lose. "Look. You said several boxes. When I called you the other day."

"Yeah, but the others are gone." She continued to sketch. "Guy took them the day before yesterday."

"Took them?"

"Well, bought them."

"You sold Relnik's papers?" He looked straight at her, something which he had been avoiding doing for most of the visit. "But Relnik's work belongs to science. Scientists don't sell their work. Knowledge has to be free, see, it belongs to humankind, in the largest sense."

"Don't worry, it still does." Riane was looking down at her sketchpad. "He was human, the guy with the money."

"How much money?"

"Does it matter?"

"It could be important." An old rule: When at sea, pin down the numbers.

"Twenty-five thousand."

"My God! I'm surprised you didn't throw in the love letters too."

"He wasn't interested in love letters."

If she had a facial expression, it would have to be a smirk, Alex decided, his eyes still shut. But when he opened them she was as unreadable as ever. "I don't know why you're so upset," she said. "You have a job, right? You get paid anyway, right? For teaching comparable sex or something."

"Well, my bad luck that moneybags beat me here, huh?" He was stacking the letters back in the box and closing his notebook. "And I bet you don't remember his name, which was on the check, but you already deposited the check, right?"

"Yeah, right. But don't be sore. Let me fix another drink and I could finish this sketch. See? Not bad, huh?"

"Do you remember anything about him? Where he was from?"

"Not right this minute I don't, but maybe if you were a little nicer. I can't think with people yelling at me."

"Okay. I'm sorry." He tried a patient expression, the same one he used with students who had lost their term papers due to multiple deaths in the family. "I just didn't expect anything like this. I didn't know that anyone else was involved. See, I'm going to need to talk to this person. We can't both be doing biographies of Henry Relnik. I've got to talk to him before, well . . ."

Riane looked at him—sketching, appraising, it was hard to tell what. "Maybe if we could just take this a little slower, you know, have another drink and"—her tongue moved out across her upper lip, jolting Alex, like an independent creature emerging from backstage—". . . see what happens."

Sex was the subject now, there was no mistaking that. Whatever the official language had become, she was speaking in the pidgin version. Something came back to Alex: the memory of sex or maybe only a cartoon of sex. He was seldom sober enough to remember anything but the broad moves and the hydraulics of the thing. But it started like this, with some reckless talk and a dare thrown in your face, only usually with a more generous supply of drink. He thought of the rum, somewhere in its source in the kitchen, and heard it speak to him in a jocular, man-to-man tone: Stay a little while, mon, don't let the girl come between us; you and I got business together. The rum had a threesome in mind, and Alex could see himself waking up in a little while, wet skin sticking to his, nothing ahead but a talk about death, the opportunity of a lifetime, the portal to alternative planes. If he stayed, he would be part of someone else's plan—maybe not even Riane's—just rolling downhill along a path already cleared.

"No thanks," he said at last, shoving his notes into his briefcase and snapping it shut. "As it happens, I just remembered I have a date."

■ ■ ■

He drove as fast as he could for half an hour before he thought to get off the freeway and find a working phone. A machine answered at Della's and he left something involving traffic and deadlines and how he wasn't usually like this. Then he got Phyllis's number from information and called her at home.

"Hiya, sweetie, I didn't know you cared."

"Look, I'm really sorry to bother you at home like this, but you know the good doctor has been turning the screws and I'm running around out here steppin' and fetchin' as fast as I can, but—"

"You okay, Alex? You don't sound right."

"It's sobriety, or something very close to it, but I'll be better soon. What I need to know is, did you find the file with the other contributors to this thing, the *Biography of the Twentieth Century?*"

"Mmm, what's it worth to you?"

"My honor, my body, whichever is in better shape."

Phyllis giggled. "I'd take 'em both if I didn't have a very hot offer a little closer to hand. But there's nothing in it, sweetie pie, I hate to say. Nothing in it but a letter to you, the contract letter you already got."

"There's no list of the other contributors? No letters to them?"

"Not in my shop, but then I can't be expected to monitor every single plot the great man hatches. Why don't you just ask him?"

"Oh, I will. Believe me, I will." And he was surprised when he got out of the booth at how unfamiliar the landscape was, perhaps only because of the trees, although the freeway, which pulls all things together, was just a few hundred yards away.

■　　■　　■

So you just keep going, one foot in front of the other. This was the essence of Miriam's plan for her: go to work, come home; breakfast, work; dinner, bed; shower, dress; work and sleep and work again. There could even be a theory behind it. "Repetition therapy" would be the name for it, the idea being that reality inheres in things that repeat, and that the great one-time events, the departures and ruptures and door slammings, can be safely disregarded like the occasional odd, irreproducible result in a laboratory. The problem, Della could see, was that there were still too many parts of the day for which there was no precise system. Going back to the apartment, for example, was not the reverse of going to work. Here things could be done in any order or even omitted without the least consequence, and nothing would really improve until night tightened around the place, cutting off her world at the windows.

There were three pieces of mail addressed to "occupant," on themes of efficiency and thrift, and one hand-lettered envelope for "Mrs. Markson." No "Della," no "Leo," just "Mrs." without a return address. Della adjusted the fan, sat down at her kitchen table, and opened the envelope. No letter either, she saw, just a printed card saying "SKD—Knowledge Designs, Interventions, Special Orders." There was an 800 number but no address.

It had to be the business card of the man who was looking for Steve. Homer must have sent it; the black-penned handwriting on the envelope was laboriously neat and a little eccentric. She had not forgotten that Homer said he'd send it along, it was just hard to imagine that anything could come of such a slender clue. When she thought of Steve, the same scenario was always in rehearsal in the back of her mind: A man coming to the door one day, grim-looking, refusing to drink anything, and asking her to take a seat, instead of the other way around.

"I have some bad news for you, Mrs. Markson," he would say.

And she would not say "About Steve?" when it was still possibly about Leo, who might not have thought to change the name next to "Notify in case of emergency," so that she was still, for purposes of death or disaster, Leo's wife. Then the man, who sometimes in the scene looked worn-down and wise, sometimes just in a hurry, would describe how Steve had been found, giving the facts as the police defined them, like time of day, manner of dress, weapon, if any, or method. There would be papers to sign. Then he would reach into his briefcase and offer her a memento of Steve, some entirely unrepresentative object, like a Rubik's Cube key chain or the playbill for a musical she had dragged him to once as a child. It would be presented to her in a plastic bag, the way evidence is preserved for fingerprints.

Miriam would say just call the number. Visualizing the worst was stupid, a form of magical thinking, a way of preempting fate. Miriam had shown her an article on this. What you visualize is what you get. Here was the card, after all, a definite object requiring a definite act.

She punched in the numbers and waited. It could still be office hours where the 800 number was, an industrial park in some lovely, well-tended part of America where it was always afternoon.

"SKD," a voice announced.

"I'm . . ." She hadn't figured out what to say and there was no name or extension to help. "It's about Kipper Markson. I'd like to speak to someone about Kipper Markson."

There was no answer, only silence and a further ringing. When a new voice said "Personnel" Della repeated her line. "Hold on," the voice said, "I'm transferring you." There was no surprise or interest in the voice, and then a long silence before a new voice, a woman's voice, Della thought, though low enough to be a man's, came on.

"So hello, are you a friend of Kipper's?"

"I'm his mother."

"Oh yes. Well, what do you know. I'm going to have to put you on hold for one second. But don't go away, please, I'll be right with you . . . Mrs. Markson."

There was silence, then music came on the line. Later Della would think that this was where she had gone wrong, that she had let the music distract her, but at the moment she found it reassuring. Only a well-run company, at the cutting edge, would think to entertain its clients with music you could actually listen to. It took her back before Steve, before Leo, to some prior form of herself, a young girl who would get up before sunrise and go out to the yard where the shrubs were crouching against the light. She would walk carefully, disturbing no secrets, toward the edge of the yard and what she believed was the beginning of the day. It had been a long time since she had seen so much promise in the mere shape of things, in a sound or melody.

"Hello? I hope you didn't mind waiting."

"Oh no, not at all. What was that music, I can't help asking."

"Ah, you liked our little composition?" The voice was unduly pleased.

"Very much. It's so familiar, but I just couldn't place it."

"There's no way you could. It's computer-generated. Once you have the equations, there's no reason not to give them a try."

"Well, I would never have guessed. But the reason I'm calling is my son. You're looking for my son, Kipper?"

"We're always looking for talent."

"I was wondering whether you found him."

"You don't know where your son is, then?"

"Not at the moment. At the moment he could be anywhere. That's why I'm calling."

"Well, I'm going to have to see if I can call up his name. Don't go away."

The music returned, stronger and simpler now. There were three layers, she realized, intertwining, playing off each other, and the melody was filled with the sadness that exists in all things as long as they are things, and separate from each other. If this was something a computer could understand, then anything, she realized, like love or regret, could be written down in a series of numbers.

The voice came back, more distant and with a slight distortion added on, so Della could barely make out the words.

"Look, I can hardly hear you." There was no way to know whether her words were clearer than the other's. "What did you say you do at SKD?"

"Knowledge systems. The first phase is information and the second phase is knowledge. We harvest information and condense it into knowledge."

"Condense it?"

"Of course, knowledge is a condensation of data. Brevity, if you like, is our goal. The universe is exploding, right? *Is* an explosion, getting bigger all the time. Well, we are the countertrend, Mrs. Markson."

The sound of her name anchored Della to the task again. "Did you find my son's name?"

"I'm sorry, we have no record."

"But you are looking for him?" He had been close for a minute and was sliding away.

"He's not in our records. No one by that name."

"But you took my call. I mean, you acted like you knew the name."

"There are a lot of names, Mrs. Markson, you must know that. And many of them are similar." The voice was echoing now, some syllables beginning to drag out drunkenly, like a fading tape. "When did you last see your son?"

"About a year ago, that's why I'm worried."

"That's not so long as these things go. There's always turn-over . . ." Here a section was lost to the distortion. ". . . new product lines . . . We have no knowledge of your son is what I'm telling you, Mrs. Markson. Or anyone by that name." There was hissing and a blur of mechanical sounds. "May I call you Della?"

"Why don't you tell me your name and I'll call you right back?"

Della strained to hear the answer. Strange underwater sounds filled the line. Maybe it was cables, not wires, lying on the sea floor, inaccessible to repair.

"Della . . . my name is Della too."

A bubble of pure silence passed through the wire between them. Then the hissing took over again, so that the last words came in a tiny receding voice: "Don't you want to hear my last name too?"

CHAPTER 5

A lex had settled on the Baycrest Bar almost as soon as he left Riane's, and now he admired his foresight. The place was dark and deeply chilled. They knew him here. He could set up office hours if he wanted, meeting with impassive students in the back booths, or use the phones, or just sit and drink until Chris, the bartender, gave his ritual speech on the drunk-driving laws. Chris was a stocky blond who took business courses at the community college and enjoyed a reputation for heavy drug use, though to look at him, the drugs in question could only be steroids. He saluted Alex with a gesture of controlled appreciation, nodding a little and pursing his lips.

"Whaddya say, Professor? You look like you been through a bad patch."

"Rum and orange juice. I was forced to drink rum and orange juice."

"Could've been worse, man, could have been H$_2$O." He poured the whiskey and returned to rinsing glasses in a sink filled with oily water, one eye on the TV that was set up high above the bar, where a light might normally be.

Alex let the astringent drink rinse out the sweet, musty coating in his mouth. The mistake, and it was amazing how many times he had made the same mistake, was in underestimating Leitbetter. There was a lot more going on than some little flight of academic whimsy, and he had been marched right into it like a pawn on a suicidal combat mission. Maybe Relnik had figured out cold fusion or a cure for cancer and left the formulas in the margins of some blathering paper on scientific euphoria. Corporate interest would run high, bids would be made. Except that there was still Leitbetter's elaborate cover story—the *Biography of the Twentieth Century*— to explain. Why couldn't Leitbetter have leveled with him? The one area in which Alex might have expected a little openness and decency was a get-rich-quick scheme, even if his own cut was going to be just a little sliver, a chance to keep hanging on, suspended between whiskey and science.

Chris let him use the phone behind the bar so he wouldn't have to leave his stool to talk. After three rings, Leitbetter's wife came on, an expensive woman, vaguely displaced from a more appropriate way of life, who was committed to tennis and furniture restoration. Years ago she had seen Alex as a possible threat—a perpetual graduate student was what she called him to Leitbetter —but now she took a comfortable tone with him. They were, in a way, members of the same staff, though serving in unrelated departments.

"He's at one of those godawful chicken-breast dinners, with speeches over parfait," she told Alex. "I won't go with him anymore. I told him, life is too short."

"My feeling exactly. Eating is a bodily function which should be conducted in private. That, in addition to the fact that I've never been invited, is why I avoid ceremonial dinners."

"So what should I say it's about, Alex? Is it about that hot new disease Hershey's got hold of? I know Richard thinks it's got a lot of promise, but it seems to me, one person walks out without washing his hands and that's it: the black plague."

"Don't worry about that. Hershey's a steady man. Tell him it's about the Nazis, that should get him interested." Alex excused himself from further explanations and waggled a finger over his glass as a cue to Chris.

The Nazis had nothing to do with it was the direction his opinions were running. That had been bait, most likely, the lure of historical evil. The first job of a scientist was to separate out the extraneous, the decorative touches, as it were, and move in on the facts of the case. Relnik, for example, could not be mad, because a madman's thoughts were at best worthless froth. Twenty-five thousand dollars said he was uncommonly sane, an unappreciated soul, just coming into his own.

Not to mention the fact that Dora loved him, and Alex still held Dora in a certain regard. There were two types of women in science. One was the perky type who would interrupt to make the tiniest correction of fact, just to show that she knew. Short and bustling, he pictured them, always scoring points like some science-fair winner, ill at ease because they were never sure they belonged where they were. And they didn't. Alex grinned to himself. If they could only hear the cracks about their pushy little bosoms and behinds.

But then there was the quiet, serene type, veritable nuns of science, who could not have done any other thing in life, except perhaps paint miniature landscapes if that was in vogue. Never very original, they excelled at filling in the missing parts of the picture: making measurements, testing the theory on previously unexamined species, and so forth. Dora must have been one of these; at least he had to assume so without knowing the exact nature of her work. Della might have been too, if she'd ever had a chance, and at the thought of her he felt a twinge of regret that he knew to be out of all proportion to a missed appointment with a former student.

■　■　■

Leitbetter returned the call somewhere in the middle of the third drink and listened in silence to Alex's story, every part of which was true except for Phyllis's role. Alex made up a more roundabout explanation of how he came to see through the *Biography of the Twentieth Century* project and Leitbetter accepted it without comment. There were far more eye-catching details, like the money.

"I can explain everything, or at least what I think it is," Leitbetter said finally. "Because it's not over, Al. In fact, I think it's just beginning. But we can't do this over the phone."

"I would say your place," Alex offered, "but I'd rather not drive. Certain problems have arisen in the blood chemistry department, if you know what I mean. Besides, Dick, I think you owe me one here."

"Well, okay, but do me a favor and lay off the sauce till I get there. What's the point of talking if you're going to be goddamn impaired?"

There were good answers for that one, which Alex had perfected over the years. The purpose of alcohol was to winnow out the excess brain cells, moving in like a lion on a herd of gazelles, eliminating the old and the weak. Survival of the fittest: a process of refining the neuronal hardware. But he had Chris assemble him a cheese sandwich anyway and an Irish coffee, the only antidote to stupor which did not carry sobriety as a side effect.

As a compromise they met in the parking lot, sitting in Leitbetter's car with the motor running for the air conditioning, facing the dumpster behind the squat building that housed the bar and the attached motel. "What if someone spotted me in a dive like that?" was Leitbetter's explanation, and Alex wanted to remind him of all the hours they had spent in worse settings, drinking and sketching diagrams on damp napkins, arguing hoarsely about experiments and probable outcomes.

"The reason I didn't fully explain what I was getting you into is frankly, Al, that it's embarrassing." He sighed and stared out into the darkness, where the neon sign of the Baycrest was illuminating the empty branches of a couple of maples, now orange, now blue, making them look foolish and depraved.

"It wasn't exactly a matter of sparing me details, Dick. Suppose we start with some first principles here. Characters, plot line, and so forth."

"Okay. But this is absolutely between us, okay?" Leitbetter loosened his tie and settled back, looking resigned and rueful. "It goes back to WOW. The truth is, I got the idea for WOW from Relnik, from an article of his I came across years ago."

"I thought WOW was my idea."

"You designed the syllabus, Al, and brilliantly, I've always said, brilliantly. But the concept was mine, you may recall. Or not really mine: I got it from Relnik. Article published in *Perspectives on Humanistic Pedagogy*, 1949. I more or less stumbled onto it while I was doing a literature search for something or other, but I saw the potential immediately. The prepared mind, you know. I saw where you could take it. I knew it was wrong, but I . . . took it."

"Well, for Chrissake. It's not exactly a unique idea: 'Science should be fun.'"

Leitbetter ignored this and continued staring ahead. "I'll never forget one particular quote from that article. I wrote it down word for word: 'The inquiring mind knows a buoyant gladness even in the darkest times, for it perceives a world transformed, where even the clouds are heavy with secrets and the dullest pebbles glitter like gemstones, arranged to show the way.'"

He turned slowly to Alex. "See? The thirst for knowledge is hardwired into our brains, hooked up to the pleasure principle. It's as fundamental as sex or hunger—part of the reason we're *here*, Al."

"'The reason we're here'? Jesus, Dick. What are you, getting religious now?"

"Well, what's wrong with a reason, huh? There's no proof life *doesn't* have a purpose. In fact, what does science show us, when you come right down to it? Levels, Al, layers and levels: baryons inside atoms, atoms inside molecules, molecules inside cells—all the way up to galaxies inside galactic clusters. A hierarchy, one level nested inside another—"

"Okay. All right. But to return to the more mundane level of—"

"What I'm saying is, why should human consciousness, pathetically limited as it is, be the ultimate level of awareness? Why not another level, a higher form of life, compared to which we're no more than bugs? It could have 'reasons,' you know, reasons for everything we do. It could have programmed us, through the wiring of our brains—"

"So you got the idea for WOW from Relnik. Now could we get to the embarrassing part?"

Leitbetter tightened his grip on the steering wheel. If they were driving they would probably be going too fast to miss the dumpster. They would be annihilated in a burst of garbage.

"At first it didn't matter. Who was going to ask if the WOW concept was really mine in the original sense? But then I was asked to give the Galway lectures—remember that? up at Harvard? So I had to put it on a little firmer basis: you know, pedagogical breakthrough, the TV generation wakes up. So I borrowed a little more freely. I had an intern, bright kid, little on the autistic side, snoop out the unpublished papers. Family wouldn't part with them, unfortunately, or none of this would have come about . . . See, it was like this gold mine and nobody else knew about it. I took phrases, sentences, figures of speech."

Leitbetter winced and studied the neon-colored branches. "I was going to credit him. When the Galway lectures were published, that was my chance. Then I thought, Who the hell ever heard of Henry Relnik? I'm going to cite some unpublished papers by a guy no one ever heard of? You know how careful I am, Al, about giving credit where it's due. But this wouldn't help anyone, Relnik being long gone and me being an infinitely more credible source myself. So the lectures got published and there it was."

They sat in silence for a moment, Alex fingering his cigarettes, but Leitbetter wouldn't think of it in a closed car. "This is all very disillusioning, Dick, but could we move along to the part where I come in?"

"So I conceived of a solution. I would simultaneously rehabilitate both Relnik and myself. The idea was, I would write a biography of the man, discover him, so to speak, and in the same fell swoop pay my debt." He paused and switched to an indignant tone. "The point is, what you're telling me is someone's trying to stop me. You see what's going on, don't you? You see what they're trying to do?"

"Trying to break into the hot market for Relnik biographies, no?"

"Blackmail, Alex, that's what's going on here. Blackmail. With the Relnik papers they've got me like a mouse laid out for vivisection, a tack through each one of its pretty little paws. Why else would anybody pay for the stuff?"

Alex tasted the cold sweet residue in the coffee mug he had brought out from the bar. "Usually," he said, working to make the s's come out clear, "blackmailers take money. They don't spend it."

"Oh, it's not just that. That would be simple. They want my name, don't you see? My reputation. There are people—the old guard, you know, the faculty is full of them—who would love to see me ruined. What I call popularization they call sensationalism. It's envy, of course. Pure envy."

"Let's not get into that, Dick. But you have been pushing it, you know: Visitors from outer space. Cryonics. Shit . . ." Cryonics, or the possibility of freezing human beings and reviving them in the future, had been the subject of one of their long-standing arguments, years ago. Frogs had been frozen and revived, Dick would say, so why not men? Technology works its way up the food chain, first you do it to bacteriophage, then bacteria, then mice, then charity patients in the university hospital. Same with freezing and thawing, the time will come.

"What about cryonics?" Leitbetter turned and faced Alex, leaving one hand on the wheel to show he was still in command. "You call that unscientific? It's the ultimate expression of *faith* in science: having yourself frozen because you believe, you *know*, that science is going to progress to the point where you can be revived, in full health, just as you were, sometime in the future . . ."

"I've heard this before, Dick. Can we get back to Relnik?"

"All right. Yes. Relnik. The truth is, I gave him life. That's one way to see it. Because of me, Henry Relnik's ideas didn't die with him. They live on, in our university and dozens, now, around the country."

Alex rolled down his window and lit a cigarette. The air in the vicinity of the dumpster was tainted with day-old garbage smells, too rich and meaty, one might think, for a straightforward drinking establishment like the Baycrest, but it was worth it for a smoke. "All I know," he said carefully, monitoring his elocution, "is I spent today reading about romance in the Third Reich under the watchful eyes of a punked-out New Age slut. This is a shabby business, Dick, any way you want to run it."

"I wish you wouldn't do that."

Alex let the cigarette fizzle out in the remains of the Irish coffee. "Okay. And what you're telling me now is probably just as hokey as Take One—the *Biography of the Twentieth Century*. Now we have the Ptolemaic version of the universe, everything revolves around Richard Leitbetter."

"Look, what is it going to take to make you see the urgency?" He was back to holding the steering wheel with both hands now and staring at Alex like an unruly passenger. "I know all this sounds stupid and melodramatic. But the basics are solid, and the basics are: I made a mistake, okay? I didn't know how bad a mistake, but I made it. Two, I was attempting to correct the mistake. Three, someone is trying to stop me, so the mistake, you see, will not get canceled. Unless we stop them, which is the next step here: getting from point three back to point two."

"We?"

"Well, of course, Alex, who else could I trust?"

■　■　■

Miriam wrote "Dr. L." on the pad and let the felt-tipped pen hover over the space next to these letters. The idea had been to sit down where the air conditioning was strongest, which was Miriam's bedroom office, with a legal-sized pad, and try to plot out some moves. Then, Miriam explained, when you've done something, you check it off, and you move on, getting closer, with each step taken, to Steve, or at least some idea of where he might have gone. Everything can't be done according to a plan, Della had once teased Miriam, when they were students together meeting for coffee after class, because then your whole life is repetition: everything you do, you've already done in your head. But the alternative, Miriam argued, was to go careening into each new moment like a total stranger, fresh off the boat, an easy mark.

"Maybe you should talk to Leitbetter," Miriam said, frowning down at the pad.

Della just sat there, pressing her lips together, twisting them from one side to the other. They had agreed that the call to SKD was not a good sign. If someone was looking for Steve, and if they had a legitimate purpose, they would have gone to Della first, they would have gone to the mother, and there would be no telephone games when they found her. Miriam had tried the 800 number herself and gotten one of those computer voices saying, "If you would like to make a call, please hang up and try again," over and over, meaning no such number at all, at least not anymore.

"Well, what if someone sees me and it gets back to Hershey that I've been talking to Leitbetter? You know, the enemy camp."

Miriam sighed. The other problem was Della herself. It was hard to see her in a situation requiring quick answers and follow-up questions. You said one thing and she would agree. You said the opposite and she would shrug and stare off toward that horizon where things and their opposites converge into a single smudged and useless point. It could be that faith healer (because that is how Miriam thought of Sister Bertha) putting a glass wall between the two women, or a wall that went just around Della.

Miriam set the pad of paper aside and lit a cigarette. The time when Della should have pursued the search was right after Steve left, when the trail was still warm and she had the leisure and resources to follow it. Why hadn't she done more then?

Della flinched. It had been hard, she said. The weeks after Steve left were not complete in memory. There were fissures and gaps. Almost a month went by between the last time she saw Steve and when she called the police, since he could, after all, have been staying with a friend, one of the people he took up with when he came back from college. The police had been noncommittal. They asked about drugs, disappointments, intimations of suicide. These things happened all the time, they said. And in Della's experience this was true. Everyone's child was grown-up and missing, or had been replaced at a certain point by a third party, some hard-eyed stranger who denied having ever been needy.

It was around that time that her mother had taken a turn for the worse. She had been declining for months, losing things, garbling her sentences in a way that sometimes only Steve could untangle. There are rules, he told Della, even in decay, for the way words get put together, and Della had been touched to see the two of them talking, if you could call it that, the prickly old lady and the boy. At the neurology clinic, they said "receptive aphasia," meaning Della's mother could speak clearly enough but in no clear relationship to what had been said by anyone else. Once she was in the nursing home, she began to complain of things she found in her food—pieces of string, switches and gears such as a child might have used to invent things. When an aide tried to feed her, she had stabbed the woman with a fork, breaking the skin. There was talk of restraint, and Della ended up going to the nursing home for every meal except breakfast, and cutting the food into tiny pieces to prove there were no objects concealed in it.

"Besides," Della said, half swallowing her voice, "when someone goes away like that, it probably means they don't want to be found."

Miriam waved the thought away. It was unhelpful, the internalized voice of the parent who says everything is doomed to fail, or something like that she had read in a book. "It's the only option," she said, "going to Leitbetter and seeing what he knows. I mean, it's your son, after all; Hershey should understand that."

■ ■ ■

Dr. Hershey removed a cigarette from the breast pocket of his lab coat, put the filter end in his mouth, and sucked quietly for a moment before replacing the cigarette, unlit, in the crumpled pack he carried at all times. The meeting was to take place in half an hour, but the fact was, he was no longer sure what to say. He could not tell them what he had concluded from his log, certainly not yet; that went without saying. Until it matures into theory, supposition must be kept in a realm of its own, sheltered from the hard eyes of skeptics. On the other hand, it would be unfair to chide the members of his lab for what he no longer believed was their fault. Morale was already an issue. That very morning Claire had reported to him, with some satisfaction, finding the Pakistani in the ladies' room crying, or at least replacing the eye makeup that had been ruined by tears.

This was not the kind of information he would have entered in the log when he began it, some weeks ago, as a record of the untoward events and peculiar obstacles that seemed to plague the work. Note-taking is essential to adversarial relationships, as with the disease itself, whose every manifestation and possible trait were recorded in ink in a number of notebooks, none of which was to be removed from the lab, that were stored in a locked cabinet at night. In fact, you might say it is the very essence of research, the taking of notes. What is an experiment, anyway, but a trap for nature, an artificial circumstance designed to close off all other options and imprison the enemy until a confession is extracted? At which moment the experimentalist must be poised to record all that transpires, down to the slightest signal or deviation that might betray the enemy's logic.

He had begun by noting the seemingly impersonal things. There was the continuing problem of contamination, if that's what it was. Samples they had prayed would contain the virus turned out, again and again, to be full of cellular debris, smears of protoplasm, loose organelles, strands of intracellular fiber. And it was a virus, he was sure of that, and would lead eventually to years of well-funded work: isolating the coat protein, mapping the nucleic acid, DNA or RNA as the case may be, and condensing the results into slides which could be shown at the annual meetings. That is how things would go in the normal course of events, in a well-run lab, in a supportive institutional environment.

But the mishaps had only multiplied. There were fluctuations in the strength of the air conditioning, which had led to the ruin of several key plasma and tissue samples. The technicians had brought the suspect samples into his office for a sniff, and he shuddered to recall the sudden insult of the odor, with its undertone of menstruation and swamps. Then there had been the accident in the animal house, attributable to the confusion of a momentary power failure, in which an entire tray of samples ready for testing on rabbits and rats had smashed to the linoleum floor, creating a spill which may or may not have been hazardous, depending on how successful they had been in their efforts to isolate the virus. No specific accusations were made, though Claire muttered about the quality of the animal house personnel, who spoke less English with every year and were believed to take drugs in the men's room.

Gradually, by imperceptible degrees, the log had expanded into a more general diary of events in the lab. The Pakistani's visa had run into an unaccountable tangle, which surely the administration could have overridden had they been inclined to extend themselves. Dr. Hershey's graduate student, a lumpish young woman of uncertain promise, had been late returning from her annual vacation at home in St. Louis, and now seemed preoccupied with inner doubts. Almost daily, there was some minor crisis in which the technicians would squeal, Claire would stiffen up, eyes bulging, and the post-docs would slam doors and leave huffy reminders on the blackboard: "Whoever last used the microtome will please remember in future to clean it thoroughly when finished and return it to the shelf where it belongs." Even the new girl, Della, was a source of concern. She was reliable and quietly bright, as one might want a wife to be, if the subject of wives was admissible during Dr. Hershey's workday deliberations. But her association with Dr. Leitbetter's poor drunken ward continued to bother him. It was Freud, he believed, who had determined that women had no true loyalties, only shifting assessments of convenience and gain.

The ideal thing would be to photocopy the log, so that he would feel free to take it home with him to review and expand on during his evenings at home. But he rejected the idea of entrusting it to someone—most likely Della, who had taken up so many of the clerical tasks—to carry to the copy center, where it would then be handed over to a gaggle of indifferent young people who were required, according to rumor, to make secret additional copies for Dr. Leitbetter's private perusal. The only alternative was to copy the log out by hand, entry by entry, behind the locked door of his office. This exercise had forced him to review the last few weeks' events more closely than would be possible in memory, and it was clear now, the one thing that he could not tell his research team: that some outside force was opposing them, some mischievous and ingenious power.

They were already seated when Dr. Hershey entered the seminar room and took his place at the head of the oval table. He set a notepad down on the table, though nothing was written on it. Not being prepared, even for something as informal as a lab meeting, gave Hershey an unaccustomed thrill of anxiety. The room was windowless, covered by gray carpeting material that ran from the floor halfway up the walls, presumably for soundproofing, though in effect serving as a growth medium for mildew and unanalyzed molds. Across the table from him, the graduate student piled cookies onto a napkin in front of her while the technicians watched, silently counting. At one point Hershey had banned cookies from lab seminars on the grounds that they created a distraction, with all the passing to and fro; the solution had been to put them on two plates, one at each end of the table, more or less in reach of all present. He cleared his throat and aligned the notepad parallel to the edge of the table. There was no choice but to start.

He began with a review of their progress to date. There was, happily, an abundance of samples—blood, spleen, liver, and now even fragments of brain and spinal fluid. The process of concentration and fractionation was well under way, producing a multiplicity of derivative samples ready to be tested for infectiousness on the usual animals. In most respects, it was a perfectly straightforward problem, a textbook case. Soon they would be harvesting tissue from the injected—and, they all hoped, infected, animals—and, with any luck at all, looking the little devil in the eye.

The Pakistani frowned pointedly and Hershey began to move it along. Difficulties were to be expected. Nature is a modest lady, she guards her secrets well, throwing up makeshift barriers, petty distractions, when she feels the cold eye of science may be about to find her out. You could hardly expect the universe to come all neatly labeled, with flow diagrams attached. In many ways science was a test, perhaps the highest test, of man's mettle and will to survive—a game, the ultimate game perhaps. The victims had come up against the disease and lost. They, however, would win.

There was now a definite restiveness around the table. The Korean had stopped chewing and was examining his knuckles. One of the technicians had begun a series of neck and shoulder stretches. Only Della seemed fully engaged, her brown eyes fastened on Hershey with touching intensity.

"I will come to the point," he said, staring down at the blank notepad in front of him. "Just as we have all been studying the disease, I have been undertaking a parallel study of the problems that have plagued our enterprise, and I am happy to report that they appear to be . . . quite unrelated. We've had an assortment of symptoms—mere accidents, really, in appearance—with fortunately no single thread connecting them. No virus, so to speak." He paused to smile and distribute confident nods around the table. "We may have had our off days, but there is, as yet, as far as I can see, no sickness here."

The Pakistani arched one eyebrow and leaned back in mild dismay, but otherwise Hershey's conclusion was greeted with a general relaxation: chairs were pushed back, cups refilled. The graduate student, emerging from a heavy-lidded slump, offered the first comment, a suggestion for a biomathematical approach involving terms like "point source" and "chi square factors" that caused the technicians to roll their eyes. Of course, they would need a much larger sample size, the graduate student went on—several thousand cases at least, before these methods would apply. Dr. Hershey nodded tightly and turned to the Pakistani, whose eyes had narrowed into a frown.

"This is no place for your sigmas and chis." The Pakistani opened the fingers of one hand dismissively. "We are dealing with the death of children, of the young who are born into innocence. You must ask yourself, what does it mean?"

Hershey made a weak joke about the dangers of infringing on the philosophy department and turned with relief to Claire, who could be counted on for some practical proposal on technique or faulty equipment. In retrospect, it was not a wise move. Later, memory would muddle the events of that afternoon so that Claire's comments or, more precisely, speech would seem to caption the startling images that followed. But there was no warning at the time, except for the manner in which she drew herself up for the honor of speaking, her small eyes flashing, arms folded across her chest.

"The young aren't always so innocent. Don't kid yourself . . ." She glanced at the Pakistani without turning her head. "With the teenager today anything goes . . ." and here she leaned forward and widened her eyes. "We're talking about drugs, the worship of idols, sex in parked cars . . ."

Hershey cleared his throat and the technicians rose tactfully to clear up the cookies and cups. But there was no stopping her.

"For He shall rise up and smite them with plague. Death will spray out from His sword in droplets of poison and toxic waste. The earth will open and spew deadly gas . . ."

The insolence of it should have angered him. Claire had never brought her beliefs into the laboratory before, at least not openly or in Hershey's presence. But something in this was a rebuke, he could not help but feel, for the rambling mendacity of his own presentation. In anger at least was clarity, and while he had never been encouraged, as a boy, to meander in the hallucinatory extremes of the Bible—Revelations or the bloody record of Genesis—Claire's words had an eerie and impelling rhythm. A serene God had some explaining to do. A God who worked his will through equations and fields of force could be faulted, at the very least, for frivolity and indifference. But a warrior God, locked in mortal and unending combat with his evil twin, forced an entirely different moral focus on the picture. He himself knew what it was to push up against the weight of a malevolent Other, human or otherwise, in the pursuit of unassailable goals. No one could be blamed who put up a good fight. He made a slight grimace and tapped his watch, a reminder that it was nearly five.

People were already rising from their chairs, making excuses about experimental deadlines and gel chromotography, trying to get out without hurting Claire's feelings, for she was winding down now to the familiar subject of the Lamb's approaching return. Dr. Hershey was struggling to compose some last words that might put a more encouraging spin on the meeting, something about diversity and unity, different cultures but common goals, when a muffled scream came through the half-opened door from the direction of the main lab area. There was an awkward moment as they all tried to get out the door at once, until Dr. Hershey established himself in the vanguard, marched across the corridor with his people in tow, and entered the laboratory.

The scream had come from one of the technicians, who had dropped the plate of cookies she was carrying and was standing with her hands crossed over her mouth, staring at the dishwasher.

"He fighting," the dishwasher announced with a grin. In one rubber-gloved hand she was holding up something gray and dripping red.

"Put that down, Mrs. Lopez, put it down very carefully." Hershey found he was having trouble with his breathing, a constriction, no doubt, of the trachea. The dishwasher shrugged and put the dying rat down on a little mat of paper towels, which began to drink up the blood, leaving the excess to pool on the lab counter, dripping over onto the floor.

Firmly, but disturbed by his heart rate, Hershey approached the sodden animal. Even the eyes were bleeding, black holes of ignorant grief, streaming outward with the dark venous flow. Hershey bent over and poked at the rat with a glass stirring rod. Wherever he pressed, blood seeped out through the short gray hairs, adding new areas of leakage to the matted spots already present on the belly, under the legs, and in the groin.

"I didn't do nothing. He come like this already in the cage. Someone should watch they don't fighting like this."

"That's all right, Mrs. Lopez. There was no fighting." Hershey wiped the end of the stirring rod with a clean towel, paused, then threw both rod and towel into the covered trash can marked HAZ-ARDOUS WASTE. He turned to the others, not sure what expression they would find on his face, hoping only that it fit the dignity of the moment. "It looks like we've done it. We've done it despite of . . . everything. We have here the first known nonhuman victim of the disease. Of course, there are assays to do, a thorough dissection. But it looks very much, you can see for yourselves, it looks like we've finally isolated the infectious agent."

He paused to wipe the film of sweat from his forehead. There were gasps and a whoop from the Korean. "The sample we used to make this animal sick"—his voice was thick but he wanted to make this clear enough so that even Della and the dishwasher would understand—"is the sample that contains the virus."

He looked around for the cage the rat had come up from the animal house in. The tag on the cage would reveal the infectious sample, which was all they needed, Hershey realized with a rare surge of energy, to define the full night's work ahead.

But the graduate student was standing next to the cage, fingering the tag like a receipt she could not decide whether to save or throw away. "This rat didn't get anything." She read slowly from the tag: "It says CONTROL."

■　■　■

It was dusk, a few days later, when Alex pulled up at Riane's house. He hadn't wanted to get there so late, but a hangover had slowed him down all day, making physical objects slippery and even small projects look hopeless and barren. On the drive over he entertained a cynical fantasy of taking Riane up on her offer, on the couch or, for all he knew of the latest trends, the kitchen table, but she seemed to have lost the spark, because he had to ask if he could come in and then she just stood there, patting the flat top of her haircut, not thinking to offer him a seat.

"So," she said, "the professor."

"I'm sorry for how I left the other day."

She shrugged and Alex tried not to notice how the sweat held the V-necked man's T-shirt to her body.

"See, I need your help. I'm really in trouble." It's easy to be humble when you're hung over. Alex said he had not quite explained his stake in the matter, because it did him no credit. The pressure, she must know, in academia, is intense. It had not seemed such a bad thing to get a grant for the Relnik biography before he actually had access to the papers, though he knew he had stretched it by stating in the application that access was assured. Now he very much needed to contact the man who had purchased the papers, to work something out, if she could tell him the name, that is.

"Who's the asshole?" a man's voice inquired from the other room.

Alex turned so quickly that his head spun and dark spots appeared in his field of vision. A thin man, possibly Asian, with his black hair slicked into a pompadour had emerged in the dining area that bordered the living room. Alex could make out that he was wearing a long-sleeved shirt and had his arms folded across his chest.

"Professor. I told you already." Riane stood her ground between the two men.

"Sure." The man flipped on an overhead light so that Alex could see he was scowling. "And what are you in the market for? Because we're a little low on stock right now, after last week's big sale."

"Well, I'm not actually in the market," Alex offered. "I'm a scholar. Man of science. I deal in ideas, knowledge. The realm of thought, you know."

The thin young man leaned forward against one of the chairs. "Aren't we all, though? In the 'realm of thought.' But someone comes along and dangles a check under our noses and we forget everything we ever knew, everything we ever believed in, and we leap, you know, straight into the shit."

Riane snorted softly and Alex tried to figure whether any of this was addressed to him. "What I mean is, I'm doing some research.

It's not a matter of money, although as I said, there are certain pressures. I, uh—"

But the thin man was looking at Riane. "What next, huh? Turning art into money? Selling the annual collage so it can hang in some corporate atrium and make the money men feel noble about their stupid, shit-shoveling, meaningless lives?"

Riane cocked her head toward Alex. "The idea is that nothing is property. Anything worth having is worth giving away. Homer would be happy to explain."

"It's not my rule, you know that—it's his."

"Well, he isn't here, is he? Or haven't you noticed?"

"What is this?" Alex took a half step toward them. "And who is 'he'?"

"Is that why you're here, huh? To snoop?" Homer demanded of Alex, and then, turning to Riane, "Tell him to get out, will you."

Riane stood there for a moment, saying nothing, then turned and left the room. In the silence while both men stared after her, Alex's thoughts turned to the pint he had left in his glove compartment. His stomach was cringing, each part of the abdominal surface drawing away from contact with all the others. He was trying to formulate a question, something that would cut to the root of what was going on between the two, when Homer noticed him again.

"You must be enjoying this." He brushed his hair back where the pompadour had fallen in long bangs over his eyes, giving him for a moment a delicate, Edwardian look.

"No." Alex loosened his collar. "I can't say I am. I feel that I've stumbled into something and—"

"What do you want here?"

"Well, as I said," Alex saw the need to establish his age and position, "I'm working on a biography of Henry Relnik. His work has remarkable implications for—"

"I know that. You told your story already, remember? The point is, who are you working for?"

"I'm not working for anyone. I mean, I'm an associate professor at the university. It's easy enough to check."

"I mean, who are you working for now?"

But before Alex could answer, Riane returned to the room with a slip of paper in her hand and scissors, sat down at the table again, and began to cut. She was composed and expressionless, withdrawing into her art, Alex figured, her dumb collage.

"Look—" Alex took out a tissue and wiped his face, mentally preparing a short speech on the theme of Henry Relnik, his relevance and contributions. But the place had become quiet and taken on the atmosphere of a well-run schoolhouse: Riane bent over her work, cutting; Homer leaning back from the table and watching her so intently that Alex stared too at the flashing scissors and the diminishing slip of blue paper in her hand.

"Wait a minute!" Alex leaned forward to assert his presence. "What are you cutting there?"

"Twenty-five thousand, man, that's what she's cutting," Homer answered without turning to look at him. Riane was working in from the edges, freeing tiny irregular shapes from the bondage of the larger form.

"Is that the check? Look, would it be asking too much to know who that check is from?" He had no confidence that Riane would remember anything that presented itself in the form of letters or words. "I mean, that's what I'm here for, right?" He forced a chuckle. "Before you mince the whole thing into molecules."

If his voice had actually traveled across the room, there was no way to know it from the couple seated at the table. Riane finished her work, scraped the pieces of paper into her hands, and tossed them in the direction of Homer, a confetti of triangles, trapezoids, and odd pieces of arc. "There. Happy now? I didn't sell anything, I gave it away."

"What in the living hell . . . ?" Alex made his way to the table. It was Leitbetter he wanted to yell at, but these two skinny punks would have to do. He drew in a long, shaky breath, leaning one hand against the table. "If I may interrupt this little séance: I came here with one simple question, which is, who bought the Relnik papers or, as it has just developed, was given them as a donation—"

"He's right, you know," Riane interrupted. There was a hint of defiance in her tone, Alex thought, though here again a facial expression might have fleshed the whole thing out. She had scraped the scraps together again and was letting them run through her fingers onto the table. "Why don't you tell him, Homer. Tell the sucker what he wants to know."

A long look went between the two, in which items unknown to Alex were counted, sorted, and set aside for a future reckoning. "All right." Homer shrugged, apparently feeling more generous now that Riane had finished her cutting. "It's a company, based in Mexico, I think, or the West Coast somewhere, sent some guy to buy the papers."

"A company? What do they make?"

Homer laughed. "You must be a professor, you think companies have to make something."

"Okay, so what do they sell?"

"Things people want. Or would want if they knew they could get them."

"He means the guy is a gangster," Riane said with the faintest trace of a smile. "Made his money in drugs, but he's gone hi tech since then."

Homer glared at her, but she shrugged one shoulder.

"Would you mind telling me," Alex tried, "what a gangster would want with the Relnik papers?"

"He's a scientist, tell him."

Homer and Riane locked into another long look filled with mutual challenge and testing.

"We don't know for sure, right? It's not like we actually *know*," Homer said to Riane before deigning to address Alex. "Probably it's a whole lot smarter *not* to know. Now, will you get out of here? We have business, Riane and I."

Alex shrugged and took a step back toward the door. "Well thanks, kids. It's been real interesting. If either of you should get a further flash of illumination . . ." He wrote out his name and phone number on a blank page from his appointment book, tore it out, and handed it to Homer.

"Wait a minute." Riane ran into one of the back rooms again

and came back with a file folder held shut with rubber bands. Alex was already at the door when she gave it to him, along with a tiny circle she drew on the back of his hand with one finger, very lightly, so that Homer could have only seen the folder passing between them. "Your portrait. Take it. I never keep my own work."

CHAPTER 6

Dr. Hershey spent most of his time locked in his office now, reviewing the lab notebooks, he said, retracing every step. According to Mrs. Lopez, the cleaning lady had found him still working at 11:00 p.m. one night, and he had refused to let her empty his trashcan. So let him eat his waste paper was the cleaning lady's thought, there was enough to worry about in the lab, where a syringe might come stabbing through a plastic garbage bag, with something on it so you'd never be the same again, some invisible dirt that science put there.

He was in no way out of touch with the lab, Dr. Hershey assured himself. Twice a day, at eleven and four, he still did a quick tour, peeking into microscopes, holding test tubes up to the light, nodding or frowning as the faces around him seemed to require. Something would always be broken, there would be a question of how many controls to run. Or, as had occurred more than once in the last few weeks, the appearance of faint, crystalline structures in an electron micrograph, possibly viruses, possibly nothing at all.

Back in the office, he shut the door behind him, checked that the drawers he had left locked were still locked, pulled out a cigarette and twirled it, unlit, between his fingers. There were far better offices, everyone in the lab surely knew, offices that contained their own seminar tables, easy chairs, even adjoining private bathrooms. He knew his own place in the upper-middle level of the hierarchy and accepted the layout that went with it: a desk, or work space, that ran L-shaped along two walls; an extra chair for whoever might come in; and one high window, situated so as to provide a rectangular sample of sky, like a colorless slice of tissue pressed between glass slides.

It was not ideal, but neither was it a place where anything would jump out at you. The journals lay in their pile, yellow scraps of paper marking the articles that would need to be copied and filed. His wife and children smiled forbearingly from within their photo frame; the ashtrays were cleaned and replaced each night. Here, unlike in the lab, nothing lived or moved without his knowing or inviting it; nothing crept around, or took new forms, or changed overnight from dry and gray to a brilliant, greasy red.

Except for the stain on the carpet, which he had first noticed the night of the incident involving the rat, the bloody "control," although the stain could have been there much longer, for he had not always been in the habit of staring at the floor. He considered it for a long moment, then took a ruler from his middle drawer, hiked his pants up to loosen them around the knees, and crouched down over the carpet: 5.7 centimeters. It was advancing at the rate of three or four millimeters a day, from the outside wall toward the center of the room, a dark peninsula stretching out into the industrial gray. Claire said this was the kind of thing you had to expect, that most of the carpeting throughout the complex was damaged by moisture, some of it far worse than this. She had offered to call maintenance, but he said no, they would want to move his things out, tear up the floor. He bent over and brought his face within inches of the stain. There was nothing, though, nothing but a smell of damp, closed-in places; of thick, impacted dust and the chemicals that are added to fabrics in the mill to make them outlive the people who tread on them.

At the knock on the office door, Dr. Hershey pulled himself to his feet and slid the extra chair over the stain. It was the Korean, Dr. Soo, sticking his head in and peering around curiously. One rumor was that Dr. Hershey did secret experiments of his own in his office, checking the results of his staff, but the same thing was said of all the deskbound scientists, and was probably encouraged by them for purposes of mystery and intimidation. Dr. Soo lowered his solid frame into the one available chair and smiled faintly, waiting to be called on.

"Well. Any progress?"

"Claire is coming up clean. So far anyway. You know this group she belongs to, BOLT? Blood of the Lamb Triumphant; a church, I guess you can call it. You want to see their symbol?"

Hershey took the paper the Korean handed him and put on his glasses. It was a photocopy of a cruciform object, a cross that seemed to be in motion—no place, here, for the Lord's repose.

"See? Two crossed lightning bolts." The Korean leaned forward and ran his finger along the cross. "Makes you want to put on your Boltman suit and go whoosh!" He did an airplane taking off with his right hand and leaned back, laughing.

Hershey compressed his lips. This was the aspect of the investigation he found most distasteful, poking into the private lives and irrational allegiances of his little crew. Since Claire was as secretive about the church as she was evangelical about the Lamb, they had had to get most of their information from the Urban Anthropology Department. It was a hardly a complete picture but probably sufficient for their purposes. According to the people in Urban Anthro, BOLT had been founded a few years ago by an unordained preacher who claimed to have received, by dictation, a previously missing chapter of the Bible, in which the Lamb figured prominently, as well as a snake. With a little effort, it would be possible to get hold of a copy of the newly released chapter, but Hershey resisted the pornographic lure of further information. It was enough to know that the angel who had delivered the dictation had wings that folded forward, more like a chicken's than a swan's, and that the church believed that the Lamb might already have attempted to return but had been butchered in utero as a fetus.

"Anyway, they're clean," the Korean continued. "No record of involvement in animal rights or fetal tissue protests. Creationism, sure, it comes with the territory. But basically they're a pretty quiet group."

Hershey nodded slowly. Only a few years ago, a young female employee had released ten cages of genetically pure laboratory mice into the scrubby wasteland that bordered the parking lots. None of them was ever sighted, though there was a temporary problem of stray cats in the area. Since then all potential employees were put through a background check for membership in groups with a record of scientific sabotage. It was hardly reliable, though, by scientific standards, more a matter of primitive rumor-gathering and hearsay.

"You think we can rely on that?"

"Well, you know Urban Anthro, they don't give you any guarantees. You have splits, you have changes in tactics, you have front groups. A group could be lambs one day and terrorists the next." He laughed at his own witticism. "They tell you what they've got, that's all, they keep on monitoring." He shrugged and pulled a small notebook out of his breast pocket. "I've got something else here too. You know Della? You know she has a son who used to work for Leitbetter?"

Hershey ran his fingertips along the arms of his chair in a tentative fashion. "Well, that in itself . . ."

"Okay, but listen to this. Son's name is Steve. Bright boy, a little weird. Hacker. Member of some kind of computer cult. 'Anarcho-fundamentalists' is how they're listed in the Urban Anthro files."

"Another, uh, Christian group?"

"Not exactly, but there isn't much information on them. Just the usual holier-than-thou, we've-got-a-plan-for-the-world kind of thing, I suppose."

"So what do you think this, ah, means for us?"

"I'd keep an eye on the mother, that's all."

Hershey stroked the breast pocket containing his cigarettes. Now he was eager to have the Korean out of his office, so that he could let the entire space fill with his disturbing new sense of the mysteries that lie behind each bland and helpful face. "And, uh, Soo, any progress with the Vista View samples?"

The Korean rolled his eyes and held up his hands. "What can I say? We're repeating the whole thing at three different concentrations. Nothing yet, nothing at all. We'll give it a few more days, and if we don't pick up anything, then . . ."

"Remember, don't just tag the cages, mark the animals themselves. Something that won't dissolve, okay?"

When the door closed again, Hershey sat for a long time before unlocking the drawer and taking out his logbook. Always, in some unarticulated way, he had believed that there is ultimately only one disease underlying all the florid profusion of medical science, one eternal, spiteful rebellion against the original and orderly design of things. But what do we know of its inner nature or intentions, when all we can see are the brutal methods it employs?

Then it occurred to him, as it had probably already occurred to the Korean, and certainly to the Pakistani, that it was possible that the tags had not been switched, that the first rodent to die of the disease had been the control, after all. In which case . . . No, he put the thought away. Cross that line and science was left behind; you entered a cartoon land not too different from Claire's poor barnyard religion, where elves lurked behind mushrooms and blood flowed from empty flasks. It was not possible that the disease had cropped up among the general animal population. There was no way.

Though there had been that spill in the animal house weeks ago, trays full of tissue samples all over the floor. Surely that had been cleaned up within minutes and all surfaces scrubbed and disinfected. He took out a cigarette and studied the floor. In nine or ten days, at the present rate, the stain would reach the center of the room, impossible to miss. In a couple of weeks it would be under his feet.

■　■　■

Della got home early that day, had a quick dinner in front of the TV, and decided to see where she stood. By nine she had spread the bills out on the table and tried arranging them in different ways—by the date due, by the amount due, by the probable consequences of nonpayment. Already there had been a call from a collection agency predicting the involvement of lawyers. A check would no longer be honored, they said, only money orders or cash in person. Outside, the water tower was taking on the aspect of a guard tower in a rural correctional institute, gray and forbidding. It was not what she had been to led to expect, this misfit between income and expenses. The job and the apartment, her wages and the rent, were supposed to go together, complementing each other, forming a sustainable life.

But there are expenses no one can foresee, arising like tolls on a long-distance journey. Food, for example, was causing her income to dribble away invisibly in outlays of cash. It was surprising to think that in her former life there had been whole days devoted to dinner, the idea of it, the shopping, the cooking and cleaning up. She used to start in the morning, reading magazines for inspiration, waiting for a plan to form around which the afternoon could be structured into errands. Even if the food was rejected, and used only to paint the plates in smears of sauce, she was not disqualified from starting again, the next day, with a new approach to dinner.

But these days the thought of dinner arose out of context, baffling her. Breakfast and lunch were embedded in the routine of work, but dinner had no natural point to it. Too much was being spent on ready-made items and take-out foods that could be eaten directly from their wrappings, then the whole thing thrown away. She would have to start going to the supermarket again and face the shame of a nearly empty cart: a bar of soap, a couple of yogurts and pieces of fruit.

It was late and only four checks had been written, leaving barely

enough for the rent. Outside, it was night, which in this neighborhood was the same as nothing, or at least she hoped nothing and
that the landlord's dog was alert. The bills were enough of a menace.
If her job were secure and offered some possibility of advancement,
that would be one thing, but in the afternoon Dr. Hershey had
stopped by her cubicle during his four o'clock tour of the lab and
said, after a moment of throat-clearing, "I hear your son is a whiz
with computers."

Della brightened. "Yes. He used to work for Dr. Leitbetter, in
fact."

"Mmm. He isn't involved in anything . . . uh . . ." Hershey rocked
forward a few times, frowning, and then started again. "He still
keep in touch with Leitbetter?"

"Oh no, I don't think so. He's—" She could say "missing" but
it sounded too irregular.

"I just want to be sure that you're happy here," he said, nodded
stiffly, and moved on before she could say anything else.

■　■　■

If she lost her job, what would happen? From the television set
in the living room came the scary music that accompanies the approach of the villain. The beautiful heroine would be sitting all
alone in front of a mirror and brushing her hair, or perhaps there
would be no mirror and she would be blind, so the first she would
know of the villain would be his hand coming over her mouth. Of
course, a chord of music could mean anything, could be a warning
about transmission problems or the need for a reliable mouthwash.
But fear recruits everything to its purpose, every sound or piece of
mail, even silence and the absence of mail.

She shivered as she gathered up the unpaid bills and stuffed them
hastily into their drawer. A wind was ready to spring up, she sensed,
a force field, with the strength to ravage the room. Nothing moved
as yet, but the intention was there and the means. Anything that
was not put away, like a spoon left out by the kitchen sink, might
be swept up as a deadly projectile. She moved around quickly,
shutting the cupboards and putting away the dishes from her dinner.

When there was nothing left out on the counters to turn against her, she checked the locks and listened to hear if her landlord was still up. It occurred to her that at his age he could die and no one would know unless it was her, and even she would probably not know but would go on living above the apartment which had become his tomb.

In bed, she set the radio to the frequency where Sister Bertha appeared, and turned out the light. She lay there for a long time, watching inner movies of abandonment and disaster, so that when she first heard the voice there was no way to know whether it had just begun or had been talking already for hours. "Why do you ask what Jesus wants of you?" The voice was bullying, proud, difficult. Della turned up the radio and waited in the dark.

"You know the answer. The answer is everything, everything you have.

"A man writes and says, 'I am ready to follow the Lord. I have come to this decision. But I hang back, Sister, from taking the step. What about myself, I have to ask, I have to be reasonable, I have to think of myself.'

"Ah, Brother, let us by all means be reasonable. Let us be reasonable about this 'self' you are so friendly with. You talk like it is some baby you're carrying around in front of you. So unwrap that baby, use the mental force of reason to see what is this burden that you carry. Your 'self' is some kernel deep inside, right? —that sees all the things you do and think? But what sees it? Some kernel within the kernel, then, that must be it, another self to see the self.

"Brother! Can't you see you're falling for the oldest trick? There's nothing there: nothing to save and nothing to carry, so put your burden down and take the step!"

Della lay with her hands straight out at her sides, staring at the ceiling fixture or the bulbous growth that had replaced it in the dark. As Sister Bertha talked, a wall that had stood for as long as she had known between her eyes and the back of her skull, inside her head, began to crumble, leaving her no place to lean up against and see the world from, as she realized she always had, crouching inside herself against this, the back wall of the mind. The fear was not gone. It played along her arms like a cold breeze in the night. But the words filled the rest of the space, not standing for something but standing alone, multiplying through an echo effect, filling it all.

"So the men fell on Jesus and left Him bleeding there among the creatures of the jungle, who stayed by Him through the night and cried, even those who had never felt the sting of tears before. And when Jesus woke at dawn, all burned with fever and wounds, He looked at the gentle animals who were weeping still and getting hungry now, and He said: Drink my blood that pools there by the tangled root! Eat these limbs of mine all cut with the ants feeding already in the ripe red wounds! It isn't much, but it's all I got, and I share with you, my friends!

"It was all He had, and He offered up his flesh for food!"

Static swallowed Sister Bertha's voice and Della turned to stare at the radio, glowing with its own light, numbers spaced erratically along a line. When the voice returned it was filled with sarcasm.

"Now I have people say to me: 'Sister Bertha, we agree with the law. The law is beautiful, the law is true, and someday we'll get to it, just like you say. We missed Jesus the first time, maybe we'll catch Him on the second coming. And if that's real soon like you say, and we're not ready with our things in order, then we'll catch Him on the third time round. Because these are big things you ask, Sister Bertha, but God's time is bigger yet.' "

"Well!" There was a pause so long that Della thought she had lost her. "Let me set you straight right here and now. Just because there was a first coming and a second doesn't mean in all God's time there is a third. There are two times only that He comes for us. Only two, and one is past and the next is coming up. And I'll tell you why there's two and two alone: The first time was the sowing, the planting of His flesh. The next time is the reaping, and the next time is the last."

■   ■   ■

The smell of the library invigorated Alex with its promise of one thing leading to another, a footnote in one article that would lead to another article and hence to another, looping through the thoughts of men already dead or senile, all mercifully preserved here at the peak of crispness. He had started out fresh in the morning, with a briefcase full of Relnik's papers and a contraband thermos of coffee, but already the library was failing him, blocking him at every turn, speaking in unknown languages. Terms like "fasciculus interfascicularis" and "substantia gelatinosa" would be glorious to pronounce in front of a class but otherwise suggested only that deep confusion between naming and knowing which is the hallmark of primitive science.

It would help if he knew some neuroanatomy, but his own work had been at much lower levels of organization: molecules, organelles, an occasional membrane. In the brain you lose sight of individual cells. It's a society, a nation of cells, overpopulated, tightly packed, barely navigable even with the maps provided by recent textbooks and a richly illustrated atlas of fine structure. Which is why, he thought with a certain chauvinistic satisfaction, the brain will never be replaced by silicon, with its neat, militarized rows of atoms. The brain is the ideal storage vessel, expanding its capacity as the load requires, plus, of course, constantly compacting its contents through the ingenious device of symbols.

The question was . . . What was the question? Whether Relnik's articles harbored the germ of a commercially viable idea? Or was it a criminal idea? Homer and Riane seemed to believe it was, or wanted him to believe it was, but the more Alex read, the more ludicrous the notion seemed. It was hard to imagine Relnik's work on the comparative morphology of the pituitary gland being worth much to anyone, least of all to a hard-nosed gangster, and the later stuff, on the septal region of the limbic system, was of interest only with historical hindsight. The septal region, Alex read in one of the textbooks stacked on the table in front of him, was one of the sites of strong emotion, including pleasure, but Relnik, working in the forties, could not have known this.

Alex shifted in his chair to prevent his hipbones from eating their way through the skin and fusing with the plastic seat. Four would be a respectable time to leave, marking a fullish day of effort, and four was inching closer. He was thinking of going out for a cigarette when he saw Della emerging from the stacks a few yards from his table, carrying a load of bound journals in front of her and looking appealingly mussed and harried.

Tucking his shirt in with one hand, Alex half rose and hailed her. "Della? Doing a little independent research, I hope? Come here for a minute, I have an amazing experience to offer you." She looked startled, and Alex liked the way her smile seemed to come out of some special storage place that was obviously not opened for casual reasons. He tried to remember if he had apologized for not showing up the other day, and felt he had, and been reasonably charming and sober about it.

"Here, sit down. Dr. Hershey can read something else for a minute." He opened the book and slid it across the table to her. "There, see? A cross section of the human brain, in fact the occipital lobe, the part of the human brain that processes visual information."

To Della, the glossy page looked like a drawing done by a child who had been instructed to fill all the space. It could be a fabric seen up close, all tiny repetitive marks. "Hmm," she said.

"Don't you see? You're seeing—the very tissue, the very slice of biological material, that you're seeing with."

"So this is supposed to be like looking in a mirror?"

"Exactly. Only it's dead and stained with a dye so we can see the cells. And isn't that a wonder too? This brain's last intelligent act occurred postmortem, when it obligingly sipped up the dye, in a thoughtful, selective way, for the edification of our own, fortunately still largely living, brains."

She shook her head and pulled the book closer for another look. Alex wasn't sure why this gust came over him, but he could imagine feeding her—scraps of information, theory, whimsy—through a mouth sweetly open like a baby bird's.

"You're interested in the brain now?"

"My brain at least is interested. Some dreadful narcissism drives it on."

"Then could I ask you a question?"

Alex nodded encouragingly, delighted that his madcap professor routine still worked with someone.

"What I want to know . . ."—Della paused and looked down the empty aisles between the stacks—"is: could music be used for mind control? I mean music that was specially designed to have a certain effect?"

"You haven't been listening to that Sister Brenda, have you?"

"Sister Bertha."

"And she's going after rock 'n' roll. Menace to young minds, right?"

Della shook her head, embarrassed. "That would be more like Claire. No. Sister Bertha doesn't care about rock 'n' roll. She's not interested in sin, well, not in little, routine sins."

"There's another kind?"

"Well, yes. She says Jesus said give up all you have—to the poor, I guess, or whoever needs it—and follow Him, but no one does. That's the sin."

"Send all your worldly goods to Sister Bertha and she'll pass them along to the poor—is that it?"

"No, it's not that kind of thing at all." She was speaking fast now, surprised that the sentences were already there, ready for use. "It's not even necessarily worldly goods. It could be things you should be doing but aren't doing . . ."

"Ah, the parable of the talents! Follow the Lord and ye shall earn everlasting bliss. Peace of mind! An elevated comfort level! Relief from workplace stress and marital complications!" She had drawn back into a stiff, one-sided smile. "Della, Della, our only hope is here." He tapped the open book directly on the occipital lobe.

"Yes, Dr. MacBride."

"I'm serious, Della; where science ends, the goblins rise up and take over."

"You don't believe in God at all, then?"

"If you mean do I believe in the fat, tranquil, half-naked guy whose perfect thought this is? No."

"So what's the point, then? I mean, if there's nothing else, then what are we doing here?"

"Point of our existence? Oh, my dear Della, you are in a mood today. Is it all pointless without some heavenly higher-ups watching from on high? Can't we humans just amuse ourselves? Relnik would have said that the point of science, for example, is to give us pleasure. Tickle the brain."

"Then why did you quit doing science? Research, I mean."

"Ah, because I had a falling-out with the prevailing assumption, which is that what we are seeking is already dead. Necrophilia, I found, is an insufficient motivation." Plus of course there was the fact that he had run out of grants.

Della gave him a rueful look and excused herself to get back to the lab. Alex rose too, wanting to end on a note of heartiness. "Just tell Hershey you had a little seminar to go to on the meaning of it all and the nature of the deity, which broke off only for lack of liquid refreshment." She was already backing off, out of the stacks, toward the main reading room. "An oversight we must correct very soon, one of these evenings, all right?"

When he looked back down at the papers in front of him he saw that he had gotten to the point where one page more or less resembled another, the same dense plane of symbols relieved by an occasional line drawing or incomprehensible photomicrograph. The stacks no longer seemed to harbor a rich supply of secrets, waiting to be strung together into something intelligible, and the low fluorescent lights were bearing down, no longer pushing him ahead. He was a taker, that was the problem, as Della's preacher might put it; he could have been a giver and he was a taker instead, nibbling at the edges of other people's research or just sucking, usually sucking, at the liquorish oozings of a culture he brought nothing to. Which, he realized, was probably exactly how Dick Leitbetter saw him.

Leitbetter: that was it. He pulled up out of his slump and sat forward in excitement. Why does it take so long to arrive at the obvious? Leitbetter had admitted to plagiarizing Relnik, so if he wanted to understand what was so important about Relnik, the place to look was in Leitbetter's works. It was late to start down any new trails, about the time when the thought of a drink changed from a comforting daydream into a maddening hiss in his ears. One last thing—the Galway lectures—that would do it, he thought,

stuffing the Relnik papers into his briefcase, one more stone to turn
and he would have earned the night ahead. Leitbetter had sent him
after Relnik and now Relnik was sending him after Leitbetter—a
neat twist, and he had Della to thank for it, for appearing out of
nowhere and jolting his brain with her innocent smile.

■ ■ ■

When Della left the library, she went to the first restroom she
could find and patted her face with a damp paper towel. It had
been a mistake to tell Alex about Sister Bertha, just as it had been
a mistake to try to tell Miriam. All Miriam had said was, Look, if
you're going to have a guru, why not someone where you get to
meet interesting people, you know, go to a meeting, get out of the
house? The whole idea, which she would have tried to tell Alex if
it wouldn't have made her look even more foolish than she already
did, was that there was no reward. You did what you had to because
it was the law, Sister Bertha said. The idea of heaven was an af-
terthought, added by smaller men who came later, propagandists
cheapening the original message. You did what you had to, that
was all. There was no reward, no justice, only the law, and the law
came out of some framework we couldn't even begin to understand,
some framework within which everything that happens, even cruelty and grief, makes perfect sense.

If she believed this, though, there would be nothing to fear. Nothing to fear because there would be nothing to lose. She saw that
what she had been doing with Sister Bertha was hedging her bets,
investing in an alternative, but not of course really thinking of
moving on into it. She needed it to be there, she just wasn't ready.
Divest yourselves, Sister Bertha said, your things and your habits,
your grudges and your hopes—and this Della had not even begun.
She peered into the mirror to see herself as Alex had seen her, and
it was a smeary image, clouded by deposits of hairspray and soap
on the glass, not someone to take seriously or even remember from
one day to the next.

But there is always a first step, Sister Bertha had said, toward what it is that you are called upon to do, and the thought of a "first step" seemed to resolve something, leaving her dizzy and detached. She dried her hands for the second time and tossed the paper towel into the pile already overflowing from the trashcan. Now was as good a time as any.

In the corridor she looked both ways, but no one was coming. There were more factors to consider, but she was moving too fast to be burdened by them. It was interesting how one thing gave way to another, the elevator door opening, closing, opening again, the corridors stretching out, then tightening up in front of her, more doors, fluorescent lights being replaced by bulbs in shades, like a living room, a softer floor with carpeting, and then a woman behind a desk smiling at her curiously. Della had come all this way, such a distance, without even feeling the motion.

"So you're Kipper's mom," Phyllis said when Della arrived at Leitbetter's office and apologized for just showing up. "You have his eyes. Or it would be vice versa, right?" She spoke into something on her desk that must be connected to the inner office, announcing that "Mrs. Markson" was here, as if Della had been expected and had come along right on time.

Dr. Leitbetter did not look up from his desk until Della was halfway across the carpet from the door. He was turning pages vigorously, making marks with a red pencil, frowning like a man coming down to a deadline. There was a story in the complex that he had personally timed the distance between the door and the desk so that he could tell, just by looking at his watch, when it was time to look up from his work and catch his visitor edging quietly across the room, red-faced and neglected. He looked up suddenly when Della was within a few feet of his desk, rose, and stretched out his hand. Della put her hand out too, but he was only gesturing for her to take a seat.

"So, Mrs. Markson, this is about your son, I presume?"

"Yes." She was flustered, expecting more in the way of preliminaries. "I'm, uh, working here now and I was wondering if you might have heard, you know, anything about where he went."

"I suppose you took the job with Hershey so you could get in here and poke around for information leading to the whereabouts, isn't that so?"

"No, of course not, I just needed a job."

He tapped the desk with a pencil, watching her like a man assessing a long shot. "Look, Mrs. Markson, let's not kid each other. You probably know Kipper and I weren't exactly on the best of terms. But whatever you heard is not the whole story. You should realize."

He tilted back in his chair and pressed his fingers together, looking responsible now and pained. Della tried to remember if Steve had ever said anything about Dr. Leitbetter, or shown any changes of mood that could be linked to his job, for better or worse. Once, she had called him to the TV when Leitbetter was on and he watched with her for a minute, like someone seeing a suspicion confirmed. It's a commercial, he said, can't you see? Forget the quasars and the birth of the universe. It's a fund-raiser, that's what he's doing.

"I tried to be understanding," Leitbetter was saying. "I gave him a very long leash, all the time he needed, all the resources. And still . . . I would say something, a suggestion, a little pointer, and he would just sit there like it wasn't worth the bother of an answer. And then there would be that smirk, always the smirk." Leitbetter shut his eyes and snorted softly. "But I'm sure you know what I mean."

"He could be difficult sometimes."

" 'Difficult.' Hmm. I'll show you how he was. Come along, let me show you where he worked." Leitbetter rose and put on the lab coat that was draped over the back of his chair. Della rose too and followed him across the carpet, past Phyllis, who looked into Leitbetter's face for an explanation, and on out into the corridor. "I want you to know he was to get equal recognition when the project was done. Well, not exactly equal, but appropriate to a junior partner. I laid this all out."

A few yards from the entrance to Leitbetter's office, the corridor was blocked by a double door, which he unlocked by punching a code into a wall fixture. On the other side was a long corridor lined with doors, most of them shut, except for one which opened into a quiet lab space where a woman sat on a high stool watching a liquid drop from a convoluted apparatus into a tube no larger than a finger. "You see, I like to keep my hand in," he said as they reached the end of the corridor. "A little experiment here and there. He thought it was silly, of course. 'You're dazzled by the details,' he'd say. 'We already have enough details. The point is to put them together.' "

Leitbetter unlocked a door and they stepped into a vast, windowless room, at least twice as large as Hershey's office but shrunken by the stacks of books and papers on the floor, like stalagmites in a natural cavern. "See, not bad for a kid, is it? There's even a window here somewhere, but he covered it over. Something about excess photons disturbing the computer-brain interaction." He snorted and ran his finger through the dust on a pile of old magazines: *Psychology Today, Astronomical Bulletin, Journal of Applied Cybernetics.*

It was like stepping into Steve's mind, Della thought, only without the connecting logic that made him sane. Every square inch of wall, some of it possibly window underneath, was papered over with posters, clippings, diagrams, computer-generated works of art. A chart of the geological ages, showing mastodons arising from horseshoe crabs, overlapped a map of the night sky, and where this was torn you could see an old magazine photo of a fetus that was still deciding whether to become a fish. It looked as if Steve had been attempting to condense all the knowledge in the world, at about the tenth-grade level, plus some of the doubts, onto wallpaper, and it was beginning to peel off now into its separate parts—the Krebs cycle, the earth as seen from the moon, the Periodic Table, the double helix, concentration-camp victims staring into a GI's camera, their eyes as blank and objective as any man-made lens.

"What was he working on here?" Della asked, strengthened by the garbled paper messages from Steve.

"The idea"—he was peeling away at a science-fiction scene of impossibly sharp mountain ranges, seen from an even higher peak, presumably trying to uncover the window—"was a pedagogical device, a way to make learning"—he gestured to indicate the subject matter on the walls—"more fun. Same idea as WOW—you took WOW, right?—only carried to an infinitely higher level of sophistication."

"That was the point of it, education?"

"Yes, of course. And it went very well for a while. The commercial possibilities were staggering, at least so the consultants said. And then, I don't know. When he came back from college I thought the project would really take off, move beyond the design stage into production. But that was when his attitude took a turn for the worse. Fell in with the wrong group, I suppose, happens a lot at that age. But let me show you something. I'd just like you to know what I was up against."

He lifted the plastic dust cover off the computer terminal that was sitting against a side wall and switched it on. The monitor lit up to show a mushroom cloud expanding in tones of pink and yellow, and when it dissipated, a message appeared in restrained green letters against the black screen:

> Leitbetter, you're so fucking lame
> Still haven't found the password yet
> But everything around you has a name.

There was a silence while they both studied the screen, Leitbetter apparently lost in thought, tapping his chin with his fingers. Della felt a prickly embarrassment move up from her chest to heat her face. "Steve wrote that?"

"He programmed it. There's a different little ditty every time I turn this thing on. You see what I mean? He must have been setting this up weeks before . . . he actually left."

"Let me ask you. The project you were working on, was it related to his game, his computer game?"

Leitbetter frowned and crumpled the peeled-off paper in his hand. "Is that what he told you?"

"No, I just wondered. I was curious about his game."

He glared at her so long that she was afraid she was about to be marched back to his office in silence, possibly fired. "There is a family resemblance, isn't there?" he said finally. "Especially around the mouth. The answer is no: this was not a game. This was not *his* anything. Least of all a game, a childish amusement. In the first place, the original idea for the project goes back, well, decades— before your son, or even you, were born." He paused for breath. "Plus, if you have followed my work at all, you know that I have been concerned about these matters, about the limitations of the human brain, for many years now, well before I knew your son. You do watch television, Mrs. Markson?"

"Of course, and I really enjoyed your—"

"Good, because then you have some faint glimmering of what I was trying to accomplish here. Retraining the mind, changing it into a powerful, non-stop learning machine. But now of course that's finished." He waved at the computer screen. "I had no idea it would turn out this way, or I would never . . ."

"I'm sorry, Dr. Leitbetter. About your project, but—"

"Oh, I'm not exactly high-and-dry." He switched off the computer, replaced the dust cover, and gestured for her to precede him through the door. "There are other possibilities. Work with the physical structure of the brain. Get in there somehow and reconfigure the wiring. Enlarge the capacity that way. Here, please. If you can find surgical instruments tiny enough, that is."

"Yes. Well. What I wanted to know was whether you have any idea where he might have gone. Where he might be."

He paused in the doorway, half blocking her, so that for a moment their lab coats brushed against each other and she was aware of his scent, which was something rare and stratospheric like ozone.

"I think I can help you, Mrs. Markson. But you can help me too."

CHAPTER 7

Alex arrived at the Baycrest with the intention of having one drink, maybe two, but not so many as to destroy the soft, enveloping sense of disorientation that had come over him in the last hours at the library. It was easy to misjudge Leitbetter, to accept him as the caricature he sometimes seemed to be, when in fact he had taste, he at least had taste. The first two Galway lectures were nothing special: parallels between memory and the immune response, the role of natural selection at different biological levels, the usual stuff. Only in the third lecture, on the old mind-brain problem, did he seem to be drawing on Relnik: the brain as a potentially self-sufficient organ, the neurons reaching out to each other, attempting contact in as many ways as possible, each new thought representing new links and chains of interaction. And what was the motivation to connect, to bond, to be united in surges of electrical current, if not a cellular version of eros, as powerful as sexual lust? The word for the cellular connections that make possible memory and intelligent thought was *synapse*, from the Greek word meaning to clasp or embrace.

Leitbetter had gone further, much further, with the sexual analogy, ranging into creativity, epilepsy, the mystery of idiot savants. There was a particularly nice riff on Freud, suggesting that the real point of psychoanalysis was to enlist the subject in the scientific endeavor, the process of discovery, and that it didn't matter so much *what* you uncovered—hating your mother, for example—as that you *re*covered the joy of discovery, which is the ultimate joy.

It might be silly, but still it was pretty, all this vapid speculation, in the way certain ideas are that may be true or untrue but have the power anyway to delight the brain, to set the circuits singing. Narcissism again, Alex thought wryly, the brain locked in contemplation of its own thick, tangled secrets. Where all this tied in to the mundane schemes of men, he did not know, but things were humming, it would come to him in time. He locked his briefcase in the trunk and entered the bar's endless, dreamproof night.

"Yo, Prof, there's someone wants to see you." Chris slid a drink across the bar and leaned over conspiratorially. "Been here since six. Life-of-the-party type." He cocked his head toward the far end of the bar, where a cluster of men were laughing and pounding their hands on the bar. "Okay to tell him you're here?"

"Why not?" Alex shrugged, enjoying the glint of new respect in Chris's eyes. "I think I can squeeze him in right now," he added, doing an exaggerated check on his watch.

Chris moved away and a disappointed silence fell over the far end of the bar. Then Alex heard his name and felt a heavy hand on his shoulder. "Kent, Kentwell Brabant," the man said. "That's Kent, not Ken. Ken's the doll." There was an echo of appreciative laughter from the fans at the end of the bar. "And I'm buying tonight if you're drinking."

" 'If he's drinking,' " someone repeated, to another burst of laughter, making Alex squirm and assume a professorial face. The man didn't fit into any categories Alex was familiar with, business or professional. He was big, an inch or so taller than Alex, probably a weekend weight lifter, but artistic-looking too, with shoulder-length hair and a couple of gold loops in one ear. Everything about him suggested money, but money uninhibited by the usual constraints of class. Alex followed him over to a booth, promising himself a few clear hours for quiet drinking later.

"Sorry to cut into your happy hour here," Brabant said, loud enough to be heard at the bar, then dropped his voice and leaned back, cracking his knuckles. "But I tried everywhere first, your apartment, your office, even the personnel department at the university."

"Well, here I am. What can I do for you?"

"We have something in common." He said this archly, and appeared to be waiting for Alex to make a guess.

"Probably not the same tailor."

"Well, what the fuck." Brabant pounded the table and did another of his hearty male laughs. "They said you were a funny man. Jesus." He shook his head in mock-scolding manner. "Let me get to the point. It's Relnik, Henry Relnik. The scientist?"

Alex felt the adrenaline response go into action, clearing away the last of the comfortable fog left from the Galway lectures. There is a point in any line of research where a kind of paranoia sets in and everything that arises seems to be put there as a clue, but Kent was right in front of him, and it was much too early to be drunk.

"What about Relnik?"

"Hey, relax, guy, I don't mean to trample on your turf. I'm a filmmaker, independent filmmaker, doing the story of Dora and Henry, star-crossed lovers divided by war. For television, you know, made-for-TV. Maybe you saw some of my other stuff: *Mariniyah*, about this White Russian princess with thirteen personalities, trapped in wartime Vienna. Lots of snow, knocks on the door in the middle of the night, so-so reviews, but the ratings were up there, way up there." He winked and downed half his drink.

"I don't really see the, uh, audience appeal."

"Love, death, and Nazis—you don't see the appeal?"

"Dora Mueller wasn't a Nazi. We're talking about two scientists."

"Whoa there, fella, I know they're scientists. That's fine that they're scientists. Beautiful women scientists are big these days, couldn't get better demographics unless you threw in mud wrestling. Nazis in the background is better yet. You watch any TV in the last decade or so? Nazis never get old. Everyone wants Nazis." He gave Alex a knowing nod, then leaned forward in sudden concern. "You know, you don't look so good. Whaddya say we go somewhere decent and eat, my treat. Huh?"

The whiskey was adding plausibility to the situation, but only slowly, by degrees. "What do you want from me?" Alex asked finally.

"What do you think I want from you? I'm doing the movie, you're doing the book. That makes us colleagues, right? Practically blood brothers. Tell me your consulting fee. Anything you need. You want we get our lawyers in on this, is that what's on your mind?"

"No. Look, let's back up a little here. Relnik was what is known to my students, unless my vocabulary has fallen a few years behind, as a nerd. A dweeb. Ditto Dora. They work in their labs. They write letters. They go for hikes. There is no hard evidence that they ever actually consummated their star-crossed love. I am having trouble seeing this exactly as a movie."

"Then you don't know how the story comes out." Kent was ogling him, amused.

"No. How does the story come out?"

"Okay." Brabant signaled for another drink, then rubbed his hands together. "The letters from Dora stop coming in, what?— '42? '43? Relnik gets back into Nazi Germany to look for her. Probably via Austria, but we don't know how. Picture third-class railroad cars with the Alps rolling by outside; the German border police coming through, asking for passports, guys pretending to sleep, their caps pulled down over their faces. Anyway, he does it, gets to Heidelberg, starts asking around. We have to figure his German is good, he has some kind of cover. She's not at the girls' high school anymore. Zoom in on hundreds of little blond girls saying Heil Hitler, adorable, fanatic faces. People freeze up when they hear her name, but there's someone who helps, someone must've pointed the way. Because eventually, he's about to give up, he finds Dora. She's living in a sort of Tyrolean-style house, sheltering a family of Jews in her basement. He joins them. It's kind of Trapp family for a while, and then Relnik and the Jews get out. The thing is, Dora won't go. It's her country." Kent shook his head sadly. "It's weird, but she wants to stay."

"She did that? She sheltered Jews?" Alex leaned forward, scraping the table excitedly with his matchbook.

"Shit, man, I don't know, but we do know Relnik drops out of sight for several months. Actually in the summer, but we could make it winter for Christmas, depending on the air-time. Whaddya say?"

Alex drew one hand over his eyes and shivered. "You made that up?"

"All right, he doesn't go to Germany, then we don't have to figure how he gets in and manages to be a tourist in the Third Reich. We do know Dora disappears at some point, right? So she gets out, plenty of people did, especially people with blue eyes and lots of money. She has to sleep with this SS guy, *Kommandant*, whatever; it breaks her heart. See, she's a casualty now too? Make it six million plus one, that's what we want to leave 'em with."

Alex just sat there, forgetting to drink, so that Brabant fell silent for a moment too and looked absently around the room for something more entertaining. In science, Alex reflected, there is one truth behind each mystery; in this man's world, there could be four or five. It was an entirely new moral universe, in which a man could lose his grip. "Look, Kent," Alex said at last, putting a fatherly emphasis on the "Kent," "You're a real fun guy. But you don't need me. You can make it anything you want, right?"

Brabant shrugged. "Suicide. You want suicide? She's thrown out of the university, cut off from her life's work. We see her in girls' high, writing on the blackboard; her hand trembles, it looks like she's going to faint. Headmistress out of *Mädchen in Uniform* is watching every move. Cut to the outdoors. It's one of those long hikes in the mountains, lederhosen if they don't make her look like one of the seven dwarfs. She's been warned about the avalanche but she just keeps going. We go from a Heidi mood to *The Eiger Sanction.* Maybe she's pregnant with her and Henry's little love child, first few months so it isn't showing—"

"What is this? What is this about?"

There was another long moment of silence before Brabant cocked his head to one side and said, in an almost singsong voice, "I need the Relnik papers."

"I don't have the Relnik papers."

"I need what you have. You have something."

"Look, I owe you for a drink, so I'm going to tell you this. What I have, that is, what I have seen, is all *published* papers." This was not entirely true, but close enough for the circumstances. "Anyone can get them."

Brabant did a little dance motion with his shoulders, shutting his eyes as if carried away by the music piping fitfully from the jukebox. "Sure, Doc, are we ready to talk about money now?"

"It's nothing to do with money. Whatever I have isn't mine to give. I'm afraid the movie is not going to bear a very strong relationship to the book. Okay?" He pocketed his cigarettes and started to slide out of the booth, but Brabant put the flat of his hand over Alex's glass, fixing it to the table.

"That's really a shame, Professor MacBride, because I have to tell you there are people who feel very strongly about this."

Alex freed his glass but froze in his seat. "Meaning what?"

"Meaning? Meaning? What is this, Film 101?" Brabant suddenly relaxed and roared, ignoring the anticipatory rustle at the bar, which had been deprived of his company for nearly half an hour. "Meaning the discussion is not over, that's all, guy. Here." He reached into his wallet and slipped a card into Alex's hand. "Think it over and give us a call, huh?"

Alex stood up as steadily as he could and gave the card a rueful glance. It said "Kentwell Brabant, SKD Entertainment Enterprises."

■   ■   ■

Della wasn't able to reach Miriam until the morning after the visit with Leitbetter—from a pay phone outside the HEC library. When Miriam picked up she felt her knees bend in relief.

"Miriam, listen, I went to see Leitbetter."

"That's great, Della, I was afraid you'd wimp out. So tell me what happened."

"He told me he'd help find Steve if I find out some things. He wants me to get him information on Hershey's disease."

"And you believe him?"

"Well, he thinks he has an idea of where Steve might have gone. He said he just has to make a few calls. Make sure his information is up to date."

"Well, why didn't he make those calls long ago? Hmm? Be careful, Della, he's using you. To get back at Hershey or something because of Claire messing up that lecture. Remember, you told me? That's how it works in science, believe me: you hurt my feelings and I'll wreck your life's work."

"I know, I thought of that. And I don't think I could, you know, betray Dr. Hershey. But you know what?—Steve went away because of Leitbetter. He didn't run away from home, he ran away from Leitbetter. At least that's the impression I got." Della dropped a quarter on the floor, but the telephone cord was too short for her to bend down and pick it up.

"He told you that?"

"Sort of. He told me how they weren't getting along."

"Well, so what. Steve's gone, he's gone."

"No, the thing is, see, he's not running away from me."

"Of course not. Jesus, Della, so much negative thinking. Why would you think he was running away from you?"

But Della said she had to go; it was coffee-break time in the lab and she had already been away too long.

Because she let him down was the answer to Miriam's question. Because she had failed as a mother, which was what had made the whole search so far a fraud. Della took a shortcut through the E Corridor, which was formally off limits due to a toxic spill several years ago but was still the fastest way back to the lab. Until now she had not had the strength to focus on the night Steve left, which was mostly noise and confusion anyway. Steve had wanted to eat early, so that he could go back to the complex, back to the computer there, and she was sitting with him at the kitchen table, watching him eat, when Leo rolled in, complaining that Steve's car was blocking the driveway. This was his own home, he said, and he couldn't even park. When Leo got to the kitchen and saw the two of them there at the table, he put on a knowing look. So what am I, just a walk-in? You got some leftovers, huh? For me?

After Steve left, Leo started in on the issue of drugs. You see his eyes? Don't tell me you didn't see his eyes. That's a sign, the first sign is the eyes. Della said, He looks like he always does, let's forget it and eat. But something was building in Leo, something he had brought back from his workday, an affront or a missed opportunity. How the hell would you know? Look at you—will you look at yourself. You're probably on the same thing, like mother, like son.

She had done what she could, Della told herself, but Leo was a big man, nearly six feet, and what she could do was nowhere near enough. Leo, stay out of his room, she had said, all of this just for the driveway? He pushed her, she was sure that he pushed her on his way out of the room, and then she was on the floor in the kitchen, picking up things from her purse, which had fallen when he rushed out: loose change, gum wrappers, a hairbrush, receipts. She knelt there, half under the table, and heard Leo searching, making the sounds of furniture in revolt, scraping and banging against the walls of its cage.

When the noise stopped, she had gone up the stairs and stood at the doorway to Steve's room. It was really not so bad was her first thought, a few drawers emptied out and the bedspread pulled back, exposing the sheet, the bureau pulled away from the wall, but the computer was all right, the only witness. At least the computer survived.

She was still putting things away, folding T-shirts and straightening papers into piles, when Steve came home, long after Leo had cooled down in front of the TV and gone to bed. He thought there were drugs, she told him, you know he has a thing about drugs. Steve just stood there by the door and nodded a little, as if he took this as a reasonable explanation. From the way he stood there, taking everything in, making an entry in some file he kept in his head, there was no way to know he would be gone in the morning, taking most of his things, like a burglar, in pillowcases and tied-up sheets. All he said, as he stepped into the room, holding something out in his hand, was: "Your key, Mom. You left your key in the door."

■ ■ ■

By the time Della got back to the lab, the others had already gathered for coffee and were leaning over the Pakistani's shoulders, staring at the glossy photos she had spread out along the counter. Dr. Bhatar was her name, and for some reason she treated Della as a visible presence, a woman like herself who knew something of life's complications. "Look, Della," she said, making a gliding motion with one hand as a summons. "Come over here and tell us what you see."

It looked like nothing: black dots of various sizes against a grainy background, then an enlargement of a dot, nearly circular but bulging in places, like an oil spot pressed down in a watery place. "Well, I don't know," Della said hesitantly. "They don't look like cells."

"The question is, do you see a membrane? Is there a membrane around them?"

Dr. Soo frowned at Della, making her feel responsible for something untoward that had been detected in the photos. "I guess so, yes." Della took the plunge. "It looks like there would have to be a membrane."

"Ha!" Dr. Bhatar swept up the photos and replaced them with

a new set from a file folder she had been holding close to her chest. "We go to a magnification of 33,000 times and what do we see? A membrane."

"Is it the virus?" Della asked.

"No," Dr. Bhatar said vehemently. "No virus is this big. Not many cells are this big. But I think we may be looking at what the virus does to the cells."

Dr. Hershey had emerged from his office and stood there clearing his throat, so that the technicians spun off to their tasks and the graduate student pulled herself up from a slouch.

"It was in the 'gunk,' Dr. Hershey, the secret was in the gunk all along." Dr. Bhatar arranged all her photos in a sequence, careful to avoid the sticky spots on the counter. "We didn't even think of looking at the bottom of the tubes, did we?" She looked at Dr. Soo accusingly.

"There's nothing at that sed rate," Dr. Soo said with a shrug.

"What the virus does," Dr. Bhatar continued, ignoring him, "is it causes the cells to fuse. To reach out to each other, touch membranes, and fuse."

"It's an artifact," Dr. Soo said, tactfully addressing the ceiling. "Electron microscopy is not a precise science. You get some impurity in the system and you get anything you want to see: the Braille alphabet, cells with smiley faces . . ."

Dr. Hershey put down his coffee cup and bent over the photos. "These are hepatic cells?"

"Yes, San Carlos liver. I get the same thing with Vista View— liver, epithelium, spleen. Everywhere the same thing—huge, fused megacells—always at the bottom of the tubes, the stuff we were throwing away . . ."

"And the brain? Did you get a look at the brain?" Dr. Hershey's face was solemn, like a man being informed of a body count.

"Here's brain," Dr. Bhatar said with a sigh. "But I don't know what to make of it."

Dr. Hershey straightened up and drew his hand slowly over his mouth. "The synaptic connections have proliferated. You might almost say metastasized." He reached for his breast pocket, then seemed to remember that he did not, officially, smoke. "It's like a circuit that's been wired through every possible connection."

The graduate student whistled softly and grinned. "Before the next one dies, someone ought to ask them what they're thinking."

■   ■   ■

When Alex woke up, lemon-colored bars of light were already stacked against his bedroom wall. At the end of his bed, near his feet, his clothes were piled up in a mound; on the bedside table, a glass still stank of whiskey—proofs that someone had been here the night before, someone like himself, but who was also purposeful, mobile, upright. He propped himself up on one elbow to check the corner of the room for demons, though it was alarmist to call them that. They were the visual side effect of hangovers, when the hangovers reached a certain degree, and they always massed in the same corner of the room, so that he would have to walk by them to get out the door, tiny black imps in a mewling heap. There was nothing definite you could say about them except their color and their frame of mind, which was gleeful anticipation of the day when he would wake up and be too tired, just too damn tired, to defend himself from decomposition.

He tottered into the kitchen, still nude, emptied a tray of ice cubes into a bowl of water, took a deep breath, and submerged his face. That was the initiation rite; then came the serious rituals: shower, shaving, coffee, cigarette, aspirins, teeth. Some people, his former wife for instance, seemed to draw comfort from the daily routines of self-maintenance, which they confused with self-care and the concern of others. But for Alex it was empty repetition, and a reminder that everything you do in this life is the lesser of two evils, the larger one being when you cannot do anything at all.

The phone rang and he propped it between his neck and shoulder while he poured milk into his coffee. "Yes?"

"How ya doin', Al. Kent here. Did you get a chance to think about it?"

Alex put the coffee cup down and put his free hand on his belly, sucking it in. Not all days were the same, some of them had consequences that reached out into the next one. As the evening before began to reassemble itself, Alex felt a jab of adrenaline, followed by the shakes. The honest answer would be that he had had a chance to think and hadn't used it, the subject not seeming to merit the effort.

"No deal, pal, I told you."

"There's always a deal. That's the beautiful thing about the social matrix. Between any two people there exists at least one deal."

Alex lit a cigarette and let the smoke move through his brain on a purifying mission. "Look, Kent, I'm going to tell you something that might make your life a little simpler. The Relnik papers are crap. Piled high and deep. I'm thinking of dropping the project myself."

"You're thinking the wrong thought." Kent chuckled. "I asked you to think about price, not quality."

"I just want to save you the effort. You tell me what you want them for—and no more soap operas, please—and I'll tell you whether it's in there. And if you're looking for the formula for the ultimate drug—the weightless, odorless, tasteless version of crack cocaine, or whatever—I can tell you right now, it's not in there."

He missed a beat on that one, Alex observed with satisfaction, just a microsecond lapse. But then he was back on instant rebound. "You know Dora's brother-in-law? We didn't talk about her brother-in-law, the one that ends up south of the border somewhere. He was a medical researcher who worked for a while at Auschwitz, sewing eyelids shut to see whether the eyes went blind after a while from disuse. Two hundred prisoners who missed the whole thing, groping around in the dark. But you know what? When they went to cut the sutures it was too late. Scar tissue, pus, that kind of thing. A terrible waste."

Alex was aware of himself as a naked man standing near an open window outside of which there was a naked tree. "What are you saying, Kent? I don't like this movie."

"I'm saying there's impatience at this end, pal, and one thing leads to another."

■　■　■

All right, he'd been warned. Alex dressed quickly and started scooping up the little piles of Relnik papers from his desk, his kitchen table, his bedside table, and stuffing them in an overnight case that he kept in his closet in case he should ever be rehabilitated and start going to conferences again. An oversized folder caught his eye—Riane's portrait of him, which was certainly his to keep as a memento of what he might someday know as the Relnik phase. Inside was a sketch all right, all nervous lines and sinews, but any resemblance was accidental. If Riane was an artist, then he was a genuine biographer.

He got to the complex at noon, called Phyllis, who told him that Leitbetter was busy charming some bankers from Singapore, and then looked around for a place to deposit the Relnik papers. His office offered few possibilities: there was no closet, only a coat hook, and the one locked drawer of his desk already housed a makeshift medicine cabinet containing vodka, sinus pills, breath mints, and candy bars. He could take the overnight case straight to Leitbetter's office and wash his hands of the matter, but that might mean endangering Phyllis, if there was indeed any danger. In the center drawer of his desk, an unfamiliar key jolted his memory. There was still the gym. He had a locker in the gym Leitbetter had constructed a few years ago on the theory that exercise oxygenates the blood and hence stimulates the brain.

When the gym was first opened, Alex made himself a vague promise to harden his body against middle age. But fortunately the gym itself declined before his resolve could be put to the test. Located in the subbasement of the A Tower, it was prone to an insidious dampness that rusted the exercise machines and turned the carpeting into a field of mildew. No one much used the place after an animal-behavior guy, dedicated to aerobic rowing, developed a fungal infection of the lungs. The locker room was poorly lit, half the toilets were clogged, and the lighter free weights had long since been spirited off in gym bags.

It took Alex twenty minutes to get there, pry his locker door unstuck, and deposit the papers. There was no rush to get back, so he sat down on the bench that ran next to the lockers to get his trembling under control and consider the depths of his cowardice. No one had explicitly threatened him; he was a scholar, an innocent academic, free to ignore the demimonde characters who were cir-cling around Relnik's leavings. And suppose the worst, that he had just received a bona fide death threat, shouldn't he be inured, by this time, to facing them daily in the form of cigarette coughs, bloody stools, not to mention the single-minded march of days toward the final one?

He took a short, sweet nip of vodka from the pocket flask he had had the foresight to refill in his office. Interesting how we are expected to die with equanimity after spending our whole lives dodging death. He pictured dying in the conventional way, as a great leap into nothing, with all the people of the world, plus the animals and bugs, lined up to get to the edge. Most of them arrived unconscious, sleeping or passed out, destroyed by fever or dementia, and rolled over the cliff without noticing any difference. Another large number went cringing and pleading right up to the edge, and had in the end to be pushed, while their loved ones sobbed wildly, as if they had never been warned that anything like this could happen. But the ideal thing would be to walk jauntily out on one's own, turn back to the crowd and blow a kiss, then step off with the sangfroid of a man entering an elevator to go to his usual floor. There was no way to do that, though, if you had not at some point abandoned the precautions and the seat belts and the vitamins and been prepared to welcome death.

"Why, Alex MacBride, I wouldn't have guessed you were the athletic type."

The voice made Alex whirl around and grip the edge of the bench, but it was only Eddie, from Accounting, a harmless pest.

"I was thinking of working off my excess energy, but just thinking about it seems to do the trick." He laughed weakly and stood up, pocketing the key to the locker.

"Myself, I'm just checking out the real estate. Seems our kindly Führer has been thinking of renting it out, if not for a commercial gym, for which it is grossly unsuited, then perhaps as a sanatorium. The magic mountain, only underground. But it's lunchtime, isn't it? Heading for the faculty club, or will you be joining the proletariat in the caf?"

Passively, but deciding there were advantages to being with another person, especially a paunchy bald man with a clipboard, Alex followed along. Food was not an ideal choice, but it had attractions when compared to blacking out. The problem, as he knew from past experience, was to get through the cafeteria line without visibly retching. Even the air was full of greasy calories, he noticed as they slid their trays along the counter, because of the way the low ceilings pressed down on the neon atmosphere, condensing it into a kind of nutrient broth.

"Notice how there are no windows in this area? Or in the so-called gym?" Eddie asked when they had settled in at a table. "The number of people working in enclosures without windows has increased by 300 percent in the last ten years, nationwide. You know why?"

Alex shook his head, concentrating on the reluctant downward motion of cottage cheese.

"Because they don't want us to see what's going on outside."

"And what's going on outside?"

"You looked recently? It looks like January out there, 86 degrees and not a leaf in sight, except for the shrubs; there're leaves on the shrubs. Ever think about that? They go for the trees, but not for the shrubs. They're making a judgment based on height."

"Well." Alex didn't want to argue about the judgment of worms. Money was Eddie's subject, possibly everyone's, in moments of truthfulness. "How're things going? In the realm of lucre."

Eddie's tiny eyes lit up above a mouthful of potatoes and khaki-colored gravy. "You haven't heard? The outlook is, we don't open for classes in September, simple reason that the grad students are refusing to work without pay, which they haven't been getting since April. They make the usual claims of hunger and homelessness, and in fact small mammals keep disappearing—guinea pigs, rabbits— roasted apparently and eaten straight from the spit."

Alex pushed his plate away and leaned back, snorting wryly, to light a cigarette. "This is true?"

"You are questioning, perhaps, my grasp of the data? Well, let me fill you in just a bit. The financial base for basic research no longer exists. First the government money dried up, then the philanthropic money. It seems that the consensus among the powerful is that we know enough already, possibly far too much.

"So what's left? The information companies, that's who. Makers of data bases and high-powered intellectual software. They'll buy up anything that passes for data, God knows what for. You have some funny outfits in the info business these days: two or three boy geniuses and a receptionist, or hundreds of people and a macrobiotic cafeteria, CEOs whose résumés include past lives as goatherds and shamans."

"I had no idea."

"Half of them aren't corporations at all. They're cults. That's what they are."

"I meant that we're running out of money here. Leitbetter must be in a panic." Then he leaned forward, feeling the first stirrings of normal intellect as glucose hit the bloodstream. "Where *does* the money come from, anyway?"

"Ah, Professor MacBride, all these years and you never wondered who was buttering your bread? That's the thing with you scientists. Money all looks the same to you; it has no background, no personality. But I can't help you, Doc." Eddie put one hand over his mouth in a speak-no-evil gesture. "Professional ethics."

■   ■   ■

Back in his office, Alex put in a call to Leitbetter and then flipped through the neurophysiology text he had checked out of the library, vaguely seeking confirmation of the wild speculations in the Galway lectures. A section on drug-addicted rodents derailed him for a while, perhaps because of the element of personal relevance. Rats would do anything for cocaine, it seemed, to the point of forgetting to eat. The same effect could be achieved in drug-free rats by electrostimulation of the brain in one particular site, known colloquially as the "pleasure center." Alex wondered what Relnik would have made of these experiments, whether he would have approved of artificial joy, of drugs and electrical currents.

By the time Leitbetter called, it was nearly five, and Alex was working his way through a chocolate bar, reading the afternoon's harvest of interoffice memos and planning a night of quiet and halfway sober reflection. "What is it, Al?" Leitbetter sounded irritable, and Alex imagined he could pick up the sound of fingers drumming against precious wood.

"Let me start with the good news. The good news is, no one is blackmailing you. No one is interested in you at all."

"What do you mean?"

"I mean various parties are interested in Relnik, but none of them because of you."

"What parties would they be?"

"Shouldn't you be a little relieved that no one is trying to blackmail you?"

"I am relieved. I'm sitting here grinning from ear to ear. The telephone doesn't convey that well. But where were we? You said 'various parties.' "

"Possibly two, possibly one, possibly dozens. It's hard to get a firm count out here. The big question is, what do they want? I've heard drugs, I've heard soft-porn movies. I was hoping you could give me a clue."

"I'm sorry, Al, I'm just not tracking. You haven't been dipping into the ethanol, have you?"

"Only what comes my way in the natural course of evaporation or gravitational pull. The point is, this guy snagged me at the Baycrest, says he wants the Relnik papers badly. He's showing signs of getting ugly about it."

"Alex, you meet some guy in a *bar*."

"Why not just Xerox another copy, huh? Toss 'em his way."

"There's a lot at stake here, damnit, I don't have time—"

"Yeah, my life maybe. What about that?"

"If you cared about that you wouldn't drink. You'd check into a dry-out farm and come back with a working liver."

"Spare me the temperance lecture, Dick. If I lay down my life for anything, you can be sure it's going to be whiskey, not Relnik."

"Listen, Al. If you hadn't dawdled, if you'd gotten those papers from the grandniece before she sold them, we'd be way ahead of the game . . . And now you want to start handing out the Relnik papers to guys that approach you in bars. You know what you are, Al? A drunk. From charming young alcoholic to addled old drunk in three easy steps, by Dr. Alex MacBride. I thought I could trust you."

Alex crumpled the candy wrapper in his fist. "So find some sober young thing to do your odd jobs for you, if you think someone sober and young and with actual options in life would spend ten minutes on this crazy stuff, not to mention night and day. Night and fucking day, Dick." And he hung up before Leitbetter could answer.

■ ■ ■

On the way home Alex stopped at a convenience store for a sandwich and a six-pack. To anyone else it might look like an alcoholic's indulgence, but he was buying time. Beer is slow, half-empty really, with all the bubbles, and he needed an hour or two before the bottle of whiskey under the kitchen sink asserted itself and demanded a quicker descent to the inevitable blurred and spinning climax of the day. The rack of tabloids near the cash register irritated him, like an echo of Kentwell Brabant, and he fumbled with the change so badly that the clerk looked away and whistled a few tuneless notes.

Alex opened a beer as soon as he got home and stretched out on the couch with the sandwich handy in case he got hungry before he was too bloated to eat. A quiet night of reading was what he had in mind, catching up on the journals, nothing to do with Relnik, then maybe some hard thinking about his career. Probably he should be sending out his résumé, after the way he had talked back to Leitbetter. Alex snorted at the memory. It had felt good for a moment, though not as good as it should have. There was still the question of what was in it for Leitbetter, for Brabant, for any of these guys, if it wasn't a matter of blackmail.

Stealthily, his mind tiptoed back to Relnik, bypassing the pile of unread journals. He had assumed, when Brabant asked about the Relnik papers, that he was from the same company that had bought up the only really interesting collection of them from Riane. Or there could be two groups on the Relnik trail, each of them with a lot of money to throw around, each of them in a hurry. Or, of course, either one of them could be a fiction. There might be only one group with the ingenuity to use different names—and the determination to get hold of every last scrap of Relnik's writings, every wistful burble, every cracked and brilliant image.

But he was not sorry, here in his underfurnished apartment with the door bolted and even the windows locked. He was no longer sorry to have a mystery set before him, perhaps especially since he had defied Leitbetter and virtually walked off the case. It was his to think about now, not Leitbetter's, and he knew that, as with any mystery, the answer is always there, the meaning of the pictogram whose half-literate tracings lie before you. But there is never any way to squeeze it out of the data by brute force. It can only grow to full form and visibility in its own time, like any living thing, and the way to get to the answer is to meet it ahead in time, at the future point where the dots will be connected and the implicit opens itself up to light. Alex poured a second beer and held the glass to the light, where it looked like some temporarily upgraded, delirious form of urine, each bubble tracing its own deliberate path to the void at the top of the glass.

If he had been fully sober he would have gotten out some paper and started writing out the possibilities. One, two, three, this or that, one thing or another. It is almost the first rule of science: Think with a pencil, put it down before it flickers out, make a clear list. But he stared, instead, at the light fixture above his head, with the dead moths trapped inside it, and let the fragments swarm freely around at their own pace. Hedonism was a theme here, the joy of science, the brain as an organ of pleasure. Then there was money and danger, passion and suicide. Brabant had thrown in these additional elements, but it wasn't necessary, Alex thought, he was already paying attention.

He did not think he dozed, but at some point the light above him grew larger and he became aware of the flies moving in around the half-wrapped sandwich. The swarming in his head had stopped and there was now a clear, blank space in the center of things, a hole that had to be filled. Before there is an answer, there is always another question. He swung his legs off the couch and checked his watch: not yet eleven, still possible to make a call without seeming crazy and drunk.

On the third number he tried and the sixth ring, he got his man, an experimental psychologist with whom he had once argued for half the night about electroshock therapy, whether it was torture or the only way to break the frantic currents of the psychotic brain. Alex hoped that the debate had ended peaceably and with no damage to his reputation, but the outcome was indistinct. He could only try.

"Saul, Alex here. You're working late."

"No later than you're calling, Al. What can I do for you?" The voice was a little stiff, possibly hurt, but Alex decided to press straight on.

"I have a question. Do you mind a question? The inquiring mind, you know, never slumbers, never sleeps."

"Are you drunk?"

"That wasn't my question. Let's do my question, then we'll do yours."

"Okay, but look. I have a time-point in fifteen minutes. A cat must die and have its brain pureed."

"Of course, and I wouldn't want to get in the way of that." Alex held the phone with his neck and lit a cigarette. "The question is: In the brain there is a so-called pleasure center, right?" There was an "mmm" and Alex plunged ahead. "It can be turned on with drugs and electrical stimulation. Everyone knows about the rats who would rather die of pleasure than eat—isn't that so?—if you stick an electrode in the pleasure center and let them press a lever to get a shot of current."

"Thirteen minutes, Al. What's the question?"

"Do you think there's a way to activate the pleasure center without drugs or electrodes, by thinking in a certain way? With conscious thoughts?"

"What is it, you run out of whiskey?"

"Bear with me, Saul, this is important. Could you?"

There was a long silence, using up time. "You mean, could you reach down from the cortex—because that's where the conscious mind is, in the upper and outer layer—and switch on the pleasure center?"

"I guess that's what I'm asking. I mean, here I am in the cortex, suffering away, and there it is, the seat of ecstatic pleasure, a little gland juiced up with the most powerful natural drugs in the world, just a few inches away. Is this possible, anatomically, physiologically? To just switch it on?"

"Jesus, where do you come up with this stuff? What you need is to get back in the lab, a few mice to dissect, glassware to wash."

"I am, believe me, I'm in a huge shiny lab with dozens of still living, pulsing human brains split open in front of me. Please."

"All right, if you're asking are there efferent nerve pathways between the cortex and the limbic system, yes, the answer is yes. But you know that already, right? If you think happy thoughts, you feel good, the natural opiates flow. So of course there's a connection."

"But could it be developed is what I'm asking. By some sort of training. I don't know what it would take. Some sort of mental gymnastics. Like in cognitive therapy. You've heard of cognitive therapy? Much nicer than electroshock. The idea is to train yourself to think positively. Sounds idiotic, but couldn't that be a beginning? Why not push it a little further? Not just feel 'better,' but feel bliss, actual bliss, at will, all the time."

"But it doesn't work that way. The brain doesn't exist in a vacuum, for Chrissake. We're wired so we get our little crumbs of pleasure only when we serve the species: have sex, for example, reproduce. That's the deal, Al. Live with it."

"So why do you do science? Why are you playing bondage with cats right now instead of going home and fucking your brains out?"

"I happen to enjoy science."

"See, that's my point. You're using your cortex to stimulate your pleasure center, only in such a feeble and ineffective way, if you don't mind my saying so. Why not just find out how to flick it on? No cats, no booze, no bimbos."

"Because that would be masturbation!" Saul yelled into the phone. "Because there wouldn't be any point to anything if we could do that. Because we would be like those dumb addicted rats dropping dead over their little levers. That's why!"

"I know."

"It would be the end of the human race."

"Maybe."

"This is my time-point, Al. Go to bed."

CHAPTER 8

By early August, intact caterpillars were hard to find, even as specimens, most having moved on to a stage of disintegration and slippery residues. A double-trailer truck, skidding on a mass of the dead, jackknifed on the freeway, killing its driver and blocking three lanes for several hours. Without shade except from buildings, certain species of shrubs were bleached out by the sun, while other forms of flora exuberated in their release from the shadow of the trees, embraced the dormant trunks, climbed walls, blocked windows, and sent tendrils out to squeeze the power lines. A solvent was invented for the caterpillar goo, but it led to rashes and left yellow stains on lawns already barren from the drought.

There was no sense of crisis, but rather a need to take a stand, to make some kind of statement in the face of what was, for once, clearly nature's crime. Children in day camps had taken to wearing green ribbons affixed to their T-shirts, indicating concern. The trend spread to parents and homeowners, who spoke of it as a way of showing solidarity with the denuded trees and an effort to compensate for the loss of color. Then there was what the media called the "inevitable backlash": cynics and disillusioned teenagers, fans of morbid rock bands advocating extremist expressions of despair, started wearing black ribbons or even black objects, including the oil-soaked feathers of dead sea birds. These were hard to come by, though, and difficult to attach to safety pins, so a market developed for plastic replicas, promoted as "accessories with a message," clean and easy to affix to a shirt. By August thousands of the small, black, man-made objects—feathers, pebbles, and beaks—could be found in gutters and dumps, augmenting and imitating the natural garbage.

All these trends and countertrends were duly noted by the Department of Urban Anthropology, whose chairman, Dr. Gelph, had the honor of giving a special lecture for the benefit of Leitbetter's visiting Japanese bioethicists. Della went along with Dr. Bhatar, ignoring Dr. Soo's comment that it was a little early to be taking a break. Dr. Bhatar dismissed him with a shrug of one shoulder and marched off with her arm through Della's, protectively, in the manner of foreign women. She believed, as she explained to Della on the way to the lecture hall, in taking in all you could and that too much time at the bench would cramp the mind. Besides, there was a certain fascination, even within the complex, with Dr. Gelph's Index of Mass Anxiety, a composite number revised each week to measure the likelihood of riots, mass delusions, and other forms of social breakdown. Financial markets watched it carefully, and some of the daily newspapers printed it in the upper-right-hand corner of the front page, along with the weather.

When Della and Dr. Bhatar slid into their seats, the lecture had already begun and the audience was hunched forward, waiting for an idea worth capturing on their notepads, an equation or significant number. "The motion of history is saltatory," Dr. Gelph was explaining, "not smooth at all, but a matter of sudden leaps and jumps." For a long time everything is more or less the same, generation after generation. Traditions arise, dynasties, customs, stable religions. Then something happens, something always happens. Revolution, war, the Mayans suddenly leaving their huge stone temples and fleeing into the jungle to live under vine-stitched shelters. Who knows why? But the equations—because there were equations now and finely honed computer simulations—suggested the buildup of some factor, some invisible substance, which reaches a peak just before the turning points, the irreversible quantum leaps.

Della looked around furtively for Alex and caught sight of Dr. Leitbetter up in the front row next to the Japanese guests. He nodded from time to time, and sometimes cocked his head back with eyes shut tight and his palms pressed together, savoring a deft inference.

The first part of the lecture was diverting enough. Of course, no one knew what the "substance" was that built up just before the outbreak of panic or mayhem, but with the Index of Mass Anxiety, the equations worked quite well, predicting the First Crusade, the riots of the sixties, the sacking of Rome. Many elements went into the calculation of the Index, and Dr. Gelph began to list them on the blackboard: the emergence of new religions and sects, revenues of astrologists and alchemists, published predictions of doom. He had an apologetic manner, shrugging and ducking his head, as if some embarrassing mess, for which he had been called to account, lay on the floor between him and the audience. For modern times, many new factors had to be added—UFO sightings, freeway shootouts, ritual eviscerations of livestock—and the list was under constant revision.

Dr. Bhatar elbowed Della, inclined her head, and whispered, "It's totally Eurocentric, you know. Mass anxiety wasn't invented by a group of white men."

Della half nodded, unsure whether it was polite to agree. A slide had come up showing the steady ascent of a line between two axes, a hill with no plateau in sight. Dr. Bhatar leaned forward and pressed her fingertips against her mouth. Even Leitbetter, in profile, was frowning and still. If a graph was drawn of her own situation, Della knew she would be at an apex between Leitbetter and the

Pakistani, with the Pakistani standing in for Hershey and the lab. Maybe this was her business in life, to be a squeezable substance between two hard sharp things, Leo and Steve for example; it being considered less damaging to the design as a whole if it was she who bore the pressure of conflict.

When the lights came on, Della spotted Alex heading for one of the side exits and hurried after him with a whispered excuse to Dr. Bhatar.

"Alex, wait!" she called out, shutting the door to the lecture hall behind her. "I didn't know you were here."

"I didn't know I was here either"—he smiled ruefully—"for long stretches of time. Gelph needs a course in public speaking, possibly an amphetamine boost."

Alex was looking more rumpled than usual, puffier in the face, subdued by exhaustion or drink. "So," Della said as brightly as she could manage, "how are the Nazis?"

"Ah, the Nazis, yes." He guided Della out into the corridor, toward the elevator. "The Nazis are dead. Dead to me, anyway; I got sick of being jerked around."

"By Dr. Leitbetter?"

"Hmm. Anyway, seems he has other fish to fry. I hear Dr. Caragiola is back in the net. Money must be raised before the centrifuges and paper clips are repossessed. The usual."

"Oh. Well. I'm sorry to hear. It was interesting, what you told me." Della looked around, but there was no one left in hearing range. "But look, I need to talk to you. About him. Something has come up and I need your advice."

"Leitbetter? So how do you figure in the schemes of our inventive director?"

Della winced. "It's a long story."

"So come to my wee office and tell me right now. I've got nothing to do but open my mail. Dust the plants. Alphabetize my bookshelves. That kind of thing."

"No, I've got to get back to the lab before they decide to dock my pay. Maybe later, after work?"

"Dinner, then. This could be our long-lost dinner." Alex brightened a little. "I'll be the perfect date, the sensitive man, the ideal listener. Eight o'clock, okay? The pizza place on the turnpike? We'll go somewhere real from there."

■ ■ ■

A new fissure had opened up in the lab since Dr. Bhatar's discovery of the enucleated cells. At first merely skeptical, the Korean had begun an open campaign to discredit Dr. Bhatar's results. He had nothing against women in science, he said, women in science had much to contribute. Emotionalism was the problem, he said over coffee, a too ready identification with the victims, leading to unjustified leaps and the cutting of corners. Not all women are like this, he added with an uneasy glance at the graduate student, it was a matter of statistical averages.

So it was better all around that Della returned from the lecture alone, to reduce the impression that she had taken a side. But when she entered the lab, no one even glanced at her, although Claire and Dr. Soo were standing right there, staring at the large sink where the glassware was washed—or, what seemed less likely, at Mrs. Lopez, who was staring back at them, a righteous look in her dark eyes, holding a wide-bottomed Erlenmeyer flask to her chest.

"Watch out, there's broken glass," Dr. Soo said, still without looking at Della. And there was, right underfoot, a scattering of jagged fragments and bits of glass tubing.

Della edged her way behind Claire and Dr. Soo and leaned against the counter near the coffeemaker. Usually people ignored Mrs. Lopez because her English was so bad as to make her seem simpleminded. No one knew where she lived exactly, or how she got from there to the complex every morning, or even where she was from in the national sense, an island or a whole country somewhere.

"Give me that flask, I have a right to check it," Claire said, pausing between words so that the sense of them would find a way across the language barrier. She stretched out one hand for the flask while the other hand picked spasmodically at her lab coat.

Mrs. Lopez narrowed her eyes and stood her ground.

"We're not saying you did anything wrong," Dr. Soo tried in a kindly voice. "It's just that the tiniest little thing"—he brought the tips of his index fingers together to make a tiny thing—"could ruin the experiments. The least little bit of dirt."

"There are standards," Claire said. "Six hot-water rinses, six cold-water rinses. Then we autoclave."

Mrs. Lopez threw back her head and broke into a wild laugh. "You think I putting the dirt? You think this dirt, huh?" She rubbed her wrist with one finger, still clutching the flask. "You think the dirt come off of me, huh? Get on the dishes? You think the dishes get brown like me, huh?"

Claire took a step toward her, still extending one hand, but Mrs. Lopez held the flask tighter to her chest and began to speak rapidly, almost clearly, using words that her children must have brought home from school. "I tell you about dirt, you wanna talk about dirt. I have eyes, I see things, what goes in these dishes. You think I don't see what's going on? I don't know you taking children, you taking little brown children and cutting him up? Cutting and mixing and putting in tubes. Why you need so many tubes, huh? Kidney and liver and heart, chop him and put him in tubes. Put him in tubes, put him in bottles, all the dead babies, put him in 'frigerator . . ."

"You stop that right now!" Claire had turned bright red and struggled to free herself from Dr. Soo, who was holding her back by one arm.

"First I think, okay, they putting him back together again. All the little pieces in the 'frigerator—mix him up, the children come back. This what doctors do, right, he fix things. Right?" Mrs. Lopez paused to catch her breath, wheezing asthmatically. "But no. I wash the dishes, I see what's going on. You taking the pieces, cut him into more pieces. You starting with one test tube, pretty soon hundred test tubes. Same baby, hundred tubes!"

"She's on drugs," Claire said with a high-pitched laugh. "She's taking something. We should have known."

"Ha, ha, *drogas*," Mrs. Lopez nearly screamed. Then her face hardened and she clenched the fist of her free hand. "But I don' eating babies, I tell you that!"

Dr. Hershey, who had heard the scream from his office, stepped into the room and cleared his throat.

Mrs. Lopez, Claire, and Dr. Soo all spoke at once, but Hershey focused on Dr. Soo and the women fell silent. "I'm trying to figure out the impurity that could have caused Dr. Bhatar's results," Dr. Soo said with an innocent shrug. "Claire said maybe the glassware. It wouldn't take much. Some kind of surfactant, you know, a little film . . . And Mrs. Lopez here, she started throwing stuff." He gestured toward the broken glass on the floor.

Dr. Hershey nodded slowly, his hands behind his back. "It's all right, Mrs. Lopez, just put the flask down." Tears filled her eyes as she looked into Hershey's large, tired face.

"I don't put any dirt, Doctor, they say I put dirt."

"That's right," Hershey said, "just set it down there."

"I do everything nice, huh?" She set the flask down on the counter meekly. "Everything *limpio*?"

"Thank you, Mrs. Lopez."

Then Claire screamed and for a moment Della thought that Claire was hurt or going into a crisis of her own by contagion from Mrs. Lopez. "The Blood of the Lamb" is what Claire screamed, but it was real blood this time, in a wet palm print and running down the sides of the flask in forked red trails from where Mrs. Lopez's hand had been. Mrs. Lopez just stood there sagging against the sink, and when she brought her hand up to wipe her eyes, the tears ran pink over her wrinkled cheeks.

"She's bleeding, Dr. Hershey," Dr. Soo said, sounding, for the first time, truly alarmed. "We have to send her to the infirmary. She's bleeding from the palm of her hand."

"Just cut her hand, that's all," Hershey said in a steady tone. "Now get her purse, Claire, and some Band-Aids." He reached under his lab coat, pulled his wallet from his pants pocket, and drew out a few twenty-dollar bills. "You can go home now, Mrs. Lopez. Take a taxi if you want. That's right, take those Band-Aids too. Get a nice rest, okay?"

When Mrs. Lopez had shuffled out of the room, sniffling and rubbing her eyes, Hershey took a pair of tongs from a drawer, lifted up the flask, and tossed it, along with the tongs, into the hazardous waste. Then he glanced meaningfully at Della and Claire, settling on Dr. Soo with a long, careful look. "All that broken glass. She cut her hand. You saw it. She just cut her hand." And he went back into his office and shut the door.

Della found her own hands trembling as she helped Claire clean up the bloody shards of glass. Yes, she had seen it: the blood and the haste to get Mrs. Lopez out of the lab. Hershey hadn't even checked whether the blood on the flask had come from a cut or straight out through the skin, like the sick rat that had been labeled CONTROL. He had just thrown Mrs. Lopez out like so much hazardous waste, and the fact that he had done so gave a certain credence to the dishwasher's view of the lab: all those chopped-up children, waiting to be processed and turned into "results."

Della washed her hands slowly and then hesitated over the sink. Dr. Soo had vanished and Claire had withdrawn into a muttered commentary on the "work of the snake," so no one noticed when she left the lab and walked quickly down the corridor to the elevator. Three floors down and another long corridor across to the B Tower, she found a pay phone and dialed Leitbetter's office. He came on right away and told her it was a wise decision, for science and everyone. He would ask the questions, starting with the outbreaks and where they had occurred, moving on to what Hershey's team had learned so far about the virus, everything she could remember. Just speak clearly and slowly, Leitbetter told her, so the tape can get it all.

■   ■   ■

Alex did have work to do, though it was nothing that would make a decent man honestly tired. For months now, Leitbetter had wanted the WOW syllabus revised and enlivened; there were dull patches, heavy with numbers and theory, that showed up in sagging grades. Alex hadn't heard from Leitbetter since the angry exchange on the phone, and reasoned that, in the interest of self-preservation,

he ought to produce a brisk and sexy new course outline. All A's
was a realizable goal for the entire class, now that grading on a
curve was a thing of the past, but that meant that the material had
to leap up and grab the slumbering mind, had to sparkle in every
detail.

So what about kuru? had been Leitbetter's thought, back in the
spring before the Relnik project took over. Begin with kuru, the
slow virus transmitted among New Guinean Highlanders through
the practice of eating dead enemies' brains. Give them the basic
facts: headhunting, cannibalism, the problem of protein deficiency,
a wasting disease. Ask them, then, how do we know it's not a
matter of ghostly revenge? How do we know it's a physical thing,
lodged in the brain, not the mind, of the warrior?

The depressing thing was that it would probably work. The slow,
plodding pilgrimage of linear thought—beginning with observable
fact, leading to hypotheses, more facts, finally theories—numbed
the minds of his students and brought forth questions about grade
points and upcoming quizzes. Unless, of course, the trail was littered
with corpses, because young people, Alex had found, come alive
when the talk turns to death: paralyzing substances derived from
blowfish, anticoagulants that might prolong a vampire's meal, foul
play in all its forms, the abuse of corpses, crimes committed by the
dead or the undead. Relnik was wrong about some wired-in love
of learning. The mind was a tool with no life of its own, propelled
to exertion only by more powerful forces, like the shuddering lure
of zombies and dybbuks.

Alex stood up in disgust. If he had a job to hold on to, and he
assumed he still did, then he would have to produce something—
memos, revised syllabi, teaching aids, lesson plans. But not now. It
occurred to him that the whole Relnik thing was on the same cheap
level as WOW: the allure of the lurid. Nazis, an impossible love,
a secret project connected, somehow, to drugs. The ideal movie for
the jaded, degenerate children that he would be expected to entertain in the fall.

He needed to start a cleaner, better life. He would go straight
home and take a shower, skipping the Baycrest, holding out for the

first, virginal drink of the day at the restaurant with Della—lovely, patient Della, who had nothing to do with all this.

■   ■   ■

The first sign that things had moved onto a different level was that the door to his apartment appeared to be stuck. It unlocked all right, but there was resistance when he tried to open it, so that his impulse was to say "Hey" in a loud voice, to whoever was leaning on the other side.

Silence. It was only a book, rather a pile of books on the floor, most of them opened and lying face down, not only just inside the door but all over the living-room floor, along with emptied file folders, unused stationery, and the contents of his desk drawers— pencils, rubber bands, newspaper clippings, road maps. He stood there for a moment stunned by the blank, factual tone of the scene, the stripes of pale sunlight where they always were late in the day, the dust motes hovering in the light, as if things had settled in this manner years ago, in some natural disaster, defining a new kind of order.

He backed out the door, picking with his feet for clear spots on the floor, and rang the bell of his next-door neighbors, the ones whose television kept time for him through so many long evenings of booze. A thin woman in shorts and tank top peered out at him but did not fully open the door.

"Look, someone's broken into my apartment. Next door. Did you happen to notice anybody? Going in and out?"

The woman shook her head. It was useless to ask if she'd heard anything. From inside her apartment came the sounds of a child crying, a TV game show, and a man yelling for the child to shut up. The woman turned and spoke to the man, and Alex made out the words "goddamn niggers."

He went back into his apartment, locked the door behind him, and bolted it, feeling like an idiot, not sure he wasn't, even now, being watched. The bedroom was in better shape than the living room, the drawers and closet messed but not emptied onto the floor. As he more or less expected, even dreaded, his valuables were still there: the watch his wife had given him on their second anniversary, the gold cuff links he had never worn, in the shape of fresh-mined nuggets. The kitchen too was in not bad shape, except that the refrigerator had been pulled out from the wall and the cupboards all stood open, nearly empty as usual, but offering up all that they had.

Coolness, he thought, leaning palms down on the kitchen table, coolness and reflection. It was paper things they had gone through and paper they must have been after. So did he call the police now? And tell them that someone, possibly a criminal, possibly a man of science, had ransacked his apartment looking for the key to the ultimate powers of the mind?

The bathroom—he had forgotten the bathroom. But it was empty behind the shower curtain, nothing seemed to have been touched. He ran water until it was cold and brought it up to his face in his palms. Then, when he leaned over the toilet to reach for a towel, he saw what was in the toilet—the natural thing for a toilet, floating at mid-depth, what you would expect to find in a toilet, a turd, a brown and solitary turd.

Alex held on to the towel to control his shaking. First, it was not his. This was not the kind of thing he could establish in a court of law, but there is a memory of the day's bowel movement that stays with you, just below the level of words, at least until the next day's load is dumped. Small or large, soft or hard, no one asks, but still you know, and this one was not his.

Alex leaned over the sink and gagged. Then he flushed the toilet and instinctively washed his hands. Call the superintendent was a good idea, have a drink was another one, but the first priority was to get away from this. He locked the apartment up and went back out to his car, where he sat, just sat, until his hands stopped shaking. Leitbetter, that was the thing. If Alex was off the case, then the case should leave him alone. Whatever he had been before all this started, a failed scientist, a drunk, a lonely miserable lowlife son of a bitch, he wanted to be that again.

■　　■　　■

For the party, Dr. Leitbetter was having a film projected onto one great white wall of the penthouse room, a film he had himself produced, of white cells, seen through a microscope, waving soft, crenellated membranes into their ambient fluid. It took Alex a moment to adjust to the dim lighting and overcome the sensation that he had himself somehow shrunk down and entered the tiny, secret world contained in all visible things. "Nice touch," said a familiar voice close enough to be addressed to him. "What exactly are they supposed to be doing?"

"I don't know," Alex said. It was a guy from History, a fellow drinker, a decent sort. "What does anything do? Hang out, I guess, test the waters. Look, have you seen the auteur anywhere? Leitbetter?"

"No, I mean what are they doing here?" The historian winked over his wineglass. "What are we supposed to derive from this?"

Alex smoothed back his hair and straightened his jacket. The guard hadn't wanted to let him into the building, but he had his ID whether he looked like a partygoer or not. He had thrown out the invitation along with the rest of his mail that afternoon, and only remembered, sitting there in his car, that this was the night Leitbetter was fêting Dr. Caragiola in the penthouse on the top of the A Tower, a space designed for receptions and banquets and built over the firm objections of Accounting. It was a successful party, Alex could tell, with a well-dressed crowd that had drunk enough to keep up a thunderous sound, topped off by squeals and the summons of beepers. Anything he said got snatched off a few inches from his mouth and recruited to the general noise.

"Oh, marriage of science and art, I suppose; a toast to Dr. C. But he isn't here yet?"

The historian shrugged. "You come from the gym?"

"The gym? No." Alex started. "Why do you ask?"

"I don't know, the rumpled look."

Shouldering his way through the crowd, Alex got to the drinks table, ordered a double, and reconnoitered. Across the room he made out a particularly thick clot of people and worked his way into the perimeter, but the center of attraction was Dr. Caragiola, with Leitbetter still nowhere in sight. Her hair, which had been grayish before, was now jet black with artful white streaks, and she was laughing, tilting her head back and pressing down on her chest with one hand. "I didn't say that, I didn't say there was 'no meaning at all.' "

"But if everything is just words . . ." It was Saul speaking, the experimental psychologist, and he frowned to acknowledge Alex.

"Have you seen Dr. Leitbetter?" Alex whispered to the pudding-faced young woman next to him, throwing in the "Dr." because she looked like a graduate student, probably Hershey's.

"Huh?"

" 'Just words'? And why are we so dismissive of words?"

"Leitbetter." Alex was almost shouting now and the word hit in a half second's lull in the talk, so that Dr. Caragiola frowned in his direction too and raised her voice.

"What I am saying is, words are not only a means of communication but of *transportation*. A word can be defined—"

"He was here a minute ago," the graduate student whispered, turning stolidly back toward Caragiola.

"—as a symbol, an impacted, condensed experience, capable of being transported from one situation to the next. A movable experience, if you will. The real question about language being not grammar or vocabulary but *destination*. Where are we going with our neat little bundles of letters?"

There was a murmur of appreciation as Dr. Caragiola turned away to shake the hand of a tall man accompanied by a small gaggle of staff, probably the provost, here to check out the progress of science. Alex caught sight of Phyllis, standing near the food table, and made his way to her side. "Oh, Al, there you are." She kissed his cheek in honor of the party. "Dr. L. is looking for you. Wants you to chat up a donor. Very big money, but he's been having his doubts."

"Where is he?"

"The donor?"

"No, Leitbetter."

"He'll be out any minute now to say a few words. But look at this, I think the caterer screwed up."

The food had been picked at and scattered from its original plates. A salmon mousse molded in the shape of a fish displayed deep wounds in its side and head, right up to the olive eyes. Little remained of the crudités except for a few carrots and scallions, lying in pools of blue-flecked dip. "Looks fine to me, as food goes, but do you think I could catch him now?"

"Damnit, it's not fine, it's all orange. Everything's orange."

"Phyllis, look, this is kind of urgent. Where the hell is he now?"

"Shhh." She pinched his arm and nodded toward a clearing in the middle of room. Leitbetter was striding in with a cordless microphone, asking for a moment of quiet. ". . . Your attention," Alex heard him say, ". . . this extraordinary film . . ."

"Someone is after me," Alex told her, *sotto voce.*

"Mmm," she whispered up toward his ear. "Who besides me?"

"This is serious, Phyll." He took a tissue out of his pocket and wiped his forehead. "I need Leitbetter to call them off."

From the center of the room Leitbetter announced ". . . the moment of cell lysis," and Alex turned with everyone else toward the wall with the movie on it. Black holes, loaded vacuoles, had appeared within the featured cell, which was agitated now, its pseudopods thrashing out in ignorant panic. The vacuoles expanded, taking up more of the protoplasm, and Alex could make out some structure within, a geometric pattern.

". . . viruses," Leitbetter was saying, admiringly. "Not a lower form of life, not a form of life at all, but an *alternative* to life." And at that moment the cell burst, discharging thousands of tiny black octagons, then collapsing like a fallen parachute while the black octagons drifted off. There was a murmur from the crowd, followed by a decisive burst of applause; then the movie ended and the wall went blank.

Dr. Caragiola detached herself from the crowd and stepped into the clearing, where she tilted her head to one side and grasped Leitbetter's free hand with both of her own. ". . . a few words," he was announcing, "on the subject she will be exploring here at the complex: the principle of *condensation*, exemplified by the virus, which is, after all, what? A mechanism for copying DNA without the tedious digression we know as 'life' . . ."

Then Caragiola was speaking, or perhaps reading from the note-cards she had drawn from her bag. "The primitives of course require a separate explanation for each phenomenon as it arises, some spirit or demon peculiar to each thing. What is meant by scientific prog-ress is that the explanations coalesce, so that they can be encoded in ever smaller volumes. We go from the poetry of clouds to the austerity of the gas laws, pressure times volume equals temperature. As simple as that."

It was a bizarre sort of entertainment for a party, but then so was the film—probably some sort of tour de force intended for the funder Leitbetter wanted Alex to entertain. There was already a discreet drift back toward the refreshment tables, no doubt noted also by Leitbetter, who was nodding furiously at the end of each of Caragiola's sentences in an attempt to enforce attention.

"Science advances from the colors of Mendel's flowers," Cara-giola continued, oblivious to her audience, "which an artist could work on for years, to the laws of genetics, which can be summarized in a few well-chosen paragraphs.

"And from those laws with their thousands of irritating excep-tions, to the clean-cut beauty of the genetic code, which can be inscribed on the back of an envelope. If that is 'reductionism,' then science stands accused." There was a tentative burst of applause, but Caragiola only nodded and lifted a fresh notecard up toward her face.

"Jesus, Phyllis, I can't take this. Would you tell him I'm out on the balcony having a cigarette? And that it's urgent?"

Of course, from Leitbetter's point of view it probably wasn't urgent at all, and in anticipation of a long wait, Alex asked the bartender for two doubles, saying one was for a friend, a crippled friend, as it happened, unable to provide for himself. Then he worked his way through the rapt crowd to the balcony, where he set the drinks down on the soil of a potted shrub and lit the first cigarette since late afternoon.

The darkness was soothing. No breeze, but the assurance that there was plenty more air where this came from; and no people, since Dr. Caragiola was still talking and hardly anyone else was likely to come out for a smoke. The idea had been that the balcony, which extended along two sides of the building, would be the site of al fresco cocktails as well as meteorological observations, and to this end it had been furnished with the potted shrubs, each trimmed in a conical shape, with a little round burst of branches near the ground. But it was too hot in the summer, too cold in the winter, and the view, which extended to a strip of neon in the south, was mostly of the employee parking lots.

Alex heard the man before he saw him, because as he turned around from the railing, almost knocking over his glass, the light from the party indoors was full in his face.

"Dr. MacBride, is that you? Dr. Leitbetter's secretary told me I'd find you out here."

Alex acknowledged his identity to the silhouette and stretched out his hand. This was the donor, no doubt, that he was expected to charm.

"Martime Stimmerman. Martime will do," the man said, joining Alex at the railing, his face still half in the dark. "You are not enjoying the post-structuralist commentary?"

The man had an accent, which, like a physical infirmity, Alex found slightly disarming. "Is that the technical term for it? The vernacular is much briefer, I think."

"Ah, but don't dismiss it entirely." Martime chuckled. "I mean, what *are* the aesthetic criteria in science? As Caragiola continually asks. You scientists search for the 'elegant' solution or theory, but what do you mean by that?"

"Simple, I guess, clean-cut."

"And simple means what? Brief, does it not? Capable of being expressed in a single statement or, better yet, equation?"

"Well, yes, you could put it that way. The trend is toward a smaller size. A certain economy of expression." Alex had the uneasy feeling he had seen him before, in some completely different context, the same fine lines of eyebrow and cheekbone, although it was too dark to tell for sure. An overeducated businessman, no doubt, like so many of Leitbetter's potential donors; perhaps an engineer-turned-executive, hoping for redemption through his moment of contact with science. "Occam's razor: the most economical explanation is the true one."

"Good, very good." Martime lit a cigarette, inhaled till it glowed orange, and then passed it over to Alex. "Here, much better for you than that whiskey," he said in a mock-stern voice, and Alex was glad that the darkness covered his surprise. It had been a long time, years ago in graduate school, since he had had anything fancier than booze, and he inhaled gratefully, eager for the wonders of chemistry to begin.

"But," Martime was saying, "what do you think is the point of all this shrinkage, this search for the smallest form of truth?"

"Oh well. I guess the goal is to find a truth that will fit in the brain. We're just beetles, Leitbetter always says, trying to comprehend the cosmos."

Martime laughed out into the summer night. "I knew I would like you. Dr. Leitbetter's secretary told me you are doing a book on the biologist Henry Relnik. A most charming young woman, no?"

At first it seemed to Alex that Martime had not said this, that the marijuana had disoriented him so quickly that he was getting some kind of echo in his head and wrapping it in a convenient voice. But why shouldn't the outer world correspond to the workings of the mind? Here and everywhere else, all the little whorls of significance were tightening, closing in on a single theme.

"She told you wrong. I was. But I'm out of it now."

"Ah." Martime sounded petulant. "But you must have learned a great deal. It would be a shame . . ."

"Look, Martime, it's not my favorite subject right now. Too ugly. Large sums of money moving around. Threats of violence. Ugly threats."

"You think it's about money?"

"What isn't?"

"But such an empty view of the world, my dear Alex. I may also call you Alex? Sit down, have a seat." He indicated the lawn chairs ordinarily used by Phyllis and her friends for lunch-hour sun-bathing.

Alex straightened up with the idea of going back in to the party, drifting on to the next encounter. But the way he was feeling, that could be a dangerous move. The systems of perception and communication that seemed to work on the balcony would be inactivated in the bright, overcharged atmosphere of the party inside. There was nothing to do but sit down on one of the lounge chairs and stretch his feet out in front of him.

"Besides," he added, "Relnik wasn't a Nazi. The biography would've only been interesting if he was. At least that was Dick's idea: Nazi scientist invents the psychology of joy, or something like that."

"Of course he wasn't a Nazi," Martime said with an indulgent laugh, "neither was Dora Mueller, not in any real sense. None of them was the slightest bit interested."

"Them?"

"You have heard of the Erntegruppe?"

"Uh, no."

"Really? But I can't believe you looked into the Relnik matter and you were not aware of the most basic facts."

"The basic facts?"

Not everything Martime said after that remained fixed in Alex's memory. It was too much, coming too fast after a day that had already strained his capacity for the unexpected. He kept thinking that Leitbetter would appear any moment and switch on the patio lights to reveal that there was no one else there, just a faint haze of burnt-rubber smoke where Martime had sat. He fit no categories Alex had encountered—too intellectual to be a corporate clone, too suave to be your typical scientist manqué. He talked, too, like someone who was used to being listened to, as if it were Alex who had sought him out, rather than the other way around.

An elite group of German scientists, Martime was saying, founded who knows when? The criteria for membership had grown stricter in the years preceding the war, the Second World War, that is. Achievement in one area must be at the Nobel level, and they meant only the level, since the actual prize, everyone knows, is so sullied by graft and petty influence dealing. But achievement in one area was not enough. Every member of the Erntegruppe was to some extent a polymath, like Relnik himself—anatomist, psychologist, and, of course, philosopher of pedagogy. He was one of the few Americans to qualify in those years, most of them being considered too crassly experimental and lacking in intellectual depth.

The war of course cut them off from their scientific counterparts in other regions. They continued to fulfill their roles in an amiable and energetic matter, but they withheld their creative minds. They taught but did not publish, or published only dry permutations of what was already known, saving their true work for private circulation among the group, and for the larger world that they hoped someday to rejoin.

As an American, Relnik had a special role to play within the group. The arrangement was that he would publish the scientific work of Erntegruppe members in respectable American journals, under his own or an assumed name. You see the dilemma, Martime said. German scientists were barred from the mainstream British and American journals. This did not matter to those who had faith in the ascendancy of the German cause, but those who doubted, or who believed that truth respects no borders, found themselves silenced in those years, cut off from the constant conversation that is science, the endless bickering and elbowing. Relnik's job was to "launder" the Erntegruppe's work, as we might say today. He was the conduit for what many, including no doubt his faculty colleagues, would have condemned as "Nazi science."

Alex shifted in his seat. "And Dora Mueller?"

"His contact within the Erntegruppe. Naturally."

"How do you know all this?"

"Information is my business. Some people generate it, like your colleagues here. I merely traffic in it." He laughed modestly. "Though sometimes I share."

Alex had the sense he was being seduced for some purpose he could not guess. "But the papers I read were—" He hesitated to say "unimpressive." "I mean, why all the interest in Relnik? All of a sudden."

"All of a sudden? There has always been interest in Relnik, among those aware of his role. Because of what he found." Martime's voice dropped to a level above a whisper. "Remember what we were talking about a moment ago: how science seeks to shrink the truth. Well then, the same thing can be achieved in other ways. You yourself said that we favor the small and simple truth because we have such small and simple minds. So: the truth must shrink or the mind must grow. 'Grow' is not right. What is the term? Mind expansion, yes. The mind that is freed from suffering, from petty inhibition, from the strictures of the self. Such a mind expands. That, you might say, was Relnik's goal: a smaller, truer truth; a larger mind to hold it."

"Drugs?" Alex interrupted, pulling himself up in the lounge chair. "Is this about drugs?"

"My dear friend, you sound so alarmed. So what if the brain of all the organs, the brain alone recalls how to make the lovely, multiringed compounds that otherwise occur only in berries and leaves and flowers? So what if these compounds can be taken from the berries and leaves and put in the brain to liven things up? But no, this is not 'about drugs.' Drugs are unfocused, inept."

"So what are we talking about?"

"Enlightenment! Isn't that clear? What the mystics have always sought. The pure, blissful unity with *what is.*"

"I thought we were talking about scientific truth."

"Yes, yes, but they come to the same thing, don't they? Mystics seek to enlarge the mind. Scientists seek to condense the truth. The point is only to get the fit." Martime held back his head and laughed. "And Relnik, you see—"

There was a sound from the sliding doors and a bar of light fell across the tortured shrubs.

"Alex, is that you?" Phyllis took a few cautious steps in their direction and peered uncertainly. "Oh, Mr. Stimmerman. Is that you, Mr. Stimmerman? Dr. Leitbetter was looking for you a few minutes ago. Dr. Caragiola's finished her talk and . . ."

"And to think I missed it!" Martime spoke for both of them. "Dr. MacBride has been indulging my taste for philosophy and we both forgot the time. Tell him we'll be right along, will you?"

Phyllis went back to the doors, turning once toward Alex with a quick interrogative lift of the eyebrows. Alex lifted his eyebrows too and shrugged with one shoulder, but he was no longer sure what these signals were supposed to mean. When the doors had closed and darkness folded back around them, Martime revived his laugh as a mild chuckle. "But you have let me digress unpardonably, I'm afraid. The point is that Relnik—and Dora of course, she did the actual work—found a way, a way that led through the brain, but nevertheless, a way to enlarge the mind, a way to the possibility of ultimate knowledge."

"Really?" Alex hoped his sarcasm was audible to Martime. "Well, I haven't come across the secret of enlightenment in Relnik's papers yet."

"But it was in the nature of the work, the crucial experiments anyway, that it could not have been published, even after the war. If experiments such as these ever came to light in a journal such as *Nature* or *Science*, it would be as a warning, an object lesson, on the dangers of scientific curiosity, which begins as a form of love but can grow obsessively, beyond the bounds of law or caution."

Martime fell silent and there was no way to see the expression on his face.

"Well?" Alex asked.

"You don't have to know," Martime answered slowly, teasingly, "if you have no further interest in this business."

Alex took a sip of whiskey, but it did nothing for the fuzziness the drug had left in his mouth. "All right. I have to know."

"I am not a scientist," Martime continued. "I could never bear to think of life constrained by so many petty laws, crushed by circumstances of pressure, gravity, wavelength. But as I understand it, Relnik and Mueller accomplished something that 'mainstream' science would not achieve for another decade. She managed to locate the 'pleasure center,' as it is now known, in the limbic system of the brain. Relnik's theoretical work had suggested it was there, and once this was confirmed, a whole new world of possibilities emerged."

"How did she do this," Alex interrupted, "with the electrodes they had then, in the forties?"

"How do we know exactly what equipment she had then?" Martime countered.

Remember that German science had sunk from view, Martime went on. Many things were destroyed in the war, and not only by Allied bombs. As the Allies advanced, papers were burned, certain industrial and scientific secrets were erased or, in some cases, carried off. Martime sighed and relit the magic cigarette before continuing.

Besides, all subsequent work on the pleasure center was done with the usual small laboratory mammals. How dependent we are on these furry little packages of organs, unburdened by souls! And for most purposes they do quite well, offering up hearts and blood and livers that are not so different from our own.

The exception comes in the case of conscious thought. Here we are on uniquely human ground, so far as there is any reason to believe. If, for example, the goal was to enlarge the mind, using the pleasure center to drive the process along and provide the necessary reinforcement . . . Well, if these were the research goals, we would not be well served by the thoughts of mice.

Martime stopped to light another cigarette. "I am not boring you?"

Alex tried to speak, but his tongue stuck to the roof of his mouth.

"I am so imprecise, it must be maddening for a scientist to have to listen to." He laughed softly, and the orange dot of light from his cigarette surpassed anything showing through the black lid of sky above.

"Go on," Alex managed hoarsely.

"Well, to come to the point, we cannot imagine a scientific paper stating, in the section on 'materials and methods,' that fifteen adult males, human beings, were sacrificed . . . Do you still say 'sacrificed,' or has the euphemism been dropped for 'killed'? Unless somehow human sacrifice was all around, ongoing, a historical circumstance, ugly beyond words, no doubt, but transformed by science into opportunity . . ." He trailed off.

"Why are you telling me this?"

"Why are you listening?"

Then there was the sound of the sliding doors opening again and lights were switched on, dozens of scattered lights, tilted up at the potted shrubs, creating the effect of noontime in a forest of floating cones. "Oh ho, so you found each other." It was Leitbetter, stepping out toward them, then pausing with a nervous smile. "I hope Alex has not been poisoning you with his cynicism about our accomplishments here at the complex?"

"Quite the contrary, Richard, you have no more effective spokesman than Dr. MacBride, I am sure." He snuffed his cigarette out in the soil of the nearest shrub and swung his legs off the chair to the floor.

"Well, good, because if you're ready for dinner now, Mr. Stimmerman . . . and Alex, I'm sorry, but the reservations were made in advance . . ." Leitbetter turned back to the sliding doors where Phyllis now stood with something about a taxi to report and the fact that Dr. Caragiola was waiting. While Leitbetter issued instructions, Martime leaned closer to Alex and smiled.

"So you have an experiment that could be performed only once, that could never be repeated . . ." Martime whispered. "The results of such an experiment would be of infinite value. Or, depending on one's moral assessment, entirely useless, of course."

CHAPTER 9

Della checked her watch and saw that Alex had gone past the point of ordinary excuses like car trouble or wrecked trucks blocking the freeway, meaning he was lost again in his work. The restaurant made her uneasy, and her dress, which had been questionable when she put it on, was revealing itself now to be hostile and consumed with its own ambitions. It had cost almost as much as she now earned in a week, but it chafed under her arms and bunched at the tummy, and in general represented her poorly, she felt, although no one could have noticed except the waitress, who wore a black skirt and stained white shirt and looked like she resented coming all the way to Della's booth with nothing more than a soda water and lime.

She drank and tried to look absorbed in the dew that had formed on her glass. Once, years ago, Steve had told her a piece of Hindu, or maybe it was African, wisdom that said the purpose of humankind was to transport water from place to place. She had forgotten about that afternoon, but as soon as she remembered it she had the feeling that she had been thinking of it all the time, that it had been underneath everything else she was thinking, at every moment, waiting for a chance to poke its way out.

Actually Steve had been talking to Maisy when Della came into the kitchen with grocery bags and started unloading them onto the table. It was not the first time Della had gotten home from an errand to find Steve and Maisy at the kitchen table together, sharing a snack. This was before Carl, meaning Steve might have been thirteen, and Della had thought at first this was a riddle or the tail end of one. "What do you mean, transporting water?" she asked.

Maisy got up and started to help with the groceries, making it more like a mother-and-son discussion. "Well"—Steve wriggled in his chair—"water by itself only goes downhill. You need people, with pipes or pots or something, to get it uphill."

"Which is where the water wants to go?" Della laughed. She was in a good mood because of the sudden warmth outside, which had steam rising straight from tawdry patches of snow, bypassing the liquid state. But Steve was frowning.

"Maybe."

"You mean the water is using us, just as a way of getting around?"

"Not 'using,' no one said 'using.' I mean, like the bees from the point of view of flowers."

Maisy nodded in a way that made it seem that she and Steve had already worked this through. "Bible says the animals are put here to work for us. But it doesn't say who we're supposed to be working for here."

"God," Della said. "The Bible says God, it doesn't say water."

"Oh, it doesn't have to be water, Mom, it could be anything. Rocks. Dirt. Anything that can't get where it wants to by itself. How would we know?" He got up from the table then, leaving the two women to move cans and boxes from the table to the shelves.

Remembering this, Della liked the idea of water better than dirt: her coming to this place, the waitress bringing water from the bar to the table, the entire human enterprise revealed through its in-

frastructure of pipelines, canals, irrigation ditches, dams, water towers, earthen jars held on the heads of swaying, earth-colored women.
And the water itself, thanks to all this, reaching out into the earth's
secret places, between the sand grains of deserts where no rain ever
comes, down through canyons, past insoluble outgrowths of rock,
tumbling and churning, finding its way to her glass. She drank
slowly, thinking how it was an odd notion for a child to have, the
idea that something might be using us, without our ever knowing
it, for some purpose of its own.

At twenty after eight, the door opened and a large man came in
and sat at the bar with his head lowered until a beer was set down
before him. Then he drank, tilting his head back so that the thin
ponytail on the nape of his neck pressed into his back. It was bright
enough around the bar so Della could see that he was the same
man she had seen in this place the first night she came here with
Alex, the man who had led her to Homer. She started to get up,
with the idea of approaching him, but was afraid of scaring him
off. The way her heart was beating, though, she needed to do
something before the opportunity fled. Maybe she should forget
about Alex. Maybe the whole point of him, his entire existence,
was to bring her to this place at this time, like water getting to
where it could not go by itself.

Della signaled to the waitress, who was passing with an empty
tray. "See the man over there, kind of heavyset?" The waitress
turned slowly to show that the question was not in her job description. "Do you know who he is?" Della asked.

The waitress nodded in the man's direction, then turned back to
Della with her jaw pulled down in an exaggerated "oh no" look.
"That one over there? I wouldn't mess with him, you want to know.
Something wrong upstairs."

"Wait a minute." The waitress was moving off, flipping at the
floor with her towel. "Please. Would you take him a note?"

Della chewed on her pen for a moment before writing on a
napkin, folding it, and handing it to the waitress. Maybe she should
have offered a dollar bill folded in also, or maybe that would be
an insult. Leo always knew how to extract the maximum from a

person in a temporary condition of servitude, but he had never imparted the method to her.

From where she sat Della could see the man looking down, studying the message, she hoped, at least not getting up and leaving. There was no way he could know it was a lie, and she felt vaguely proud of her ingenuity. In principle, a lie is no worse than its function; the only problem with lies being their tendency to self-destruct, to contain some barely visible flaw that bursts open and wrecks everything. For example, if she had really heard from Steve she would know where he was, she would not be searching for him right now. Unless there was some reason, of course, a call out of nowhere, an envelope with the zip code smudged off, and inside:

Dear Mom,
Where I am now I am not supposed to write because of the nature of the work and the need for security, but I was afraid you would be worrying and . . .

She felt her eyes sting, and when she looked up from the tissue she had dug out of her purse, the large man was standing by her table with his hands in the pockets of a denim jacket, looking like he was on his way out but standing there anyway.

"So?" He glanced at her quickly and returned to staring at the floor. "You got a message from Kipper?"

"Uh-huh. Can I buy you a drink or something?"

He slid into the booth without looking at Della and tested the edge of the table with his fingertips. "Okay, yeah. A beer."

"I saw you drop Kipper off at the house a few times. But I don't think we ever met."

"Yeah, well. I'm Hannibal," he said, without offering a hand, "Hannibal Murphy."

"Oh yes, of course." Della smiled, glad to have gotten his name so easily, because that was another weak part of the lie. Up close, he looked older than she had at first thought, maybe well into his thirties, with a few wrinkles fighting their way through the acne scars and already a problem of nose hairs.

"So what was the message?"

"What he said . . ." Della drew in her breath, waiting for inspiration. "He said he was sorry he left the way he did. That he, uh, says hello."

For a moment Hannibal's face seemed to enter into a dispute with his lower lip. He blinked hard a few times, still holding on to the edge of the table, then let go with a long whistle and looked up at Della just long enough to check whether her pupils were dilated or anything else was awry. "Well, for shit's sake," he said finally, and squinted back in the direction of the bar with an exalted look, like someone who is trying to hold on to an insight that is already beginning to slip out of reach.

"Was there anything for Homer?" he asked, with another quick look at her face.

"Any what?"

"Any message."

"No, he didn't mention anyone else."

Hannibal shook his head at the floor, snorting with satisfaction. "So that's that, huh."

"That's what?"

"Well, Homer . . . Did you go to Homer?"

She nodded, surprised that he remembered their first encounter.

"Homer always said his attitude was like, fuck you, on to better things. But Homer was jealous. When Kipper left he tried to run things himself, but I said, Forget about it, I don't need this shit."

"This was like a club?"

"A club?"

"What Homer tried to run. You and Kipper and Homer."

"Computer network. You know, log in, hang for a while, maybe cop some software. Most of the people I never met, you know, face to face. I only met Kipper in person when he came back from school and I started doing some hardware for him." Hannibal shot Della a shy, proud look. "Did he tell you about the hardware I did for him?"

"For the game? Homer was telling me about the game."

"Well, he can't take any credit for it. I mean, Homer could pull off a cool hack now and then, but he's no gamer. He got scared, that's what. It was too big for him."

"Scared of what?"

"You could get too involved, you know how games are. Homer said I was getting too involved and I'd end up like Kipper's old pal who hung himself." Hannibal sighed and shook his head. The exaltation was fading.

"You mean his friend Carl? Carl got too involved in a game?"

"Sure, you can get too involved. Even Kipper said that. He warned me, but you know, you think things are going to last forever."

"What is it like, the game?"

He took a few gulps of the beer the waitress banged down in front of him and smiled at a distant point from which he seemed to gather motivation. There were different versions, of course, rough drafts by the dozens, but the principle was always the same, that what you did in one level you took on to the next. That was why it was so hard to stop, because wherever you were in it was always the middle, with everything that happened so far just a prelude to what was coming next.

But you had to see the visuals. Hannibal's eyes grew moist. There was this artist who did the visuals and they were awesome beyond belief. Like there's this place, he forgot which level or which version it was, where you're in the tall yellow grass which goes on forever and the sky is purple at the edges. And you're waiting, see, watching the wind move through the grass in waves because you don't know what'll be coming at you next. You had the sun, actually two suns in the sky—a big one and a smaller star—because it gave you more to figure as far as where the light would be, in your eyes or the other one's, whatever you had to fight. Because in this way it was like your average, off-the-shelf, shit-for-brains game. You had to fight, see, they were coming at you all the time.

He went on about the way it worked, how everything was a clue. Something you could use, a warning maybe, a weapon, a way of getting out. He thought he had it: the third white knight after seven black, the suns aligned, and what he already knew from the level before, adding up to a scheme for getting out of the plain and out through the mountain pass, into the black night of space. An algorithm, a mathematical plan, a visual pattern, sometimes a melody. Not like this, he said, wincing toward the bar, where stuff don't add up.

"Was that the point of the game—to win these fights?"

Hannibal blinked dumbly. "The point was to take the scrolls to the wise woman, that was the goal."

"What wise woman?"

"Shit, I don't know, a character, that's all. That was just the goal. You start out with these scrolls, and you don't know what's in them either, not on any level I ever got to, and I got pretty far. You had to get them to the wise woman, past all the obstacles in the way. That's how games work, there's always some mission like that."

Then he was back to the way you play, the challenge of it, the stuff you had to figure out. You didn't do this all in your head, of course. You had the data banks built right into the game, everything you needed to know. Fourier analysis, orbital calculations, Tarot symbols, you name it, man. This is why Kipper left—because of the data banks; he figured he could use help upgrading the data banks.

"The data banks?"

The knowledge base, he told her. Like an encyclopedia built into the game—the one real weapon you had. He kept expanding it, throwing shit in—foreign languages, chemical formulas, astronomy, whatever he learned—he'd find some way to condense it and build it into the game. This is where it maybe got a little out of hand. He wanted the game to be everything, see. He couldn't stop himself. He wanted it to contain everything that's known, down to the last byte, "the sum of human knowledge." He just couldn't stop.

Della thought of the clutter in Steve's office, the stacks of books and journals, layers of clippings on the wall. Of course, he must have been working on the game while he was working for Leitbetter. In fact, Leitbetter could have lied: Steve's game and Leitbetter's "pedagogical tool" were probably the same thing.

"But who could play this? It sounds so technical."

"The game adjusts to your level: how else could you play? Kipper studied AI in college, artificial intelligence. The game figures out what you can handle, see? and what it takes to keep you going. How many times you need to get it right, score a little win so you don't give up: the game adjusts to that. It draws you in." Hannibal stared off at some point behind her, the double suns still glinting in his eye.

"So what was he planning to do with the game? Market it somehow?"

"Market it? Shit no. Kipper wouldn't do that. 'If it's worth having,' Kipper used to say, 'it's worth giving away.' "

"I see. Right. Well, do you happen to know where he went to get this help with the data banks?"

"Nah. Is he coming back?"

"He didn't say."

Then a look of immense sadness came over Hannibal's pitted face. "But what the fuck, huh? I blew a fuse, man. It's all gone, what there was. I can't do games, forget about it. I repair bikes." And he got up, ignoring Della's hand as it reached out for the sleeve of his jacket, ignoring her urgent "Wait!," and walked out the door into the neon glow of the parking lot.

■　■　■

When Della got home she slipped off her shoes, turned the radio on to Sister Bertha's frequency, and called Miriam to tell her about the encounter in the bar. In the middle of talking there was a knock on the door and Miriam said, Don't get it, look at the time.

"Burglars don't knock on the door," Della told her, trying to peer out the kitchen window to see who could be out there, if it could be, for example, a repentant Alex.

"But rapists might."

"Okay, hold on, I'm going to look." But before she could figure out how to look without opening the door, she heard a voice above the pounding, saying, "Della, I know you're there. We've gotta talk. Please."

"It's Leo," she whispered into the phone.

"Well, don't let him in!"

"I'm not letting him in, but I'm going to see what he wants."

"Then call me right back, okay?"

Della unbolted the kitchen door and looked out through the screen door, which was also locked. It was Leo, all right, on the landing of the stairs that led up to her apartment, and she could see him in the outside light trying to force a smile through the crust of irritation on his face. He shook the screen door by the handle. "Will you let me in or what? It's buggy out here. I'm getting bitten all over."

"Do you know what time it is? I have to work in the morning."

"Would I be here if it wasn't important? Jesus, *you* have to work in the morning . . . It's about Steve, Della, is that important?"

She unlatched the screen door and he pushed in past her, staring around the kitchen and into the living room like a landlord checking for damage. Then his eyes landed on Della and did a complete tour. "Well well, aren't we looking good."

She stepped back behind a kitchen chair so that less of the dress would show. "Why did you come here, Leo?"

"I have to have a pretty good reason, right? And where the hell have you been all night? The 'working woman.' Screwing one of those professors, huh? Well, what's it like with them? You finally learning a few advanced technologies, I hope?"

She pulled the chair more tightly to her. Most women are killed by people they know, she had read in a magazine, so that the safest thing would be not to know anyone, and otherwise to break off all contact at once. He must have seen some of this in her face, because he straightened for a moment, then sagged forward with one hand over his face.

"Oh my God, Del, I didn't mean that, I didn't mean that. I don't know, it's been so long since I've seen you, and then I see you and it's like I can't handle it, I fall to pieces." He took a tissue out of the pocket of his sports jacket and wiped his face. "Could I sit down? Please. I need to sit down." He was already walking into the living room, where he sat down on the couch and patted the tufted plain of upholstery beside him to show that she should sit down too.

"I've learned some things, Del. Maybe I don't express it too well, but I've learned some things. I've learned twenty years isn't something you just blow off because the communications happen to be jammed. We were a family, weren't we, Del? You, me, Steve. Not exactly the Swiss Family Robinson, but life is a journey, you play the cards you're dealt."

"Twenty-*two*."

"Yeah, I meant twenty-two." He was looking around the living room as he spoke, for clues of some kind or things that should have gone to him, and Della could only edge her way into the living room and sit stiffly in the chair across from him. "I just want to know what this has to do with Steve."

"Steve. All right, Steve. Maybe I should be asking you."

"Asking me what?"

"About Steve. Where he is. Like you hear anything around the campus?"

"No, nothing." She frowned and rubbed her arm. Leitbetter had thanked her solemnly for the information she gave him about the disease, and said he'd call right away, as soon as he had some information for her. Days had gone by, though, without a word. "But what's the rush here? I mean, the first six months I don't think you even noticed he was gone."

"But he's in the area, Del. He might be in the area right now."

"How do you know?"

"Because I get around, Del, I get around." He leaned back and rested his arms on the back of the couch. "See, it's a big world out there, but not so big you don't get a little overlap here and there. One person wants something, maybe another person has it. And Steve, all right, I misjudged. Will you accept that? I misjudged. Him sitting at that computer all day like a goddamn office temp, how was I supposed to know? But, Della . . ." He bent toward her again so that she could smell his cologne mixed with traces of sweat, the only man she had ever slept with, the father of her son. "The kid's on to something big. But you know that, don't you?"

"I know he was working on computer games."

"That's what I thought at first too. 'Computer games,' big deal. But suppose you've got a game that everybody wants to play. Suppose you start playing, you don't want to stop." His face was pink under the tan and his eyes were glowing. "We are talking major product, Del. You market it in installments, the price goes up a little with each hit. This is millions easy. You following? Millions for a fucking game.

"So Steve comes back, you let me know. We get together, the three of us, we talk it over, I maybe give him a little business advice, take him to meet some people. We're set for life. Steve's set for life. Maybe you and me, we spend some time, take a little vacation, talk things out. That's where we went wrong, Del. We didn't talk."

"Well, it's up to Steve, isn't it? I mean, it's his business."

"Della, look." Leo was smiling, but his features had stiffened again. "Steve doesn't know anything about business. Did he ever have a paper route? I mean, we're talking about a kid who never even had a fucking paper route. All I'm saying is, we show him the advantages. We lay things out. You and I, he'll listen to you. We set things up. We introduce him."

She looked up from the frayed spot on the armchair that she had been reweaving with her finger. "You mean we sell him. You want to sell your own son."

"Jesus, Della." He stood up and hit his shin against the coffee table. "Shit. What kind of way is that to talk?"

She stood up too and found herself only inches from his face. All the furniture in the room was encircling them, waiting for some ritual to begin. "Della, will you fuckin' come to life?" He squeezed her bare arm so that she knew there would be marks the next day. "You always were on a higher plane, huh? You and Steve on a higher plane. Me, I just made the money. And look at you now: I paid for this dress so you could go whoring around with your tits sticking out . . ."

The phone rang and he loosened his grip, letting his hand slide down her arm. "So, okay, get the phone."

Della walked to the kitchen, holding on to her arm where he had hurt it, took a deep breath, and got the phone on the fifth ring. But it was only Miriam wanting to know whether Leo had gone yet. "He's going now," Della said, and he was. Miriam's presence on the phone seemed to remind him of something, because he checked his watch and whistled, pausing at the door to say "Think about it, huh?" and blow her an ironic kiss.

■   ■   ■

There was no way to put the apartment back the way it had been before Leo's visit, although nothing had been rearranged or moved, not even a cup or glass for water. He had just come in and sat down as if he owned the place. No, it was worse—she had let him in herself—and at the thought of all the thousands of ways she had deferred to him over the years, waited on him, smoothed things out for him, she felt the shame rise up in her like a bad smell from between her legs.

She was still sitting in the kitchen, all the shades drawn tight, when she heard Sister Bertha's voice come slicing through the static. "You say you lost too much already?" Sister Bertha was saying. "So you forgot what I told you how Jesus died. I thought I told you that already, the story of how Jesus died." There was another blurt of static and Sister Bertha began to speak in a strange singsong tone while Della sat there and let the words come in and make pictures in her head.

At first it was the familiar story of the Crucifixion: Jesus being nailed to the cross, the two thieves, and the rest of it. But there were details Della had never heard or couldn't remember, like one of the thieves asking Jesus to use his power to get him down off the cross, and Jesus seeing the blood dribbling down the man's chin and the eyes climbing back into the skull, and saying, "It's too late, brother, give up hope and you will be free."

And at that moment, Sister Bertha said, hope passed out of the man with a soft whistling sound and entered the morning air, from which it could never be gathered back again. Then the other thief laughed at Jesus and said, "You fool, you killed that man." But Jesus only sighed and said, "Give up your anger, brother, and go with him."

"No," said the thief, "because this anger is all I have."

"But didn't I say," said Jesus, "that you must give up all you have?"

The thief smiled again, cracking the dust that had caked in the sweat of his face. "I tell you what, Jesus, I'll give up my anger if you will give up your sweet holy face and weep and rage like any man at what they've done to you."

"Oh no," cried Jesus, "I cannot give up love."

And the thief brushed his lips with a dry, stiff tongue and said, "But you told us give up everything, everything we have."

So Jesus looked down at the gleaming world that he must leave and for the first time he felt God's law as a weight on him, heavier than any cross. "All right," he said. "Tell me how I may know anger, so that you may die in peace."

And then the thief began to talk, and to tell the story of Jesus' life, and how he had cured the sick with his breath and fed the hungry with his flesh, and still the people picked up stones and bits of pottery to hurt him with and thorns to scratch his face. Who did this? asked the thief. Who guides the fall of every leaf? Who hardened their hearts and sharpened the thorns and set this up as a mockery, all that you have done?

And as Jesus listened he felt a humming in his chest like the angel of death at work inside him, clearing out a space where his heart had been. When he thought of Judas's kiss, of the soldiers picking their teeth as they cast lots for his seamless robe, the humming grew to a roar, and Jesus opened his eyes and said, "This must be the thief's anger coming to me now." And when he looked around him, the world no longer gleamed but boiled with the blood that ran down over his eyes and out from his mouth, and Jesus saw that the anger was now his and not the thief's.

Then he grew weak from straining against the nails and trying to bend his fingers against his palms in fists and cried out to the thief, "So have I saved you, then? Is your soul now light and free?"

And the thief looked up at the vultures gathering around their heads and laughed so loud that they rose back into the sky like smoke. "Fool," he said. "You have only condemned yourself to return in rage, with plague clearing the path before you, to this prison of time and place."

Then the static took over from Sister Bertha and Della turned the volume down to a low background noise. Steve would like that story, she thought. He would like the idea of God being caught in a trap of his own making. Then she was sorry she hadn't done a better job of explaining Sister Bertha to Alex, that sometimes she wasn't religious at all, but more like a dare to the religions there already are.

■　■　■

Alex awoke to the neurological fact that the part of the brain everyone was interested in, Relnik and Dora especially, was dead in him, a gray cinder at the center of things. Rehabilitation was out of the question, but there were still steps, steps that had been out-lined eons ago, in the night before, like calling Della and trying to explain. But at Hershey's lab a foreign voice answered and said she wasn't there. Would she be back soon? Not here, not here, the voice just kept repeating, and it seemed to Alex that the heavy accent was trying to bend her name into "Dora"—an obvious trick con-sidering that Della and Dora seemed to have become the two leading ladies in his meagerly populated life.

The next idea was to call Leitbetter, tell him about the apartment being ransacked, find out how much he knew about Stimmerman —a full and honest discussion, in other words. But Phyllis said Leitbetter was seeing Stimmerman off at the airport. Fresh money had been promised beyond the usual grant, earmarked apparently for Hershey's disease, but now Stimmerman had to get back to his base in Mexico City, she knew because she had made the reservation herself.

Mexico: Alex felt it should mean something, but he couldn't think what. He poured himself a cup of coffee and, when he opened the refrigerator, with the idea of milk, and saw the unexamined containers, the aging condiments, the sordid brown lumps like hardened syrup on the white enamel, he remembered the dream.

After leaving the party, he had gone back to his apartment, where the mess seemed connected to the fact that he had stood up Della once again; sweet, sad Della, who had the power, he was sure, to blot up all strangeness and evil. There had been nothing to do but go to bed with the whiskey bottle within reach on the floor, the one thing that was in his control. Sometime between the last tilt of the bottle and the scent of the first fumes rising from his lungs in the morning, he dreamed he saw Riane and Martime locked in sex on a cluttered floor. Riane was on top, and Alex marveled at how that posture seemed to thrust out every bit of fat on a woman's body, small as these were in Riane's case, more like hors d'oeuvres than any kind of substantial offering. She looked up at Alex, who must have been present himself in some form, then bent herself into an inchworm's shape to work on Martime's hairless nipples. Alex felt no more pleasure from this scene than if he had been watching a cat devouring its back-yard prey; but as it faded, he saw Martime looking at him, composed and faintly challenging, and the last thing he saw was Martime's face.

Riane's portrait—it was the face in the drawing Riane had given him, supposedly a portrait of himself. Alex was shaking so badly that he poured an inch of vodka in his cup to smooth out the coffee. Mexico clinched it; that was where Homer had said the company was based that had bought up the rest of the Relnik papers. The drug traffickers, or former drug traffickers. He picked up the phone, dialed the travel agent who arranged his rare ventures away, and asked for the next flight to Mexico City. No, he would not be needing a ticket.

At the airport, the signs, with their peremptory commands, put him into a weak sweat, but inside the terminal he began to feel shrewd and purposeful again. A man with matted hair approached him for five dollars, to buy a bus ticket, he said. Alex gave him two and went into a gift shop, where he bought himself a cheap canvas overnight bag, a candy bar, and some mints. He breezed through security, the X-rays finding nothing but newspapers.

There must have been two hundred people in the boarding area, practicing for the flight by sitting side by side and staring pointedly at the fixed spots each had chosen to study. Alex loitered for a while, then went into the men's room to bolster his resolve with a splash of cold water, and there, standing over the sink, was Martime.

"Well, what a coincidence." Martime gave him a slow, questioning smile. "You are also going somewhere?"

"Just to see you."

"I see." Martime looked at Alex's overnight bag appreciatively and began soaping his hands. "I like it when people make an effort."

"Look, Martime, you weren't exactly honest with me last night." A man exiting from one of the stalls raised his eyebrows and walked out quickly without washing his hands. "You didn't tell me you bought the Relnik papers, the family's collection. You paid $25,000 for them. Remember?"

The two men looked at each other in the mirror, where their images looked at each other too. "So." Martime shook the water off his hands and reached for a towel. "The grandniece said this? Or her hacker friend?"

"No, no one told me. It was just one of those lucky accidents that light the path of science from time to time, like Fleming finding the penicillin growing on his petri dishes." There was no way to know whether it was really an accident at all, Riane giving him her sketch of Martime instead of her sketch of himself. But why else would she happen to have a sketch of Martime, unless she had just had a visit from him? Of course, Alex couldn't have put it together without the dream. The sketch was too abstract, all curls and soft noodly lines.

"You told this theory to your Dr. Leitbetter?"

"Not yet I didn't. Does it matter to you?"

"Come, my friend, the atmosphere is not conducive." Alex shouldered his bag self-consciously and they set out, the one tall and rumpled, the other short and precisely dressed, like any two people who have nothing more in common than a destination.

"Look," Alex said as soon as they had settled into the snack bar. "You told me you were in the information business, but it is drugs, isn't it? What do you expect to find in Relnik's papers—some technique for narcotizing the human race like those rats with electrodes in their brains?"

"You think that was the goal of Relnik's work?—'narcotizing'? Then you have understood nothing." He shook his head in silence for a moment and then leaned forward. "Relnik asked a simple question: Why do we live this stunted existence? Why do we live in ignorance and grief when the seat of pleasure is only this far away, inches from the cortex, waiting there, virtually dormant, in the middle of the brain? Why not activate it and thus activate the entire brain? The mind, you might also say. Why live in darkness when enlightenment is anatomically possible?"

" 'Enlightenment,' if I recall, is not the same as mere euphoria, especially artificially induced euphoria."

"My friend! You think there is not a technology of enlightenment? But there is! Beginning with drugs, yes, but only beginning. Every tribe has its magic mushroom, its fermented brew, ecstatic forms of dance. The next step was fasting, self-mortification, the mental discipline of prayer. With Zen we go to a new level: the *koan*, the little puzzle, the involvement of the intellect . . .

"Then there is the computer, compensating for the tragic limitations of memory and logic. But the computer is only a prosthesis, a wooden limb added on. It is nothing compared to what could be done by training the mind itself, for the mind is not a machine— such a misleading metaphor! The mind is an animal, groping, desiring, metabolizing, with so little help from the wakeful speck we like to call 'ourselves.' This is what Relnik—"

Alex rolled his eyes at the pictures on the wall of the snack bar, familiar foods photographed so close up that they looked like challenging new forms of terrain. "Spare me. I'm a scientist, remember? A believer in reproducible results and testable hypotheses. Save the mysticism for the mush-heads, okay? Like Leitbetter."

"Your Leitbetter at least knows better than to treat science as a cage for the mind to hide in. Listen, you have read some of Relnik, bits and pieces—what does he say about the connection between pleasure and learning?"

Alex sighed loudly. "He asserts that there is a connection, that's all. He *asserts*."

"Yes. He 'asserts' a link: Pleasure facilitates learning and learning is the greatest pleasure of all. So. If you have some way of harnessing the 'pleasure center,' as it is now called, to drive the process of learning—"

"Some way which Relnik presumably worked out with Dora and left somewhere in the goddamn papers?"

Martime nodded. "Now, if you have some way of tightening the link between pleasure and learning . . . Using pleasure to stimulate the process of learning and then the pleasure of this learning to keep the whole process going—you are following, yes? Then think of the implications: how much sooner we might comprehend, for example, the origin of the universe. The wave-particle dualism. All the great unsolved mysteries of your science."

"I'm supposed to believe this is all for science? A little boost for the inquiring mind? Shit. You want to market this . . . thing. Instant bliss—chemical-free, organic, do-it-yourself bliss. That's what you want, right?"

Martime cocked his head and smiled sadly. "Look at you. Your eyes are bloody, your hands are shaking. What is the last thing you have ever enjoyed? I mean other than your whiskey and rocks. A good meal? Sex perhaps? You will pardon me, Alex, but you are the picture of self-neglect." He stood up and reached for his attaché case. "You are in no position to judge the virtue of anything.

"Drugs, for example." Martime tossed coins on the counter. "What do you know but propaganda? Hmm? Who is to say whether the white powder, for example, that inches its way from the Andes to the lungs of your countrymen is not, on balance, an absolute blessing, a pharmaceutical miracle on a par with penicillin? Not someone who has never known the despair of your shanty towns, or are they still 'ghettos'? Surely not someone who has never inhaled the product himself and found shelter from the pain. Here, come along."

They stepped out through a crowd of teenage soldiers and gray-suited, remorseless business travelers, Alex trailing heavy-footed behind.

"In your country criminals are executed by—what is it? Lethal injection. A drug for everything. Think of it, Alex. Does the doctor first wipe the skin with alcohol?" He tilted his head back and laughed.

They had reached the boarding area where the line of passengers was disappearing through the door that would close, any moment now, behind Martime. Alex took a deep, painful breath, reached forward, and grabbed the shorter man by the arm. "Listen. I don't really care what you're up to, okay? My apartment's been ransacked. My life has been threatened. I've had enough. Forget I ever asked. I'm out of this."

"Oh, how terrible! Really. But it's too late for that now. Sadly, much too late."

"Too late for what?"

"Too late to be uninvolved. Everyone is involved to some measure. Even that fellow over there . . ." Martime nodded toward a businessman staring slack-jawed at the departure and arrival monitors on the wall. "By being here at this moment, by our noticing him, perhaps him noticing us, he too is involved." He laughed. "You can stay, you can leave. You are still 'involved.'

"Ah, my friend, I regret. It is time now to board. What I am saying is, you really don't have anything else. Think about it, what else are you going to do?"

CHAPTER 10

The news of Homer's death took many forms in the days that followed it, beginning with the local television report that Della caught while she was dressing for work, tuned in to see whether the heat would break and give way to something kinder. At first she felt awe, approaching pride, to find some point of contact with a public tragedy. The converted garage he lived in was shown marked off with yellow police tape, and she had walked up to that door herself and knocked on it only weeks ago. According to the news, he had been shot twice, with no signs of a struggle, late enough at night for doors to be locked but still early enough for televisions to be on, canceling the sound of shots. Homer was identified as a freelance computer consultant with parents in the dry-cleaning business. A high-school yearbook picture showed the deceased looking unformed and ill at ease.

Della called Miriam without waiting for the weather to come on, getting her only half-awake. It was scary, she told Miriam, Homer was Steve's friend. Although even as she spoke she knew that Homer and Steve had probably not been friends for some time, and it was not clear whether the decline of their friendship, if there had even been a friendship to decline, moved the tragedy nearer to her or farther away. "It's a bad sign, someone getting killed like this."

"It's not a sign. Astrology is signs. Superstition is signs. There's such a thing as crime, you know."

"You think it doesn't mean anything, I go to talk to him about Steve and then a few weeks later he gets killed?"

"So tell the police, you want to talk to the police."

They would take Della for a nut was the implication. There are mothers of lost children everywhere, seeing patterns in out-of-town bus schedules and reports of vagrants in faraway states. It frightened her to think that she and Carl's mother, and now Homer's mother, might have this much in common.

The news came to Alex later the same afternoon when he went out for groceries and the newspaper. He had spent the day restoring his apartment, reshelving the books in belligerent disorder just to clear the floor again. The newspaper was mainly to distract himself from the sandwich, which he ate absentmindedly, letting mayonnaise and tomato seeds dribble onto the lower half of the pages down near the less important news, about garbage disposal problems and labor disputes. When he came to Homer's murder, he put the sandwich down and forgot, for once, that he owed himself a cigarette for eating.

No signs of forced entry, he read, suggesting that the assailant was known to the victim or appeared harmless, even arriving, as he or she did, well after eleven at night. Next to the news story was a short feature entitled "Area Youth: A Vital Resource Wasted?" The problem was not hard to pinpoint: the tragic retreat from reality that mars so many young lives, usually in the form of drugs or gangs or fantasies of wealth. Homer was different; smarter than most, he had withdrawn while still in high school into a ring of computer hackers and other variously gifted young miscreants.

Homer's computer ring, the article went on, had been suspected of various inexplicable transgressions, though no charges had ever been brought. It was believed, for example, that they were responsible for the transfer of thousands of dollars in credit to the accounts of persons registered with the Health Department as tuberculosis carriers, on an alphabetical basis. They may also have meddled with an electronic data base subscribed to by multinational corporations, inserting erotica of a highly literary but nonetheless shocking nature into the daily financial reports. These are the kinds of things young people do, the article concluded, in the absence of a firm set of values.

Alex cut the article out of the paper and then dialed Riane. No answer after six rings. Well, let the police try, then, and see if they could get anything coherent out of that one. Then he called Leitbetter's office and, after the requisite five minutes of verbal foreplay, got Phyllis to interrupt Leitbetter's meeting and beg him to come to the phone, saying things had escalated into drugs and possibly murder.

"Listen, Al," Leitbetter hissed into the phone, "I don't have time for one of your tantrums. I have a major funding crisis on my hands, in case you hadn't realized."

Alex counted to three and decided to let the "tantrums" part go. "A kid's been killed. Friend of the grandniece."

"Really?"

"It's in the paper. Computer hacker."

"I see. Well. So?"

"I've been trying to tell you I'm in danger. Because of this goddamn Relnik—"

"I don't see the connection. If anything, it means we have to hurry, right? Gather up data bits while we may. You're still on the case, aren't you, Al? Combing through the Relnik papers, et cetera?"

"Dick, could you give me thirty minutes? Fifteen?"

"Yes, of course, but not right now. I'm trying to work out some alternate funding—"

"Yeah, well, the funders are one of the things I'd like to talk to you about."

"Stay away from the funders, Al. And the booze."

What was it with Leitbetter? The on-again, off-again attitude, as if he already knew the whole story or just didn't want to be in the one-down position of listening to what somebody else knew. All right, it was Leitbetter's project, he called the shots, but whoever killed Homer didn't necessarily know that Alex was only a hireling, not much above the level of an errand boy.

He sat down to review his little system of defenses. The locks had been changed right after the break-in, and he locked the windows now too, even though it meant the apartment was stagnant with heat when he returned in the evenings. He avoided the Baycrest, not that he feared any encounter in the bar itself, but the parking lot was unpredictable, especially after dark. He had reviewed his evening pattern of drinking and realized that between the first awareness of drunkenness and the end of awareness itself there was a sloppy, vulnerable period maybe forty-five minutes long. Whiskey, he realized with a cold sense of doom, had gone over to the other side.

He was also avoiding his office, with the long, empty corridor outside that was only half lit due to some energy-saving plan concocted, in all likelihood, by Leitbetter himself. In this, the absolute dead point of summer, hardly anyone used the corridor except for the mouse-faced chemistry adjunct who had an office three doors down. Even the graduate students who usually crouched fretfully in their cubicles were away on their low-budget summer backpacking trips, munching trail mix and cataloguing environmental wreckage in the national parks, unless Eddie was right and they actually had done something stupid and bold like go out on strike.

Eddie—there was the stone unturned. If anyone knew who was pulling Leitbetter's strings, it would be Eddie. And Eddie ought to know about any peculiar funders, like Martime. Alex stood up so fast that his breath went short, then spent half an hour regretting the mess on his bookshelves. He needed something to take to Eddie, not exactly a bribe, but something to distract him and break the ice, and found it finally in an old college zoology text—*lepidoptera*, that was the word. It was 3:30, just time to drive to the complex, do a quick pass through the library, and find Eddie before the five o'clock exodus.

■ ■ ■

The library had four fat volumes on lepidoptera, of which Alex chose the fattest and newest-looking to lug out of the stacks. In over 500 pages of fine print and line drawings there was no way of locating a particular caterpillar on the basis of looks alone. Alex wandered idly to the colored-plate section in the center of the volume. No recognizable grayish creatures were featured, but why should they be? The emphasis was on the bizarre and mendacious: caterpillars built to resemble leaves and twigs, moths impersonating jungle fauna. Camouflage seemed to be their major achievement, and it bothered Alex that whole species would choose to base their lives on deception. Here was the pupa of an orange-tip butterfly looking like any other thorn on a branch. Would they copy anything, given enough time for natural selection? Paper clips, cigarette lighters, bits of Styrofoam packing material?

After only two false starts Alex found Eddie's office in the administrative area. Eddie could have seen the book on his own, but it was unlikely, since non-faculty personnel had no library privileges.

"Well, well, Professor MacBride. What have you got there?" Eddie grinned, always eager for what he thought of as a creative interruption, and began clearing off a chair for Alex. The office was larger than Alex's but no less claustrophobic, windowless and smelling of human scalp oils and dank postprandial emissions. Alex remembered there was some story about Eddie, something admirable and pathetic like a live-in retarded brother or incontinent parent, that was supposed to account for any failings in the realm of hygiene and charm.

"Caterpillars, Eddie. Lepidoptera is the general name."

"So? Are they in there?" Eddie leaned forward to reach for the book.

"Nope, nothing even like them." Alex offered him the book, opened to the colored plates so Eddie would have something to look at. "But the interesting thing is that no one has even looked. I asked the librarian. This book, for example, hasn't been checked out in five years. You'd think somebody would take a peek, just out of idle curiosity."

"Ha. There's no idle curiosity in hell. All the curiosity is employed full-time churning out publishable results. You know that." Eddie fingered a spotted yellow caterpillar disguised, apparently, as a snake. "So tell me, what are they up to?"

It took Alex a moment to realize he meant the caterpillars. "Oh well. They're not too smart. Lepidoptera don't have brains, just a ganglion where a few nerve cells come together; exchange notes, so to speak. They're programmed, that's all, genetically."

"Good. So the program is smart. What's the program?"

"The program? Oh well, it's the same for any larval form: eat, eat, eat. The transformation of vegetable matter into animal matter, in as large a quantity as possible. But the question is, why doesn't anyone care? I mean—"

"What's next?"

"Oh, a winged form, I suppose." Clearly, judging from the abstracted look on his face, Eddie was hooked now, lost among the lepidoptera. "What I've been wondering is," Alex went on, "who funds Leitbetter? His special projects and so forth? Anything, uh, insect-related?"

The transition was weak, but Eddie looked up conspiratorially. "You thinking maybe genetic engineering? Like we have a new species on our hands?"

"Could be, could be. Half of so-called nature these days is man-made. Anything like that turns up, of course I'll let you know."

"You will? Anything you find out about these little beauties?"

"Why not? You're the only one who seems to care."

Eddie stroked the lepidoptera book thoughtfully. "All right, there are some funny companies out there, I told you, in the funding business. This one prefers to be anonymous, you know what I mean. You're not going to tell Dr. Dickhead if I happen to mention the name?"

Alex swore solemnly in the names of Galileo and Einstein.

"The Harvest, nonprofit outfit dedicated to the 'advancement of human knowledge,' ha ha. Headquarters somewhere south of the border and an outpost in Silicon Valley. They fund 30 percent of the complex and 90 percent of Dr. Blightbetter's personal projects, including cutie-pie Caragiola. Only they've been stalling us on a check for weeks, which is why we may be boarding up the windows in October. Such windows as there are. The Harvest Enterprises."

"I see, and, ummh, what's in it for them?"

Eddie grimaced and riffled through the files in his desk drawers, coming up finally with a thin brochure printed on heavy, cream-colored paper. Alex reached for it, but Eddie shook his head and began to read aloud: " 'The Harvest offers significant funding for projects designed to accelerate the process of learning and scientific discovery. Areas funded include (1) Pedagogical tools for the facilitation of science education, (2) Chemical and surgical interventions aimed at the enhancement of human mental capacity, (3)—"

"Let me just see that, okay?"

"That's enough." Eddie buried the brochure back in his files and folded his hands over his paunch.

"Well," Alex exhaled slowly. "Sounds benign enough."

"Sure, and look where it's got us. Lightfeather going on TV talking about the second coming of the great extraterrestrial Visitor from space. Caterpillars swarming all over and nobody sees them: you tell me why."

"What are you saying, Eddie? About this Harvest company."

Eddie gave him a brief, close-mouthed smile. "What company? We're talking about caterpillars, right? Anything else leaks out and you can count on your paycheck getting permanently digested by the mainframe. *Comprende?*"

From Eddie's, Alex went back to the library to return the book, but found himself slumping into the first chair in sight, out of shakiness and a need to slow things down and stare at them one at a time. The Harvest, he was thinking: the idea was somehow familiar. Then it came to him, out of some old cupboard in the back of his mind where things like his ex-wife's birthday and the formulas for amino acids were stored. Of course: the word for harvest in German is *Ernte*. *Ernte* means harvest. He should have asked what it meant when Martime first said the word, but he had been mixing it up with *erst*, the word that means first.

So Leitbetter's chief benefactor, The Harvest Enterprises, was probably a spin-off of Dora Mueller's Erntegruppe of Third Reich scientists, if it had existed at all, and involved in drugs, enlightenment, the traffic in information—all the ingredients of a crazed paranoid tract. That would make Martime Stimmerman a descendant of someone in the Erntegruppe, a grandson or something, hence the German surname, the Mexican headquarters. And Brabant? He could be part of the same incomprehensible effort, the criminal side Eddie seemed to be hinting at. Or something entirely different.

For a moment something seemed to gel in his mind, dots connecting themselves, forming some statement or odd-shaped polygon. Then whatever it was faded into the chaos of tiny, jostling, creeping thoughts, and Alex's gaze drifted down to the book in front of him, which was open to a tropical moth dressed up as a mask for a tropical owl. One plate showed the moth, and next to it was the beaked and menacing original. What held Alex's eye was not the resemblance between the original and the copy but the subtle divergence, making the moth less like a photocopy or an abstraction, and more, he felt uneasily, like an interpretation.

He covered his eyes with one hand for a moment and looked again. If you could define the difference, the blunt primitivism of the style, you might begin to understand the character of the artist, and hence, generally speaking, what you were up against.

■　■　■

The morning she learned of Homer's death, Della got to the lab ten minutes early thanks to some freak opening in the rush-hour traffic. These things happened sometimes. Just as there could be a huge, snarled tie-up at the unlikely time of 2:00 or 10:00 p.m., there were occasional sudden clearings when the freeway seemed to tilt and spill its contents smoothly through all the exits. Dr.

Hershey was standing in the main lab room when she arrived, in deep thought, or just waiting for someone to come along and get the coffee started.

"Oh. Della." He gave her an odd look that implied there was surprising and not entirely welcome information stamped on her face. Nothing had been said about Mrs. Lopez since her departure, although Claire had given the new dishwasher a stern talk on the use of protective gloves and the correct disposal of waste fluids. Hershey looked away and squinted in the direction of the windows. "Doesn't look like the weather is going to break yet, does it?"

Della looked out obediently. Already, the haze-filtered sunlight was giving the day an antique cast, making it seem like a rerun dredged up from an earlier decade. "Kind of depressing," she offered, "day after day."

Claire's entrance, with a loud "A-hem," was the true start of the day. Hershey had decided to rush into print with Dr. Bhatar's preliminary findings, because it was time, he argued with Dr. Soo, to stake their claim. He picked an obscure journal—one on whose editorial board he happened to serve—so they wouldn't risk rejection and a delay of months. Still, there were gaps to fill in, experiments to be repeated, shaky bits of data to be massaged into shape. By midmorning, tangy smells of chromatography solvents filled the air and magnetic stirrers whirled in their flasks. Soiled glassware and loops of tubing piled up in the sink, where the new version of Mrs. Lopez stood elbow deep hour after hour in suds and steam. Even Della had a role to play, transforming Dr. Hershey's handwritten drafts into printouts so crisp and neat that they looked like self-evident truth.

At eleven she slipped out and called Dr. Leitbetter's office from one of the pay phones in the main lobby. Phyllis remembered her, which was encouraging, but no, he hadn't heard anything, and couldn't come to the phone if he had.

Della snuck back into her cubicle without being noticed by Claire. The thought that Dr. Leitbetter might have tricked her, that he might never tell her anything about Steve, seemed to alter the computer screen, heightening the contrast and blocking all vision peripheral to the phrase at hand. At least he had done nothing, nothing visible anyway, with the information she had given him about the disease. Hershey's lab had not been impounded; no one had come around to snoop.

When she got up to take Hershey the latest printout, she saw that it was already lunchtime and the lab was empty except for the rodents, a whole penitentiary of them, stacked in cages against the wall.

"Della?" It was Dr. Bhatar, peering out from the door of the darkroom. She crooked her finger toward Della seductively. Since Hershey's decision to overrule Dr. Soo and go ahead with publication, Dr. Bhatar's face seemed fuller, almost rosy against the dark tan, as if she were pregnant, which is how the technicians treated her now. Della would hear them snapping at each other, "Dr. Bhatar needs the assay now." "Dr. Bhatar said three mils and that's all." Pregnant with the baby Einstein.

"Look at this, will you." Dr. Bhatar was standing over a shallow tray of liquid containing freshly developed photomicrographs, tilting the tray from side to side so the liquid moved in waves. "Now what do you see? I need an unbiased view."

"I can't see if it's moving."

"All right." Dr. Bhatar took the top print out and laid it out wet on the counter. "Now tell me."

"Circles." Della remembered an IQ test that went something like this. The trick was to suppress the imagination and be as brutal as possible. "A bunch of gray circles. Some kind of a wall."

"Excellent. Now, any other shapes you can make out?"

Della bent over the shiny wet surface, but not so close that the whole thing dissolved into dots. "A diamond. Inside one of the circles. No, not a diamond. A hexagon?"

"Yes." Dr. Bhatar looked up from the print and stared straight at the wall. Then she turned to Della, leaning on her fists, and said it again slowly. "Yes."

"Well, what is it? Is this the virus? I mean the hexagon?"

"So it would appear. They are not found in normal brain."

"Oh, the brain." Della looked more closely and made out another hexagon in its own circle. Even without the virus, the print looked nothing like the blown-up brain images Alex had shown her. "And the circles, what are the circles?"

"The 'circles'!" The Pakistani threw back her head and laughed. "My dear Della, the circles are the synaptic vesicles. We are looking inside a nerve cell within the human brain. The vesicles are—what should I say?—the mechanism of nervous transmission, the way one nerve cell communicates with another. See, they are traveling, these circles—in life they were traveling—to the edge of the cell, the cell wall, where they will release their contents into this space—"

"You mean the virus?"

"In this case, yes, the virus; but normally they are releasing a chemical, a very special chemical, that tells the adjacent nerve cell to, uh, fire. That is, to do the same thing to its neighbor, to pass the message along. You are following?"

Della frowned. She had been doing so well with the circles and hexagons, it seemed a shame to fail at this point. Something came back to her from a book Alex had lent her when she was taking WOW, and "synapse" is of course a well-known word. "Neurotransmitter, right? That's what's in the vesicles?"

"Very good, Della, neurotransmitters. Acetylcholine for example, but never mind. The point is, the virus has entered the brain. It has entered the cells of the brain. In fact, it has entered the most important part of the cells of the brain, the functional part. Yes, the vesicles that transmit the thought."

"The thought? Or the transmitter?"

Dr. Bhatar crinkled her face impatiently. "The vesicles contain the transmitter that passes the signal to fire from one cell to the next. The thought: well, who knows really what a thought is? But we suppose it is a certain pattern that arises . . . A pattern of cells firing in sequence. That is a 'thought.' "

Dr. Bhatar began to examine the other prints in the tray, slowly, one by one. In the silence, Della heard her stomach growl and coughed to cover the sound. "Does this have something to do with why people die? From the virus?"

"Maybe, maybe not. We don't know. Most likely it is the attack on other organs that kills them. But you see how clever our virus is. It stays inside the cells where the immune system can't get at it. In other parts of the body, it causes the cells to fuse with each other. But here in the brain, it causes the nerve cells to form new linkages, new synapses, each cell reaching out, linking with all its neighbors. And the virus uses these linkages to travel, to spread. It uses the very mechanism of nervous transmission as a means, yes, of transportation."

She set the print she was studying back down in the tray and stood there for a moment in dazed silence. Then she reached down and grasped Della by the wrist. "You see the beauty of it? How the virus is spreading through the brain along with the thought. And why not put it so? There are waves of light and also particles of light, the photons, you know. In thought, the particles are the vesicles, the little packets, the quanta of thought. And the virus has entered into them. Yes, the virus is moving on waves of thought."

■   ■   ■

After work Della drove to the mall with the idea of taking a walk in the air conditioning. It was late enough so that most of the afternoon shoppers had gone home already to dinner, but a few people still strolled around, enjoying the power to spend or reject which the mall seemed to confer on everyone, even debtors like herself. She moved along in a slow, definite trajectory, trying to shake off the residue of the day. The holy glow of science, which had seemed to emanate from Dr. Bhatar's huge dark eyes and reflect from every surface in the lab, had faded quickly in the afternoon. After Della dropped the latest printout off with Dr. Hershey, Claire had snagged her and pulled her into one of the microscope rooms, no more than a closet, and tapped with a pen on the notebook she was carrying.

"I know what you're up to, Della." She was nodding without blinking, demanding full attention to her eyes.

"What do you mean?" But Della knew she was already failing by not managing to act surprised. Claire could have found out about her visit to Leitbetter through some acolyte, a secretary or another technician, who could have seen Della going in or out of his office. That would be damaging enough, without Claire's even knowing what Della had told him over the phone.

"I know what's going on. With you and Dr. Hershey."

"What with me and Dr. Hershey?"

"I know how these things work, believe me, I know what you're up to." And she banged her notebook down on the microscope table, and turned and left the room.

Thinking back, Della was struck by the indignity of the situation, two women facing off in the tiny room like jealous wives in a harem. Anyone coming in might have thought that Claire had found the evidence of Della's wrongdoings in the old gray phase-contrast microscope that took up most of the space in the room. She was safe because Claire had the wrong accusation. Or she was in danger because at least Claire knew it was she, that she was the bad element, the one who would turn out to have given the lab's secrets to Leitbetter.

What did women do if they had no jobs or families? She could divide her time between the library, reading magazines without paying for them, and the mall, looking at things without buying them. At least she would get out, that was the important thing. She paused in front of a clothing store where signs announced ABSO-LUTELY FINAL CLEARANCE, EVERYTHING MUST GO, and, it seemed to Della, THE END IS NEAR.

Around her, family groups moved by, their shoving and bickering offering a glimpse into long-run dramas that are normally per-formed in kitchens and cars. There were old women with their grown daughters trailing grandchildren desperate for snacks. There were teenage boys with their hunted looks, and girls who met, heads down, in circles, debating the next move. Della watched a young mother with a tattoo on one bare arm moving furiously ahead; the stroller she was pushing might have been a minesweeper; the older child who dragged behind looked like a prisoner of whatever war the mother was serving in.

Della had never been like that. Even when Steve was little they had walked along side by side like a settled, older couple separated only by the accident of height. Sometimes she would leave him in the computer store, as other mothers might drop their children off in the temporary child care set up for Christmas shopping. She paused and looked for the computer store, but it was gone or changed into something else. In those days, she had enjoyed buying the small things that Leo needed, shirts and underwear, and the way the salesmen circled around, half flirting, trying to divine her tastes and steer her toward additional, related items. So when the man approached her, dressed too well to be the average daytime shopper, she thought at first he was a clerk from one of the men's stores, come up to tell her that something she had ordered months ago, a special color or size, had finally arrived.

"Mrs. Markson? Della Markson?"

Della said yes, and he shook his head so that the long, straight hair snaked around on his shoulders. "I can't believe this. I tried to reach you at the university but they wouldn't put the call through. And here you are. Jesus." He reached into a breast pocket. "See, this is all I had to go on."

It was a clipping from a local newspaper, a weekly given away free in the supermarkets, showing her and Leo and two other couples at the annual dinner for the realtors' association, six months ago at least. Della remembered the dense press of gray suits and Leo's eagerness to get into the picture.

"I'm sorry. Kentwell Brabant." He put out his hand and she gave him hers. "I'm a producer with *Nightzone*. The 'far side of the news'?"

"Really? I saw the one about the scientists who've had themselves frozen."

"Cryonics, with Dr. Richard Leitbetter. Shows you the kind of quality stuff we do. But look, you probably have to be somewhere for dinner. Can I take just a few minutes of your time?"

Della tried for a light tone. "You want to put me on TV?"

"Maybe. Jesus, with those eyes? And the bone structure. The

bone structure is amazing. I'd love to get you in front of a camera, Mrs. Markson, no pressure, just completely conversational. Very informal. I talk, you talk . . . about your son, of course.''

Later, when she told Miriam about the encounter, she would leave out the fact that the man was attractive, even sexy, though in a processed way that made her think of manicures and male smells just barely controlled by expensive, man-made scents. But it is a condition of experience that you never know how to weigh things as they happen, whether the voice matters or the words, the logic of the words or the faint hope the voice inspires. She pointed toward the group of tables arranged around the snack stand and let him lead the way and order sodas.

"You were just wandering through the mall," she asked him when he came back to the table with the drinks, "and happened to run into me?''

"The very person I've been looking for all day, yes, incredible. Because I was expecting someone older. Kipper is, what, twenty?''

"Twenty-one.''

"But you work out, don't you, Mrs. Markson? I can tell from the shoulders. Most women neglect the shoulders.'' He looked from her torso to her face and Della had the sense of a physical message passing between them, with information about certain strokes, touches, hidden sensitivities. "If more people worked out, the world would be a more beautiful place, wouldn't it? Not to mention saner. But you've heard about this computer hacker who got killed, Homer something?''

"Homer?'' She coughed to cover her surprise. "It was on the news.''

"Good, the news.'' He was leaning forward, moving his paper cup in circles against the table in a slow, rubbing motion. "You get something like this, execution-style, and our little ears perk up. We see a segment, five minutes, maybe eight. But I'm going to need baby pictures, Mrs. Markson, family photos, diplomas, letters. Kipper in short pants, Kipper in blue jeans, Kipper in prom tux. Normal is fine, boring is fine. Whatever you've got. See, people think television is all fake, re-enactments. But let me tell you from the inside, most of it is God's own vérité."

"But why Steve? Kipper. Homer must have had other friends."

"I'm sorry." He shook his hair again. "I got ahead of myself, didn't I? Okay, look. Start from square one. We have Carl, Carl Whitman. Hangs himself in the two-car garage. Why not the standard carbon-monoxide exit? we wonder. But anyway, suicide. Maybe we model it just a little. The mother rolls up the garage door and we're coming in over her shoulder, the kid hanging in silhouette. No known influence of rock 'n' roll. Sorry, Mrs. Markson. Jesus. I forgot you knew the family."

Della felt her stomach tighten. "How did you know about Carl?"

"A little research. Computer-related deaths, see? We weave them together, look for the thread—the sick side, you know, the unnatural. Like they're on to something, see, these kids, and now someone . . . or something, something very powerful, very intelligent . . . because these are smart kids, we know that. Look, want to find a real drink somewhere? Frankly, I've been in better-looking bus terminals."

She hesitated. "Listen, I don't really think I can help you."

"Oh, but you can." He sounded charming again, assured. "You stayed home while Kipper was growing up, a devoted mom. Our viewers like that, the human touch. We have a sensitive boy, very involved with his mom. And Dad is what? Tuned out, missing in action. It's a standard pattern. These things don't go away. These things grow. This is one way to run it, Mrs. Markson, the sickness within."

Della pushed her chair back an inch and looked around for support. There should be other mothers around, a caucus of mothers, but the mall was nearly empty now.

"How do you know all this? That I stayed home."

"Nosing around, Mrs. Markson." He blew through his straw, cigarette-style, and winked. "Intelligent conjecture."

"Well, it didn't make him sick."

"Oh please. This is the modern age. There's no stigma attached.

But of course, you're the mother. Every mother wonders, What are they doing? In their rooms all the time, the doors locked, maybe sounds coming out, maybe music, maybe nothing at all. But in this case we do know something. A computer network, the news mention that? Think about it, Mrs. Markson, Kipper and Homer were both members."

"So what if they were? They weren't close, they weren't even friends."

"Okay. Now we're getting somewhere." Brabant looked around to see if anyone was listening, but there was only the wind playing with the plastic sheeting near the roof of the mall. "They were friends but they had a falling-out. Happens all the time. We bring a psychiatrist on, some guy to talk about the adolescent ego, how the boundaries are thin. Or woman, of course."

He frowned and shook his head. "Only we already have you as the mother. Can't have just boys and female authority figures, can we? Formula for rage, and that's not what we're going for. We're going for that chill on your neck when you don't know what you'll find when you turn around, because you realize you've had your back turned half your life, didn't you?"

He was looking at her from somewhere low in his eyes, waiting for a response to register.

"Look, if you're saying that Steve, Kipper, was in any way . . ." She couldn't finish the sentence because even to say "involved" could be some kind of an admission.

Brabant shook his head and whistled. "There I go again. See? I get carried away. Sorry. You want another soda or something?"

"No. I want to know what the point of this is."

"The point is, between any two events there is at least one plausible connection. Kipper knew Carl. Kipper knew Homer . . ."

"Listen, Kipper is missing. You know so much, why don't you know that? I haven't heard from him for over a year now." Della thought of just standing up and walking away, through the wide-open internal boulevards of the mall and out to the parking lot, where it would still be light. But he was holding her down with his eyes, which had a pink glow in the pupils from reflected neon or some new connection he was making.

"Missing." He bit his lower lip and studied the napkin. "Good. I mean, that could work for us. It's not as good as dead, but it's a step in the same direction. I mean, strictly from the viewers' point of view. Someone is missing, right? Then a little time goes by and they're 'presumed dead.' Objectively speaking."

"Look, I'm sorry but—" Della put the strap of her pocketbook over her shoulder and started to stand up.

"No, wait. Jesus, the whole thing, I'm so into it I don't know where to draw the line sometimes. But look, Mrs. Markson, missing is good. Missing gives the viewer a role to play. There are people out there who take photos of the TV screen every time a missing person comes on. They carry the photos around in their wallet and when someone comes along, see, they can check. This is why we need the pictures, Mrs. Markson. You get a million people looking out for the lost boy. People in a position: toll collectors, flight attendants, emergency-room nurses, waiters. Think of it, Mrs. Markson, everyone looking out for your boy."

"Yes. All right. I'll think about it."

"And do me one favor, Mrs. Markson. Watch the show. Please. It's on tonight, ten o'clock."

Della nodded as she backed off.

"And if you don't see my name in the credits, it's because I just started, all right?"

■   ■   ■

Della drove home the fastest way, although she hated the freeway at night, when the speed limit seemed to be suspended. All the time people were killed in accidents where their cars went "out of control," and Della could see now how that happened: it was a matter of giving up, at the individual level, a surrender to the car and whatever cars generally wanted, just as on a larger scale everything was already arranged for the convenience of cars, whole neighborhoods were removed to make way for them, fields cleared to give them places to rest. All you had to do was loosen your hands for an instant and say, Drive, go wherever it is you've been wanting to go, deep in your engine, all this time. Show me the true destination.

Steve would not kill someone. It needed to be thought out loud, so to speak, word by word. He would not kill another human being. But there was the game. The game was hard to explain. She had to admit that most people would stop if they designed something addictive, something that could leave people stupid or dead, they would not keep going with it, perfecting, refining. They would find something else to do with their time.

Dogs barked when Della got out and slammed the car door shut, the landlord's dog and stray ones that assembled at night to go through the garbage. She walked quickly through the floodlights that the landlord had installed on the corners of the house and rested before climbing the steps. Maybe this was the issue of scientific responsibility that Alex had talked so much about in class. To the scientist, it's just a game, what you can do with ideas and equations. To the rest of us, it's an atom bomb. But did it change things if the whole thing was a game, if the result was a game as well as the process?

When she got in, she switched on the TV and found *Nightzone* already five minutes into the show. An astronomer, beamed in from an observatory in a desert somewhere, was explaining that there are structures in the universe that cannot be accounted for: high-energy strings millions of light-years long, bubble formations holding thousands of galaxies in place, a "great wall" hundreds of millions of light-years high, made of thousands more galaxies piled together. The screen showed all this in artists' conceptions that made the universe look like a lumberyard or a project abandoned in the midst of construction.

The phone rang and it was Miriam. "You're home, good. Are you watching *Nightzone*? Leitbetter's going to be on it. I saw the announcement."

Della leaned forward and pressed the remote to turn up the volume. It was Dr. Leitbetter, with his sandy hair falling over his forehead, exactly as he had been a few days ago when he was talking only to her. Yes, there is extraterrestrial life, he was saying. How could there not be, given the scope of things? There was even the possibility of beings so far beyond us in technology and strength that they could reshape the universe for some purpose of their own. The great wall: was it intended to divide two hostile realms? The strings could be devices for transportation or communication; no better explanation had been found.

"Extraterrestrials," Miriam said. "His favorite theme."

See, Dr. Leitbetter was explaining, we have always imagined just two levels: life and the universe, man and God. Life envisioned as a thin, greasy coating that appears only on the rare planetary body blessed with the right temperature and chemical makeup. But "life" is a generous word which could include many things. To assume that we are the ultimate form of consciousness, beyond which lies only God, or whatever we are to call it, the prime mover perhaps, could be an error rooted in provincialism. Look at our position here at the edge of the galaxy, far from the churning center of things.

It was like being in WOW again, Della thought, the opening lecture, delivered by Leitbetter himself via the TV monitors that jut out from the walls of the lecture hall.

"Can we expect any contact with these beings?" the host asked, and Leitbetter was going on about the possibility that they had already been here, perhaps in the form of some inexplicably superior human, Jesus for example, Buddha, Darwin.

"It's his idea of the Visitor," Della half-whispered into the phone.

"And if they come again," the host inquired deferentially, "what can we expect? What do you think they'll want from us?"

Leitbetter brushed his hair back with both hands, and Della could see he was enjoying this, that the interview was going as planned. Well, of course, he said, they'll be interested in the highest products of our species, our art and our science. But especially our science. Art is idiosyncratic to each life form on its own little planet. Science, however, is the study of the universe we share in common with all forms of life, wherever they are. And any intelligent being, seeking to comprehend the universe in its entirety, would want to know what each species had discovered from its own peculiar vantage point, with its own science and instruments and tools . . .

A commercial came on, sad faces turned to smiles, mothers hugged children, hair gleamed and dentures remained in place.

"I heard him give a talk once," Miriam said. "The whole point of the Human Ecology Complex, he said, is to put together all knowledge of human life. In case we should ever be asked. Get it?"

"Well, why not?" Della said from her end. "If they're intelligent enough to get here, they're probably not just going to use us for food."

"But, Della, don't you see? This is the ideal theory from Leitbetter's point of view. It means the only people who matter on earth are the scientists, and especially Leitbetter himself. This is how he gets his grants."

The dark-suited man had returned and was prompting Leitbetter on the "spiritual implications." There are angels, he suggested, myths of godlike beings, giants on the earth.

Yes of course, Leitbetter responded, all the ancient religions speak of Intermediate Beings, he was saying, intermediate to God and man. Only modern religions, with their hatred of clutter, have simplified the story down to us alone in the world with God, but even these have their prophets, their emissaries or representatives from a "higher realm." The birth of Jesus, for example, was heralded by unprecedented astronomical phenomena, and archaeological research might eventually show that Jesus himself, no disrespect intended—far from it, in fact—was one of these Intermediate Beings, an emissary from another world, which—

"Oh no!" It was Miriam's voice, startling Della. "He's really gone around the bend this time. 'Jesus was an E.T.'!"

It would have been a most disappointing visit, Leitbetter was saying, arriving here at A.D. 0: the beginnings of atomic theory, some rudimentary algebra and geometry, a bit of primitive astronomy, but no real chemistry, no evolutionary theory, no Newton, no Heisenberg, no Bohr . . .

"But the Scriptures speak of a second coming," the dark-suited man said with a nod and smile, indicating time was running out. "The question is, will we know when it happens?"

Della leaned forward, resting the receiver against her knee so Miriam couldn't interrupt. "The question is," Leitbetter was saying with a little half-smile, "will we have anything to offer when it does?"

CHAPTER 11

A lex called Della from the complex with the idea of asking her if she had read about this kid Homer, and making a nice yarn out of it, the tie-in with what Della still called "the Nazis," for example. But when the answering machine came on he realized that it was a dumb thing to leave on the tape. If the police talked to Riane, she might mention him, and then what would he say? That sometime in the forties a beautiful scientist named Dora Mueller had implanted electrodes in the brains of concentration-camp victims and set off a series of neuronal impulses that flowed through Mexico and up to here and now circled around in a holding pattern, tighter and tighter, getting ready for the crash or whatever violent arrival was taking shape?

Better to leave a more personal message, something whimsical, pleading, self-mocking. And the whole business with Relnik receded until he got home in the evening and found a message from Brabant on his own machine, the only message except for something from Phyllis about the syllabus meeting, a nice juxtaposition, he couldn't help notice. First Phyllis with her "Alex, yoo-hoo, are you the-re?" Beep, beep. Then Brabant's "Hi, guy. This is your buddy from the Baycrest, remember? Time's passing, and taking stuff with it as it goes. Know what I mean? Check you later, pal."

In the morning he got up and made a breakfast of eggs and cottage cheese, toast and juice. He was surprised at his own lack of euphoria. It was twenty-four hours since he'd had a drink, much too early in the process to take the absence of nausea and trembling for granted, yet this was how millions of people got up in the morning, he realized, straight from bed to bathroom, from bathroom to kitchen, and back to bathroom without stopping to cower or cling to the wall. He did it with pills of course, two sleeping pills at eleven o'clock after checking all the windows and double-locking the door. You have to do it with pills until the habit returns and the entrance to sleep becomes a soft zone of comfort instead of a trench filled with sharpened spikes.

He would pay later, he knew that. On the drive to the complex he tried to assess the effect the syllabus meeting would have on his chemical balance. An hour or two of futile intellectual competition would lead almost certainly to weakness and rage. He tried to imagine what other people, meaning non-drinkers, did to reward themselves for reaching the end of the day. Television in most cases, gardening, loose clothes, dinner, sex—but it was hard to believe there wasn't something else, some more potent measure that almost everyone used but nobody talked about. Otherwise, how did they divide day from night and move from one kind of thing to the next?

Then the thought came to him, in the shape of a terrible fear, that maybe there were no rewards at the end of the day, that the day was all you got. He had forgotten what extended sobriety was all about: world without retching, without headache or trembling. World without hope.

But the meeting room was empty when he got to it, just the chairbacks, which he knew from experience to be viciously hostile to the human form, facing each other around the table in apparently perfect agreement. Alex checked the memo, which he was carrying along with his notes on the WOW syllabus in a battered manila folder. Yes, he had the right time and the right place. Something else was wrong.

Saul's lab was just down the corridor, closer than any working phone, so Alex headed for it, nourishing the warm, growly sense of grievance. When he opened the door, Saul cocked an eyebrow in his direction but went on with the story he was telling. A couple of Asian women, post-docs, Alex guessed, were laughing politely into their hands.

"So I said to this guy, Eduardo or whatever, I didn't order two thirty-pound iguanas. I ordered six ten-pound iguanas. What the hell am I going to do with a thirty-pound lizard?"

There were giggles from the devoted audience. Saul had never done anything brilliant or noteworthy, which is why he still got to work at all, as opposed to sitting in an office devising grant proposals.

"I thought there was a meeting this morning," Alex said as the post-docs flitted back to their microscopes and racks of smeared glass slides.

"There was a meeting this morning. Nine a.m., right down the hall. Fine, uplifting meeting too." Saul was still smirking from the success of his iguana story. "Dr. L. proposes that we reorganize the syllabus around the theme of death. Biochemistry of decomposition. Cell self-destruction. Liquefaction of the tissues. The only thing that will hold their attention. So he says."

"I know, I told him that myself."

"Yeah, really. 'Knowledge of science is the confrontation with death.' Our physical natures. Pile of cellular debris, ultimately atoms. Very gripping material. Of course, all this assumes we'll still be in the education business in September, and there remains a margin of doubt."

"Why didn't someone tell me the time was changed?"

"Oh, come on, Alex, if someone told you, would you even know?"

Alex didn't stay to answer that. The problem with drinkers is that they get either covert adulation or total contempt. Adulation from the occasional naïf who sees drinking as a rakish, bohemian gesture. Contempt from the barren, healthy-minded majority who see it as a degenerative disease. There is a need for a rational middle ground, a recognition of the craftiness and planning required for the drinking life. It's hardly a dashing existence, so chained to absolute need. But neither is it a lifestyle for the foggy-headed and forgetful, all the business of monitoring supply and knowing the hours and locations of liquor stores.

Not to be paranoid, the changed meeting time was an ominous sign. Alex stopped in a men's room to look at his face, at what he hoped would be the bloodless blue eyes of a hardworking man, but the stench drove him out. Another blocked and overflowing toilet, more disrepair, not even a sign on the door to warn you away.

At the elevator bank, he hesitated for a moment over the question of whether to go up to his office or down, down to the basement and the gym. The rational thing would be to go down to the gym, collect the papers from his locker, and make multiple photocopies of them, because it would be a mistake, it occurred to him, to be the only person with the Relnik papers, this set anyway, and possibly the Relnik secret. Maybe the precious secret was in the papers Martime had bought from Riane, otherwise he was the one, right? The one left holding the cat, or the bag, or whatever it was that got you counted out.

But it had settled in his mind as a fact that the gym was to be avoided. The gym was a tomb. No doubt Phyllis had a backup copy anyway, that being, he trusted, a well-known secretarial concept.

Maybe it was because the gym was out of bounds that Alex decided he had to steel himself for the trip through the half-lit corridor to his office. You can't have phobias hemming you in from all directions. He needed to sit down, smoke, and study something neutral and unchallenging, preferably a wall. What they don't tell you is that not drinking is slow, hard, ball-busting labor, which is why only the sober can do it, the firm-of-mind and steady-of-hand. It wasn't that there was nothing to look forward to, he was realizing as the day wore on, inexorably, toward cocktail hour. It was that there was too much lying ahead, too much in the line of detail and humiliation and car problems and backaches and threats. And him without the magic spray, the wonder drug, the laser beam.

So when he opened the door and saw the bottle sitting on his desk, full of self-assurance and the finest booze, it seemed at first like an obvious simplification, the solution to a tricky, multifaceted problem. Here I am, it said, the answer. No note, no wrapping paper, not even one of those red yarn bows the liquor stores call "gift wrapping." Alex cleared his throat and studied the label, which spoke of fields of soft heather, ancient wood, traditions defended for centuries against the forces of thrift and convenience.

Then he sat down facing the miraculous presence and put both hands up over his face.

■ ■ ■

Rats do not vomit. It's too wasteful and goes against the rule that says non-self must be turned into self and kept that way as long as possible. Instead, rats convulse, stretching their legs straight out so there's nothing to stand on, lending the entire length of their bodies to the waves of revulsion that move from neck to tail, tail to neck, never satisfied, getting nowhere. But the hardest part of the experiment wasn't the rat and its suffering. The hardest part had been the task of wrapping the bottle up in newspaper, seal still intact, and leaving his office without even a sniff of the famous aroma. At least the seal seemed to be intact, although there was the slightest ridge in the plastic where it could have been broken once and glued back into shape.

It cost less to bribe the men in the animal house than it had to buy a bottle of the same exalted brand at the liquor store on the turnpike. Not that Alex really needed the same brand or any whiskey, for that matter, when lab alcohol would have done for a control. But he wanted this done right. If he couldn't nail the perpetrator, he could nail down the facts. It even occurred to him to do the experiment blind; that is, not knowing which bottle was which. But there was no point to that, and if he didn't know which bottle was bad, neither would he know which one was good.

For the animal house workers it was a good joke, an excuse to stand around elbowing each other and saying universal words like *borracho* and *loco*. Only one of them, a young guy who was rumored to be a troublemaker, watched with a sad, straight face as the control rat lurched around its cage and finally slumped in drunken comfort against the wire netting. In his eyes this too was science, maybe the best of science, the kind that finds the toxins and uncovers murder plots. He even seemed to understand that this was about language as much as science, a way of translating "bottle" into "dying rat," and dying rat into This is it, MacBride, time is up.

■   ■   ■

When he got back to his apartment, Alex locked the door behind him and put the bottle marked *C* on the kitchen counter. The poisoned bottle was another warning, he reasoned, not an actual attempt at murder, since his adversary would at least give him credit for being a scientist and running the appropriate tests. Brabant he assumed was the perpetrator, although it was true he had not actually seen Martime board the plane with the door sealed fast behind him. There could be hirelings, of course, but the message was clear: We know your little weakness, ha ha, and are prepared to exploit it as needed.

At his desk he took out a pad of paper and two sharpened pencils, like someone preparing for a test. It was time to sketch out the situation and try to grasp it as a whole. But what was he supposed to put at the top of the paper? The Relnik case? It was beyond Relnik now; Relnik was only the instigation, the first cause. All right, leave the paper untitled and list the participants, in order of appearance: Leitbetter, Riane, Brabant, Homer, Martime . . . with lines between any two who could be definitely linked, like Leitbetter and Martime, Riane and Homer, poor Homer. Oh cruel, linear world, where young men die and older ones are left to soldier on through endless tracts of thirst!

The diagram seemed worse than stupid; it was ugly, cluttered, arrows and lines going this way and that, the work of a lesser mind. It was true what Dr. Caragiola had said: Truth is the great simplifier, the great packager, making things neat and, yes, making them small. Then he remembered the conversation he'd had with the librarian, the other day when he'd been looking up lepidoptera. She had been complaining about the problem of theft, and how microfilms facilitate the crime: The smaller things are, the faster they leave. This could account for the human impulse to condense, so admirably expressed by the scientific endeavor. The difference between a pattern and a mere pile of things was that you could remember the pattern, you could take it with you.

But what did that have to do with anything? He pushed back from the desk and found himself in the kitchen, leaning against the counter. Why fight this on top of everything else? was his perfectly reasonable thought. The cap came off with a twist and the fumes blew up through his nasal passages, where they took the form of the breeze the becalmed ship has waited for through weeks of glassy water and slow, twisting hunger. Then he drank and knew in the same instant that one of the great issues of his life was finally settled: that what we are given is not enough. The unmodified universe, even with its blue skies and galaxies and soft fingers to kiss, was not enough and never could be. We are born into a condition of unbearable deprivation that he, for one, would not accept. Maybe this was the attraction of Della, that she lived in full sobriety and knew just how bad it was.

Now the diagram looked more alien and futile than ever. His mind flipped back to Martime and the librarian, the scientific endeavor as a process of condensation, expressing the sum of human knowledge in ever smaller, more elegant forms, making it, he now saw, more *portable*. But that meant one thing in the case of a library, with volumes shrinking onto microfilms and being carried off in the pockets of lab coats. What would portability mean in the case of all knowledge, all human knowledge; in other words, where would such knowledge be going?

Then something, maybe the whiskey soaking into drought-racked tissue, made him think of Leitbetter's idea of the Visitor. What was it? Alex never paid much attention to Leitbetter's more extravagant fantasies, designed to keep the viewing audience from switching the channel. Ah yes: that someday They would come, or maybe just One, and demand to know what we'd found out in our years on earth, how the universe looked from our tiny perch. And then the Visitor would what? Pack up our findings and take them away. That was why it had to be portable—the sum of human knowledge was going somewhere, to what is called in science fiction "off planet."

He indulged the digression, imagining Leitbetter carrying the precious gift of human knowledge up a huge flight of marble stairs to where the Visitor waited, angelic and mild-faced. It was the perfect solution, both to the riddle of human existence and to the problem, from Leitbetter's point of view, of how to win proper recognition for his own accomplishments, administrative as well as scientific. What would it be, this offering? A diskette? A slim volume full of elaborate mathematical notations? Leitbetter would no doubt apologize for its bulkiness, relative to what could have been achieved given a few more centuries of work, a few more grants for the "advancement of human knowledge." The Visitor would sigh patiently and accept it, then vanish off into the void.

It was lovely, this line of thought, like something straight out of a Leitbetter TV special. Even Relnik fit in, with his mushy notions of intellectual joy, because what do scientists call the simplest theory, the theory that ties things together in the smallest, most portable package? They call it "elegant." They admit that it gives them pleasure.

His diaphragm convulsed in the beginning of a laugh. He wondered if Leitbetter had gotten the idea of the Visitor from Martime, from The Harvest, and whether this was their motivation too: preparation for the moment of extraterrestrial contact. Now if only he knew what it was all about, and how he was supposed to survive it.

■　　■　　■

Della sat in the car for a moment, savoring the air conditioning. The day was already oppressive, a jungle sun pushing down through morbid, rot-soaked haze. When she got to the lab she would have to wash her face and powder it again. Pat under her arms with paper towels. Africa is what it looked like, acres of dirt lots edged by brown stubble, a clump of bare, black-trunked trees in the distance.

"Della!"

He was coming around from the driver's side of the car parked next to hers, dressed for work in one of his creamy tan summer suits. "Leo?"

"Yeah. Della." He tilted one palm upward in an explanatory gesture. "Della, look."

"You followed me here?"

"It's not hard when someone doesn't change lanes for five miles at a stretch. When they stop on yellow, you know."

"I don't like being followed."

"What's the matter, I'm embarrassing you? I don't have those leather elbow patches, huh?"

"Forget it, I have to get to work." The lot was beginning to fill up and there was a carful of women disembarking a few yards away. No one looked at Della but they would hear her if she screamed. They would at least have to turn around.

"So I have only one question, Del. Where is he?"

"Steve? How come you're suddenly so concerned?"

"It's just that . . . They're leaning on me, you know what I mean? They assumed a small debt I happen to have incurred, I mean the parties that are interested in Steve. So I thought, you know—"

"What parties are interested in Steve?"

"That's not the point. The point is, they're getting kind of impatient, if you know what I mean."

Della turned away and started up the walkway toward the complex, but he rushed up behind, breathing audibly.

"Della, listen." He rubbed his cheek and looked up toward the sky, the source of the heat, with one eye flinched against whatever else might be up there. She had never seen a look like that on him before. Maybe he was noticing for the first time that the direction of things is not necessarily the same way you were planning to go. That you could be involved in packaging, arranging, and putting things together, while the general tendency is toward tearing apart.

"You'll let me know, huh? First sign of the kid."

■   ■   ■

At lunch, Alex waved to Della and came shoving his way across the cafeteria with a coffee cup in one hand and a dish of Jell-O in the other. She thought she should say something light and ironic: Well, Professor MacBride in person! But a fit of primness came over her in his actual physical presence and all she could think of was "Is that lunch?"

"They say there's something odd about the stew—little white fibers of meat about the size of a rodent femur." He looked better than usual, cleaner and more clear-eyed, but tense, like a man who is trying to be cheerful in spite of an obvious rash. "Jell-O is safe. It's not cooked, it's mined. In huge great shiny slabs the size of a railroad car." He shook the Jell-O to make it vibrate. "Look, I'm sorry, Della, about the other night. It's a joy to see you. My heart bounds dangerously."

Della closed her magazine. "I got your call."

"Oh yes." He frowned, trying to remember what message he'd left. "It's turning out to be a pretty vicious business."

"The Nazis? I thought you weren't doing that anymore."

"Guess I never really stopped. And they were Nazis, all right. I don't know how much I told you, but . . ." He paused and looked around. "Anyway, I spent the morning reading about Nazi medical research. Using concentration-camp inmates. Remarkable conjuncture of Enlightenment science and Neanderthal barbarism. Strange there isn't more on it, actually."

"So she was a Nazi, this German scientist?"

"I'm beginning to think so. At least after today's bout of reading I am. But the awful thing is how dumb most of these experiments were: putting people in cold-water tanks and seeing how long they'd last. Cutting off testicles. Starvation. Removal of the internal organs, one by one."

"What was the point?"

"My question exactly. I mean, if you're going to use the most expensive research material in the world, if you are going to use live human beings, then you might as well do something elegant. I mean, if it were animals it would be one thing. Guy in pathology used to tie dogs down and have a hammer pound the leg joint at regular intervals: 'Effects of Repeated Trauma on Cellular Recovery Mechanisms.' You see what I mean? Dumb. No imagination, just hit 'em, freeze 'em, slice 'em up."

They turned toward the sound of raised voices on the other side of the cafeteria. "Product of a sick mentality!" "What gives you the right . . ." It was Claire's table, or actually two tables, since her following had grown to the point where one table would no longer hold them and some of the faithful had to stand, mixed with the curious and hecklers loyal to more traditional faiths. Della could see a security guard approach the table, lean on it, nod, shrug, and move away.

"It must be a spiritual test, working with her every day."

"She barely speaks to me. She thinks I'm undercutting her with Dr. Hershey."

"And you are, no doubt you are." He looked up furtively. "You know what I'd like to do sometime, Della? Go out and look at the night sky. Get a blanket, a pair of binoculars, a jug of wine. Count the shooting stars. Find the Pleiades. You know there's a religion, I forget which tribe, where the Pleiades are God?"

"I'd like that."

"A jug of wine and thou."

Their eyes remained stuck for a moment and Della was the first to look away. "But do you think we'd see anything? This isn't a good area for stars."

"Of course, of course." Alex laughed. "Can't really see anything worth seeing anyway, what with the satellites and airplanes and searchlights announcing new gas stations. Ever think about that,

Della? A tribe today would never find the Pleiades, never figure out astronomy, eclipses, order, logic, symmetry, mathematics . . ."

"A tribe wouldn't be living around here. They tend to locate where the sky is clear."

"But if they did . . ." He knew he should be pleased to have the conversation back on a neutral, speculative course, but he felt, oddly, hurt and derailed. "If they did, what kind of a religion would they come up with? What kind of science? No orderly progression of point sources moving across the sky, just some confused traffic in flashing lights and beams and miscellaneous UFOs."

"So? Whatever they came up with, maybe it would be closer to the truth."

"My my, you're cynical today," Alex said approvingly.

"Well, you brought up the Nazis. Your beautiful scientist—Dora?—she did experiments on human beings?"

"Well, probably not directly in a hands-on sense, but she may have designed the experiment." Alex tilted onto the back legs of his chair and breathed in deeply. "Her name doesn't show up in any of the records, at least not in any records mentioned in the books I could get hold of, and it seems unlikely that a beautiful blond Mengele would somehow escape the historians' attention. But it is known that twenty-four inmates of Auschwitz were requisitioned for use in experiments performed in a research hospital near Heidelberg, where, I am fairly certain, Dora's brother-in-law worked. Lovely town, Heidelberg. That's where Dora was and where Henry used to spend his summers. Anyway, the interesting thing is that they were not just any twenty-four inmates. The requirement was that they have some professional background in biology or medicine."

"Maybe they were using them as technicians?"

"But you see, there's no record of them after that, at least not that I could find mentioned. It's not like I have primary sources, of course, but it looks like they just get ground up and put into test tubes. So to speak. I still have the problem of accounting for nine of them, because the allegation—I said 'alleged' here—is that Dora's experiment used only fifteen."

"For what? What did she do?"

"Experiment, alleged experiment. But then there would have been the trip, of course. A day or two in an unheated railroad car, food, if any, at the discretion of the keepers. Plus the natural attrition due to madness and suicide. There are hints that one of them was a neurologist, very distinguished Viennese neurologist. Had been, anyway. Who knows what shape he arrived in. When he got to Heidelberg. After no doubt seeing his family raped, bayoneted, gassed, whatever. A neurologist reduced to mere neurology himself, the state just above unconsciousness, where the feet keep moving, the nerve cells keep firing, but there is no product, you know, no thought."

"That's terrible."

"Science run amok."

"What about Dora? What did she do?"

"See, that's what I'm trying to pin down. Maybe it was Dora who instigated and designed the experiment. Maybe twenty-four was really fifteen. Or maybe this is all crap, invented by someone who thought I was running out of conversational topics. Would you find me just as interesting, Della, without the Nazis?"

■　■　■

Back in her cubicle, Della tried to regain the numbness of work. Alex was not worth thinking about, Miriam said, he was too far gone, too much of a wreck unless he started in recovery now. She concentrated on making Hershey's draft leap from paper to computer screen, letting the words use her as a pathway and a form of locomotion: from paper to eye, from finger to screen. She finished entering the most recent batch of corrections, saved them on the computer, then checked to see that they were really saved. Some days the mainframe was overtaxed and you got odd effects. Files would drift away and come back half chewed. Touch one key and garbage symbols, weird hieroglyphs from the computer's subconscious mind, would pour out onto the screen. Error beeps would sound at the end of every line.

She was poking around, pressing the function keys, when suddenly a door swung open into another space. Think of it as spaces, Steve had once said, rooms leading to other rooms, closets connecting to closets through secret passageways, cupboards in all the rooms. The resemblance to TV, he said, is not incidental. Only this is three dimensions or more, and you are in control. And now she had left her narrow workspace within the computer, the program where words and phrases are polished and stored. She must have gotten out into the mainframe, because the menu before her said TYNET, ACCOUNTING, E-MAIL, PAYROLL, SYSTEM SUPPORT, and PERSONNEL.

Della moved the cursor onto PERSONNEL and pressed ENTER, but she already knew it was useless. This door would not open to her. You can get into the mainframe now and then, Miriam had told her, but the administration's programs are accessible only through approved terminals. Data-entry people can't be poking into Payroll, and so on. Information flows up, not down; in, not out. Della sighed and got up to take the printout to Dr. Hershey.

The door to his office was open, but he was not there. In fact, the lab was empty except for the new dishwasher, who was taking a break, sitting on a stool and tapping her foot.

"Where is everyone?" Della asked.

"I don't know. They say meetings." She was younger than Mrs. Lopez, darker-skinned, and didn't like being asked where she came from. "From here," she would say. "What you think?"

"Claire too?"

"Maybe not back till four, she say. Same with the doctors. Look, you got a cigarette? I sit here, I'm going to lose my mind."

Della said why didn't she go to the cafeteria and pick up a pack. It would be all right with no one around, and if anyone came, Della would tell them she had gone on an errand. It would be fine.

After the dishwasher was gone, Della went back to her cubicle and stared at the empty screen. She had no plan, but a plan would imply guilt. Without a plan, you were in the realm of "I just thought . . ." And that would be the truth, she just thought it would be a good time to learn something about her son, who was missing, you know? The longer someone is missing, the closer they are to dead, or to "presumed dead," as the man from *Nightzone* pointed out, which is the stage that comes between missing and dead. It's a progression, she would explain, which she was hoping to interrupt.

She walked back through the empty lab to Hershey's office, shut the door behind her, and stood for a moment to adjust to the smell. It was a sharp, nitrogenous smell, something she recognized from the early spring before the buds are out, when the air is still crowded with spores. Maybe while everyone else was out there investigating death, Hershey was in here synthesizing life in some damp new invisible form. The carpet crunched and blanched as she walked over to the computer. Of course, the leak—that was it—was turning the carpet into a growth medium, the whole room into a tissue-culture chamber. Della pressed on her upper lip to keep from sneezing and slid into Dr. Hershey's chair, in front of Dr. Hershey's personal computer terminal.

It took her a few minutes of stumbling around before she got back into the mainframe. This time, when she pressed Personnel, the door swung open and she glided in. Name was the next choice. She entered MARKSON, STEVEN and there was a moment of stillness before the message came up * NOT FOUND *. All right, he did not want his given name. He wanted his taken name. She typed in MARKSON, KIPPER and pressed Enter.

But the grid labeled KIPPER MARKSON was almost empty. The social security number was filled in, also a slot for BALANCE, which listed $32 in library fines. Payroll code, job title, birth date, dates of employment, and evaluations were all blank. Della scrolled down through the vacant file to the last slot, which was labeled CONTACT. Someone had started to fill this in, or it had been filled in and then erased in a power surge or memory overload, because all that was left was THE.

She turned off Hershey's computer and went back to her cubicle. Maybe she had never left it. You are somewhere, then you are somewhere else, but part of you is always in the first place, unchanged, following an earlier script. If you come back empty-handed, it doesn't matter anyway, because nothing has changed.

There was just a little gap, a few minutes' gap, between one moment in her cubicle and the next. That plus the fact that she was trembling and the soles of her sneakers were wet.

■   ■   ■

She was still frozen to her seat in the cubicle when human sounds returned to the main lab, but unnatural sounds, foot stamping, muttering, a cry or scream. She wondered if she had left behind some evidence of her trespassing—footprints, maybe, in the carpet—and these were the sounds of general indignation. But she found only Dr. Bhatar in the room, staring out the window, for once not wearing her lab coat over the lush, peach-colored silk tunic and pants.

"What happened? Is there something wrong?"

"Oh, Della, dear Della." The Pakistani turned around and Della could see her dark eyes were magnified by tears. "I will be married, that is what. I will go back to my country and lie in the bed that is made for me there. All of this will be an interlude. My maidenhood, my young life. Oh, Della, you will remember me sometimes? You will remember Santiya Bhatar?"

"Go back?" Della saw that the door to Dr. Hershey's office was fully closed now, but there was no other sign of change. "Why would you do that?"

"Because what else am I going to do? Oh yes, I will wake up sometimes by the side of my husband at night and think, Why not work up the third dilution and try it perhaps in a primate?" Tears ran down her cheeks and she wiped her nose with the purple border of one sleeve. "I will think: Everything in the world is a word that Allah has spoken and I will never know now, with the virus, what is the word Allah is trying to say."

Della put her hand, gingerly, on Dr. Bhatar's arm, the part that was covered with a sleeve. "No, you can't leave, you have to finish your work."

"Work? You don't know? The work is finished. Dr. Leitbetter has our work now. He has taken over the disease. We are finished."

Della leaned against the counter and watched the bland white surfaces of the room arrange themselves around Dr. Bhatar's brilliant presence. "Dr. Leitbetter said this?"

"He announced it today—'his' discovery of the virus. Dr. Hershey has the press release."

"Where is he?"

"In his office with the door locked." Dr. Bhatar gestured toward the closed door. "He fired Claire, the stupid peasant Claire, but it is too late, eh? Locking the door after the pig has got in."

"He fired Claire? Where is she?"

"What does it matter?" She grabbed Della's ringless left hand and held it up. "Look at you, Della, you are free."

Della rushed into the corridor and found only Dr. Soo, pacing in front of the ladies' room door, fists sunk deep in his lab coat pockets.

"A change of direction," he said, looking vaguely over her shoulder. "Administration. The lab goes on. He needs us. I mean, we have assurances. To develop the vaccine, the dirty work. Natural selection, isn't it? The strong rise, the weak creep along behind."

"What happened to Claire?"

"She has to surrender all her notebooks. The keys to her desk and her locker. Turn in her film badge, ID card."

Della pushed past him through the ladies' room door. There was a couch in the anteroom where the women's lockers were, a concession to the unreliability of the female body, and the technicians were sitting on it side by side. From the inner room came the sound of Claire's voice in a steady monologue, punctuated by thuds.

"She won't come out," the technicians said.

"She's in there menstruating into a beaker so she can hex the lab the old-fashioned way." It was the graduate student, leaning against the wall, giggling.

"Oh gross," the technicians said. "Do we need this?"

"What's she saying?" Della asked.

"That she's innocent, what else?" the graduate student filled in. "Innocent as the Baby Lamb."

Della approached the locked stall that contained Claire's voice and fist, banging against the metal wall. "And they defiled the temple, yes, with the filthy oils of their lust . . ."

Della looked at the graduate student and grimaced weakly. "What do they think she did?"

"Xeroxed all our data and trundled it up to Dr. L.," the graduate student whispered back with dramatic glee.

"The Ram, the Ewe, and the Baby Lamb . . . They defiled the fleece of the Baby Lamb" came from the stall. Thud.

"I still don't see . . ." Della said.

"Microbe-hunting, witch-hunting." The graduate student smirked. "Same thing, right? Claire's female, she's crazy, so she must be guilty."

Slowly the door of the stall opened and Claire stepped out, red-eyed and pale, her perm flared out in rays of bleached gold frizz. She looked straight at Della. "Come to see your handiwork, huh, Della? How it all turned out?"

"Listen, Claire—"

"No, Della, you listen." She took a step toward Della and Della stepped backward into the anteroom. "You can't give your soul to the Lamb when your body belongs to the Snake!"

The graduate student was giggling openly now. Della took another cautious step backward. "Listen, Claire," she started, "listen to me. I know you didn't—"

"You! I feel sorry for you. Look at you!" The technicians nudged each other and stood up, muttering about security and how this had gone far enough. But Claire was gaining momentum, shaking a fist closed tight around a wad of damp tissues. "You crawl on the earth. You scamper and hide and try to stay out of sight—the perfect lady, right? The lady who serves the *Snake*."

■ ■ ■

Probably it didn't make any sense, she blurted it out so fast: I did it. I went to Leitbetter. My son. I have a son, you know.

But it didn't matter, because the way ahead was now so clear. Down the corridor and left into the main lab, then through the lab and right to Dr. Hershey's office. She could hear scraps of noise behind her, voices being soothed by the larger sound of air conditioning, but she didn't look back to see which of them was calling or denouncing her. There was such a long way to go, beyond the corridor, beyond the office and the lab, miles to go through waste spaces and abandoned areas that she could already see in her mind.

At the door of Dr. Hershey's office, she paused and half turned. No one had followed her. Dr. Bhatar was gone. In the sour afternoon light, the equipment which had once been so intimidating seemed arbitrary, pathetic. It was just so many extensions of kitchen appliances, ways of shaking, stirring, slicing, heating, cooling, storing—and utterly feeble, she could see now, against the growing forces of disorder.

She knocked and waited.

"Yes?" Dr. Hershey's voice finally answered. There was no anger in it; in fact he sounded helpful, alert. "Is that you, Della? Come in."

He was kneeling on the floor, a pipette in one hand and a glass slide in the other, a soft, diffident look on his face, as if decades of lunches had reverted to baby fat.

"I'm looking for the virus," he explained, holding out the glass slide as evidence. "Or maybe not virus. Microorganism, I should say."

Something in Della's face seemed to make him reconsider. "Oh, of course I don't expect anything from light microscopy, but you have to take a peek, you have to scan. We're going to squeeze out as much of the fluid as we can. Concentrate it by evaporation. Spin it down. Work it up properly. Catch the little devils in their lair." He poked with the pipette deep into the tufts of carpet. "Find out how they do it, you know, the mechanism."

"Dr. Hershey." Della fought the impulse to sneeze back the crowded air. "I came here to tell you, it wasn't Claire."

"Hold this, will you?" He handed her the slide and Della had to concentrate on holding it steady, so the drops of fluid he had collected wouldn't roll off. He rose to his feet in three disjointed launches and set the pipette down on his desk.

"Here." He took the slide from Della and dropped a cover slip onto the fluid, flattening it against the glass. There was a sly look on his face when he turned back to Della, like a bright young man who is on to something that others refuse to see. "We're going to find the virus. Yes. The source of floods and leaks, things like that. Seepages. There has to be cause, you know, a germ, a microorganism, and we would be the first . . ."

So it was finally Dr. Soo who had to take Della's film badge and locker key and call Personnel to suspend her parking permit.

CHAPTER 12

Without a job to go to, Della found the day collapsing around her like a punctured tent. There's always something to do in a house, her mother used to say: scrubbing and waxing and rearranging. But it was better to sit in one room and let the others gather up emptiness, shutting her out. She got up at six even without the alarm clock, and by nine, when everyone would have climbed up the hill to the complex and started the day's work, she would still be sitting over her coffee, staring at the water tower, alert to any fluctuations in the air around her, any little suggestions as to the plan of action.

You should keep a journal, Miriam said, so you can measure healing and growth. But in a real journal Della would be compelled to explain how it felt to wake up at 1:00 a.m. to some distant scratching sound and realize that, except for the walls around her, and the wiring and insulation, she might as well have been sleeping in public, open to anything, with the whole of the night only inches away. Her own writing was too feeble and sissified, reclining there passively on the page, swooning at the vigor of real events.

"6:45 a.m.," she wrote in the notebook she had purchased the day after she was fired. "Sister Bertha for about 30 secs. Says 'Why are you still rowing when you already got to shore?' (???)"

Della pondered this entry and frowned. A few hours of note-taking and study, even just the posture of study, seemed to provide some sense of structure, anchoring the whole vague, fear-laden day ahead. What did she mean by the "shore"? Della stared out at the water tower and let her mind drift. A few years ago it had been mistaken, in the moonlight, for a UFO, the landlord told her, and the picture that appeared in the paper showed portholes and odd bristling antennae, which was ridiculous, of course, when you saw the real thing.

The shore would be the other side, what we are heading toward, the second coming. We are almost there, Sister Bertha had said, because surely we are not there yet. No more effort required, just lean on your oars, drift up to the dock, the time has come.

She wondered if Steve had ever listened to Sister Bertha. Music, she had always assumed when she came into his room and found him with the Walkman on, but then why not a noisy stereo and source of family arguments like other people's teenage sons? He might like Sister Bertha if he heard her. He might find in her mono-maniacal tone some parallel to his own obsession. He might have been able to explain, if anyone could, what it is that Sister Bertha wants us to do: what it is that has to be given, and who is waiting to get it.

But all this was useless, irrelevant, dumb. Nothing she had written in her notebook led anywhere, that was the common theme. Homer, SKD, Leitbetter, *Nightzone*—just diversions, brief flare-ups of hope and confusion. She should be thinking ahead, Miriam said, making that call, for example, to the place that had an opening in data entry. Prioritizing the bills. Calling her lawyer to explain why there would be no check this month. Trying out a support group for unemployed women that featured stretching exercises and motivational readings. Looking for a cheaper apartment.

But each option, when she followed it out in her mind, led down a wormhole of failure and deepening disgust. By afternoon there was nothing to do but lie on the couch with the TV on, half listening to it, half listening to the static from the radio. She flipped idly from channel to channel, letting the television poke into her mind like a thick, coarse, rubber-gloved finger. "In less than five months . . ." "Falling thirty-two points . . ." "A wonderful, wonderful human being . . ." Only, she moved on so quickly that it came out as a "human bee," which seemed to accentuate everything hateful that had come over the day.

■ ■ ■

She was still on the couch when she heard footsteps on the stairs leading to her apartment. It was her landlord and someone else coming up behind him. "Young lady to see you," he said, casting a scowl over his shoulder, and then, in a hiss to Della, "You got a check for me yet?"

The "young lady," when she came into view, looked like one of those rebels Della had seen on TV, almost hairless and with an earring on only one ear. At least Della assumed they were rebels, because the look of it, with the thick boots covering more skin than the skirt did, made her feel witless and old.

"I didn't know you were upstairs. I thought it was the whole house. Is Kipper home?"

"Kipper?" In her confusion, Della fumbled with the latch on the screen door. "No, he doesn't live here. He's been gone for over a year."

The woman's eyes skidded away from Della's and fastened glumly on some private point of reference.

"But come in. Please," Della said, "if you're a friend of Kipper's."

"I'm Riane, you probably guessed."

"Riane? Well . . ." But Riane was looking around the kitchen and beyond it into the living room, even tilting her head to try to see around the corner to where the bedroom was. "He never lived here," Della explained. "We had a regular house."

"He come by or anything?"

"No. Sit down, please. Here."

"Because you're his mom. You would know, right?"

"I suppose. I hope so. What makes you think he's around?"

"I tune into fields. Kipper has a very strong field, you know."

"Oh. You mean extrasensory perception?" Della had read about psychics who prey on the relatives of missing persons.

"No. Sensory." Riane had stopped scanning the room and was focusing on Della's face. "I could tell you're his mom. Same pattern of vibrations in the aura. Mine is dead."

"Your mother? Oh, I'm sorry."

"I know he's around because there are signs, see? I pick up the phone the other day and get this music, you know, made out of beeps from a touch-tone. Right there, I just pick it up and there is this tune. Kipper used to design music, you know, computer-assisted design."

"He did? I didn't know that."

"And the microwave, the microwave went on by itself. Plus the sign at the bank, one of those electronic signs that goes around and around? Well, it's been stuck for a week saying TIRED OF WAITING?" She paused and looked around for some further sign. "Well, if he comes by or anything . . ."

"Wait. Please don't go yet. You were one of his, uh, group? With Homer?"

Homer's name had no obvious effect on her face. "Yeah, the artist. I did the artwork. For some people that was just decoration. But Kipper always said, The art is half the game. I mean, if the mind was just a computer it would be one thing."

"So you worked on his game?"

Riane nodded and addressed herself to an invisible flaw in the fabric of her skirt. "Kipper must have said something about me."

"Well, I don't know. He didn't talk much about his work. After a certain point."

"I mean about me in particular." Riane looked up quickly from her lap.

Della felt a warmth rising in her, carrying promises as well as warnings. You could say the girl was attractive if you were willing to modify your standards in a certain direction. The hands, for example, were slender and long-fingered, as an artist's hands should be. But the nails were clipped off haphazardly and the face was bloodless and cold. "You knew him pretty well, then?"

"Mmm. He said there was a problem with his dad. Libra and Leo, there had to be trouble, right?"

"Libra? Oh yes." Libra was Steve's sign and Leo was Leo's. Della stood up nervously and offered Riane something cold to drink. The idea of someone like Riane in Steve's life was so new that she spilled the juice and had to wipe it up. For a moment she was embarrassed, imagining that it was Riane's kitchen and she was only the guest.

"So." Della set down the glasses. "Do you know where he went?"

"Well, Kipper wasn't supposed to tell anyone, that was part of the deal . . ."

"What do you mean 'deal'?"

"I know what he told me. Which isn't the whole thing." Riane rocked a little as she spoke, swinging one leg up and down. "It was supposed to be three months at the max, like computer camp, is how Kipper put it, you get food and a power source. What else do you need? That's what he said. It was supposed to be a privilege. You get what you need, they leave you alone."

"So he went somewhere to work on his game?"

"The game, yeah. That was the whole point."

"This is what I don't understand. The game. I mean, a game is a game. A game isn't real. It sounds so—"

"What?" Riane's eyes narrowed.

"Nothing. I mean, I know what Homer said about the game."

"Yeah; well, Homer didn't understand. That was part of the problem. It's an artform, see. You want to know, this is what Kipper said: A painter works with paint, a sculptor works with stone. With a game what you work with is patterns of thought. A game is an artwork using patterns of thought."

Riane seemed to be reading aloud from a statement written on the wall. "It's like a way of sculpting the brain," she added in her own words. "You play the game, the brain changes. It opens up, see, stuff flows in."

"I see," Della said finally. "I mean, the idea of the game as a kind of art. But who would know where he went? What about his boss at the university? Dr. Leitbetter. Did he send him to this place?"

"Send him? Anything that happens, you think there's one cause, there's really convergence." Riane nodded and widened her eyes. "That's how things happen, they get pushed by convergence."

"But when you didn't hear from Steve, from Kipper, and all that time went by?"

"Well, Homer said there was nothing to worry about." Riane returned to the study of her skirt. "He said that's how it works at these places. Very tight security, you know."

"What happened to Homer? Do you have any idea?"

"What happened?" Riane looked up, startled, and rose to go. "I don't know. It could have been lots of things. The forces were all converging in just one way."

■   ■   ■

The full story of Leitbetter's coup over Hershey leaked out slowly and in several different versions. Admittedly, Alex had been preoccupied for the last few days, getting iron grates put up over the windows of his apartment, for one thing, pricing alarm systems, even having a long technical discussion about handguns with Chris, the bartender, who offered to sell him one with the serial number filed off for just a few hundred dollars. But even with all this to keep him away from the complex, there was no real excuse for hearing nothing at all about what had happened to Della. In the only version that found its way to Alex, the big news was that Claire had not been fired, and this was taken as evidence that Hershey himself had come under her spiritual tutelage and had been recruited to the service of the Lamb.

So when Alex finally heard the story from Della he felt dumb and unprepared. "He fired you?"

"I resigned, same thing."

"Della, this is terrible. Why didn't you call me right away?"

"I was embarrassed. I am embarrassed."

"You mean you did it? But, Della, why in God's name?"

She told him in short drooping sentences. Her son. Did he know she had a son? Who used to work for Leitbetter. Grown now, twenty-one. Leitbetter was supposed to help find him. A simple exchange. The risk had been there all along, only she thought she would at least learn something. About her son, that is, and where he went.

"You mean you gave Leitbetter Hershey's data?"

"I told him what I knew."

"And the sample, you took him a virus-rich sample?"

"I didn't take him anything. It was all on the phone."

"Oh. Well. Because he'd got hold of a sample too, you know, so you're not the only leak."

Afterward, he was sorry for the way he said that, implying mitigating circumstances and some sort of crime. He was supposed to be clearheaded because of not getting drunk, but instead he had a sleeping-pill hangover, thick webs deep inside his eyes growing tighter and blocking the view. In fact, he had handled the whole thing abominably, letting the phone call taper off as if Della had drifted outside his jurisdiction and there was no more reason to talk. It was a lot to take in, the thought of Della enmeshed in her own system of plots and allegiances. He had thought of her as simple and guileless, an absorbent substance, the ideal woman.

He felt a tension in his jaw that only liquor could loosen, but it was too soon, there were rules now. He poured himself some fresh coffee and observed how firm his grip was, how steady his hand, although the dark stream was miles away and he had the sense that he was not doing things directly but only reading about how they were getting done. Della had mentioned some involvement with Leitbetter and he had let that slip by, too, like a piece of junk data that doesn't fit the hypothesis.

Leitbetter had used Della and tossed her away, that was the shameful part, the double deception. Probably he barely knew Della's son in the first place; there must be any number of bright kids who "worked for Leitbetter" for a summer or two, stuck away in some dark cubby with a computer for company or apprenticed out to a lab. Della had got caught between the gears, that was all, in the war between Leitbetter and the faculty. You could see the complex or any large-scale institution as a machine where the powerful squeeze up against each other and the weak get ground down to powder.

On the drive over to the complex he let himself into an old fantasy of purity and health. He would take a humble job at some remote mountaintop observatory, copying numbers from one page to another, sweeping if necessary. Simple stir-fry meals, regular hours of sleep. Eventually there would be a flicker in the data, a wink from out there, a quasar calling out through the light-years to him alone. But first there were some soiled, mundane things to take care of, just to get them out of the way.

The faculty lounge at this time of day was one of the more reliable gossip markets. Even in August there were always a few drinkers around, recovering from hours in the company of mice and machines or just waiting for the traffic to subside before going home. Alex shouldered up to a tall black figure at the bar and gave him a hearty "Hey, Darryll, how's it going?"

"Excuse me" was the only response, and the molecular biologist headed off to one of the tables, a drink in each hand.

Alex shrugged and decided there was no other choice, he would join the table of women by the window, although Greta, the immunologist, made him uneasy with her habit of peering through his skin to the sites of incipient illness, the fat-engorged liver and blackened lungs.

"Afternoon, ladies," he said with a gallant dip of the head.

Greta gave him a slow up-and-down look, assessing muscle tone, no doubt, postural defects. "If it isn't Alex MacBride."

"In person. May I join you?"

The other women looked from Alex to Greta, wide-eyed. "Sorry," she said levelly. "This is girl talk."

Alex retreated to the bar and thought of how dogs, in this kind of situation, shook themselves to shed the embarrassment. So let them talk about their periods or whatever it was. Fucking bull dyke. Then he did shake himself, involuntarily, and thought of upgrading his drink order to something more manly, but let the thought drift away.

Saul had come into the lounge and was looking around tentatively for someone to join. When Alex hailed him his expression changed to a scowl. "You have some nerve, Alex, coming in here."

"Oh, come on, Saul, it's only ginger ale."

"I don't mean that." He sat down, leaving a seat empty between Alex and himself, looking around warily.

"So where should I be? Rehab somewhere?"

"I'm talking about Hershey, Alex, or is it already out of your mind, the memory traces dissolved in ethanol?"

Alex held his face steady, sensing that the slightest tremor could be held against him. Saul returned the stare, then looked down in disgust. "What happened to Hershey could happen to any of us. You know that. This isn't science anymore, this is banditry. When a man's work can be stolen from right under his nose. This is barbarism."

"Right." Alex said it slowly, optimistically, like a tutor with a slow student.

"So maybe Hershey was slipping. But that's no excuse."

Alex nodded cautiously. Across the room he could see the three women look at him and then close ranks again.

"Jesus, Alex, why did you do it?"

"Do it?"

"Don't be funny, all right? Everyone knows you've got your nose stuffed six inches into Leitbetter's rectal cavity. Doing his 'special projects.' Like espionage, huh? With your girlfriend conveniently planted in Hershey's lab, your little spy. Let me tell you something, we get Leitbetter on this, and there's a damn good chance we will, you're furniture, MacBride, you're finished."

This was beyond insult. Alex studied Saul's pale, stubby face and thought of throwing a punch that would smash his extra-heavy prescription glasses into his watery eyes. It was so easy to cross the line dividing words and comment from the ancient language of force. Holding that lovely little .38 in his hand in the kitchen of the Baycrest, he had felt the clear temptation. Just fuck it, all of you, shut up and leave me alone. Screams, a spray of red, the hot surge of competence and release. But he hadn't bought the gun and he wasn't going to hurt poor earnest, hardworking Saul. "What do you say we have a real drink?" he said, and rapped the bar with his knuckles to get the bartender's attention.

Saul shook his head tightly. "I don't want to hear any of that malarkey. The 'Leitbetter perspective.' Shit, science isn't about glorious 'Visitors' coming out of the sky. Science is a game, Al, period. You sneak up on it, whatever it is, and try to choke it till it tells you something, the finding of the day."

He grimaced and looked around the room again. "This is madness, utter madness, where he's been taking us. You didn't have to help him along."

"Who says I did?"

"Everyone knows what happened. You and your 'special project.' Nazis, ha ha. A nice little cover for microbiological espionage, huh?"

"And Leitbetter? How does he explain how he got the stuff?"

Saul looked momentarily confused. "He hasn't said anything. Just a press release saying that he's isolated the virus. Meanwhile, Hershey's on indefinite medical leave. So what?"

"So obviously I need to have words with him. Is he around?"

"How would I know? I'm not his boy."

The bartender slid over the usual double with rocks and Alex raised the glass toward Saul. "You know why you're so bitter? Because you're a failure, Saul, just like me. Only you're still pretending to have a career, a meaningful life, a contribution to make. You admire my openness, that's all. I do it with a little more flair."

Then, in the manner of someone performing a magic trick, he

took a long swallow of the drink, set it back down, and strode out of the lounge.

■ ■ ■

It was a long hike to Leitbetter's office and Alex didn't like roaming around the complex after hours. Not that he'd ever seen anything beyond a few loose mice, but the thing was, no one would miss you. Unless you had an actual class scheduled, no one would miss you for days.

But Leitbetter had gone too far this time, crushing Hershey, crushing Della, and if Saul was a fair barometer of faculty opinion, it looked as if Alex was next. Why had he ever imagined himself exempt?—that was the question that made Saul's insults relevant. He'd thought he had some special status, the childhood buddy, so to speak. He'd thought he'd always drift along in Leitbetter's wake, nourished by the crumbs, safe from the storm, and so forth. This was his big mistake.

But no more of that. End of illusions, end of era. He moved quickly, fortified by righteous anger and what he had managed to swallow of the drink. In his mind he savored the speech he would deliver to Leitbetter: (A) You tricked Della Markson into spying for you and then you stood by when she got fired. Yes, you know who I mean. (B) You're letting the rumor flourish that I had some part in that sordid transaction. Which is entirely incidental and insignificant compared to the fact that (C) You tossed me out into the Relnik business knowing damn well it was neck deep in armed and vicious thuggery. You probably even know why everyone is armed and dangerous—the secret, that is, of my own forthcoming death. And (D) Well, damnit, people aren't beetles, Richard—he would call him that, but mockingly—no matter how dumb you think they are.

Della, for example. Then he began to wonder how much he should get into that with Leitbetter. There was something almost maudlin about the story: abandoned wife, searching for her lost son, etc. It was the part about a son that he tended to forget, since the idea of a family didn't fit with his conception of her as a student, his student, empty and waiting to be filled. Better to dwell on the theft of Hershey's work. If the faculty actually believed that he, Alex, had had a hand in that, then he might as well go back to drinking full-time, because he would never get a job again, not in academic science, anyway.

He checked his watch. The E Corridor was the fastest way between the towers and Alex wished he knew of an alternative. All these years and he didn't have a clear map of the complex in his head, just a set of instructions for his feet: Go straight, then turn left, take the nearest elevator . . . If there was a diagram it might require more than three dimensions, what with the skyways that linked the towers at odd angles, the elevators that stopped at some floors and not others, the sealed-off areas, the shortcuts through working labs, the walls where doors and windows should have been. He wasn't even sure if a floor plan existed. But then there were so many things he didn't understand and had never bothered to find out: Why lightning is forked and never straight. Where the caterpillars came from and where they went when they died. What was really in the Relnik papers, if anything at all.

He passed the old, contaminated labs with their skull-and-crossbone warnings and imagined he could see inside to the bodies of dead scientists, preserved by the cleansing force of unnatural, fanatic isotopes. It was just that he and Dick went back so far, that was what hurt, to the time when Dick had been an overeager guy who liked to stay up late and talk and then bustle out into the campus fog, still talking, shouting even, under the streetlights and on into nearly empty buses. Plus the fact that Dick had known his own younger self, a drunkard, to be sure, and a verbal show-off, but the kind of person people made room for at crowded tables and rose to greet in bars. Take Dick away and there was no witness to the past. Failure was everywhere and eternal.

■   ■   ■

In the outer office a red-eyed Phyllis was keyboarding furiously. "What's the matter," Alex said, "forced to work through happy hour?"

"Never mind. Allergies. And no, you can't go in. Alex! I *said*—"

But Alex had already entered the deep, reliable air conditioning of Leitbetter's inner office. The shades were drawn, so that the only light came from the desk lamp, illuminating a disheveled Leitbetter standing behind his desk, sorting papers into foot-high stacks. "Al, listen, I'm awfully busy, if you don't mind."

"Well, I'm awfully pissed, if you don't mind."

"I know, we never had our little talk. But as you can see."

"Goddamnit, Richard, listen to me. Do you have any idea of what you've done, the way you've been—"

"Now, let me see." Leitbetter looked up quickly, mockingly, and then back down at his papers. "I'm a pitiful degenerate version of the scientist you once knew, right? A narcissist, a martinet, a vain and callow bully. You think I haven't played every possible criticism over and over in my mind? Ripping off the faculty's research grants with 30 percent overhead rates. Underpaying the peons. Cheapening science with my crude sensationalism. Stealing Hershey's disease. But you know something, Al? I don't give a flying fuck, as we used to say when we were young and clearheaded." He laughed and began to sort through another file full of papers.

"You're stepping down?"

"Out. Out of the whole blighted era. What does it say about our time, after all, if someone as wicked as I am supposed to be could be running one of the world's largest and most respected research institutes? An institute dedicated to the selfless search for truth. Not the kind of century you'd want to hang out in, is it, Al?"

"You don't seem to be taking this too seriously, Dick. People are trying to kill me. Other people think I helped lift Hershey's data for you. I don't know which is worse, but I want a statement right now, on tape."

"Fair enough, I owe you that. Tape's on, see?" Leitbetter cleared his throat and appeared to be speaking for the tape now, first looking at Alex and then casting about for a more congenial audience among the objects in the room. "The business with Hershey's disease, or the Leitbetter Syndrome, as I expect it will henceforth be known, was one last attempt to salvage the financial situation. The fact is, Hershey was getting nowhere with the disease. Arguably, he was fucking up. Probably the whole business would have escaped my attention if it were not for that religious lunatic in his lab, in direct violation, I might add, of complex-wide security rules . . .

"Stimmerman, you see, was willing to fund the disease, but he wanted it in competent hands. That was his condition, that I take it away from Hershey, and the amount promised would have kept us all afloat for another six months at least. Will, if it ever comes in. That's why I did it, Al. For this place, for all of you.

"And let me say here for the record that Professor MacBride had nothing to do with my recent microbiological coup. Bradley Soo himself brought me the viral sample and he will now be leading the effort. Della Markson kindly assessed me of Hershey's progress, if you could call it that, as seen, of course, through a layperson's eyes."

Leitbetter switched off the tape and cocked his head teasingly at Alex. "But it's only natural for people to think you were involved. Everyone knows you're having an affair with the Markson woman—"

"An affair? What are you saying?"

"Not that you had the courtesy to fill me in on your new alliances."

"Fill you in? Who the fuck do you think you—" Alex lunged across the desk, grabbed Leitbetter by the collar, and shook the smile off his face. It was insubordination, assault and battery, but it felt good and useful and clean—until Alex noticed that Leitbetter wasn't bothering to resist.

"Don't hit, all right?" Leitbetter shrank back limply. "No bruises. I can't have any bruises."

"Why? Camera crew on the way?"

"No, real thing this time. So to speak." Leitbetter shook himself weakly as Alex loosened his grip. "Now take it easy, okay? I hear rumors, I assumed you were somehow in league with her."

"What's to be in league with? She was my student. We had coffee. And how am I supposed to find the time for an affair, huh? with these goons chasing me all the time. Not to mention it's none of your fucking business, anyway."

"Really?" Leitbetter adjusted his collar, still looking wary.

"Really what? Now look, you're going to start from the beginning, all right? Sit down; but if you give me any more bullshit I'm going to be on your side of the desk so fast you won't know what hit you. And by bullshit I mean that story about Martime Stimmerman. He doesn't care about the disease. That's just a cover. He's after the Relnik papers. In fact, he bought them up from the grandniece the day before I got there. Relnik's scientific papers, lab notes, the whole thing. I could have told you this weeks ago, only you never could 'squeeze me in.'"

"Oh, I know. It's Martime's people who got me chasing after the Relnik papers in the first place."

"They: The Harvest Enterprises, right? Or some such agricultural notion. Here's another thing I don't get, Dick: why you would let a shady outfit like that virtually take over the complex. Gangsters, for all practical purposes."

"Stimmerman told you the name?"

"You paid me to investigate, didn't you? The Harvest Enterprises: ostensibly an information and software firm based in Mexico City. A branch in California somewhere."

"Well, if you'd investigated, you'd know they're not gangsters, Al. They're visionaries."

"From the beginning. What is this Harvest business and what do they want from the goddamn papers? For a start."

"All right, all right. They started funding us, oh, five years ago." Leitbetter pushed his hair back with both hands and stared past Alex into the gloom. "Let's just say I had no idea how large their operation is, the range of methods. When they first asked me to hunt up the Relnik papers, they said, 'They're in your region.' Region? And what was I, branch manager? 'Neighborhood,' they said. 'That's all we meant.' And I still didn't see that they had carved up most of the scientific world, that they already had Beckworth at Harvard, Zinsser at Cambridge, D'Albert at Louvain. I was only one fly in the web. Yes, a very small part of the scheme.

"They paid me well. I was privy to all their special reports, data bases, conferences, luxury retreats. Still, I didn't like the idea of being sent on an errand. Relnik's grandniece wouldn't sell the papers, so some new approach was required. I was annoyed, frankly; I mean, I can't just run around on errands. My face is recognizable, they should have known.

"So I sent this, uh, research assistant. Partly to get him off my hands, of course, and—"

Alex interrupted. "You said intern before."

"Does it matter? Intern doing the work of a research assistant. So he dug up whatever articles he could in the library, went out to visit the family, somehow managed to get the grandniece to let him look at the papers there, and, uh . . . Well, he drew up a report, at my request, of course, which I sent along to Stimmerman at The Harvest. And they were extremely interested, what can I say?"

"Keep talking, Dick. What was in the report?"

"I don't have much time, really."

"So let's not spend it trading punches. You'd get hurt as bad as I would."

A trace of a smile came over Leitbetter's face. "Remember that time when I had to pull you out of the Ratskeller before some frat boys destroyed your face? You got two of them before I got you out."

"I thought it was three. Now goddamnit, will you finish the story."

"Well, all I can say about the report is that it took him a month to put together and it ended with a request that he be given full time to work out the, uh, psychocybernetic aspects of Relnik's theories. That's a new discipline, I suppose—computer-brain interface and so forth. Other than that, it was mostly diagrams, mathematical notations. Over my head. All I could make out from the bits of narrative is that it was something highly speculative. Technological. So do I know what's in those papers? What the big secret is? If anything? The answer is no. That's what you were supposed to find out."

"Where is this research assistant?"

"I don't know that either. Long story short, they brought him out to California and gave him a job, but it didn't work out. I don't know the details. Really."

"So?"

Leitbetter breathed in deeply and continued. "All I know is that I got a call from Stimmerman sometime back in the spring. He was upset, extremely upset. He blamed it all on me."

"What all?"

"The kid leaving, taking things with him. It wasn't supposed to happen. Anyway, Stimmerman said they were going to have to start all over. From scratch. They wanted a completely fresh look at the Relnik papers, the idea being to reconstruct, I suppose, whatever—"

"Which is where I came in, right? The fresh look. Why didn't you tell me all this so I could have had some idea of what to look for when it was my turn to go running after the Relnik papers?"

"Because I had no idea what to look for myself. And the rest of it—well, The Harvest prefers to remain in the background. They've been victims of ridiculous rumors in the past, because of the size of their assets, of course, as well as their . . . theories, and I, well, have always honored their desire for anonymity. That's why I couldn't fill you in. I'm sorry it had to be that way. Now, would you mind if I get back to work here? I'm going to have to make my exit very soon, cryonically, that is."

"Don't change the subject, Dick. I'd like to know why you didn't just give them all the papers and let them do the 'reconstructing' themselves. Especially when I started getting these threats."

"Oh, I did. I mean, I gave them . . . just about everything. But there had been some, well, erosion of trust. Stimmerman had gotten the idea that I was perhaps engaged in some sort of double cross, starting with when the kid, uh, left them. He blamed me for that."

"And were you? Engaged in some little game of your own?"

Leitbetter lifted a paper from one of his piles, glanced at it slowly, defiantly, and then replaced it in a second pile. "Well, I was thinking we might just take a look, you know, ourselves. There's obviously something of a great deal of value in there, and I don't mean just the commercial applications."

"You mean you've had me risking my life on the off chance I might be able to help you squeeze some patent or something out of the Relnik papers? Why, you probably never gave them all the papers you had. Or that I have. They probably figured I had something they don't have."

"Conjecture, Al. Sheer conjecture."

Alex leaned across the desk again. "Damnit, Dick, do you have any idea what you've done? You ruined Hershey. You got Della fired. You've got me living like a fugitive, trying to shake off the thugs who've been following me around. The thing with you, Dick, everyone is expendable. Completely expendable."

Leitbetter stood up on his side of the desk and shouted back into Alex's face: "Everyone *is* expendable, if you want to know the truth. Compared to what has to be done. Compared to the only thing that matters. Do you know what Gelph's data mean? On the Index of Mass Anxiety? They mean there is a goddamn good chance human civilization is going to collapse before the Visitor gets here. Yes, collapse. We may only have a few decades, a few *years*, to gather up all of human knowledge and condense it into portable form before—"

"You actually believe that shit?"

"You never listened, did you? All these years. Yes, of course I believe it. I still agree with them on everything that matters. The general outlines, anyway. The need to gather up knowledge, condense it, preserve it for the moment of extraterrestrial contact. My God, Alex, what do you think I've been *doing* all this time? Living for? What is *anybody* doing? There's only one thing that matters, one purpose, one goal—"

"Dick, this is—" But there was no point. It came to Alex with the force of a terrible giddiness that all the silly, cartoonish themes running through WOW and Leitbetter's televised interviews were not just cynical efforts to popularize science to the bored and slow-witted public. They were what Leitbetter actually believed, his personal metaphysical infrastructure, a religion almost: giant beings in space, the Visitor coming to gather the fruit of all human endeavor and inquiry.

". . . and I'm going to be there," Leitbetter was saying. "I'm going to be frozen."

"Frozen?"

"Deanimation. Liquid-nitrogen refrigeration. Am I making myself clear? Time travel, ha ha, the only form available."

"Dick, what are you saying? Nobody's ever been revived. The name for that is suicide."

Leitbetter straightened himself, switched on the tape, and addressed an uninhabited spot in the middle of the room. "Deanimation, I want it known, is my free choice. Everything has been arranged, calculated. It's a reputable firm. None of this business of half price for the head alone, everyone packed in a suburban meat locker. The cryotorium is located in a quake-free zone, stocked for all eventualities—post-nuclear, post–meteor hit, post–ice cap meltdown. Ice age they can do nothing about, of course, but I can easily ride that out.

"My wife will be comfortably provided for by the amount now in our joint account. Another sum has been transferred in my name to a Caribbean bank. With the interest that will have accumulated at the time of reanimation, I will be able to pursue my interests in financial tranquillity. As for the date of reanimation . . ."

There should be some satisfaction in this, Alex thought, too stupefied to move or interrupt. How many times are we surpassed by a friend only to see him destroyed by his own illusions? But the gloom was softening Leitbetter's features, making him look foolish and hopeful. Alex tried to think of something to say that would subtract twenty years from the scene. Words came to his mind, anecdotes, jokes, whole narratives, things that young men talk about on that upward slope of life's beginning, before the plateau has come into sight, the inevitable descent on twisting paths through landscapes strewn with bones. He started to speak, but he was afraid any sound that came would be something less than speech.

"It's all right, Al." Leitbetter hugged his arms to his chest and shivered. "I want to go. It's my dream, it's my life, everything. I want to be there when the Visitor comes."

There was a buzz followed by Phyllis's voice on the speaker phone. "They're here now. The cryonics people. Dr. Brabant and his team."

CHAPTER 13

"What are you waiting for?" It was Sister Bertha, rising from the static. Della sat up straight, expecting to see a figure at the foot of the bed, made out of shadows, pulling on the sheet. "How long before you come to life?"

Then chaos again, the fretful, jaw-tightening sound of unprocessed radio waves. Della knew better than to search for Sister Bertha with the tuning dial. It was better to lie there, gauging the menace of the morning light, and wait till she came back on.

"What did Mary feel when she heard the news? I'll tell you what she felt. When Mary heard she was afraid. Why me? is what she thought. For Mary was a quiet girl, easy to take for dull. She rose to fetch her mother, but the angel said, 'It's you I come for, Mary. God knows all women by their name and He has picked you out.'

"Now, it was not as one-sided as they make it sound, because the angel turns to Mary then and says, 'Are you willing, girl? It's up to you.' And Mary did not answer right away.

"At last she said: 'You want me to take the Lord into me, to dwell in me and make from me some flesh to wear? Am I a vessel that wine pours from that does not flavor the wine? Any plain woman can bear a child of her own, so why should I be less?'

"Then the angel felt tired and leaned against the wall. 'Oh, Mary,' he said, putting his hand to his forehead and letting his wings droop down, 'you think God is not shaped by what you humans do? You think the Spirit works in clay but no clay touches It?'

"Because here is the truth that the angel said: The ship leaves its mark on the sea. The leaf deflects the wind. All that God touches touches Him. Why, each thing that falls bends the lines of force so the next thing must take a different path. Yes, creation lives and works back on its Maker!

" 'Oh, Mary, please!' the angel said. 'All these years the marching of men, the trampling, the scuffling, the sneaking around, have left their mark on God. He feels it when the branch is broke and the sandal presses down on grass. The fist that shakes in air, it beats on Him. I have seen His face, dear Mary, and He is aging fast.'

" 'Yes, He is sick and aging,' the angel said. 'And if He cannot get Himself reborn through you, the world itself will soon wear down. The stars will fade and the sun will be a candle flame at noon.'

" 'Believe me, Mary, many will see God's human face, but only you will know what lies beneath the skin. Surely, that is enough.' "

There was a silence, not static, just silence itself. Then Sister Bertha's voice returned.

"And we will never know, will we, how it felt to contain the Lord, whether He entered her as liquid or as fire. You want to know, the Book says nothing. And did she cry then, or shriek or tremble? Or did she laugh, to feel the form of things, the pattern out of which all things are made, turn inside out and enter her? We do not know, my friends. All we know is, she said yes."

■　■　■

From the window of her second-story apartment, Maisy saw the white woman heading down the sidewalk that ran through the grass to building N4, where Maisy lived. Everyone else was looking out too, even holding babies up to stare, because you didn't get white women coming alone to this place, not even caseworkers would come alone anymore, just junkie-type women too chewed up by the drug to wait on the street for their dealer to show. The one time before was a redheaded woman kids found in the stairwell, turned from white to blue, with the syringe still sticking up out of her arm and wobbling when they came to move her.

After the knock Maisy counted to seven before getting up and opening the door. "Why, Mrs. Markson," she said, noting the other doors along the corridor each open a crack for purposes of entertainment and spying. "Well, don't just stand there in the hall, come on in."

"I'm sorry, just barging in like this."

"You got my message I left for you with the agency?"

"No. You left me a message?"

"I didn't know how to reach you, so I left word with the agency. But here, why don't you come on in and give your feet a rest."

They sat down at the table, which took up half the living room, and Maisy tried to reckon with the fact of a white woman who was not there to deliver some kind of official warning or instruction. Della didn't even look like a member of the employer category anymore, with her hair moving around in various directions and half circles hanging from her eyes.

"Steve came by. Couple of days ago, came and went."

"He was here? He's alive, then. I knew it."

"I only saw him for a minute or so, then off he goes again. Children let him in before I got home. My sister's children are with me now."

"How was he?" Della asked. "I mean, did he look all right?"

"Well, clothes a little messy, but then he's been on the road. Men chasing him, he said, and I said, Police? And he said, No, nothing to do with police. They've been chasing him a long time. Weeks. Wherever he goes, they show up soon enough."

"Why didn't you tell me right away?"

"Mrs. Markson, I tried. I left a message with the agency, I told you that. Where was I going to reach you? I didn't know where you'd gone to, and I wasn't about to call Mr. Markson. Steve said he would go see you except maybe the news get from you to Mr. Markson one way or the other and he didn't want his father in on this . . . You all right, Mrs. Markson?"

Maisy could see she was rocking in her chair. It looked like waves were coming over her and maybe she couldn't take anything in unless it hit her near one of the crests. Things were never 100 percent with that woman even in the best of times, when she had her house and son. "Look," Maisy said with the intent of being reasonable and nudging the visit toward a courteous end, "I wish I could help you, Mrs. Markson. I always liked that boy. But he was out of here real fast. You know there's people want to know what your boy knows, whatever he figured out."

"They could offer him money, then. Why would they be chasing him?"

"He has no use for money, Mrs. Markson, a boy like Steve."

"Della. You could call me Della."

"So the money didn't work, they took to chasing. Think about it, everyone's being chased by someone. No one chasing you, how're you going to know where you're supposed to go? Even the people doing the chasing, usually someone's right behind, chasing them."

"What if they hurt him?"

"Well, look. Not much we can do, right?" Maisy sighed and looked around, trying to signal the end. "Same with all the children. They fall into your hand and then you look one day and they floated off. Everything you did for them, it just floated off too. Isn't that just the way, though? You give and give and there ain't no giveback coming. Sooner or later, everything's taken away."

Della sat there, not moving, not even rocking, taking this in. "You listen to Sister Bertha, don't you?"

There was a long silence in which Maisy calculated this was not going to end so fast. "I guess so. I get a chance, I listen some."

"So do I. I found her on the Walkman. You left it, you know."

"I don't need it. I got a radio here and a TV set."

"Did he say where he was going?"

"Didn't say and I didn't ask. Men chasing him, I don't want them chasing me."

Still, Della sat there staring at the couch where Steve perhaps had sat. "Sister Bertha says give up all you have. Why, do you think?"

"Jesus said that too, Mrs. Markson."

"I don't see why someone would have to give up their son."

"Oh, Lord." An expression between worry and distaste came over Maisy's face. "There's nothing about why. How are we going to know why? Maybe what she wants us to do is just one step in some whole plan. Maybe God looked down and didn't like what he saw, the way everything's piling up in a few people's hands. Maybe nothing's going to move ahead until people give stuff away and break those piles down. Maybe it's the things want to move, you got to think of that too. It's a matter of motion and everything's blocked.

"Because you look out this window, tell me what you see. The trees are dead. No leaves on them since May. The children got worms in them, sores on their faces. The men they just stand there all hours of the day. Everything's stuck, Mrs. Markson. Nothing's moving along. Sister Bertha says stuff's gotta move along.

"Why, your son could have told you that, could have told you a lot better than me."

"Steve listened to Sister Bertha?"

Maisy turned to her slowly. "Now, what do you think?"

■ ■ ■

Someone was holding his hand. Wrist, he corrected himself, not hand. There were fingers on his wrist. Alex jerked his arm away and tried to sit up in the same motion, but black circles rolled smoothly into place before his eyes and began to fuse, forming a chute, a tunnel he was required to enter. At the last moment he pulled himself back, exposing a stretch of naked belly in the process, landing with his head on the pillow.

"Mr. Stimmerman," a voice was saying, the voice that went with the fingers. "He's awake now but a little weak. I'll order up some juice."

"Alex, at last. A rough night, yes? You seem much calmer now, that's good."

It was Martime, and it was not a hospital or a jail. A hotel room, more likely, judging from the color scheme of peach and moss green and the absence of movable objects. Alex winced against the light, but darkness brought no improvement. Pain was everywhere, pounding out a single message: Learn! Learn! But learn what? What was the lesson supposed to be? With further effort he could see that the headache was his and not a feature of the room, and that there was a television set, flickering blue without the sound. Alex groaned and pulled the sheet up over his chest. If they wanted to kill him they could; there was no point in making a fuss.

"Where are my clothes?"

"Poor thing. It is disconcerting to wake up naked and in a strange place, I am sure, but you might be a little bit grateful. We have been up most of the night."

"What happened?"

"By the time we arrived, the action was mercifully over. We found you in an abandoned laboratory in your Human Ecology Complex, bound and quite tightly gagged. The expectation seems to have been that you would eventually die behind a locked door proclaiming HAZARDOUS RADIATION ZONE. That is why we had to dispose of the clothing, though the doctor assures me the dose was nothing a nuclear power plant employee could not handily absorb in a day. No great loss, that suit, by the way."

"The E Corridor" was all Alex could think of to say.

"You put up quite a struggle, perhaps confusing us with your prior assailants. It took four of us, you should be flattered to know, to get you showered and out of that place. You were quite a handful, my dear Alex, until the sedative took hold."

Alex struggled to find the images that would go with Martime's account, but there was no memory beyond Leitbetter's face, hanging there in the darkness, luminous and filled with hope.

"Dick? Did you get Dick out?"

"His office was empty by the time we arrived. There were signs of a struggle, but the struggle was probably with you. And it was ridiculously easy to find you, I might add. A trail of blood from the blow on the head, here a drop, there a drop, led us to you."

"Oh God, they got him."

"Yes, Dr. Kentwell Brabant, director of the SKD Institute, so-called, for Cryobiology and Life Extension 'got' him." Martime laughed.

"You knew they were going to do this?"

"The thought had come to me. Your Dr. Leitbetter was not the most discreet of individuals."

" 'Was.' My God."

"Well, what am I to say—'will be'? Really, the tense is not clear in such cases. You have the past and possibly the future. Only the present is missing."

"You think they'll actually freeze him?"

"Why not? He signed papers, didn't he? This way we are not looking at murder. We are looking at voluntary deanimation in the service of life extension. It happens more frequently than anyone realizes and the clients are overwhelmingly scientists. Much the same as for your sperm banks: men who have position, power, even fame, and wish to add only immortality to the list. A fine reward for so much vanity, don't you think?"

"Dick was my friend, at one point."

"Ah, Alex, I would waste no tears on that one. He tricked us. We funded him generously, and in exchange he was supposed to have sent us—how shall I put it?—Relnik's secret. But he intended all the time to keep it for himself, of that I am quite sure. Otherwise, how to explain, for example, your role? A biography of Henry Relnik, ha ha. Your Leitbetter was—how would you say?—playing both sides of the court—pretending to work for us but actually embarked on his own private project. Yes."

Alex shut his eyes with the intention of starting again, finding a new way into the day, the morning, whatever, finding a door that led somewhere else. "Look, I need to borrow some clothes."

"I have sent my assistants out to find you some. I cannot guarantee the fit, but I daresay they will be an improvement, whatever they bring. In the meantime—oh, thank you, Hector—here is the breakfast." A short compact man, a Mexican of somewhat more ancient lineage than Martime, Alex guessed, placed a tray on the bed next to him, whispered to Martime, and left.

"Yes, any minute there will be clothes now. The hotel is most obliging. A nice lightweight suit that some other guest will lose in the dry cleaning. So while we are here, enjoying a rare moment of leisure, perhaps we could resolve this Relnik business. I will admit I was hoping to find some especially illuminating samples of his work among your Leitbetter's effects, but alas."

"You went through his things?"

"Mmm. Please. Take a bite, a sip."

"What about the papers you bought from Riane?"

"Ah, you did not know? The papers that I purchased are unfortunately worthless, even the cryptologists agree. Lab notes, columns of numbers, the occasional anatomical sketch. Possibly I was deliberately defrauded by that unhealthy-looking girl. So all that remains is the set of papers you have—the ones that Leitbetter gave to you."

"And you want them."

"More than ever I do."

Alex took a bite of egg and fought the impulse to gag. If he ate, he would vomit; if he didn't, he would faint; and somewhere between those alternatives there must be mere queasiness and an upright stance. He had nothing to bargain with, but then, it was no longer so clear what he should be bargaining for. "You have my wallet?"

Martime smiled. "Slightly irradiated. I would not carry it too close to the gonads, if you have any thought of a family."

"And keys?"

"Mm-hmm. And when you are perking up a bit we will go out, won't we? And pick up the papers?"

Alex let his head roll back on the pillow, only half feigning exhaustion. He needed to find a way to get beyond the blank wall in his memory to see who had ambushed him. He had assumed

Brabant, but it could have been Leitbetter, or even Martime and his movable staff of confederates. This was the third time he had been with Martime, and he realized he had no clearer conception of him than he had had on that first night in the dark of the terrace. He had no obvious nationality—"Martime" sounding Spanish and "Stimmerman" German—and no clear commitment to gender. No personality either, and no consistent motivation—otherwise why had he told Alex so much? Even his coloring, with dark eyes pitted against pale blond hair, seemed to be a compromise of some kind, a cancellation of forces. Gangster or friend, philanthropist or thug? Alex propped his head up and narrowed his eyes for focus. "I have a question."

"Only one?"

"You told Dick you were interested in the disease. With me it's always Relnik. I mean, what's your game, if you don't mind my asking?"

"My game?" Martime laughed, the blue light from the TV dancing grotesquely across his face. "They are different approaches, that is all, to the same problem your Dr. Leitbetter spoke so eloquently about: the smallness of the brain compared to the enormity of the task—a brain, at best, designed for strolling in the Serengeti with a pointed stick for a weapon. Only so many neurons, so many connections between them, and hence only so many thinkable thoughts—"

Alex groaned. "I asked you a straight question."

"For shame, Alex. You want the plot without the guiding metaphysic, like any foolish child in your WOW course. I am explaining that this is a very special virus, one that is capable of rewiring the brain, multiplying the number of synaptic connections, expanding the number of thinkable thoughts, the entire capacity. For what is intelligence, if not a measure of the sheer density of synaptic connections? You see the potential.

"Hershey's lab was close to seeing this, or rather that devilishly clever Pakistani was. Obviously we could not leave this precious virus in the hands of your microbe hunters, to be stalked and pulverized and fractionated and forced to confess its true nature."

"My God, Martime, whatever else it does, it kills people."

"For now, yes. But no germ or virus can survive if it continues to destroy its hosts. You know this yourself. A less virulent strain will evolve, as happened once with tuberculosis, syphilis, any number of things."

"You mean you're going to just let it run its merry course until it settles down and lives peaceably in the brain?"

Martime cocked his head to one side. "A small experiment. That is all. A sideline. It may come to nothing, of course."

"You would do that? Jesus. So it must have been you, then, who ransacked my apartment. Tried to feed me poisoned booze."

"Ah, my friend, your feelings are hurt—a condition you would like me to experience too. But The Harvest is like anything else. There are factions, disagreements as to methods and urgency. You have met my cousin Kentwell Brabant. He takes one approach, I take quite another. Personally, of course, I cannot approve of the things that you mention, I hope you will accept my word."

"You're *cousins?*"

"You did not know that? Yes, yes, cousins—I thought it was obvious. Dora had a child, Henry Relnik's child, who was brought out of Germany with the Erntegruppe and raised by Dora's brother-in-law and his wife. In Mexico. That child was my father. The brother-in-law had also a daughter of his own, who grew to become Kentwell's mother. We inherited the family business, so to speak, Kentwell and myself."

Alex propped himself up on his elbow, staring dumbly at Martime's face, still blue-lit by the TV light. There were lines which could have come only from Dora, the sweep of cheekbone, the eyebrow's lift. But the smile that was always looking for some excuse to break through—could that be Relnik's, living on after so many years?

"Well. Enough." Martime stood up briskly and switched on a lamp. "You are much better now, I can see. It is time for our little errand."

"Our little errand?"

"To get the papers, Alex. And look, your clothes have at last arrived. Excellent. Here, Hector will help you to dress."

Alex insisted he could do it himself and stumbled into the bathroom with a towel around his waist. He washed and tried to judge the time from the stubble on his cheeks. One in the morning? Four? The clothes were tight, the pants a little short, but the shoes, at least, were his own. He had the feeling of a man who is about to be executed and is allowed to put a few last hygienic touches on the body that will soon be trash. The feeling only grew as they walked out through the corridors, Martime in the lead and Alex between Hector and what appeared to be another Hector, equally squat and silent.

They came out through a back door into a parking lot. "So, Alex, how are you holding up?" Martime had a hearty, optimistic tone, more appropriate to morning than the dead, empty center of night. "We go to the Human Ecology Complex, am I not right? I doubt very much you would keep anything so important in your apartment. In the complex—what do you call it? Hell?—there is no shortage of space."

Alex shivered although the air was hot and clingy. They were standing in front of a black car of indeterminate make which one of the Hectors was unlocking. Of course, it could have been Martime and his pre-Columbian thugs who had ransacked the apartment, not Brabant at all. Alex held back, trying to arrange his feet on a stable part of the ground, one that he could count on not to shift and buckle. "What if I don't want to do this?"

A jolt of tension passed between the three other men, the motion of feet edging imperceptibly apart for the improvement of balance and thrust. Alex shrugged and slid into the back seat, as indicated, next to a Hector. "No problem. The complex. The bowels of hell, in fact."

They drove along the turnpike, slowly, obedient to all the lights. Alex saw that some semblance of normalcy had been maintained during his absence from the outdoor world. At least a few of the fast-food places still had lights on and cars in the parking lots. He knew he should think, should prepare for whatever was coming,

but for a plan you need a goal, and for a goal you need an orientation, a point of view, and he could no longer remember his.

"Alex, listen." Martime was leaning back from the front seat,
cold neon lights moving over his face as they drove. "It is important
to me that you do this willingly. Can you believe that I actually
care?"

"What does it matter? For you everything is justified, right? Because you happen to know the meaning of life."

"Purpose, Alex, not meaning. For what, after all, is your 'meaning'? A warm feeling, an artistic nuance, a wisp, a touch of kitsch.
'Meaning' is merely human. Purpose comes from somewhere else."

"The Visitor? Or rather, the Intermediate Beings who are going
to send the Visitor? I heard this already from Dick, his fatal delusion.
He got it from you, didn't he?"

"Delusion, Alex? Think. What have human beings been doing
for the last fifty or so millennia? Reproducing, is it not so? And
occasionally figuring something out about the situation in which
they find themselves. The 'universe,' as the situation is known. What
is the purpose of all this reproducing? To make sure that there will
be some humans still living when the Visitor arrives. And what is
the purpose of this learning, this figuring out? To make sure that
when the Visitor comes, those who are here will have something
to report." Martime laughed. "The ideas of The Harvest are not a
delusion. They are an explanation."

"And what if your Visitor never comes? What if no one out there
gives a shit?"

"Ah, it is possible, remotely possible. Anything is possible, but
some things are too sad to be true."

"Too sad? Look, as far as I can see, Relnik's big point was that
learning is pleasurable in itself—which is a pretty good justification
for science without dragging in the extraterrestrials." Alex leaned
forward toward the front seat until he felt Hector's hand on his
arm, pulling him back. "Damnit, you've got Relnik twisted all
around, even if he is your granddad. The point isn't to use the
pleasure center to drive the mind to learn. Pleasure is a good enough
end in itself."

"Well put, Alex. But do we not also seek to learn things that will be painful to know? Did you not, for an example, make an inter-library request for further information on medical experimentation in the death camps? Do not ask how I know; I have been funding your complex for years now and have many sources within it. The point is, your foolish philosophy of hedonism goes so far and no further. The desire to know is stronger than anything. And this is because—do I have to tell you? you who are a scientist?—the universe *desires* to be known. It demands to be beheld."

"Fine. So what's the rush?"

It was Martime's turn to stare out the window. They were on the service road now, only minutes away from the complex, going through flat empty places with leafless trees and abandoned construction equipment.

"There are those who believe that we have very little time to prepare for the Visitor. Even some who believe that the Visitor is already here among us, right now."

■ ■ ■

The half-lit corridors went on and on, leading to stairs, leading to elevators, leading past locked doors and plastic bags in piles, yesterday's waste. Alex made no effort to prolong the walk. When-ever he faltered, the two Mexicans moved in closer to him on either side, like human crutches, so it was best to keep moving ahead. Martime remained behind with the car, and somehow this was not a good sign, being relegated to deaf-mutes, illiterates, Aztecs. They did speak to each other from time to time, but in a language all clotted with consonants, which Alex only knew to be different from Spanish, more ancient and basic.

They paused at the door to the gym while one of the Hectors played with the keys, then passed the key ring to Alex. "Thanks, fella," Alex said in what he hoped was a firm, colonial tone. "Ready for racquetball?"

It was dark inside, even with the lights switched on, so many of the bulbs were out, and the dampness enclosed them like fog. Alex was pleased to see doubt flicker over Hector's face. The other one stayed behind in the corridor, which was good in one way and bad in another—the idea, that is, of a lookout. Hector nudged him with an elbow and Alex shuffled, as slowly as possible, to his locker, where the papers were stored.

The locker opened, and Alex had a moment to contemplate the end of all things, all sensation and thought, and whether it would come via garrote or gun or some prehistoric obsidian blade. But just as he lifted the papers out there was a clatter behind him. He turned to see Hector, thrown off, lunge in one direction and then the other. Racquetball, indeed. A ball had slid off the shelf of the locker and bounced into the darkness, but Hector could not know it was a ball. Alex reached up onto the shelf, located a second ball with his fingers, and sent it hurling out, in an awkward backward throw. There was a shout from Hector, coming from the area of the sinks, and Alex knew this was his chance, if he wanted to continue with thought and sensation, meaning, at this point, thought and pain. And even if he didn't, he had to follow his feet.

There was a door near the showers that led to a little cube of a room that had been intended for nutrition counseling, meditation training, men's consciousness-raising. The room had never been used, except possibly for homosexual liaisons and one other purpose, which was to get to the tunnel system that connected the towers. Alex could not have drawn a map or given directions, but the memory was embedded in his muscles from the few times he'd come to the gym, pulled along by some burst of camaraderie, and needed to escape for a drink. With the circle of light from Hector's flashlight nipping at his feet, Alex dashed through the meditation room and hurled himself into the tunnel.

He stumbled ahead with one arm held out, the other clutching the packet of papers to his chest. There should be a door in ten or twenty feet, and if it was locked he would be dead, dead and in the same stroke buried. But the door was hanging off its hinges. Alex pushed through just as the flashlight caught up to him and headed to the right, hoping, believing, there was another branch on the left to soak up the Hectors. Now the floor was wet under him, the ceiling brushing against his hair. His calves hurt, that was the new thing, the pain advancing from ache to localized blaze. You've got to warm up first, he remembered Saul telling him, a century ago, when they'd gone to the gym to try out the courts. Otherwise you're going to cramp out.

Alex slowed down and let his fingers search the wall. There should be another fork soon, and every fork in the tunnel was a promise of life. Behind him he could hear footsteps, impractical leather slapping into permanent, underground puddles. One man or two? At the fork he went right again, although there was light that way, meaning danger or safety, depending on how it was used, yes, depending on who got to it first. And then he was in one of the main passageways of the intertower tunnel system, walking on dry floor, not really walking, of course, because he needed so much help from the wall just to keep standing and edging ahead. There were low-wattage fixtures in the ceiling and a sign on the wall, some graduate student's idea of a joke, saying TO PYLORIC DUCT AND INTESTINE. HE WHO HAS EATEN, HERE BECOMES FOOD.

At the next fork there were three choices. Alex took the widest and brightest, hoping the Hectors would go for the darkest and smallest, which was where a hunted man belonged. He was in an almost normal corridor now, with finished walls and doors along the sides, locked, though, and never used. Once, the idea had been to house low-level administrative functions down here in the basement, recordkeeping and hard copies of files, but the clerical workers complained of dampness and spots appeared on their lungs. Papers went limp and clung to each other without regard for content or relevance. Copying machines rusted and jammed.

He was out of shape, Alex reasoned, so far out of shape that every step made him some kind of hero. The floor had taken on a comforting, seductive look. You just had to lean against the wall and let the feet slide forward, the legs follow the feet, and so on until the head came to rest. They would catch up and lift the papers off his chest and then just leave him here, leave him for dead. Which was what, really? Maybe not nothing. Sleep is nothing. Death would be different—the dark, ignorant core of all things that exist.

In the distance he heard voices—their voices?—and fear confused his forward motion with a general trembling, a high-frequency vibration from his feet to his neck. He could just throw the papers down and run. It was the papers that they wanted, after all, not him. But then there was the problem of whether they would notice the papers, when it was a man they still thought they were hunting. Here especially, in this length of the corridor, there were papers all over the floor from where a plastic garbage bag had burst, disclosing the products, most likely, of some professor's day, the memos, the scraps bearing calculations, the announcements of meetings in major hotels. Alex could prop the Relnik papers up against the wall and write something, if he had something to write with, if they even knew words like "*Alto aquí!*"

He kept moving, or rather, the papers kept moving and dragging him along as they went. Because that was the other interpretation, it occurred to him, that he was still only the decoy, the courier, doomed to run around carrying signs he could not read. The Nazis, he thought wildly; he was saving something from the Nazis, saving something for the Nazis perhaps, some little tendril from the main stalk of history that had decided to come alive and take root here, in his own life, drawing nourishment right out through his skin.

Another fork took him back into the half-dark, a narrower place, with quotations from Dante spray-painted on the wall. Clever of course, this being the basement of hell, but in Italian and wasted on him. He leaned against the wall to slow his breathing and noticed that outside of the racket his body was making, the poundings and gasps, it was silent everywhere, which could mean the Hectors were far away or very close. He waited for the sound of footsteps or doors banging, fascinated by the movements of the two men, as if keeping in touch with them was a separate and competing project that needed attention, quite apart from the business of getting away.

"Alex!" The voice came echoing through the tunnel, around bends, flowing under doors, making right-angle turns. "Alex! Wait! Why are you running?" It was Martime. One of them had gone back for Martime, meaning there were three of them now, enough to begin to close the odds. Alex lurched toward perfect darkness, which was only an instinct, not a plan. Now there were footsteps again. How far away? In a parallel space, or in the same random pathway as himself? Ahead was a tiny circle of light, maybe the fabled end of the tunnel, the dawn of the day when all that had been broken would be made whole again. He moved one foot ahead of the other, into the pain.

"Alex, is it the Jews?" Martime seemed to be speaking through a megaphone, the voice was so frighteningly close. "You are worried about Dora's Jews?"

Alex hugged the papers to his chest and inched forward toward the light, which was either small and close or large and unattainably far away. The Jews, yes, how perceptive. Because whatever secret Relnik's papers contained had been squeezed from the brains of living men, just as whatever mental breakthroughs Hershey's disease might lead to would come at the cost of—how many lives?

Then he bumped his forehead where there should not have been a wall. He had arrived at the light and it was a button in the wall, an elevator button. Alex leaned into it and prayed to Faraday, Volta, Ampère—anyone concerned with electricity and the movement of objects against their will. A huge wheezing sound began, coming from far away, from the heart of the complex, and Alex's heart jumped to hear the complex still functioning, all wired together into one vast and makeshift machine.

"Alex!" Martime's voice came floating clearly through the dark, borne along on the sure clicks of his heels. "Come out! Please! I understand your revulsion. Yes. But the experiment worked. She found the pleasure center. They died, Alex—think of it—they died in ecstasy!"

The elevator creaked to a halt and Alex almost fell through the opening door. He pushed the button for a floor that he thought would be safe, and then, as the elevator started to rise and the pounding of Martime and his men on the door below grew fainter, he tore open the package containing Relnik's papers and peered inside. Expecting what? Some assurance that the souls of Dora's victims had indeed flown out in ecstasy from the dank enclosures of their skulls, out through the holes that Dora had drilled through living bone?

But the papers were stuck to each other in a sodden mass, impossible to separate, like papier-mâché, the ink turned into a water stain. The neglected basement of Leitbetter's empire had sucked out Relnik's secret.

CHAPTER 14

C hris was a real pal, letting Alex sit in the kitchen, out of sight of the bar, and drink coffee followed by whiskey chasers. Then he'd brought out the pistol and said, "Change your mind on this, Professor?" And Alex acknowledged it wouldn't be a bad thing, in the company he kept, to have a gun at least as a prop. No, he didn't need a lesson, he had hunted as a boy and he wasn't planning to actually shoot. The idea was at some point you pulled it out and the others would back off in respect.

"Trouble with you," Chris said, "professors and so on, think everything comes from ideas. You get in certain situations, man, there isn't an idea in sight."

"I'm not planning on sinking to their level, I have my pride."

"Yeah? I had a guy come in here after hours with a gun of his own. Shot the motherfucker twice before the police got here. No questions asked."

"Ah, but questions are my business. Ask first, shoot later."

"Just words, man. You gonna die for words?"

Maybe Chris was right and he was in love with words, or at least ideas, otherwise how could he have gotten into this bizarre and lethal mess? He should have washed his hands of the whole thing the minute he learned that Leitbetter's *Biography of the Twentieth Century* was nonexistent, a private hoax. He should have found some other way to supplement his income—tutoring, whatever—and called Della up and begun a proper courtship then and there, weeks ago. All through the long day of hiding in the complex, the image of her eyes, her serious face, had flickered in front of him like some artist's conception of safety and reason. He'd ended up going into a seminar room to hide out from Martime and the Hectors, dozed on and off for a while, and then decided to stay until five so he could leave the complex in the confusion of the general exodus. At first he was too numb to think. He lay down on the carpet, remembering all the times he had sat upright in a room like this and dreamed of stretching out on the floor, under the table, in view of ankles and knees, while the talk droned on above him. His mind drifted to Martime and whether there was really any danger from that quarter.

Martime obviously wanted him to believe that The Harvest was the more legitimate end of the business, and that all the nasty physical stuff, like poisons and drugs and beatings, was Brabant's work. Alex had read about international corporations that ran covert "black hand" operations, just to smooth the way ahead, and he liked the idea of good and evil partitioned into separate divisions on the organizational flow chart: The Harvest here, SKD over there; Martime working on the science end, if you could call it that, Brabant running alongside, softening up the opposition. But of course you can't really divide things up so neatly, Alex dimly reasoned, any more than you could dissect Relnik himself into pure filaments of hope on the one hand and a mass of sodden evil on the other.

It was nothing like a hangover, this pain the night had left him with, it was too profound and physical, too deeply rooted in the joints. Alex strained again to remember the part of the night before the hotel, the fights, in particular, he was supposed to have had, but it was like the effort of pulling on a frayed string attached to something heavy and far away. One thing at last returned: the soft, exalted look on Leitbetter's face when Phyllis had announced the "cryonics team," making him seem twenty years younger and almost trustworthy again.

At the thought of Leitbetter, Alex sat up and rubbed the bump on his head. What was it that Leitbetter had told him? If you left out the part about cryonics and the overblown cosmic musings, it was an account of Leitbetter's troubled relationship with The Harvest. But it was a vague account, it seemed now to Alex, not the whole truth, or not entirely true. He remembered his own feeble attempts to diagram the Relnik business—the balloons connected by dotted lines and the dim awareness of some missing element that would tie all the others together. Maybe if he tried to explain the whole thing out loud to some patient listener . . . to Della, of course.

Later, in taxicabs and sitting at the Baycrest, he could not distinguish the elements of the epiphany that had come to him there in the seminar room. He had moved on from Leitbetter to thinking of Della, wanting to see her, aware of her suddenly as an event in time rather than a fixture on the shelves of his mind, as something with a beginning and a possible end. She could have gone back to her husband, for all he knew, moved away to find another job, maybe gone somewhere to find her son.

Her son, he thought. Of course.

■ ■ ■

Della let him in on the third series of knocks, after peeking out with the chain still on the door. "Alex," she said, "look at you."

He had a lopsided, pleading expression that said he could see it from exactly her point of view: someone falling into your place after dark, no visible means of transportation, trousers spattered to the knees with mud.

"Okay if I come in?" He stumbled in and sat heavily on one of the kitchen chairs. "Look, your son. You mentioned a son who used to work for Leitbetter. What did he do? I mean, what kind of work?"

"Steve?" This must be the convergence Riane was talking about. All lines, straight or crooked, real or imagined, were beginning to pull in toward one central point. She sat down herself, awkwardly, testing the chair. "I just got some news about him today. Someone I know saw him, not far from here, just a few days ago."

"He's been missing, right?"

"Yes. But I don't know what he did for Leitbetter exactly. It involved computers, and it was something related to WOW . . . Why?"

Alex nodded slowly, staring out at the water tower, which was moonlike by this time of evening.

"Are you all right?"

"Just that I could use a drink, if you don't mind."

"I have something. Wait." She returned to the table with a bottle and a glass. "It's a little sweet, but maybe with ice—"

"No, sweet is good. Wonderful. Anything." He filled the glass and held it up to the light to better appreciate the clear green of the crème de menthe, the lost color of leaves in the shade. "The reason I asked is at some point Leitbetter had an intern, a kid in other words, who got sent out on the same errand I've been on—researching Henry Relnik. The kid gets a look at the Relnik papers—maybe the same ones I've read—and he gets this big idea. God knows what, because I couldn't find much in them myself."

He paused for a slow, syrupy sip. "Maybe he didn't find anything in the papers. Maybe there isn't anything to find. Maybe he had a sexual awakening in the hands of Relnik's grandniece and that's how he got his big idea."

"So what about this . . . kid?"

"He gets sent out to this outfit that's been funding Leitbetter. They give him a job. I presume in California. The Harvest Enterprises, some kind of software and information company that does a lot of funding in the sciences. They've got a huge international network of scientists including—"

"The Harvest Enterprises?" She remembered the personnel files in the mainframe at the complex. Where it said THE after the word CONTACT could have been the letters T-H-E. "Let me ask you, is the grandniece named Riane?"

He was surprised, not only by the question, but by something he had never seen before in Della's face, though it could have been there all along. A definite outline had emerged, marking off territory still unknown to him and waiting to be explored.

He asked a few questions about dates and nodded at what she told him. "That would fit," he said. "Because this kid who worked for Leitbetter, he didn't last at The Harvest. There was some kind of falling-out. He leaves. Or more likely, *escapes*. They get irritated, desperate, I don't know. That's where I come in. They tell Leitbetter to take another look at the Relnik papers, see if he can figure out what the kid found in them . . . Or who knows? Maybe Leitbetter was doing it all on his own, hoping to reconstruct—"

"And what did he have this falling-out about, do you know?"

"Oh, doctrinal differences, I suppose. This is the strange part. You've probably heard Leitbetter's theory of the extraterrestrial Visitor who's going to show up someday and ask what we earthlings have been doing down here, what we've managed to figure out about the universe.

"Well, Leitbetter got all that from The Harvest, and they—The Harvest, that is—seem to think that whatever this kid gleaned from the Relnik papers is going to help them get ready for the Visitor. Possibly it's even what the Visitor is coming here to fetch. I mean, none of this is rational. They are actually convinced that there's something of cosmic significance in the Relnik papers. In what this kid got out of them, anyway."

"And Steve was part of this . . . cult?"

"If it was him, yes. He worked for them, anyway, for a few months."

Della took this in for a moment, then shook her head. "But, Alex, I have to tell you. It's only a game, what Steve was working on. A computer game."

"A game?"

"Yes, an ordinary computer game." She shrugged and gave him

a guilty-looking smile. "Well, not ordinary. But basically like all those games. You know, full of monsters and battles and magic. You have a mission. There are obstacles. Complicated clues. That's all, like a videogame in the arcade."

"Jesus Christ. They were going to kill me for a computer game."

"Well, if it makes you feel any better, it's probably worth a lot. That's what Leo thinks, anyway, my ex-husband. It's supposed to be addictive: you start to play, you can't stop."

"A game. Some goddamn hacker's idea of fun. I'm sorry, Della, I didn't mean your son. I'm sure he's a genius, a great kid."

He got up and started pacing and running his hands through his hair. "You mind if I smoke? I could blow it out the door? . . . Thanks. It's just, this has been a rough few weeks. And all that fancy metaphysical bullcrap, I suppose that's how they lure the scientists into their web. Leitbetter ate it up, I mean the extraterrestrial part, and it gets a lot woollier than that. The 'purpose of life.' Oh shit. All it was was a computer game. An addictive computer game! The ideal thing for a gang of ex-drug dealers. A hot new product line, in other words."

Then, before Della could say anything, there was a clatter outdoors, followed by the hoarse barking of the landlord's dog.

■　　■　　■

It took them nearly twenty minutes to decide that it was only the wind, knocking over a garbage can and setting off the dog. Della checked all the locks and Alex took out the handgun he'd bought from Chris to make sure it was loaded. They both went to the front window together and peered out at the street, which was empty as far as they could see. "Just the wind," Della said, the first wind in months, turning the night into a Halloween scene, with sighs and bangs and naked branches scratching at the walls of the house.

"Look, Della, this is not a good situation." They were standing in the living room, where Della had pulled all the blinds down tight. "They could be here any minute. They could have followed me."

"You think so?"

"I should go. I'm endangering you just by being here. They chased me all night through the tunnel system at the complex. They're probably still after me for the Relnik papers, and then, what a surprise, they come here and find I'm with you, the kid's mother."

"No, don't go." She took a step toward him and grabbed hold of his arm. "Stay. Please."

He had to look away from her eyes for a moment, trying to think things through. "Of course. What am I saying? We'll both go. You have a car, we'll—"

"No. Look. We'll stay here. We'll call the police."

"And tell them what? I have this cut on my head, but there's no proof anyone is after me. So I wound up under a table in a seminar room sometime this afternoon. I can just see how that will be interpreted by my friends in the scientific community."

Della frowned. "So stay, okay? You stay. You have a gun, right? In case someone shows up."

Then she was leading him over to the couch, sitting him down away from any window, adding a little more crème de menthe to his glass. Her hand was still on his arm when she said, "Please. I'll make up the couch, okay?"

Something in the chaste intensity of the plea made him want to pull her toward him. "Okay, but I'm going to stay up all night and keep an eye on the door." He took her hand, the one which had slipped down from his sleeve. "And, Della, I'm sorry. All those times—"

Then he did pull her close to him in an awkward hug, half-facing on the couch, and they stayed that way for a minute or two, listening to the sounds, miniaturized by distance, of loose cans and bottles being pushed along the street by the wind.

"I could give up biology," he said as they pulled apart, checking to see if their faces had been changed in any way by the embrace. "I could take up Dellology, the study of Della. I could be the world's leading expert. I could write whole articles about your earlobe, give lectures—"

Then she reached up and put a finger on his lips. "Just stay here, all right?"

They fell into lovemaking, though this was not how Alex at first defined it in his mind. He was absorbed, that was all, in some act of private worship that was required for his salvation. Only for a moment, when they hit a snag—another sound outside, making Della momentarily tense—did the old fear come back, that he was being drawn into something too risky and demeaning to go forward without the cover of drunkenness. But it was only the wind again. She smiled and held his face between her hands, and then it seemed to him that the tempo picked up, and he saw it was also the tempo of flight. Behind him the terrors of the forest, ahead the undulating plain. He had to slow himself down, remind himself he was no longer running, that safety would never take a better form than this. He put his hand on her breast and was surprised at the heat of her skin compared to all the cold places he had been, Leitbetter's office and the tunnels of hell. "You're very warm, Della, you know that? I like how you feel."

She said she liked it too, how she felt right now, and later she would reason that there ought to be some slack, even in Sister Bertha's philosophy, for a moment of grasping and holding, since everything else involves letting go. His hand moved to her arm, then up along her shoulder, where it traced a pattern, moving up to her neck. His lips followed, soft and sweet from the drink. Then the kiss ended and he held her, saying Della over and over.

■   ■   ■

Della woke up to a tapping sound that was at first hard to sort out from the agitation of branches outside and Alex snoring beside her on the bed. She nudged him, but he just muttered and rolled over, returning to the sleep he had entered only minutes after making love. It had been all she could do to get him into the bedroom, stretched out and covered, and now there was this.

On the way to the door, she stopped in the living room and felt around on the coffee table for the gun that Alex had brought. The handle was made out of wood, which surprised her, because you tend to expect something cold to the touch. There was a definite tapping now, someone at the door. With the gun in her hand, she edged through the kitchen, which was dark except for the faint water-tower glow. Then she heard it, a male voice, at first indistinct, then again more clearly, repeating some word, and the word, she finally realized, was "Mom."

The wind slammed the door shut after him and sent loose papers fluttering from the counters. Somewhere another door slammed shut in sympathy and Della jumped, feeling herself caught between doors opening and closing, endings and beginnings rushing together.

"What happened?" Steve said, blinking into the light and brushing past Della. "He get the house?"

"No, I just didn't want to stay there anymore. How did you find me?"

Steve scowled and looked down. "The computer bulletin board. Don't you remember? You posted a message."

"But there wasn't an address."

"You have a phone number, you can always get the address."

If you were a hacker you could, which of course she should have known. She reached out and touched his sleeve with her fingertips. "Your hair got so long."

There were other things she could have pointed out, like the fact that under his eyes was dark purple and that the denim jacket he was wearing looked as if it had been rolled into a ball and used to clean windows; but one thing at a time.

"The better to blend in with the bus terminal crowd." He had turned away and opened the refrigerator. "I just need some juice or something. I can't stay long."

"Here, I'll get it. You sit down."

She busied herself with the food, almost relieved not to be looking directly at him. Everything was becoming a test that she sensed she could fail. How many times do you get a second chance with something that really matters? The trick was to stop acting so dumb and surprised and display some rudiments of control.

"Someone is after you, right?" she said, setting the food down and sitting across from him at the table. "Maisy told me."

Outside, the wind freed a garbage-can lid and drove it clattering down the street. Steve frowned out the window at the water tower.

"Steve, if someone is after you, we should call the police."

"Can't do that, Mom."

"Why not? You can't just keep running."

"Because of what happened to Homer. You know what happened to Homer, they're going to try to pin that on me."

"Pin it on you?"

"Mmm. Because I had a motive." He gave her a trace of his old one-sided smile, just a little tighter around the corner of his mouth on account of tiredness and possibly weight loss. "You see, Homer knew all along. From some hack he had done two, three years ago. He knew what The Harvest does and what their methods are like. That's where I was, The Harvest Enterprises. He knew what I was getting into. But he just said, Go ahead. No lunatic dad, no sleep-walking mom, no Leitbetter to drive you nuts."

Della cringed, but he eyed her levelly over the rim of his glass.

"Just do what you want, solid work, that was the idea, and I wouldn't have believed Leitbetter if Homer hadn't said so too." He snorted. "*Homer.* Then, when I finally got out to him, through the computer, he wouldn't respond or pass stuff along. Nothing. I was completely cut off."

"So you were like a prisoner there?"

"Oh, it wasn't so bad, day to day. You had a swimming pool, hot tub. The food was okay. Incredible hardware, data bases—" He paused, staring over Della's shoulder with a wary, glittery look. "What's that on the counter? You've got a gun now?"

"It's not mine. It belongs to a friend." She tightened the bathrobe over her chest. The best thing would have been for Alex to wake up and come out in person or otherwise just vanish as something too hard to explain. "It's my friend Alex. He's asleep, actually. In the other room."

"Oh yeah?" He gave her a quick, noncommittal look. "Is it loaded?"

"I think so."

"Well, look. I don't want to keep you up. I just need to crash for a few hours if I can on the couch."

"Of course you'll stay, and not just a few hours. In the morning we can talk, okay? Figure out what to do."

"Mmm."

This must be the moment, the second chance—take it or leave it—because something viscous and turbulent was bubbling up through her veins. "Steve, look, I'm sorry."

"About what?"

"About that night, the night you left."

"We do what we have to, right?"

"I didn't let Leo into your room."

"It doesn't matter."

"I tried to stop him."

His face was calm when he looked back up at her, as if he had already moved on to other things. "It's all right, Mom. I had to go, anyway. It's what I had to do."

■   ■   ■

When she had made up the couch, he surprised her by saying, sit down for a minute, he had something to show her. There was a flat gray object in his hand, something wrapped in plastic—computer diskettes, she could see when he took the plastic off.

"What is that, your game?"

He didn't ask how she knew what it was. He just nodded, eyes glowing, and fingered the three diskettes.

"Is it finished, then?"

"Finished? You never really finish a game. Like I could have got it down to two diskettes if I had the time. Maybe one."

"What's wrong with three?"

"Less is better, as a general rule. You want to see how I carry them? I have this pouch sewn into the jacket. I thought of having them surgically implanted, under the skin. They can do that, you know, I read it somewhere."

"You would have had that done?"

"If I had to."

Della pictured the disks as a ridge under his skin, maybe a square plateau on his chest, and then a knife cutting through the skin and blood all over the diskettes. "Steve," she asked in spite of herself, "is this why Carl killed himself, because of the game?"

Steve wrapped the diskettes up again and returned them to their pouch carefully, checking the seal. "It was a different game then, the one that killed him, a primitive version. See, at that stage all I had to work with was negative reinforcement: you made a mistake and an insult would scroll across the screen. Personally crafted, but dumb stuff, like the size of your weenie or how you were never going to get anywhere, being such a jerk. Well, it kept escalating and Carl couldn't take it. He forgot it was just part of the game."

He gave her an odd twisted look and patted the jacket containing the diskettes. "Maybe it was an experiment too, to see how far you could get with that kind of approach.

"But that was like the earliest stages." He appeared to reflect, or maybe study the sounds of unrest being made by the wind. "See, the mammalian brain is an amazing thing. You have reason plus feeling, meaning pleasure and pain, and the feelings can be used to drive the process of reason. You see what I mean? First I used pain—meaning negative reinforcement—because it was all I could think of to do. But Carl, well . . . what happened to Carl showed the limits of that.

"So I switched to pleasure, which is far more effective—using positive reinforcement to drive the cognitive process. I mean the process of learning, which is pretty much the same kind of effort as playing a game. See, the neural pathways are there, linking the pleasure center to the cerebral cortex. All you've got to do is put the pathways to work, and then everything you figure out, everything you learn, brings its own little shot of pure pleasure."

He went on like that for a while, throwing around terms like "endorphins" and "positive feedback" and "synaptic cascade." You're making excuses, Della wanted to say, and—I don't understand you, anyway. Then he slumped into a half-reclining position, propping his head up with one arm, and it occurred to her that he might be sick as well as tired, and that the glittery look could be coming from fever.

"I'm not sure I understand," she said. "How did you know how to do something like that?"

"Oh, Leitbetter put me on to it, not that he had any idea, asshole that he is . . . But yeah, that was when the fun began. Not everyone thought it was a good idea. Homer, for example, had his so-called moral objections. But I had to see how far you could take it. If a little discovery gave you a little thrill, and that made you want to find out more, then where would it end? I mean, what would it feel like when you had it all together in your head? So I kept going, it didn't matter what. Hannibal, for example . . . what happened to him . . ."

He looked down for a moment, fingering the sheet. "Look, if there was a way to do it just with computers, without any humans, I would have done that. But computers don't feel any pleasure, at least not yet, so there's no way to motivate them, you know, to keep on going till they figure everything out.

"Besides, Mom." He flashed her the old nervy, challenging look. "They kill hundreds of rats at the complex every day. White mice. Rabbits. Guinea pigs. Rhesus monkeys. Slaughtered in some low-IQ experiment."

"You're into animal rights?"

"There are no animal rights. No right to live when the virus is in your bloodstream or the predator has your neck in its mouth. I just mean for every species there is a truth—a rabbit truth, a mouse truth, a bug truth. The universe as seen from its perspective, whatever the species is. The best it can figure out."

"I see." She remembered how when he was very small he would get this way, overtired and unable to stop. The trick was to go along with it and try to make it into a meandering dream-type thing, so he wouldn't even know when he entered into sleep or feel he was giving anything up. "And what is the human truth, then?"

"Ah. You think it's a word, but maybe it isn't a word."

"What do you mean, a word?"

"A statement: the name of God, the final equation, the Grand Unified Theory of Everything. Something you could write down, you know. Put it in a bottle, put a cork in the bottle, throw it into the sea."

"So if it isn't a word?"

"A process. Something you have to experience. Actually do."

"A game, maybe?" She thought he might smile too, but she could see the light glinting in his eyes, deadly serious.

"Yeah, a game."

"I listen to Sister Bertha too, you know. And I can't see Sister Bertha saying that truth, the Truth, is a game."

"What does she say, then?"

"Oh, you know. I know you know, because Maisy told me you've been listening for years. Sister Bertha says give it all away, whatever you have."

"Yeah." He smiled and half shut his eyes. "Those are the instructions."

CHAPTER 15

Finally Della slept and entered a vast dream landscape marked off with mathematical equations and signs. She was all alone in a broad yellow field, trying to comprehend a diagram filled with arrows and musical notations, trying to see where she had to go next. Then the arrows turned on themselves and the diagrams tightened into a pattern of irrefutable symmetry and she heard Steve's voice, Steve's little-boy voice, saying, Wake up, Mom, come on, wake up.

But when she got up with the vague idea of checking on him and tiptoed into the living room, she found the couch empty, only the crumpled sheets to prove that he had been there at all. She hurried into the kitchen expecting a note, but there was nothing on the table that hadn't been there the night before. Dishes were stacked in the sink and a few newspapers were scattered around, opened to the want ads she had been meaning to read. Then she noticed that the gun, Alex's gun, was no longer on the counter where she'd left it.

She sat down and let the sweat turn to a coating of cold over her skin. This time there would be no more mistakes; Steve would not get away again. But she needed a plan, as Miriam would say, and she sat there for another minute letting the outlines of the room define the logic of what had to be done. Lines met in angles, angles pointed, forming vectors, showing the way.

Before she left, she crept back into the bedroom where Alex was still sleeping and looked down at his face. A good face, she thought, whatever else, and a body she could fit up against. She kissed his forehead and tiptoed out, locking the door behind her.

Only in the car did her nerve fail and the morning cold turn to a surface whose touch made her draw back in pain. Her plan, considered in the light of a day that would soon be bringing the neighbors out to their cars and men to the warehouse to work, seemed implausible, even insane. For a moment, she slipped into panic, like an alternate gear where heavy breathing and straining accomplish nothing at all. The car key trembled in her fingers, her muscles ached from invisible effort. She bowed her head over the steering wheel and breathed deeply, counting the breaths.

When she shook herself and looked up again, she saw that the sun was about to rise. The wind had died in the night and left the sky scrubbed and clear. Think what Steve would do, she told herself, do what he would do and you will be where he is. The car started and she checked in the rearview mirror, but the only cars around did not seem to be following her. To be sure she went five blocks in the wrong direction before turning onto the road that led to the freeway and picking up speed. The freeway was clear, almost empty, and as she cruised down the ramp, a tide of yellow sunlight rolled out from the east.

She turned up the radio and filled the car with static from Sister Bertha's frequency. Overnight the haze had lifted and now each object wore a dark outline against the brilliance of the early-autumn sky. It was as clear as the sunlight around her: he would go to Sister Bertha, of course. That was probably why he had escaped from

The Harvest in the first place—not to see Riane, not to see her, but to find Sister Bertha.

Minutes later, when Della was slowing for the exit, Sister Bertha finally broke through the static. *Free will*, she was saying, and: *How many times?* Then a few words came through before being eaten again by the static. *Free will? Maybe you had it once and you used it all up.*

The voice was clear, much clearer than Della could hear it at home, meaning her theory was right, that Sister Bertha must broadcast from somewhere in the direction of where Maisy lived, since Maisy had found her first. It was the only clue Della had to go on, so she assumed it was true. Maisy listened, so Maisy must be close to the source. But on the exit ramp Della was shaken by indecision disguised as a fresh outbreak of panic. When she had been sitting there in the kitchen, it had seemed so simple and clear: she would follow the voice wherever it led, first in great arcs taking in miles at a time, then making smaller adjustments as necessary until she came to the building or house or whatever it was that Sister Bertha broadcast from. But now she no longer felt sure of her ability to judge small changes in volume. Plus there were so many things, like sun spots and power lines, that could interfere with the sound.

She pulled up to the curb next to an empty lot, a safe distance away from the figures she could see picking through the piles of rubbish and discarded mattresses and tires. She did not realize she was leaning her head against the steering wheel until a knock on the window brought her upright. It was an old man smiling ingratiatingly, showing off his gums. "Mornin' ma'am," he said, "beautiful day." Not so old, she realized, maybe less than forty, but the outdoors had already carved a pattern in his face, like a second face imposed on the first. She rolled the window down a few inches, and a rude, waxy smell invaded the car.

"Good morning," she said.

"You lookin' for smoke?"

Startled, she stepped on the gas and pulled away from the curb, but not before seeing his lips draw back. "Well, fuck you, lady," he shouted. And "I wouldn't let you suck my dick."

A block or so later, she checked the rearview mirror and caught a glimpse of her eyes, which were darker than usual and foreign, looking exactly like Steve's. You are really doing this, the mirror eyes said. You are following a definite plan. If she had any doubt, there was the fact that the old man's words left no feeling of hurt or shock. She had entered the realm of purposefulness, where Steve had been all along.

There was one car behind her that she thought she had noticed earlier, but it was too far back to see the driver's face or even for sure if the driver was a man. Now she wished she had paid more attention to all the cars that Leo had owned so that at least she would have names for them more precise than "large, new, reddish-brown." This could be Leo following her or just the kind of car that everyone drove and she had never noticed before. When a yellow light came up, she shot through and hoped she had shaken the car, whoever it was.

She was driving down city streets when Sister Bertha burst through the static again. *Nothing? You're afraid you give it all away you're left then with nothing. Is that what you think?* She was getting louder, no question, and Della pulled over to the right and slowed to a crawl. It didn't matter what she said anymore, only that she spoke, calling out to Della, showing her the way. Buildings pressed in on both sides, huge empty factories with their windows blacked out leaned overhead, narrowing the sky to a river of blue. *What is this nothing? You ever held it in your hand? Because look what you got there, you still got a hand.* Clearer and clearer. Della turned down the volume so it would be easier to tell when the voice got louder, in between the patches of silence and static.

She was close to the downtown area now, where the buildings seemed to fuse into a single dingy outgrowth of granite. Women didn't drive here alone, as far as Della knew. Everyone sensed that the city had been erected on top of some act of cruelty, committed long ago and hastily buried, something so terrible that it cried out for vengeance, over and over, in the form of robberies and murders and rapes. Della checked her rearview mirror again, and now there were two of the reddish-brown cars that could have been Leo, but the sun, bouncing off chromium, kept her from seeing whether he, or anyone, was in them.

Suddenly Sister Bertha's voice filled the car. *Why do you think God's so lonely for us?* Della jerked forward and turned the volume down until it did not hurt her ears. *You think he has everything so what can it matter, what you have to give. God can't be lonely, you're telling yourself.*

The voice was so close that Della knew it was time to abandon the car and finish the journey on foot. Steve would have done this, she told herself, he would have seen there was no more need for the car. She got out, the Walkman around her neck, and looked up and down the street. But the buildings were noncommittal, no churches, for example, or radio antennae, and the only written words were COFFEE and BAR, making the choice easy enough.

■   ■   ■

The coffee shop was cool and nearly empty, since it was still too early for lunch. "Yes?" the waitress asked, not looking at Della but watching the door.

"Soup. Soup of the day," Della said, and then lowered her voice. "I'm looking for Sister Bertha. Have you heard of her?"

"I don't know your sister, miss," the waitress answered warily.

"Not my sister. That's her name: Sister Bertha."

"Oh yeah, a nun?"

"No, not a nun. She's a radio preacher and she broadcasts from somewhere around here."

"That's nice. What are you going to drink?"

"Coffee, please. Look. I'm really looking for my son. My son—" She caught herself in alarm. What was she going to say? That her son was a follower of Sister Bertha and that he had invented a computer game which might contain the summation of all human knowledge, or at least be worth millions of dollars?

"First it was your sister," the waitress said, smiling with mock indulgence, "now it's your son."

"My son is missing," Della whispered. "That's all. I think he went to find this preacher, Sister Bertha, and she's somewhere around here."

The waitress pursed her mauve lips. "She black or white?"

"I don't know." Della was startled by the question. She had assumed Sister Bertha was white, meaning in some sense neutral and of no race at all.

"Well then, how are you going to know when you see her?" The waitress winked at a nearby customer and turned away.

Della looked around awkwardly, but no one seemed to have noticed except a fat man on the other side of the counter who raised his eyebrows and lowered them in a quick little signal of interest. When had he entered the coffee shop? Before her or after? It didn't have to be Leo who was following her, it could be the men from The Harvest, hoping she would lead them to Steve. And the thought made her heart skip a beat and wobble ineffectively.

She paid quickly and went back out into the street, where the lunch crowds were just beginning to surge out of the buildings. For a moment she was overcome by the sunlight and a surge of fear. What if Sister Bertha did not speak for the rest of the day? Della had gone days at a time in the past without ever catching a word. All around her, office workers rushed by with scared, pinched faces, dragged by impersonal forces. Della slipped into the entryway of a building and adjusted the Walkman over her ears.

What would Steve do now? She tried to think, and at that moment Sister Bertha started to speak again, saying: *As simple as that.* Then the static closed in over her voice and Della was alone in the crowd.

The idea was to get to the open sky, because it was the buildings that were blocking Sister Bertha now. Della noticed she had become very light, lighter than she had ever been. She was making the motions of walking but actually floating inches above the pavement, where not even friction could slow her. A man went by wearing a Walkman and for a moment she imagined it was Steve. Soon he would turn and walk the same way she was going, to where Sister Bertha waited for her followers to bring her their gifts. Everyone had something to bring, some small, precious object that summarized a life. Della clutched the Walkman to her head and let the currents of air carry her along.

She was delivered by the street to the edge of a park where the sky opened out on all sides, and it pleased her that the very design of the city was laid out to assist her, because when she entered the park Sister Bertha came back. *What you see is all there is.* The words made Della stop and lean shakily against a bench. They were neither loud nor soft but exactly appropriate to the size of her head, seeming to come from within. *For you at least it is all that can be and all that will ever exist.* She saw one perfectly formed cloud in the sky and knew that it had been amassing light for thousands of years before this, light that had been reflected from ancient cathedrals and glassy seas and deserts where whole nations lay buried. *There is no then and now* was the message of the cloud, because this is all there ever was.

Currents of wind carried her toward the top of the hill that led up from the entrance to the park. Behind her was the city, and below her, in the middle of a field of dried-out grass, stood an abandoned bandshell designed to attract crowds and focus their thoughts. Della stopped by a tree to gather her strength. There were other trees, scattered around, in what must once have been orderly formations. The caterpillars had left them with only a few gray chewed-up leaves in ghoulish imitation of fall. But without leaves it was easier to see their intentions—a detachment pressing forward here, a rearguard there.

A man walked by, the same man with the Walkman she had seen on the street, but he was careful to give her no sign. There were other people scattered around, some of them carrying radios, some of them wearing Walkmen, some looking to the sky for instructions. The longer she watched, the more telling their movements became. An old woman fed squirrels objects she took from her purse, but with each wave of her arm she moved experimentally in one direction or another, testing the signals in the air. Everyone else, when you watched, was moving tentatively this way and that, judging their distance from the source. A man would turn his head and appear to be staring at nothing at all. A child would drop a ball and chase it, letting the motions of the ball be her guide. If you watched these movements long enough, they became universal, unending, part of a general flow.

"Steve!" she called out, "Steve!" And she was surprised at the strength of her voice, echoing between the low hills.

■　■　■

He was sitting on a bench when she found him, bent forward with his head in his hands, a Walkman pulled down tight over his ears. She was shaken to see how much had gone out of him, just in the few hours since they had said good night. There was a film of sweat on his forehead, plastering down stray hairs, and his eyes looked like someone dead had borrowed them and was looking out through them even now. Della realized she had no plan of what to say. The whole plan had been to find him, with no allowance for the fact he was a grownup and could go where he wanted without telling her.

He smiled faintly. "You knew where to find me, huh?"

"I was afraid you were sick."

"Doesn't matter. I'm so close. She's around here somewhere."

"I know."

Steve started to rise, then slumped back down again.

"I'll go with you, all right?" she said, adding in her own mind: And then we'll go back, find a doctor, get you to bed. She took a step toward him, prepared to help him to his feet if he'd let her, and then froze at the sound of her name.

"Della!" It was Leo trotting up through the bushes, red-faced and panting. "And Jesus Christ, the kid himself."

He stopped and wiped his forehead with his sleeve. "So how do you like that? The one leads to the other."

"Leo, what are you doing here? You followed me, didn't you?"

He turned toward Steve, ignoring her. "Long time, kid, not even a postcard."

Della felt the sunlight condensing around them like a cage. We have been here before, she thought, the three of us, fixed in our places, over and over, before in the past.

"I just want to talk, all right?" Leo took a step closer. "Look, why don't we go somewhere, get some lunch?" He was squinting against the sun, and Della could see he was getting impatient standing there like a supplicant while Steve sat silent, hunched on the bench.

"What's the matter, did I interrupt a nature walk here?" He looked at Della accusingly and then back to Steve. "You better snap out of it. You're in trouble, you know that? Because of what happened to the Oriental kid."

"I know that. *Dad.*"

"Yeah? Well, this is serious. Some bald-headed girl has come forward and the police are probably looking for you now."

Steve just looked at him blankly.

"But something could still be arranged, you know what I mean? You've got the game, right? The computer game . . . Jesus, what's the matter with you two?"

He took another half step toward them and then paused, as if blocked by the light. It occurred to Della that maybe he too could sense some unusual presence in the air.

"What am I—the only sane one here? Everyone else in never-never land? . . . Della, you talk to him. Is this for the mutual benefit of all, or what?"

"Leo, this isn't the time. Can't you see he's sick?"

"Well, in that case, for Chrissake, let's get him to a doctor."

He took a step forward, one hand stretched out. But Steve was already on his feet, swaying slightly, then turning to run. Leo lunged after him, and Della stumbled after them both, tripping for a second so that the smell of dried grass and cigarette butts was thrust into her face. Then she was running, calling out foolishly, "Wait!"

The sound of the shot stopped her, and for a moment there was perfect silence, as if all possible sounds, now and forever, had been sucked right out of the air. Della saw Leo stop and then fall in slow, fluttery stages, head tilted back in surprise. Then he was on the ground, eyes still staring with that baffled look up at the sky and the blood fanning out over his shirt like some brazen red flowers that had been placed on the dead. What had Dr. Bhatar said about blood? That it is the carrier of death as well as the river of life, that it knows where to go. She knelt down beside Leo and looked up at Steve.

He dropped the gun and wiped the palms of his hands on his jacket. "Mom, I can't . . ."

He looked at her before he turned away, but it was a look that said he was already gone. Then he was stumbling through the bushes down the hill to where the bandshell was.

Della stood up, trembling from being so light. What was it that Sister Bertha had said? *Do not ask to understand the law, because the law was not made in your world.* High above, the lone cloud furled its outlines against the dark blue roof of the sky. *You are not alone, if you must know, but neither can we help. We brought you the law, which is all we can give, and the time has come now to return the gift.* Della felt she could have stood there forever, palms held out toward the sky, but there were voices already in the distance.

She picked up the gun and held it stiffly down by her side, waiting for the police or whoever would come.

CHAPTER 16

On that first terrible day when Della disappeared Alex woke up in something worse than a haze, a new state he had never, in decades of drinking, even approached. Hypoglycemia, he reasoned, because he had no memory of eating for days. He was snowbound, blinded by the radiant light that bleached the simplest significance out of objects around him. It was the bottle of liqueur, almost empty by now, that finally put a caption under the things he could see, and it said, You failed completely. You lost her and now she will never return.

Of course, at that point it was still just the booze speaking in its morning tones of remorse. He had no way of knowing where Della could have gone, though a look in the refrigerator made him hope she'd driven off to a supermarket and would be back any minute with bacon and eggs. No rush was his thought, in fact he welcomed the time alone to polish off the liqueur, smoke a few cigarettes to settle his stomach. They would go somewhere, and he pictured a leafy mountain retreat. They would lie low for a while, taking long walks and making love at any time of day. And then he remembered the gun, but it seemed to be gone now too.

He learned what had happened in part from Miriam, in part from the five o'clock news. He had gone back to his apartment to pack a bag with the TV news on in the background. A fight was how they presented it, some pushing and shoving that ended in shooting. Leo Markson, described as a business consultant, was shot dead once through the chest, and the photo showed a handsome, arrogant man beginning to run to fat. Della Markson, his estranged wife, had confessed to the murder. Tensions over money were cited, a fractious divorce.

Somehow he got from there to Miriam's, whose address he still had in a file. The magical idea was that Della would be there, because he had seen them so often together. But it was just Miriam, red-eyed and righteous, and Alex had to ask where Della was.

"In jail, of course. No bail's been set."

"Have you seen her?"

"For a minute. No more visiting till Monday."

"And?"

"She didn't say much. In fact, she didn't really say anything at all."

Alex lit a cigarette and leaned over Miriam's coffee table, using his matchbook to clear roads through invisible dust. He should tell her he had been with Della the night before, but something in Miriam's face warned him not to. Why hadn't he stopped Della from going out would be the obvious question. Why had he let her take his gun? Miriam would expect him to go to the police—which could mean having to account for Leitbetter too.

"What," he said, and cleared his throat and started again. "What were they fighting about, do you think?" Because it was vaguely in his mind that it might have been him, if Leo was the possessive type and knew where Alex had spent the night. There were stories

like this all the time: Ex-husband returns and finds ex-wife in bed
. . . Whole episodes could have elapsed while he slept, phone calls
and threats.

"Probably he threatened her. She was like battered, emotionally
speaking. She needed a group."

"I didn't realize."

"So," Miriam said before Alex stumbled back into a cab in the
night, "at least she got Leo."

■ ■ ■

Della would not see him, or anyone, it turned out, except for the
lawyer Miriam had arranged. Alex presented himself at the women's
house of detention two days in a row, fresh-shaven and reasonably
sober, only to be told that Della wasn't coming down, wasn't leaving
her cell. Prisoners have a right to visitors, the guard told him, and
also a right to have none.

He checked into a motel, using a fake name and paying with cash
in case Martime and the Hectors were still on his trail. He was
afraid, too, of being implicated in Leitbetter's death, or whatever
it was. It would be the kind of thing Brabant might do, set him up
for a murder charge. But the police never came and the newspapers
brought no news of Leitbetter. The gun too was a source of worry,
but apparently it hadn't been traced.

Miriam kept him informed about the case, calling late one afternoon with the news that a dead boy found in the park on the same
day as Leo's murder was not, as had first been thought, a random
drug-overdose victim but Della's missing son. That must be why
she went to the park, Miriam said, because she knew her son would
be there. The police were reopening the case, since a witness had
seen Steve running from the murder site shortly after the sound of
the shot. But Della herself still had nothing to say, and had been
placed under psychiatric observation.

After that, he would lie for whole days on a king-size bed with
a quart of whiskey for company, staring at the parking lot outside
his window and drinking until the stupor resembled sleep. He had
missed everything that night, lost in his crème de menthe coma: her

son calling, or even showing up; her husband and his threats. And where was Alex? Where was Alex ever? He covered his face with his hands, thinking of a lifetime of omissions and neglected cues, going back through his marriage and his so-called career—the fumbled lectures, half-finished projects, unreturned calls, promises washed away in the unending flow of drink.

Nothing could make up for his crimes of omission. He could be torn alive by small, sharp instruments. The shreds of his flesh could be pounded till they were reduced to individual cells. The cells could be lysed so that the protoplasm streamed out in pain, the DNA degraded down to its subunits, the subunits destroyed in a blast of heat, the atoms smashed, the nuclei bombarded until they disappeared in a blaze of fission . . . And it would still not be enough, not even a stopover in the hell he had earned.

■   ■   ■

He ran out of money after a couple of weeks and took a job he found in the want ads, at an industrial laboratory a two-hour drive from the environs of the Human Ecology Complex. In some half-baked, superstitious way, he believed that safety lay in putting some distance between himself and the complex, with its crumbling buildings and giant antennae reaching up to contact the Others, whoever they are, the "Intermediate Beings." He found an apartment a few blocks from the lab, and managed to confine his drinking to weekends and evenings, not that he couldn't have performed the job half-drunk—measuring the adhesion of bubbles to plastic tubing and ways of speeding up the flow.

Della was still not speaking or seeing visitors, though a nurse at the psychiatric facility assured Alex she was "making real progress" and had accepted the last bunch of flowers he'd sent. But no, there was no way he could talk to the psychiatrist on the case without being married to her or some kind of relative. Even in a case like this, with criminal aspects, ethics apply.

He had been settled into his new apartment for more than a week when he saw Della again, and Leo and, for the first time, their son, on a TV program late at night. Propped on one elbow on his foldout couch, he saw her looking ill at ease in a cocktail dress with Leo at her side, and then it was the face of the boy, identified here as "Kipper." In the boy's face, Della's eyes had been brought into sharp focus, Leo's mouth had an added curl of humor or daring. It was too thin a face, Alex thought, looking like it must slice the very air when he walked, but the kind of thing women went for, as far as Alex knew. The boy's face faded and was replaced by a man in a dark suit saying, "What dark secret destroyed this family?"

Nothing was said about Kipper's game, though there were hints of genius and mental disturbance. The screen showed low, dark-wooded buildings against the California hills: a compound belonging to The Harvest Enterprises, where Kipper had worked, described here as a software and information firm. Not a word about Nazis or extraterrestrial Visitors. Then it was Homer on the screen in his smudgy high-school picture: the friend who was killed not too long after Kipper left The Harvest, if "friend" indeed was the word. A love triangle was hinted at, and the screen showed a high-school version of Riane, masses of curls surrounding the same cold, sullen face.

Then the host turned to Leo's murder and other mysterious events in the park. Here Alex sat up and cursed the flickering screen of his secondhand TV set. It would be hard enough to follow with the clearest reception the conflicting stories and wriggly theories produced by the police. Some witnesses had seen Kipper running down the hill, away from the site where his mother was found with his father's body. Possibly he had been running away, horrified by his mother's act, or maybe he had even done the shooting himself—the police were still undecided. But others said there was a third party involved, a woman who was waiting in the bandshell, and that Kipper went up to her before he collapsed, and that he had stood there for a moment, speaking to the woman or holding her hand.

But no woman was found in the bandshell when the police arrived, nor had any third party come forth. On the subject of the woman the witnesses seemed to have come under a spell. One saw an old black woman covered in rags. Another saw a tall figure with high cheekbones and burnished skin, a face that was achingly sad, holding her arms outstretched. Still another saw a thin, dark-haired woman, Hispanic perhaps, or Italian or Jewish, who had been standing in the bandshell all morning, preaching in majestic cadences to the air and up to the hills, obviously raving mad.

The man in the dark suit returned to the screen and announced a new development in the case, a *Nightzone* exclusive. Marks found on Kipper's body were originally thought to be bruises, but closer examination showed a peculiar kind of lesion, causing bleeding right through the skin. The palms of his hands, for example, were still wet with blood when the body was found. Now a round face appeared in a corner of the screen and Alex recognized Bradley Soo, from Hershey's old lab. Well, yes, he was saying, this could be a sign of the Leitbetter Syndrome, as it was called, which Soo had been investigating in the Human Ecology Complex. No, there was no way to be sure at present that this was the same disease that had infected the rats in the animal house. After all, the complex and all the labs within it had been sealed shut, and would remain so until the extent of the danger could be fully assessed.

As Soo faded, the screen filled with the familiar erratic buildings of the complex, surrounded by barbed wire and signs saying NO TRESPASSING. EXTREME BIOHAZARD. "So we may never know," the host's voice was saying, "what killed Kipper Markson or lured him to his death only minutes after his father's murder." With a wrap-up statement about forces incomprehensible to science and logic, he turned to a story about a bird that was being used by spirits as a channel.

Hershey's disease! Alex got out a pad of paper and a pencil and sat down to remember what Martime had said about the disease: that it rewired the brain, or something like that, vastly increasing intelligence. They could have infected the kid when he was working at The Harvest's California headquarters, as a way of speeding up his work. No doubt they had created the virus themselves, and administered it to Kipper in an attenuated form, so that he would be able to finish the game. Alex struggled to imagine the subjective impact of a disease that rewired the brain so that every neuron connected, insofar as possible, with every other one it could reach. All things would seem to be connected, since the patterns of cerebral circuitry must mirror, in some rough way, the patterns of sensory input we are pleased to call "the world." All things would condense into a single tightly drawn pattern in the mind.

Alex paused to appreciate the historical symmetry. If the idea for the game had originated in an experiment using human subjects, and if the game's inventor was, decades later, the subject of another such experiment . . .

But, as he thought about it now, there was really no hard evidence of any connection between Relnik and the boy. Maybe he had just wanted to believe there was a connection, so he would have an excuse for going to Della's that night. Because, after all, Relnik didn't write about games. Martime never mentioned a boy or a game, and Leitbetter's remarks were allusive at best. The kid could have met Homer and Riane through the computer network, nothing to do with Relnik at all.

Why, it could be anything, Alex mused, watching the bubbles squeeze by through his instruments, day after day in the lab. The whole connection to Relnik could have been devised by the boy as a nasty little joke on Leitbetter. The kid might have found out Leitbetter's guilty secret somehow, the business of plagiarizing Relnik. Then, when he got to The Harvest, he might have told his hosts that the game was derived from Relnik—just so they'd be sure to trip over the proof of Leitbetter's plagiarism when they went searching for the source of the game.

It was possible, then, that Alex had been playing some game of the boy's devising throughout the whole Relnik project. That the connection to Relnik was a bone thrown by the boy to distract Brabant and Martime and embarrass Leitbetter. That Alex's own involvement was entirely adventitious. That the whole thing was a "game" in the clichéd, metaphorical sense, implying a waste of time. What had Della said? That her son's game was "ordinary," full of monsters and magical quests, so why not a larger game full of lurid stories of Nazis and human experiments and drugs and hi-tech schemes for cosmic enlightenment?

■　■　■

When the papers arrived from Copenhagen, Alex could not at first remember having sent for them at all. He had written to the university for his mail, he could remember that much, on the theory that the trail must have grown cold or that Martime and Brabant could have found him by now if they wanted. There was a stack of administrative correspondence advising him of the termination of health insurance and pension rights, overdue library books, unpaid bills at the faculty lounge. The university regretted the unfortunate events which had led to the closing of the Human Ecology Complex but assumed no responsibility for any property left in one's office.

As far as Alex could determine from the bureaucratic prose, the disease had spread into the general population of laboratory animals, possibly many months ago, early in the summer when Hershey was still in charge. There was nothing to do then but give the complex over to the animals, since there was no way to hunt them all down, including the tribal rats that lived free in the tunnels and fed from the dumpsters outside. Many of the infected rats were presumed to have starved in their cages, but the stronger ones could easily have chewed their way out, and Alex pictured them running free through the empty corridors, feasting in the cafeteria kitchen, nesting in laboratory drawers, massing in the great auditorium. They had been prisoners, but in the end they were the heirs to the place.

The thick stack of papers was from an institute in Copenhagen dedicated, like several others, to the memory of the victims of the Holocaust. This one specialized in the abuses of Nazi science and also in the fate of scientist-victims, Alex slowly recalled, and it was his historian friend who had given him the contact. A cover letter in English offered hopes that the enclosed information would be helpful in his research project, though he must bear in mind the shakiness of all such information, given bombs and fires and deliberate efforts to destroy the evidence. But yes, fifteen Jewish scientists, male residents of various death camps, had died in what appeared to be a Nazi experiment conducted somewhere near Heidelberg, about a year before the defeat of the Reich. Nothing was known of the atrocity's authors, but there were hints, from the state of the bodies, that the experiment had involved the brain.

After that it seemed to Alex's co-workers in the industrial lab that he drank more heavily and worked more erratically, when in fact he had merely stopped drinking at night. He would get home at six in the evening, eat something he had bought along the way, and let himself nap in front of the TV. Then, shortly after midnight, he would wake up unprompted and prepare a full pot of coffee before settling down to his task. There were the papers to translate, with a dictionary, word by word, since his German had never been much. There were notes to inscribe on cards, books and articles to read, speculations to record before they slipped away. By dawn Alex would be sandy-eyed, tired and achy. He would shower and then stretch out on the couch with a glass of whiskey in his hand and watch the sky shudder and give birth to light. Then, with a full night's work behind him, he would tuck a half-pint bottle into his pocket and head back off to the lab.

Because in the end there is work. There is always work, meaning not jobs or paid-for labor but what we are truly called to, however modest that may be. We may be mere beetles in the scheme of things, as Leitbetter never tired of saying. But we have our beetle tasks. Already, the file folders of notes were filling up, each one of them neatly labeled HR, for "Henry Relnik: A Biography." It was an ironic title, since the story included so much more than Relnik himself: a little nod to Richard Leitbetter, a way of making him, posthumously, an honest man.

The victims of the experiment, if the records from Denmark could be trusted, were men not too different from himself: scientists, physicians, humble plodders on the path to truth, not mystics waiting for the fulfillment of some cosmic mission. One was an elderly man with a side interest in phrenology; another, a young man when he died, had already done momentous work in electrophysiology, and it may have been he who designed the fine electrodes that could be used for probing the brain.

Only one of the victims, a Viennese neurologist, had been famous enough to leave some trace, despite the Nazis' efforts to destroy all record of Jewish genius and accomplishment. At the end of the long biographical summary, after endless listings of published papers and honorary degrees, came a brief sentence or two about his hobbies. In between experiments and concerts and dinner parties and long discussions over coffee and torte, the neurologist had been addicted to games. He was considered unbeatable at poker and bridge, and had designed a three-dimensional version of chess.

It was ridiculous, a wild coincidence, an example of the present reaching back to alter the past and bring it into some kind of magical conformity, all things folding into one small and perfect shape. Alex pushed back his chair and began to pace. Suppose there was a theory of games that was also a theory of mind. Who would think of such a thing but a neurologist who was also addicted to games? And suppose this theory of mind had implications for the physical brain and how it works and can be made to work better and better. Suppose further this theory could be expressed in a game, a game that encapsulated the human experience of searching, surviving, questioning, learning . . .

■   ■   ■

Once the police had established that it was Steve who killed his father, there was no legal reason for Della to be held. The psychiatrist advised a couple of more weeks, just to let things settle, and Della agreed, having plenty of uses for the time. She would sit with the Walkman on, letting the static buzz in her ears, and practice making an inventory of the exact situation: who else was present in the room, what they were doing, the time and number of hours till dinner. If you could get the communicable conditions down right, like the weather and positions of the chairs, you would be free to move about in the world. Or at least this seemed to be the lesson of the place.

But Sister Bertha did not return. Ever since the day in the park, the static had gone on without a whisper of a break. Della decided that her inventories were not the point, that they could be the opposite of what she was intended to do. The important thing is not what is present but what is missing at any given time. That was the real lesson of the place, and perhaps of psychiatry in general. The goal is to figure out what is being omitted or evaded and try to drag it out into the light. And in her own mind the biggest gap had to do with Steve's final moments there in the park. This is what she had come up to over and over, and fallen back from every time, empty-handed.

There would have been just two of them, Steve and Sister Bertha, and in her mind their figures were outlined in black against the glare of the noonday sun, so that when Steve reached out, their outlines merged, and their hands seemed to fuse together. The disk-ettes she imagined being stained with his blood, just as she had envisioned that night in the apartment, because it was his blood on the gun that had proved he shot Leo, so there could have been blood on the diskettes or the plastic they came in. There was music, too, when she focused on this final encounter, the same music she had heard when she called SKD, telling of the endless strangeness of things and how nevertheless a pattern can always be found.

What was missing from the picture was Sister Bertha's face, and no matter how many ways Della came at the scene, or adjusted the light, or rearranged the bandshell and trees, the figure of Sister Bertha remained a vague silhouette. Probably nothing could be done about this. Della had watched *Nightzone* one night on the TV in the patients' lounge and seen a segment about an astronaut who had returned to earth absolutely catatonic, with an expression of unchanging surprise. He had remained silent like this till his death, so that no one ever knew what had surprised him so much.

Since a few other patients also had Walkmen, and sat bobbing their heads all day in tune to private rhythms, no one at first thought it strange that Della kept hers on day and night, and even loosely around her shoulders at meals. Her vigil came to an end when the activities director, a bright-faced young woman who wore a tiny teddy bear affixed to her chest, slipped the Walkman off Della's head and set it playfully on her own.

"Why, this is static, Della," she said with a frown. "You've been listening to static all this time. That isn't right."

The psychiatrist was even more disturbed. He was a pale, lashless man who wore a white lab coat in his sessions with patients, prepared for bloodshed and tears.

"You were doing well, Della, and now . . ."

"It wasn't always static, what I was listening to."

"Well, it is now. You were tuned into a part of the spectrum where there's nothing, nothing at all."

"If there's nothing, then why is there static?" Della asked, although she had learned already that logic is not a priority of science as applied to psychiatry. The goal is merely consensus.

"I don't know. It's cosmic rays or something, causing static."

"Cosmic rays?" Della leaned forward. "From space?"

He sat silently for a moment, looking hurt. "We discussed all that, Della. I thought we had put that behind us."

Della nodded, embarrassed. In the intemperate days that followed the news of Steve's death, she had once tried to tell him the whole thing, as she knew it, beginning with Relnik and ending with her quest for Steve in the park. The psychiatrist had been silent then too, for perhaps thirty seconds, before saying, "Della, would it hurt your feelings if I told you I'd heard this all, in rough outline, before?"

She had stared at him as he explained that he had the greatest respect for paranoid delusions, without which there would be no religions, or probably nations. But when you mix together Nazis and extraterrestrials and mind-altering computer technologies, you are traveling down one of the main thoroughfares of the contemporary mind. A well-worn path, not to say trite. Oh yes, the second coming too: that's fine, that's usually in there. Some people think reality is boring and oppressive. They should only have to sit in his chair and hear the same fantasy ingredients strung together, again and again.

"Well." Della knew she had to provide some sort of explanation for the Walkman and put things back on an upbeat, cooperative basis. "I was listening because I was hoping to catch Sister Bertha again. I told you about her. But I know now, I guess. She isn't coming back."

"Good, Della, I'm glad to hear that."

■   ■   ■

Still, Della was apprehensive when it came time to leave. If nothing ever happened in the facility, neither was anything meant to be remembered. The meals were the same, the daily schedules barely varied, so that the whole experience served to cleanse the mind and leave it limp and passive. At the bus station, on her way to see Alex, she was suddenly overwhelmed by the complexity of unregulated interactions going on every second—people jostling her, lining up, cutting in. It would be one thing if she were returning to something, but everything she saw, including a barefoot old man asleep on a bench, had the rude look of things newly invented.

Objects circled for a moment, a prelude to panic or fainting. She sat down in the waiting area and tried to remember what Sister Bertha had said about the first land animal, and how it had felt to climb out through the surface and into a world which you had been told all your life could only mean death. She imagined the first harsh, unsupportive touch of air, the first glimpse of dry emptiness, devoid of ripple or nuance. You would want to go back, Sister Bertha said, into the world that you knew. You would gasp and cry at the loss of all things familiar and at the hurt of that loss, like coarse sand abrading the scales of your chest. But still you would move on, driven by the surf and propelled now too by the stubs of your limbs, until the surface of the water was not something above you but something behind. You would lie there slithering and gasping, and the still air would feel as hard on your skin as the wind.

Della shook herself and stood up. It was not so difficult after all to buy the ticket and find the appropriate gate. The general idea is to mimic people: smile when they do, step forward with them, put your suitcase on the overhead rack, and stare out the window in case there might be something to see. The bus rolled out through seedy urban streets to the highway, and Della marveled at how much the winter resembled the summer that had gone before, the same white hazy sky and leafless trees.

The way out was to see things the way Steve had seen them, or Kipper, to use the name he had given himself. Otherwise his death was meaningless, just a sick boy, obsessed and possibly deluded. So she concentrated on the facts as she had come to define them: that the game which had been incubated in incomprehensible evil was also the highest product of human endeavor. That Sister Bertha was the long-awaited Visitor, emissary from the Others, who are undoubtedly out there, and that she had taken the game away with her, as a summary of all we are capable of and all we have learned, here on our poor little backwater planet . . .

At The Harvest they would never have believed Kipper when he tried to tell them that Sister Bertha was the one they were waiting for. But the proof was that she was gone now. She had gotten what she wanted and left. Or she had left and all wanting had ended— the causality was not always clear.

Della shivered and imagined the bus continuing forever, forgetting to stop. Because it was a cold world without purpose or mission, if the Visitor had come and the visit was over now. It was the end of the human race, as far as the universe was concerned. No further reason to care about us. Just "Thank you very much, we'll be on to the next planet now," continuing with the harvest, ha ha.

But still, she felt, there is something honorable about a religion that says that the encounter with God, if we're to call it God, has come already and gone. Alex would like the idea. He would say, Fine then, if whatever inhuman purpose has been served, then people can get on with their lives. And Della pictured generations going on, out of habit, or perhaps for some reason that had yet to be devised, some reason entirely of their own. No one would realize that the need had been filled, the requirement met, and that there was nothing to do but move on now, repeating the gestures, doing what we know how to do, again and again, without hope or regret.

At least try to move on, she thought as the bus maneuvered into the station, Alex's station. She would know in the spring. She would see if the leaves came back.